Also by Linda Broday

a MAN of LEGEND

LINDA BRODAY

sourcebooks
casablanca

Published by Sourcebooks Casablanca, an imprint of Sourcebooks
P.O. Box 4410, Naperville, Illinois 60567-4410
(630) 961-3900
sourcebooks.com

Printed and bound in Canada.
MBP 10 9 8 7 6 5 4 3 2 1

Dear Reader,

When I was a young high school girl, I had no idea at all what I wanted to be. I loved books but I didn't think I was smart enough to write one. I thought only college graduates wrote books, not someone with a high school education. When a counselor pressured me to choose a path, I told her I wanted to be a lawyer, heaven forbid, just to shut her up. A good portion of graduating seniors haven't a clue either. It takes getting out into the world and aging some to choose a direction.

The theme of this story is dreaming. Some characters' dreams are quite lofty and others more down-to-earth. While one girl sets her sights on traveling to Stockholm, Sweden, one young man's goal is altered by an accident.

There is magic in dreaming and sometimes, if you're lucky, you dare to reach for the impossible. I hope you'll nurture your own goal and never give up on it.

It's been a lot of fun writing about the Legend family, but it's time to say goodbye. Fear not, though. We have many exciting adventures awaiting with new people and places. Stay tuned.

Happy Reading,
Linda Broday

To everyone who's harbored a secret dream deep inside and is afraid to speak of it because it might vanish. I hope this story will give you courage to reach for whatever will bring the greatest joy to your life. The size of the dream isn't important. It's the striving for it that makes the difference. You matter. You are good enough.

One

JUST BECAUSE TROUBLE HAS COME VISITING DOESN'T MEAN YOU have to offer it a place to sit down. That had always been Crockett Legend's motto, and it had served him well. Until now. Looked like it might be too late at this point for any type of homespun cowboy wisdom. The die had been cast.

Rays of an apricot sky through the idling train's window sent a reminder that his early-morning travel could yield yet more surprises, and it was best to be prepared.

If possible.

He rubbed his face with his hands and glanced around at the people still filling the car. A group of men in rough work clothes were talking about going to the oil fields, hoping to find work in the Texas boomtowns that had recently sprung up overnight. In fact, the black gold and talk of getting rich seemed on everyone's minds these days.

A swish of delicate fabric brushing his legs interrupted his thoughts as a woman hesitated, probably scanning the car for a choice of empty seats. Finally, she mumbled something under her breath and took the seat across the narrow aisle from him. The faint scent of sage and wildflowers wafted around him. He glanced up with idle curiosity, and jolts of the familiar rushed through him.

Paisley Mahone.

He sat up straighter. He'd not spoken to her in three years, ever since her father and oldest brother had launched an all-out war

with the Legends over a section of land. Joseph Mahone accused
Stoker Legend of cheating him out of it. But the truth was, Mahone
had lost the land outright in a poker game to Stoker. Now the situation had become a powder keg.

Crockett took in Paisley from beneath the brim of his Stetson.
Three years hadn't made a lot of difference. Her hair, still the color
of ripe sunflowers, was swept into a low knot on the back of her
neck. She stared straight ahead, her light-green eyes glistening.
A little plum hat perched on the crown of her head matched the
color of her simple dress.

A stir raced along Crockett's body, telling him he'd not spent
enough time erasing Paisley from his mind.

Dammit! She was still so beautiful—still so unreachable. Still
so forbidden.

A long sigh escaped his lips.

As the iron wheels began to turn and gather speed, carrying
him away from Fort Worth, Texas, and the business he'd tended
to, his mind took him back to a sweltering summer day when they
were kids. The ride to the swimming hole to cool off.

One corner of his mouth quirked up. He'd dared Paisley to go
in naked with him.

Back then, she'd always been quick to take a dare. Memories
piled up. The pointed tips of her breasts tight against his chest.
Her wet, silken body sliding over his in the warm water. Sultry
kisses of fire. Everything about her was branded in his brain.

Then came the damn feud when she'd chosen her father's side.

In those days, he'd called her Firefly, and the pet name had fit.
Now, she'd likely slap him good. As angry as she was, he didn't
want to press his luck.

Outside, a horseless carriage raced alongside the train in an
apparent attempt to outrun it.

Crockett snorted. Another fool short on brains. Texas had long
reached its quota of stupidity.

A bit of the devil got into Crockett. He leaned across the aisle and touched a forefinger to his hat brim. "Morning, Paisley. Nice to see you."

She slowly raised her long lashes, her mouth in a tight line. "Crockett," she hissed.

After the single word, she turned to the window, clearly dismissing him. But he was like a bull charging an interloper, not content to share a pasture or a train ride without more.

"How've you been?" he asked quietly.

Swinging back around, she spat, "I might have no choice but to be on this train with you, but don't expect me to carry on a conversation."

He tried to block out her beautiful features—so close and yet so far. Tried to maintain some semblance of composure. But the little freckle at the corner of her mouth stole his focus. He'd especially loved how that freckle had seemed to wink at him when he kissed her.

She could deny their close friendship, the times they'd spent together, and the secrets they'd shared beneath a moonlit sky, but that damnable freckle made her the same girl she'd always been.

"I'm sorry about—"

"Who? Daddy? My baby brother? Mama?" Her chest heaved, and she shot him a look of contempt. Her voice dripped ice. "If not for your family, they'd all be alive. Before this is over, you Legends will probably send us all to our deaths. Don't pretend we're friends. Or that you care."

The stinging rebuke let him know how far they actually were from friendship. Hell!

However, blaming him for Braxton's death was unreasonable. If her baby brother hadn't run afoul of the law and ended up in Crockett's court, he wouldn't have been sent to prison, where a group of inmates beat him to death.

As for her father, Old Man Mahone had died a few days ago

of what his short-fused oldest son, Farrel, claimed was poisoned water. He accused the Legends, vowing to see them pay.

Colleagues had cautioned Crockett about getting involved, but he had a family obligation to figure out if the water had been treated with arsenic and, if so, who'd done it. He knew damned well his family hadn't.

If he could prove it and end this feud…

"Believe it or not, I am sorry," he said softly. "Help me prove we had nothing to do with that."

"You Legends, with more money than God, always twist the facts to make them show what you want. Excuse me." Paisley rose. Clutching her skirt, she hurried down the narrow aisle toward the next car, her spine stiff.

Dammit! How could he fix things if he got no cooperation?

A year and a half ago, upon entering the bar, he'd been appointed judge of the 46th Judicial District in Quanah, Texas. Shortly after, Braxton Mahone stood in his courtroom charged with manslaughter.

The facts were indisputable. Braxton had fought with a man in a saloon, pummeling the guy with his fists until he'd gone down, where he'd struck his head on an iron footrest and died.

Crockett released a weary sigh. He'd been over this a million times.

The resulting sentence had been appropriate. He still stood by his decision, even though it poured kerosene on the fire already started between his grandpa and Paisley's father. The two neighbors had been going at it for years. In the beginning, it had been the land, then fence cutting and missing cattle, each time gradually progressing.

Now they were facing a murder charge. Couldn't get more serious than that. He wasn't about to let the family name get dragged through the mud. Everything they'd worked for, their hard-earned reputation of being fair and honest, had been for the good of their neighbors, the community, and Texas.

Paisley's wild accusation that the Legends had caused Caroline

Mahone's death was beyond ludicrous. The woman had died on her own property after an accidental fall from a horse.

Now it seemed nothing would settle the dispute—certainly not Joe's death. Far from it.

The door at the end of the car flung open, and a passenger screamed. Crockett glanced up to see a masked gunman clutching Paisley flush against him as a shield. Anger and a healthy dose of fear widened her green eyes, but she appeared calm otherwise.

He sucked in a quick breath, his jaw tightening. Through narrowed eyes, he watched every twitch the gunman made. He had to find an opening.

"Folks, put your money and jewelry in the bag when my compadre comes around. Any trouble and this pretty little lady will get hurt!" the robber yelled.

Women gasped, stifling screams with their handkerchiefs. One lady fainted. Fabric rustled as men reached into their pockets. Children sobbed, sensing something terrible.

If the piece of horse dung hurt Paisley, there wouldn't be a safe place left in all of Texas.

Crockett eyed the train robber's accomplice weaving toward him with a burlap sack, collecting the passengers' valuables. He noted a slight limp and young, frightened eyes. This was the robber's son or he'd eat his hat. Crockett slipped a hand into his boot for the piece of steel he always traveled with and waited.

He turned his attention back to Paisley. Her calm exterior was beginning to crack around the edges. Crockett hoped she'd be ready when he made his move.

Just a few more feet.

But before the kid with the sack made it to him, a potbellied man in a bowler hat jumped to his feet, weapon drawn.

"I ain't giving you one red cent!" Bowler fired directly into the kid, who went down screaming, then swung the gun on the older robber.

Paisley let out a loud cry as Crockett stood, his Colt in hand. "Don't shoot!" he yelled.

Bowler whirled. "Don't tell me what to do. I'm protecting my valuables."

The train robber raised his gun and fired into the ceiling of the passenger car to an abundance of yelling and shrieking. "Put down those weapons or I *will* shoot the lady."

Thankfully, Bowler obliged, then stepped over the kid, who was curled up in pain, and took his seat.

Crockett faced the robber. He moved out into the aisle and held up the Colt. "I'm laying it down. Don't do anything foolish." He met Paisley's eyes and nodded slightly. She nodded back.

Good. At least they'd work together on this one thing.

As he started to place the gun on the floor, she stomped on the robber's foot with her heel and jabbed him with her elbow. The man yelped in pain, releasing her. Paisley leaped aside, giving Crockett a clear target. Taking advantage, Crockett took the shot and sent a bullet slamming into the robber's chest. He slumped to the floor in a pool of blood.

Paisley immediately yanked off her jacket and ran to the kid, applying pressure to his stomach wound. "Can someone hand me whatever you have? I'll try to save him."

Not wasting a moment, Crockett jerked off his light coat and put it under the boy's head, then went to check on the older robber. No use. He was dead. Grabbing the robber's arms, he pulled the man to a row of vacant seats, then went to help Paisley.

"Does anyone have a blanket?" he yelled.

"I do," a woman answered, handing him one.

Another passenger offered up a second one.

With murmured thanks, Crockett spread them over the boy. Paisley never glanced up. Her bloodstained hands didn't slow their movements. She stuffed the wound with as much cloth as she could and wrapped torn petticoats around the boy's midsection to hold everything in place. Once, she forced his eyelids open to look. Paisley Mahone oozed confidence and appeared to know what she was doing.

Crockett squatted beside her. "Are you a doctor now?"

"A nurse. For the last year, I've worked with a doctor in Fort Worth." She lifted her anguished gaze, and her chin trembled. "But now I have to go home to bury my father."

"I wish—"

"Apply pressure to his stomach," she said quietly. "Everything else can wait for later."

Crockett nodded and did as requested, moving his fingers over hers.

For the next hour, he worked by her side, watching her, admiring her. Paisley was as dedicated to nursing as he was to the law. Maybe respect and admiration was a place to start rebuilding what they'd lost. But it would take both, and right now she wasn't giving him the time of day.

Three years without speaking had been rough. One morning, he'd gone to the boarding house where she lived in Fort Worth and waited across the street for her to come out. He'd just needed to see her. He might've gotten the courage to speak, except when she emerged, a gentleman got off the trolley and kissed her cheek. Paisley smiled up at the stranger, and Crockett's heart shattered.

It'd been easier to blame their parting of ways on the feud between their families than to take a hard look at himself. But the cold truth was he hadn't supported her decision to seek something more than marriage. He winced. He'd discounted her desires because she was a woman, and women didn't have careers. What an insufferable ass!

He deserved her scorn, her anger. And more. They'd had something special, and he'd thrown it away like it didn't matter. Like she didn't matter.

"Do you think he'll make it?" Crockett asked.

"I don't know. He's in shock." She put a red-stained hand to her forehead. "If we can get to a doctor, he might."

"The nearest town is Decatur. They should have some kind of hospital." Crockett got to his feet. "I'll go up and speak to the engineer, see if he can get more speed out of this locomotive."

"Thanks." She gave him a grateful smile, a little of the frost seeming to thaw.

In a short time, he came back to report. "The engineer says he has this thing going at top speed, and he's telegraphed the sheriff up ahead." He glanced at the poor kid. "How is he?"

"The blood has slowed some, and he seems to be holding steady." She got to her feet, grabbing hold of the back of a seat to keep from falling as they lurched around a corner. Her face reflected genuine caring. "He's so young, with his whole life ahead of him. Why would he do this?" Her voice broke, and she seemed ready to collapse.

Without thinking or considering the ragged state of their relationship, Crockett tugged her against him. "I got you. Because of you, the kid might have a chance to mend his ways."

The feel of her in his arms was almost more than he could bear. He closed his eyes to savor that short-lived moment before she pulled away. The coldness had returned. Nothing had changed between them. Suddenly weary, he dropped into the nearest seat.

As they sped along the tracks, she kept working to save the boy—washing his ashen face and moistening his mouth. Crockett tried to anticipate what she needed and offer it before asked, trying to make things smoother for her. They reached the bustling town of Decatur in record time, and rushed the young man to a ten-bed hospital where a doctor rushed him into surgery.

Crockett accompanied Paisley back onto the train, her hand around his elbow. "Please consider what I said. Bury your father and let this feud between our families be done."

"It will never be over until your family returns the Mahone land and pays for my father's and Braxton's deaths."

"Joseph lost that land to Stoker. You know that."

"Do I? Funny, there were no witnesses, and we only have your grandfather's word."

"Are you suggesting Stoker cheated your father out of it?"

Her eyes flashed. "That was his claim—before he conveniently turned up dead."

"If you have proof, I'd love to hear it," he answered quietly.

She blew a strand of hair out of her eyes. "Doesn't your family have enough land, enough money, enough power? Or will you not be happy until you get your hands on all of Texas?"

His temper flared. "I challenge you to back up those accusations with fact. Every bit of land my family bought is aboveboard and legal."

"Are you sure about that?" she ground out through clenched teeth.

"I'll stake my reputation on it."

"Do you have to be such a Legend? Really? You're not always right."

"I know the values my family stands for and the line they don't cross. Can you say the same of yours?"

Her hand around his arm trembled slightly before she pulled away. The freckle by her mouth wasn't winking this time. Far from it.

Framed by the sunlight shimmering in her golden hair, Paisley took several steps toward the idling train and turned. "Thank you for saving me, Crockett. But don't think this changes anything. Because of your family, I've lost everything." Her chin quivering, she turned. As cool as a winter breeze, she swept up the steps and into the passenger car.

"We'll meet again, Firefly." He wasn't done trying to talk sense into her.

She was hurting and lost, but he'd wait for however long it took for her to regain her footing. Now that he'd seen her again and felt the sparks, he wasn't going to let her go. He'd chip away at the wall surrounding her until it fell.

He had too much to lose to give up on her.

Two

It neared midnight, and Paisley Mahone sat in disbelief in the quiet house, her mother's journal open in her hands. She rubbed her eyes and pulled the lamp closer, rereading the shocking entry a third time.

There was no mistaking. Suddenly very weary, she closed the book. Her mother had been secretly meeting Stoker Legend. The two had been lovers.

How could you do this, Mama? How could you betray us?

Her thoughts went to her mother's accidental fall. Had it truly been an accident? If her father had discovered the betrayal… No, that was crazy. He'd seemed genuinely distraught at the funeral.

Exhausted, Paisley wiped her swollen eyes. She felt a hundred years old. So much heartache. Then seeing Crockett on the train and being unable to restrain the angry words.

It was all too much. She was more alone than at any time in her life and it was the kind that gnawed and gnawed until there was nothing left. What would become of her? Farrel didn't love her; he could barely stomach the sight of her. She had no one.

She turned down the wick and lay in the darkness. Staring, thinking, blocking out the memories.

∽

The sunrise the following day had little to commend it. The somber sky was gray with a few subtle streaks of pink shooting through it. Crockett sat in the breakfast room at Lone Star head-quarters with the rest of the family.

"Take me to the Mahone place." Stoker Legend pushed back his plate and stood, all six feet four inches. "We'll all go and pay our respects to Joseph. We had our disagreements, but that's over now."

Crockett lifted an eyebrow and chose his words carefully. "I'm not sure they think it's over, Grandpa."

"Sure it is. With Joe gone, there's no more reason to fight. Farrel and Paisley aren't a part of this." Stoker adjusted his hat on his head, cast a look of disdain at the cane Houston tried to hand him, and marched from the breakfast table without it. Albeit with a slight wobble of his legs that failed to obey the stubborn command.

With such a start, it was a sign the day would not go well. Crockett went for his hat.

By the time ten members of the Legend family got into two surreys and drove the twenty miles to the Mahone place, the sun had risen to the ten o'clock hour. They parked next to several wagons and a buggy in the yard and got out, Houston helping his father.

A flock of vultures sitting on a fence row cawed loudly and rose slowly into the still air. Their wings caught the updraft, and their lumbering bodies lifted into the sky. Anguished sobs escaped from the inside the house. The land, silent and bare of new spring growth, seemed to be weeping as well. At least to Crockett. No one had worked the fields in quite some time. The barn also listed to one side. Everything appeared in need of repair.

What had Joseph and Farrel been doing? Clearly not farming.

He trailed his grandfather's slightly bent but proud figure as he slowly mounted the porch steps, each lift of his foot appearing to add another year to his ninety-one. Sons Houston and Luke flanked him. The youngest son, Sam, sheriff of Lost Point, followed closely behind. All had shed their guns for this somber occasion.

With the remaining top step to go, the door of the house flew open. Paisley and her brother, Farrel, stepped out with rifles raised, their faces a mask of stark anger.

"Far enough!" Farrel barked. "You ain't welcome here."

"We came to pay respects to your father." Stoker's deep voice was firm, with only a small tremor. "Joe and I had our differences, but we tried to work them out as men. Braxton losing his life in prison was none of our doing. He had to answer to the law."

Paisley drew herself up, chin raised. "The Legend brand of law has killed our family. We're hanging on by a thread, but we're going to fight to keep what we have, especially our lives. Go home, Mr. Legend. As Farrel said, we don't want you here."

A puff of wind lifted the hem of Paisley's skirt to reveal slim ankles. Crockett studied her face. She had avoided his gaze, keeping her attention on Stoker. Her swollen eyes, as green as a summer field, held sorrow. He ached to take her in his arms and comfort her. But she'd made it amply clear that she spurned his touch, his kindness, his very presence.

Despite the animosity, he stepped forward. "A special ranger from the Cattle Raisers will be here in a day or two to test your water. If it was poisoned, we'll find the culprit who did it."

Farrel tightened his grip on the rifle. "Get off our land. This is your final warning."

Houston shook his finger. "This feud is over. Spend your time and energy in taking care of this place."

"It'll never be over. Not as long as I'm alive!" Farrel shouted. "Now get!"

The Legends turned to go. They were almost back to the surreys when Paisley yelled, "I know your secret, Stoker Legend! I know about you and Mama. You stole her from us!"

Everything stilled, even the chirping birds who'd made a nest on the porch. Both Sam and Luke murmured low oaths, and their wives gasped. Houston stiffened as though struck from his position next to Crockett.

Shock and disbelief rippled through Crockett. He spoke when he finally got his tongue to move. "Do you know what you're talking about, Paisley? We'd like to see proof."

She didn't reply, simply sobbed into a handkerchief.

"You walk around like you're so high and mighty, Stoker Legend! How about now?" Farrel shouted, pointing the rifle at him. "You ain't nothing but trash! Filth! Get out of here."

Stoker and Caroline Mahone? She'd been dead for what now? A year and a half?

The old man had always enjoyed the company of ladies and had taken more than a few to bed, as was common knowledge. But surely not Caroline Mahone. Yet…maybe it explained the yawning chasm that had tripled in size almost overnight between Stoker and Joseph.

Crockett stared at his grandfather, waiting for an explosion so typical of the man he loved. At the very least, an immediate denial. The moments ticked by.

Stoker's faded blue eyes shot twin flames. "Your mother was a grand lady, Miss Paisley. Don't you dare sully her name or think ill of her. Don't you dare disrespect her memory."

Not one word of denial. Crockett could only surmise that the accusation was true.

Without anything further, Stoker let his sons help him into the surrey. As they turned the rig around, Crockett glanced back. Farrel stood glaring after them, but Paisley had dropped to her knees, her chilling cries following them. Two women emerged from the house and helped her inside, her spirit broken.

The only thing that kept Crockett in his seat was the fact that staying would just make everything worse. And right now, they all needed to cool off.

Paisley parted the sheer curtain and glanced out at the surreys leaving. She hadn't planned to speak of her mother. That had just slipped out. The truth was, she'd stumbled on her mother's journal only that morning while looking for suitable burial clothes for her father.

Her mother had written of her admiration for Stoker Legend and their deep friendship. She'd talked of how the Legend patriarch treated her like a woman, of his kind heart and soft touch, saying that he was the kind of man she wished she'd married.

According to her, Stoker was everything Joseph Mahone wasn't. Caroline claimed Joseph was distant and callous and cared nothing for her.

Paisley blew her nose. She knew her mother's assessment to be true enough. Although she loved her father, he'd spent a good portion of his life being cold and unapproachable. That was one reason Braxton had turned to liquor. He'd stayed at odds with the man who'd sired him and had died all alone in a dark prison. An icy shiver ran down her spine to think of her younger brother's last tortured minutes on earth.

But this other. Her father had to know about her mother and Stoker, and she could well imagine his rage. He'd been jealous of Stoker for so long anyway. Jealous of his wealth, his fine ranch, his friendship with governors, senators, and other important people. Especially the close bond that Stoker had with his sons, their wives and children.

"Would you like some hot tea or a bite to eat, Paisley?" her sister-in-law Hilda asked, patting her shoulder.

The thought of food made her ill. "Maybe some tea. Thank you."

In the other room, her brother was hatching some kind of plan to ride onto the Lone Star Ranch after dark with the other men. The thin walls couldn't muffle his shouting that they needed to hurt the Legends bad. Her stomach twisted. If he didn't stop, he'd wind up dead just like the rest of her family. Then she'd be all alone with Hilda and her son, Tye, and nothing but bitterness left, her face pinched like some old crone.

But she'd have about as much luck as a snowball in hell of making Farrel listen. Once he set his mind, there was no changing it.

Four-year-old Tye quietly entered the room and climbed into Paisley's lap. Silent and wide-eyed, he stared up and patted her face.

"Hey, little man, would you like a cookie?" Paisley glanced at Hilda. "Do we have any?"

"I baked some this morning because I needed something to do with my hands." Hilda reached for a sugar cookie on a plate and handed it to her son.

In her early twenties like Paisley, Hilda always wore a warm smile that showed her pretty dimples. She and Farrel didn't have much in common, but their marriage seemed to work—what little she could see—at least when Farrel tamped down his thirst for liquor and women.

Her brother wasn't the easiest man to get along with, but since it was just him and Paisley now, she'd make more of an effort. Still, she wanted no part of whatever he had planned for the Legends.

No good would come of that.

Hopefully, Farrel hadn't lied about the poison in the water. She wouldn't take odds on that. He manipulated facts to suit himself. Still, she did notice that her brother was hauling water from up near the boundary that separated the Mahone and Legend lands. Thank goodness.

They could do without more sickness and death.

Tye wiggled down and wandered off to play with his dog, Lucky. Such a sad little boy. Paisley took her tea out to the porch and stared across the land grown up in weeds.

Crockett's words about testing the water rolled around in her head. He hadn't said that to pacify them. He meant to get to the bottom of the problem.

The man she'd been smitten by at sixteen hadn't changed a lot in the years since she'd seen him last. He'd filled out his large frame a little more. Gone was the lanky boy hurrying off to make his mark in the world. Crockett Legend still took her breath away with his rugged good looks. There had always been a raw attraction between them. No denying his sexy smile and dark eyes had promised heaven to a young girl. It was a miracle to have kept her virginity.

Yesterday, one look at him on that train and Paisley's heart had raced. At that moment, she'd known she was lying to think she was over him.

"Steady as a rock" described him. He'd first gone off to try his hand as a cattle broker in Fort Worth with his sister, Grace. Though young, he'd done well but wasn't satisfied. He'd returned to the Lone Star with his sights turned to the law. It had been no surprise when he got accepted into law school. All the Legend men were smart, but Crockett had a little extra. They'd gone their separate ways when he'd left to become a lawyer.

Now, she straightened her spine and drew her anger around her like a wool shawl. He'd sentenced poor Braxton to prison, and they'd had to bury him next to their mother. That had been unforgiveable. Now their father would join him.

So as far as Crockett went, she would close her heart and build a thick wall around it. That would be the only way to survive his close proximity.

Paisley inhaled a breath of air that seemed to carry the stench of death and gripped her teacup so hard it almost broke. A sob escaped. Though she'd deserved some measure of happiness, her mother had betrayed them with Stoker, setting too much disaster in motion. Farrel was livid, and there wasn't any telling what he'd get it in his head to do. The knot in her stomach said it'd be bad.

This desolate piece of barren land was all that remained of the Mahones.

After she buried her father, she'd have to decide if she had a future here. If not, where? With the doctor she'd worked for in Fort Worth closing his practice and returning back east, that job had disappeared. But nurses were needed everywhere. It was simply a matter of finding the right place, and she wouldn't settle for just anything.

While she sorted out her life, she'd think and make wise decisions.

ఌఞ

The ride back was quiet, although everyone was looking at one another with questions in their eyes. The bombshell had shocked them all. Crockett couldn't believe what he'd heard.

Stoker stared straight ahead as though the day were ordinary in its sameness.

A million questions flew through Crockett's mind. When? How often? Why had his grandpa decided to take another man's wife?

At last, they pulled up to Lone Star headquarters. Stoker got out and looked his sons in the eye. "I'll answer your questions just once, then never speak of Caroline Mahone again."

Crockett followed his dad and uncles into the parlor. He needed to hear everything in case a legal problem arose.

The door opened, and dark-haired Noah Legend strode in, his hat in his hand. This uncle had been adopted as a child and had grown up in Stoker's shadow. As a boy, he'd wandered into Luke's campsite after losing both parents, and Luke had brought him to the ranch. Stoker had always treated Noah as a full-blood son, given him land, a name, and a place in the family. Tall, with a whipcord body, he portrayed a man who knew who he was and what he wanted.

Noah nodded to Crockett and took a seat, hanging his hat on his crossed leg.

"Glad you could make it, Noah." With a worried sigh, Grandpa sank into his usual armchair of cowhide leather. Houston poured him a stiff drink and put it in his hand. Stoker tossed it back like a man of thirty. "Years ago, I was out riding early one dawn and found Caroline sitting alone on a rocky ledge, crying. Of course, I stopped. Joe had made an ass of himself, and it wasn't the first time, but Caroline had gotten enough of his rough, mean ways. We sat and talked, watching the sunrise together."

"What were you thinking, Pa?" Sam ran his hands through his hair. "She was a married woman."

"Aye yi, yi," Luke muttered. "Dios mío!" He began to pace, the silver conchos running the length of his pants catching the light from the window with each stride. "This is bad."

Stoker jerked around. "Stop! You don't get to judge, Luke. She was a beautiful woman in pain, and I offered a shoulder. I gave her tenderness, and she made me feel young again." He pointed his finger. "But that's as far as we went. There was no wild affair, even though I wanted her, loved her, in that way. She didn't feel the same about me though."

Well, at least thank God for that. Crockett glanced around the room at the somber faces. Gone were looks of judgment. And all stood firmly behind the man staking his name and reputation on the Lone Star.

One leg propped on the other, Houston wiped a spot of dirt from his boot. "I take it Joe found out."

Stoker nodded. "He followed her one day. We came to blows, and he told her if she ever left Mahone land again, he'd kill her. Then he began a larger campaign to ruin me. Said he'd take everything I had." Stoker swirled the contents of his glass. "Joe filed lawsuits claiming we cheated him out of the section of land that once belonged to Caroline. Some you knew about and some I never told."

"We've had hell keeping the Mahones from riding onto the ranch," Noah said low.

Sam's forehead wrinkled. "Is that section the Jessup land that's smack in the middle of the Lone Star? Last time I was out that way, it still had the old family home on it."

"The same." Stoker ran a hand over his weary face. "Joe gambled it away in a poker game—to me. And that stuck in his craw all these years."

"I assume you have a legal deed to that property." Crockett sure hoped so. His grandpa had always had a sharp business mind.

"That land isn't ours anymore." Stoker looked down at his wrinkled hands. "I'm not used to explaining what I do." He raised his eyes. "But this once I'll make an exception."

Houston met Luke's and Sam's gazes. "I suggest you do, Pa. This affects us all."

"We need to know what's going on," Luke added. "Do not keep us in the dark."

Crockett watched his grandpa run a heavy hand along his jaw. He loved and admired this principled man of steel but often disagreed with his methods.

"I saw how badly Caroline Mahone needed something of hers alone to claim," Stoker continued. "She needed to be her own woman and have something her husband couldn't take from her." Stoker raised his voice an octave as though challenging anyone to disapprove. "So I gave her back her birthright. To my knowledge, Joe never knew."

"She's been dead for over a year and a half. Who owns that six hundred and forty acres now?" Houston asked.

Stoker glanced down at his worn hands, appearing to disappear down the trail of the past.

"Pa?" Luke repeated the question.

"Before she died, she spoke of changing the deed over to Paisley. I don't know if she did." Stoker sipped on the bourbon. "In any event, we don't own it."

Paisley didn't know anything about it, or she'd have said something to Crockett.

Ever since Stoker had won the land from Joe, they'd treated it as their own because it was. Learning different would change things.

"And that's a big problem. I wish you'd told us sooner." Houston released an oath. "What are we supposed to do? Take time to ride around it when we need to go through? Fence the section off from the cattle? It'll be mighty inconvenient, and Paisley has already taken her brother's side."

"We'll keep doing as we always have until the new owner comes forward," Stoker growled.

Sam thrust his hands through his dark hair. "And if Farrel gets his hands on it?"

"Yep." Crockett could damn well see all sorts of legal and other complications. "I'm sorry for my role in this. If Braxton had just appeared before any other judge."

"When you have a powder keg, one spark can set it off. You aren't to blame." Sam rose and stood next to Luke. "The problem now is how to diffuse Farrel Mahone. He seems hell-bent on carrying on the fight."

Stoker waved a hand. "If he wants a war, he's got one. We've fought rustlers, outlaws, droughts, blizzards, and spilled a lot of blood keeping this land. I figure we still got a little left."

They had sacrificed a lot to keep the Lone Star intact. At present, the family had amassed somewhere around a million acres that had begun with a small piece of land General Sam Houston had given Stoker as payment in fighting for Texas independence. Crockett had grown up listening to all the stories and knew the heavy cost some parts of their past had taken.

Owning land cemented the fact that a man belonged to something larger than himself. Crockett understood that and clung to the sections he held with a vengeance.

"I think we should present a reasonable offer to buy the land from them." Crockett's statement echoed in the still room.

"No," Stoker answered. "Don't tip our hand. Waiting seems more prudent for now."

"I agree." Houston got to his feet. "Also, until we settle this, we'd best post guards around our adjoining land. I guess that's all we can do for now."

"I'll go over to the land office and make some discreet inquiries and see who's listed as the owner." Crockett started for the door, but a shadow crossing the old man's eyes stopped him in his tracks. There was more to this. Something his wily grandfather wasn't telling them. "Is there more you want to say, Grandpa?"

Houston grunted. "Pa, this isn't the time to hold anything back."

"Don't you think I know that?" Stoker snapped. "But I made a deathbed promise to Caroline not to breathe a word of this, and I aim to keep my vow."

Sam exploded. "She's dead, Pa! That releases you."

"Not in my eyes." Stoker drained his glass. "Don't ask me any more about this. My lips are sealed. This doesn't concern you, so leave it alone."

Thick tension snaked around the room. Houston threw up his hands, and Luke muttered something in Spanish. Noah sat like a stone. He wouldn't be much help anyway, since he always sided with Stoker.

Crockett cleared his throat. "I guess this meeting is adjourned then."

Sam paced. "I'd offer to investigate Joe's death, but I can't. Not in any official capacity, since we're family. And any unofficial probe wouldn't be wise and would further anger Farrel."

"Stay out of it, Sam." Stoker tapped his fingers on the arm of the chair.

Quiet filled the room so that the loud chirp of a bird outside the window came through clearly. Crockett shifted. "I'll soon find out if the poison water is true." He adjusted the hatband of silver conchos on his dove-gray Stetson. "That should help."

He rose, and Noah stopped him as he went out of the room. "I tell you one thing. If anyone hurts that old man in there, they'll deal with me, and trust me, they won't like the ending."

Crockett's gaze followed Noah's tall figure out the door. Anyone had better think twice about tangling with his uncle. He gazed back at the center of it all. Stoker Legend evoked loyalty, respect, and love. But his extremely private nature could make things ten times worse.

As with secrets, they ate at a man, nibbling away a bit at a time until there was little left. Looking at Stoker, he could tell this one had taken a toll.

Who else would it carry over to? The family? Paisley? That question lingered in his mind like a stinging nettle as he strolled out to the porch for some air. The noonday sun sitting high in the sky was such a pale hue it barely had a tinge of blue to it. Thoughts raced through his head.

The family had never faced problems like this, and to survive and keep the ranch intact might not be doable.

Three

THE CLOCK IN THE HALL OF CROCKETT'S TWO-STORY HOME struck midnight, and he'd yet to close his eyes. Too much to think about. He stepped out on the porch, and the dead silence shot a warning. With only a thumbnail of moon, the sky was blacker than pitch. A rustler's moon. Trouble was brewing.

Ice swam along his spine, telling him to find a weapon and fast.

He hurried inside for a rifle and was on his way back out when all hell broke loose. Riders with flaming torches swarmed over the northeast section of the Lone Star, shooting and yelling. There looked to be two dozen men, but with the dark shadows to distort things, there could have been more.

One horseman tossed a torch into Houston's barn that sat two hundred yards away.

"Fire!" Crockett shouted, running full out. "Fire!" He reached a bell at the end of his walk and gave it several good rings.

In seconds, men ran from everywhere. His dad raced from his house and jerked one of the raiders from his mount, slamming him to the ground, then lurched for another. His mother ignored the mayhem and beat a path directly for the barn and her favorite chestnut mare.

They converged at the burning building, and Crockett held her back. "Wait here, Mama. Let me go in after them, and you can catch them when they run out."

"Hurry!" Lara's eyes swam with tears, and her chin quivered. The flames showed the faint lines of the thirty-year-old scar running down the right side of her face, left by an attacker.

His seventeen-year-old sister, Hannah, ran screaming from the back door of the house. "Get Mister Pete!" She raced toward the inferno, her legs churning.

Crockett grabbed her arm. "Stop. You can't go in there."

"I have to save him!" Tears flowed down her cheeks. "I can't let him die this way."

"I know, and I can't either." Crockett stroked her back. "Stay with Mama, and I'll go get him."

"Hurry! We're running out of time." Hannah stayed at her mother's side, the two women clinging to each other. "Get them out."

More shots rang out, reminding Crockett of the danger and the lives they stood to lose. "You two get low and stay out of the line of fire." Clutching a bandana to his mouth, he ran inside, then inched through the dense, billowing smoke.

Almost immediately, his eyes burned from the thick, smoky haze blinding him.

The crazed horses screamed with fear, the sound sending chills up Crockett's spine. The din of them trying to break down their stall doors with their forefeet struck home their desperation. Crockett hurried down the line, letting each animal out, praying the shooting had stopped. Blinded, he could only go by feel. Smoke went up his nose, and he coughed with each breath.

Almost done. Just two more. Still the fire raged hotter with each passing second. He couldn't breathe or see, and the heat was blistering his face.

He was down to his mother's and sister's horses when the flames ignited several cans of kerosene and blew him backward. Addled, Crockett shook his head and got up quickly, but not before the hungry flames ignited his shirt sleeve and denims. He beat at them and managed to put out the fire.

Behind him came the frenzied screams of the traumatized horses. Saving them became paramount. Even if he died in the attempt, he would save them.

A large bucket of water appeared in his stumbling blindness. He wet the bandana and tied it around his mouth, freeing up his hands. Then he drenched his clothes.

Slowly, his heart hammering against his ribs, Crockett felt his way through the impenetrable haze, relying on touch alone. Burning embers from the rafters fell in front of him, and he jumped back just in time to avoid getting pinned. The whole place had become a raging inferno. He had to finish and get out or he'd die here.

Inch by miserable inch, he fought his way forward. Time seemed to stand still in this last-ditch effort to free the animals. Heat from the fire scorched his exposed skin. Though he was tempted to give up in despair, he kept going until at last he lifted the latch on the stall holding his mother's beloved mare, releasing it.

Finally, he fought his way to Mister Pete. The large gelding shot past, knocking him down.

Crockett crawled to his feet, aware that the way was blocked behind him. Keeping low, he plunged forward away, from the initial start of the blaze. A cool breeze fanned his face, and he followed the fresh draft to where the back wall used to be before the explosion blasted it away.

Gasping for air, he burst free and collapsed on the ground in a heaving, coughing mess.

Hands reached for him, although he couldn't tell who they belonged to, his smoke-filled eyes long since blinded.

"I got you, son," his dad said. "Lean on me."

The words were a cooling balm. Crockett clutched his father's arm. "Did I get them all?"

"Yes. The last two are accounted for."

"Crockett!" Hannah screamed and threw her arms around him. "Thank you! I don't know what I'd have done if Mister Pete had died."

"Happy I could do it, sis."

Then his mother hugged him, crying. "Come and let Doc treat your burns."

His parents led him into their house, where young Dr. Edward Thorp waited. From the very first, Grandpa had kept a doctor on the payroll at the ranch. Doc Jenkins had been the previous one and spent thirty years patching up cowboys, delivering babies, and treating the employees and their families.

Now the job belonged to Ed Thorp, a man in his thirties and everything Jenkins was not. Tall and slender, Thorp embraced practicality and didn't give a rat's hind end about his appearance, often wearing wrinkled shirts with the sleeves rolled up. But he was good, damn good, and didn't cater to Stoker, much to the old man's considerable irritation.

Questions swirled in Crockett's mind as he sat patiently while Thorp washed his eyes and smeared a liberal amount of salve on them that relieved the burning and dryness. Then the doctor wrapped a bandage around his head that plunged him into darkness. Panic shot through him for a moment at not being able to see anything before calm set in. This was only for a little while.

He could endure anything for a little while—especially if it saved his sight.

"We'll have to keep this on for a few days to let your eyes heal," Doc said. "The smoke damaged them. Your other burns are much easier to treat. I'm putting a salve on them, and I want you to lather it on as thick as you can."

"I'll see to it, Doc." Lara pushed Crockett's hair back.

Even though he was a grown man and a judge, his mother's touch always soothed.

Grandpa Stoker burst through the door. "How bad, Thorp?"

An irritated noise rumbled in the doctor's throat. He finished applying the salve. "He'll live."

"Dammit, Thorp. I know that much. Can he see?"

"Some, but with luck, he will have a total recovery."

"Luck?" Stoker barked. "I need a sight more than luck, Thorp. Hell!"

"The next few days will tell more, Mr. Legend. His eyes need rest right now." The doctor patted Crockett's shoulder. "Those horses would've died if you hadn't saved them."

"I only did what anyone else would've done."

From the sound, Stoker was pacing the room. "You have Legend blood, and I'm so damn proud of you."

His grandpa's words shot warmth through Crockett. Stoker never gave idle praise. When he mentioned something special, it was filed away and long remembered.

"What about the raiders? How much other damage did they do?" Crockett asked quietly, irritated he couldn't see. Next to breathing, sight was the single most important thing to him.

What good was a blind man when he needed to see danger coming? Hell!

His father spoke up. "We sustained no other damage, son. I caught one of the riders, but he won't talk. We'll haul him in to the sheriff. I'm betting this was Farrel's doing, and if so, he's wasting no time carrying on Joe's war. I can't think of anyone else with a motive."

Crockett agreed. "Yeah. I figured Farrel might do something like this to hurt us."

Revenge was a strong motivator, and Farrel had gotten plenty worked up. Paisley crossed Crockett's thoughts. Since she shared her brother's anger at them, she wouldn't try to rein Farrel in. Crockett didn't think anyone could at this point.

What a shame. Farrel might not be a bad person, but he let greed and hatred eat him alive. There didn't seem to be any clear way out of this feud, except maybe trying to talk to Paisley again.

Silent curses blistered his brain. He couldn't even see to ride over there. Dammit!

If he could just do something. Anything.

❧

Ever since Paisley was a little girl, she'd found solace in the night. Now with darkness cloaking her, she threw a warm shawl around her shoulders and wandered onto the porch, leaving the quiet, shadowed house. Hilda and Tye had long gone to bed, and Farrel had ridden out with his friends, intent on some devious plan.

Best not to know. Or to ask too many questions. He had a mean temper.

Her mother's journal, especially the last entry she'd read, lingered in her mind. It spoke directly to her, voicing concerns that Paisley wouldn't be strong enough to stand up for what she believed was right.

I wish Paisley would listen to her heart, her mother had jotted. *War and anger breed hate. Joe and Farrel will stop at nothing to distort the truth, and I fear they'll turn her to their way of thinking. I wish I could make her understand how important it is to stand your ground.*

Her mother hadn't known the lengths the Legends would go to in order to get what they wanted. The Mahone family was shattered, Paisley's father lying stiff in the parlor. Troubled by her thoughts, Paisley stared up at the thin slice of the moon, drawing her shawl tighter around her body. While her father hadn't always spoken the truth, there was one indisputable fact. He was dead from drinking the water. And fear rose for the rest of them. Although they were no longer drinking the water, Tye seemed a little less playful, a little weaker with each sunrise, and Hilda was losing the bloom in her cheeks.

They had to be showing lingering effects of poison. Probably the same poison that had killed her father.

She left the porch and wandered out into the night. She gave the rickety barn a scornful glance and wagged her head. It was shameful to let a place fall into ruin. Farrel needed a whip taken to him. But then he'd never had a sense of pride. He'd taken after their father.

The lop-eared dog of little Tye's trotted from the barn, and she knelt to speak softly to the pooch. "This is a sad state of affairs, isn't it, Lucky?"

The dog whined softly as she stroked his head. He rolled over, and she rubbed his belly for a moment before venturing farther, to the draw that beckoned a short distance from the house. Her curiosity led her to the place that Farrel had strode from yesterday with two rough-looking strangers.

Her brother was hiding something. Her gut told her that much.

Deep, dark shadows bathed the draw, but as Paisley picked her way down the easy slope, she made out some type of strange iron equipment with sharp points both in piles and scattered around. A little farther was a wooden platform. She cautiously stepped onto it and peered down a hole cut out in the center. Someone had positioned it over a hole in the ground that looked approximately six feet deep with some thick, black sludge nearby.

What was Farrel doing? She stared, her forehead wrinkling, trying to make sense of it.

Lucky sniffed around, then got distracted by a rabbit and took off chasing it. A lot of help he'd be. Paisley walked up and down the dry wash and spied several yawning holes of various depths left open for someone to fall into. Tye could disappear into one, and they'd never find him.

A charred piece of wood caught her notice, and she picked it up. Something had burned it.

But what? Several other pieces lay scattered.

After a while, she wandered back toward the house, stopping at the swing Farrel had put up for Tye under a lone apple tree. She sat down and swung back and forth, her mind going back in time when she and Crockett were best friends.

The summer of her seventeenth birthday she'd almost given herself to him. Lying in the tall grass that day, she'd never seen anyone so handsome, so charming, so full of life as Crockett Legend. He was leaving for law school the next week, and she didn't know if she'd ever see him again. Whispering that he'd never forget her, he plucked a strand of hair from her eyes and covered her lips with his. The sensual kiss had stirred something deep inside her and tempted her to throw aside everything and become his.

"I've never known anyone like you, Paisley. I want to marry you. Please say yes."

As he'd unbuttoned her dress and slipped a hand inside, she'd somehow found enough strength, weak and wavering though it was, to resist and follow her own plan to become a nurse. It never would've worked anyway with their families at odds.

Not then and especially not now.

Did she truly think the Legends capable of killing her father?

Paisley covered her face with her hands. She'd known the Legend family most of her life and never would've believed them responsible. But power and greed did strange things to people. And Crockett might not know all the inner workings of the family, since he lived away from the ranch and wasn't involved in the day-to-day activities.

Although it was impossible for them to get back what they'd lost, she wanted to think the best of him. She owed him that. And for lots more.

Memories swirled through her head like a roulette wheel and stopped on their last encounter before she'd left for nursing school and him to study law. Their conversation had been a strained politeness of two strangers.

"I think we would've had a hell of a marriage, Paisley. If you ever find yourself in need of a friend, send word. I'll be there in a heartbeat."

Even now, her reply sounded odd in her head. "Thanks, but I won't. It's best."

Then, he'd lowered his head, tipped back her head, and lightly kissed her. "For the good times. Never forget. Goodbye, Paisley."

As the moon shone down on her now, she touched her fingers to her lips. "For the good times," she whispered softly, tears running down her face. Slowly, she made her way back.

Those days were long gone, leaving nothing but sorrow in their wake.

The house was still quiet when she returned and went straight to her room. The cool breeze through the open window brought the fresh scent of the land. She dragged a big gulp into her lungs, counting herself lucky for her family home away from the bustle of Fort Worth. She turned to her mother's open journal on the bed.

Had her mother truly sold them out for the gentle touch and kind ways of Stoker Legend?

Paisley picked it up and sat down, flipping to the next page, and stared at the single sentence in large letters.

All is never truly lost and will find its way back in its own time.

Four

WHAT WAS HER MOTHER TALKING ABOUT?

Paisley drew the coal oil lamp closer and read it again. All was never truly lost? Some things most certainly were. Case in point, her friendship with Crockett for one. That was over and done. But her mother wouldn't have known much about that, since Paisley had never confided in her.

Maybe Caroline was talking about Stoker. Maybe they'd had a fight—a lover's quarrel—and made up.

The silent house creaked, as though trying to talk. A second later, horses galloped toward the house along with a lot of whooping and hollering. Paisley rose and went to the open window, making out Farrel and five of his buddies. They sounded drunk.

"I guess we showed Houston Legend," Farrel crowed, punching the air. "I doubt Crockett got all those high-dollar horses out."

"Killing horses wasn't part of the deal." The angry statement came from Digger Patrick.

Paisley's blood ran cold. Oh God! They must've done something to Houston. And horses? She rubbed her arms. In her estimation, there was nothing worse than hurting a horse. And any man who did was the scum of the earth.

"Did anyone see if Crockett made it out of the fire?" This came from John Barfield, Farrel's boyhood friend.

A fire? Crockett? What had they done?

"Who cares?" Farrel dismounted along with the others. "He deserves to die for what he did to my brother. I thought we agreed on this."

Digger snorted. "You agreed, and we listened. I liked Braxton, but he was wrong to keep beating that guy. I was there and saw everything."

Farrel grabbed the dissenter by the shirt. "Get off my land, Digger. I expect loyalty. If you can't show me that, then we need to part ways."

"Fine by me." Digger jerked away and climbed on his horse.

Anger rose to see her fool brother throwing away an old friendship. Farrel had grown up with Digger Patrick. She wanted to march out there and smack her brother's head good, but he was in no shape to listen to reason.

"Keep your mouth shut, Digger!" Farrel hollered. "Anyone finds out about what we did, I'll come looking for you."

"We'll all come marching to your door," John shouted. "It's us against them. About time they suffered."

The old friend kept riding and soon disappeared from sight. Paisley leaned against the window as Farrel and the others passed a bottle around. Everything in her wanted to race out and confront him, but not while he had a head full of whiskey. That wouldn't be smart.

She closed the window and readied for bed. She'd get a good night's sleep and bury her father in the morning. Then Farrel had some answering to do—about a lot of things.

Morning didn't come soon enough. Paisley had tossed and turned a good portion of the night. She'd heard Farrel come in near dawn, blundering his way through the house, overturning chairs and falling against the wall. He looked like hell when he appeared at the breakfast table.

"Morning," Paisley muttered over her teacup. "Late night?"

"My business." Farrel reached for a biscuit.

Paisley stood her ground, putting starch in her spine. "I heard you and your friends last night. You rode to Houston Legend's and I'm guessing you set fire to his horse barn."

Fire blazed in her brother's eyes. "That doesn't concern you."

"If Crockett is dead, it concerns us all! Don't you get it? I heard what you said."

"No sister of mine is going to keep time with a Legend! I know you're still sweet on him." Farrel rose so fast, his chair overturned. "You and him are done."

"Stop it and listen to yourself. If he's dead, every lawman in the country will come down on us. Can you afford that? They'll find the holes you've left in the ground, the equipment, and everything else you've been up to your eyeballs in."

Hilda and Tye came through the door, her sister-in-law staring from one to the other.

"The holes?" he sneered. "I've been working my fingers off trying to make this place pay off. I fixed up a barrel with sharp points and dragged it across our land. I'm fixing the pastures so that when the rains come, the water will soak into the ground instead of running off. A sight more than you've been doing—*sis*. You're just like Mama. Always accusing."

Hot words burned her tongue, but she held them back, aware of little Tye's frightened eyes.

Farrel stomped to the door. "I'll bring the buckboard around and get Daddy loaded up. I'll expect you at the service. That is if you can remember whose side you're on."

"I'll be there," Paisley said quietly, brushing Tye's hair from his red-rimmed eyes. She'd help Farrel with this, then set to work to get to the bottom of what was going on. She didn't believe his song and dance for a moment. There was something bad wrong, and she was going to find out what.

Before it killed them all.

⤫

Crockett's head felt as though it weighed a ton. Light from the window filtered through the bandages swaddling his eyes. Paisley was burying her father this morning. His heart lurched. He should be there.

He felt his way to the drawer that held his clean shirts and got one out. The color didn't matter. The only important thing was getting there.

Quickly dressing, he left his private dwelling on the ranch and ate breakfast with the family. It seemed everyone had a million questions about his eyes, and he answered as best he could. The worry in their voices pricked him. The absolute worst thing was causing his family concern, yet he couldn't change what had happened.

After a short lull in the questions, Crockett jumped in, his voice quiet. "Can someone take me to the Mahone family's burial plot?"

His dad replied, "Son, they don't want us—or you—there. You heard them yesterday. To go will only make matters worse."

Crockett fumbled for his coffee. "I heard Paisley and Farrel, but if I don't try, I can't live with myself. I'll stay back and give them some distance, but this is something I have to do."

"Then I understand. Follow your gut."

At least Paisley might see that he hadn't given up and was willing to fight for her. Any amount of hope would be welcome. It was hard to live with this ache around his heart.

"I'll take you." The sweet voice belonged to his mother sitting beside him.

"I appreciate your offer, Mama, but I can't put you in harm's way in case bullets start flying." Crockett fumbled for her small hand. "I think it's best if someone else did."

"No, son." She squeezed his fingers, and he heard tears in her voice. "They have no reason to hate me, and like you said, we'll stay back. Caroline was my best friend, and I never got to say goodbye. Maybe I can today."

A chair scooted, and Crockett knew by the heavy sound it was his dad. Then came Houston's voice. "You know, I think you make a lot of sense, sweetheart. You might be the best one for this."

Crockett imagined his dad was patting his mother's hand like he did so often. Houston didn't show much open affection, yet Crockett knew without a doubt his dad deeply loved Lara.

"Now that we've settled that, I'll finish getting ready." Crockett pushed back his chair, and Hannah took his hand.

"Let me help you. I can comb your hair and whatever else needs doing."

Together, they set off across the compound to make him presentable—just in case Paisley got close enough to notice.

⤬

Cold spring rain fell all the way to the Mahone family burial ground. Crockett huddled in a coat next to his mother.

Lara Legend pulled the wagon to a stop and set the brake. "There's only a handful of mourners, Crockett. They've turned to stare, but no one is coming toward us."

"Good." He felt for the side and climbed down, then his mother took his arm.

"We'll stand at the iron gate. Maybe they won't mind," Lara said.

Sobs reached him as they made their way, and he imagined some belonged to Paisley. It seemed strange, but without his sight, his hearing had sharpened as well as a sixth sense. It took little effort though to feel the heaviness that had dropped over the group like a woolen cloak.

A memory crowded into his head of the dozens of letters he'd written her in the three years since they'd gone separate ways, letters he'd never mailed. Words had spilled out onto the pages of things he'd never told her. But after waiting outside her boarding house in Fort Worth and seeing her with the other man, he'd known he'd truly lost her.

It was odd the new hope that had surged when they'd met on

the train. If he could just have another chance. He'd learned from his mistake.

How he wished to hold his beautiful Paisley in his arms now, to comfort and tell her she had nothing to fear.

But didn't she? Farrel could be hard to deal with on the best of days.

Nothing was going in the healing direction. Just the opposite. He'd never seen a bigger mess.

His mother leaned close. "Paisley turned to look. Oh, Crockett, she's devastated."

Dammit, if only he could see. Or do something.

"Even though Joe was an ill-tempered cuss, he was still her father, and she loved him." That was the way it should be. Children should love their parents—even when they weren't worthy. "Do you see Farrel?"

"He's standing next to the preacher, his face set in anger. He's staring at us," Lara whispered.

"Let me know if he starts coming this way."

The small group began to quietly sing hymns of long ago, passed down for generations.

After a few songs, the preacher said last words over Joe, and folks began to leave. Lara and Crockett had turned toward the wagon when Paisley stopped them. "Thank you for coming, but I wish you hadn't. Your being here will only inflame my brother more."

"We had to, dear. It wouldn't have been right to stay away," Lara replied gently.

The rustle of fabric met Crockett's ears, and he assumed his mother was hugging her. The faint scent of Paisley's perfume drifted around his head, arousing such longing.

"Crockett, I heard about the accident. I hope you weren't seriously hurt." Tears wrapped Paisley's low murmur.

An accident? Though he wanted to set her straight, this wasn't the right time, so he didn't try. "I'm truly sorry about your father."

Letting her scent guide him, he pressed his lips to her cool cheek. "I want to help."

"You can't." Her voice held sadness, worry, and maybe a great deal of weariness.

His focus on Paisley, Crockett wasn't aware of Farrel until he spoke.

"How dare you disturb my father's service? I told you to stay away."

"Stop it, Farrel." Paisley spoke in a tone that sliced the air like a sword. "Be civil. Folks are staring."

"Are you're giving the orders now, sis?" Farrel's low growl held a threat. "Is that what you want to do? If so, you'd best think again."

"We're just leaving." Lara took Crockett's arm. "Excuse us."

"Go back to the Lone Star before you get hurt worse than you are, Crockett!" Farrel yelled.

Anger burst inside him. Crockett spun, his fists doubled. "Let's have this out. You and me. Right here."

Farrel grabbed him by the neck and threw him to the muddy ground. Crockett came up swinging, the other man's heavy breathing telling him where to strike. Instead of a solid hit, Crockett's blow glanced off Farrel's jaw. Before he could attempt another, Farrel drove a fist into Crockett's belly, doubling him over.

The wind left him, and he knelt on the ground, gasping for air. Farrel pounced on him, grinding Crockett's face into the mud. One corner of the bandage came off, and he could better judge where everyone stood by shapes and shadows.

"Farrel, stop it!" Paisley demanded. "Let him up."

"No. I'm gonna kill him."

"Enough!" Lara yelled.

Then a shot rang out.

"The next bullet will go into you, Farrel." Steel laced Lara's firm voice, and Crockett assumed she'd fired the small gun she carried. "Have I gotten your attention?"

A grunt left Farrel's mouth, and he slowly got to his feet. "Miz Legend, take your boy and go home. But this ain't near finished."

"Don't be caught on Lone Star land, Farrel. I'd hate to think of what might happen."

The not-so-subtle threat was out of the norm for Lara, yet Crockett knew she fully meant everything she said. She'd reached the limit of her patience. Any person who thought his mother soft was a lunatic. Lara held more strength than any twenty women, and she'd come by that the hard way. No man would ever catch her by surprise and vulnerable again.

She took his arm and led him to the wagon.

"That went well." Crockett grinned as they turned around and headed for home.

At least Paisley seemed less hostile, which was a lot more than what he'd hoped for. And she was standing up to her lowlife brother.

Firefly was sprouting wings.

Five

PAISLEY RETURNED FROM THE FIASCO AT THE FUNERAL AND went straight to her room. Overhead, the rain played a soggy melody on the tin roof. She'd always loved the rain, but today it failed to bring the peace it usually did.

Seeing Crockett with the bandages around his eyes had shaken her. How serious was the injury? She wondered if the damage to his eyes would be lasting. For him to lose permanent sight and never see a sunrise or brightly colored birds…that would hurt something deep inside her. Farrel had done this to him; that was plain. The jeering words she'd heard her brother and the others speak last night refused to leave her head. They'd wanted him dead and had evidently meant to kill him.

Farrel's hatred went far deeper than she'd known.

The fight today had proven it. Her brother had frightened her. His violent tendencies seemed to come more frequently and persisted longer as he aged. They'd just buried the only one able to control him. She shuddered to think what might happen now.

Her mother's voice whispered in her head. *Listen to your heart, Paisley. Be strong. Don't let your father and brother destroy you too.*

Paisley stood at the window and pushed the curtains aside. The wet, gray landscape reflected her mood. It was all more than she could bear.

The door creaked open, and Tye slipped inside. Sadness oozed from him. He huddled on the floor, resting his head against the side of the bed.

She went to him and knelt down. "Hey, sweet man. Is something wrong?"

The four-year-old pressed his face into the length of quilt hanging down.

"You can tell your aunt Paisley. Maybe I can help." She pushed back his hair that had gotten too long and kissed his cheek. "When I was a little girl, I used to get scared and sad a lot. Do you know what I did to make myself feel better?"

Raising his face, the boy shook his head.

"I used to tell myself stories about people who knew magic. A good witch was a favorite one I used a lot. She could mix up potions and cast spells, and she always made me feel better, more powerful."

"Could she make big people stop being mad?"

"She sure could. She threw some fairy dust on them, and they stopped hollering."

"What was her name?"

"Jinx. She was my best friend." Until Paisley grew out of her make-believe world and discovered there was no one except her mother to protect her from ogres and bogeymen. She sat beside him and lifted Tye into her lap. "What kind of magical person would you like to create?"

He scrunched up his face. "A wolf that can sometimes be a scary man."

"Do you mean a man that changes into a wolf?"

"Yes. With red eyes with fire coming out and big teeth. Mean people would run."

The kid was way too young to know about such. Who had he heard it from?

"I see. Who told you about these wolf people?"

"Bobby."

Hilda's eleven year old brother. She might've known.

"Who are these mean people you would scare? Are you talking about anyone we know?"

Tye nodded. "He's real mean to my mama and makes her cry."

It took her no time to figure out it was Farrel. He didn't try to hide his sharp tongue and quick blows. It broke her heart that too often Tye was on the receiving end, and the poor kid was now searching for some way to fight back.

"I know, honey." Paisley put her arms around his frail body. "Big people aren't always nice. But sometimes they still love us."

His set mouth said it all. "No, they don't."

She gave up the argument that wasn't worth it. Plus, Tye was right. "Hey, let's give our werewolf some awesome power. What will he be able to do?"

"Eat the bad ones."

The answer also disturbed her. He was too young to be thinking about killing.

"Let's think of other things first." She was quiet a moment. "I know. How about if your werewolf can make big people real little? And what if he makes them squeak like a mouse instead of talking?"

Tye laughed. "That's funny. He would run around looking for a hole but couldn't find one. And then Lucky would step on him." The bit of laughter added welcome color to his cheeks.

"Tye? Where are you, honey?" his mother called from the hall. "Please answer me."

The boy put his arms around Paisley and held on tight. Whatever had happened still terrified him. It wasn't like him to hide from his mother though.

"He's in here, Hilda" Paisley shifted and whispered in his ear, "It's okay. I promise. Remember, we have power."

He leaned back to look up at her. "It's a secret. Don't tell."

"I won't. Cross my heart."

A smile formed, erasing some of his sadness.

Her dark hair curling around her face, Hilda opened the door and relaxed when she spied him. "There you are." Her dimples were nowhere in sight.

Her sister-in-law came closer, and light from the window revealed a red place on her jaw where a fist had connected.

Paisley turned to Tye. "Sweet boy, I'll bet Lucky wants to play fetch. He'd be so happy if you went to throw a stick for him."

The frown returned, and he shot a glance to his mother.

"Honey, we'll be right here. Some sunshine will be good for you," Hilda assured him.

"Okay. Lucky wants me to pet him."

"Yes, he does." Paisley helped him up. "But don't go far." The holes on the place were dangerous.

Once, she heard the back door shut, she focused on her sister-in-law. "Sit down, Hilda. We need to talk."

"Farrel will get mad. Everything is fine. Really."

Paisley gave a soft snort. "I can see that." She took Hilda's hand and pulled her down beside her. "How long has this been going on?"

The woman looked away, twisting her hands. "It started about a year ago and has gotten steadily worse. Farrel means well. I'm clumsy and forgetful and way too slow to see to his needs. It's really all my fault. I should try to do better."

"Stop." Paisley put her palm over Hilda's and kept her voice soft. "Stop making excuses for him. You're not to blame for this, so stop."

A long sigh escaped Hilda's mouth. "I don't know what to do. He gets so angry."

"I think a long visit with your mother is in order. Put some space between you and Farrel. Let him think about what he's done. My brother is far from a nice, calm, gentle man. He has violent tendencies and always has, just like our father. Don't let him destroy you and Tye. Leave and go to your mother's."

She'd once met Hilda's mother and disliked her instantly. Nothing ever suited the woman or was good enough. She complained about everything. But maybe losing her husband with three kids to raise had made her that way. Other than her mother, Hilda had no other kin to turn to.

Hilda shook her head. "I can't. Mama said I made my bed and now I have to lie in it. She warned me from the start about Farrel, only I wouldn't listen. I wanted to see the best in him."

That was human nature—especially when tender feelings were involved.

"Then protect yourself by whatever means are at your disposal. An iron skillet can leave some damage." Paisley watched Tye through the window playing chase with Lucky. The boy didn't seem to have much energy. "Are you sure you and Tye aren't drinking the water? He still seems so listless."

"I'm positive. We only drink what's hauled in."

"Good. I guess it takes time to leave someone's system." Paisley patted Hilda's hand. "I've always wondered something. Why did you marry my brother? Didn't you see what he was like?"

"Honestly, I didn't. Maybe I didn't want to. Farrel hid his true self until long after we were married. It's odd, but he treated me nice. Bought me things. We talked of the future like we had one. Then he changed and got mean, and I discovered what I'd gotten into, but by then it was too late."

"That's true with a lot of us. Don't blame yourself."

"I can't help it. Now I have Tye to protect."

"Other than leaving or taking a skillet to Farrel, I have no advice." Paisley squeezed Hilda's hand again. "I'll do whatever I can, but that's not much." She was just as frightened of him. If only Jinx were real and had magical powers. Only Paisley had grown up now.

"Thank you." Hilda got to her feet. "I've got to get dinner on and keep an eye on Tye."

Paisley sat on the floor for a long while after Hilda left, thinking about everything and nothing. If she left, Hilda and Tye would be all by themselves. If Farrel hurt them more, she couldn't live with that on her conscience.

Yet if she stayed, her own life was in danger. What to do warred inside her.

Finally, all the sadness leaked out, leaving her limp. She rose and opened her mother's journal. The next page had a recipe for lemon chess pie. Only the directions were a bit odd. It directed the cook to squeeze the lemon into a bowl and section five eggs.

Section?

That made no sense. Had her mother gone completely daft?

The next page had a recipe for sour dough starter. It too was strange, with instructions to seek counsel before adding the sugar.

She gathered the journal and went into the parlor.

Farrel glanced up from the newspaper with a frown. "What?"

"I was reading Mama's journal, and I've come across several very odd entries that I don't know what to make of."

"That thing ain't nothing but an old woman's garbage. I read it, and you can throw it away for all I care. Ain't worth nothing to us. Not worth one hill of beans to anyone. Mama was stark raving crazy." He turned back to his newspaper. When she didn't leave, he snarled, "Don't start on me about messing up Crockett's ugly face. He had a butt-whooping coming."

"He can take care of himself—even while unable to see." She perched on a straight-backed chair and folded her hands in her lap. "I'm more concerned about Hilda and Tye. Why do you have to be so mean to the ones you're supposed to love? Stop hitting them."

A pair of strangers rode up outside. Farrel stood and glanced out the window, putting on his hat. His piercing eyes sought hers, and she wanted to shrink from what she saw, but she didn't move a muscle.

"Are you telling me how to treat my wife and son?"

She straightened her shoulders. "No, I'm saying I'll get the sheriff next time."

An angry growl sprang from his throat, and he took a step toward her. "Threaten me and you'll end up in a wooden box.

Don't think having family blood'll save you." He shook his fist. "Stay out of my way!"

Cold fear danced through her, but she didn't blink. Not even when he gave her a shove and stomped past. She didn't release her breath until her brother slammed the door and went to meet the strangers. A glance outside showed him grinning and shaking hands, then they hurried toward the back.

Chills around her spine turned to ice. A bad omen.

She was helpless to stop whatever Farrel planned but would sure try.

∽

Dr. Thorp cleaned and rebandaged his eyes, and already Crockett was encouraged by the blurred shapes and faces he could see. After Doc left, Crockett went out to sit in the sun on the sprawling porch that stretched across the front of his house, glad to have his own space on the ranch as well as in Quanah, thirty miles west, where he worked.

The town, named for the famed Comanche chief, came near to washing away in a flood the year after winning the county seat election in 1890. Then came a fire three months later that destroyed a good deal of businesses. Fair to say, the residents showed remarkable resilience, rebuilding bigger and better after each disaster, and maybe that's what Crockett most liked about the town. They never gave up no matter what calamity beset them.

Perseverance said a lot about a town—and a man. For Crockett, if there was one glimmer of a chance, he'd keep trying to win Paisley back.

The warm rays did little to fix the simmering irritation at himself. He shouldn't have let Farrel get under his skin, leading to the fistfight that he had no hope of winning. He knew better.

However, to back down would've been the coward's way out.

That was never Crockett. He was a Legend, and going full bore was in his blood. The Legend way was riding straight through hell, taking his licks, and coming out the other side with the problem fixed.

Yet Farrel had disrespected his own father by starting a fight at the funeral, and that seemed far worse than Crockett throwing down the gauntlet.

Footsteps sounded on the wooden porch, and the rumbling in the visitor's throat before he spoke belonged to his dad. "Doing some thinking I see. Your mother gave me the lowdown."

"Yessir." Crockett's lips formed a slight smile. "It sure felt good though to get in some blows. I just wish I had been able to see."

"At the end of the day, do you think you made anything worse?"

Crockett was silent in thought a moment. "Nope. Yet I can say with certainty it's no better either."

"Then don't let it bother you." Houston let out a long sigh, his boots scooting against the wood floor. "We do our best to get through. Sometimes we have regrets and wish we'd done things different. But it's a win anytime we can say we didn't make the situation worse, so pat yourself on the back. Over the years, I've had a lot of both kinds. You live to be as old as I am, you'll probably say the same."

"Thanks, Dad. I've been mulling it over, and I don't think I could've changed the outcome. Farrel was spoiling for a fight and has been for years." A moment's silence curled between them like the smoke from a pipe. "What do you think is going on over there?"

"Wish I knew, son. They haven't worked the land in quite a while and everything has fallen into ruin."

"How do you suppose they're getting money to live on?"

"Good question. Find that out and you'll have all the answers." The chair squeaked when Houston stood. "I have a little more work to do before dark. See you at supper."

Crockett sat listening to the calls of birds and the distant bawling of cattle. He had to find something to do or he'd go crazy. Where was that special ranger with the Cattle Raiser's Association? They needed to start investigating Joe Mahone's death. The sooner they determined what happened, the faster they could put an end to Farrel's outrageous and unsupported claims.

A shadow crossed Crockett's bandaged face. For a crazy moment, he fought down panic. Being blinded by the smoke had made him vulnerable.

But someone *was* there. He could feel them watching, could hear their breathing.

He forced firmness he didn't feel into his voice. "Who's there? Speak up."

Six

"Judge, it's me. Julia Bishop" came a soft voice. "I brought Race with me, sir."

His law clerks. Their identity settled, Crockett relaxed. "Miss Bishop, you're a welcome sight. You too, Race. Well, not exactly 'sight' since I'm unable to see at the moment." He motioned them forward. "Sit with me. I was just thinking how much I needed something to do. I'm about to go mad. I prefer staying busy, and this inactivity is killing me."

The air fluttered as the pair took chairs next to him on the wide porch.

Race Grant had applied for a job about a year ago. Julia had been with Crockett even shorter than that. Both were top-notch, and his courtroom had run smoother with their skills.

"How are things in Quanah?" He tilted his face toward where he thought they'd sat.

"Pretty peaceful," Julia answered. "Chief Quanah Parker and three of his wives visited the Matador Ranch and made the news. The reporter took a nice picture of them at Ballard Springs."

The old Comanche was living the good life these days and taking full advantage of the press. But then being friends with the president came with all sorts of benefits that the shrewd chief was quick to grab.

"Somehow that doesn't surprise me." The fragrance of sage and wildflowers drifted on the breeze. Crockett inhaled the scent that brought some measure of peace. Spring brought rebirth over the land—even though it was rife with discord and falsehoods.

Race Grant interrupted his thoughts. "We didn't know about the trouble until we got here. The telegraph your father sent simply asked us both to come."

"What happened was no accident." For the next few minutes, Crockett gave them a brief version of the events. "Doc says with luck I should regain my vision in a week or so. I've taken a month's leave to focus on recovering." He paused a moment. "I need to work. But first, could I offer you some refreshment?"

When both clerks declined, Crockett leaned forward. "So let's get to it."

Over the next several hours, they went over Crockett's docket, deciding which cases could be postponed. The urgent ones would have to be assigned to another judge. Then they worked on the current files Crockett had already begun hearing.

"I think we made good progress. How long do you propose being out?" As always, Julia's cultured voice spoke of education and refinement that seemed incongruous with her impish reddish-brown curls and tinkling laughter. At twenty-six, with her share of beaus, it puzzled Crockett why the pretty woman had never married.

He pondered her question before he answered. "I should return in some capacity within a month, but I expect I'll be traveling between my office in Quanah and the ranch for quite a while."

Who knew how long before things would settle down with Farrel? If ever.

The feud showed no signs of abating. One fact remained. The best shot seemed with Paisley.

And who better than Crockett to extend an olive branch? Their previous relationship gave him better insight into her. Or did it? Maybe he only wanted to think so. He hadn't done so good lately.

"When you get back to town, I want you to check the land records and see who holds the deed for a section of land here on the Lone Star. Telegraph that information to me here."

"Sure, Judge." Julia took down the information, and judging from the rustle of paper, she had begun to gather her things. "I'll do it right away."

"Hey, do you mind if we ride for an hour or two this afternoon?" Race asked. "We don't get much of a chance, being stuck in town, and I miss it."

"I'd love that too." Julia's soft voice held wistfulness.

"Absolutely. I'll take you over, and you can pick one out. I'll get my sister Hannah to advise you. She'll let you ride any except her favorite, Mister Pete." Crockett rose and let Julia take his arm.

Dammit! He felt like a doddering old fool having to be led around.

Though he knew it was just supposed to be temporary, a part of him wondered if the doc was wrong. Maybe this would go the other way and end up permanent. He didn't think he could live as a blind man.

As luck would have it, Hannah was with the horses. "If you want a smart one that won't give you any sass, I recommend Missy for you, Miss Bishop. And Gentleman Jim for Race."

"Sounds good." Julia released Crockett's arm. "I'll saddle her, Hannah."

Race had been around horses all his life and took firm command of the three-year-old gelding. His confident voice let the horse know he wouldn't put up with any shenanigans.

After the pair left, Crockett draped an arm around Hannah and kissed her cheek. "Thanks, sis."

"I was happy to do it. I'm glad they came. You needed to dive back into work."

"How did you know?"

"I've been watching you. You've been like a caged lion."

Crockett growled. "At seventeen, you should be setting your cap for someone who tickles your fancy, not watching after your big brother."

Hannah gave a soft snort. "I've decided to be like Grace and have a career."

"Even our independent and headstrong sister finally married," he countered.

"But not after first establishing a name for herself as a newspaper reporter for the *Fort Worth Gazette*. She showed that women can do more than cook, sew, and raise children."

"That she did." Crockett shifted as memories circled in his head of the danger Grace had put herself in while tracking down and rescuing a bunch of orphan boys from a Thurber, Texas, coal mine. But it was while working hand in hand with Deacon Brannock in that endeavor that led to their marriage. "Okay, Hannah. What kind of career do you want to forge?"

A long pause ensued before Hannah replied, "I want to take Mister Pete to the Olympics. We've been jumping hurdles that Dad set up and practicing a lot."

Crockett sucked in a breath. He'd known she ate, slept, and breathed horses, especially Mister Pete. And she'd read every article she could find about the Olympics held in St. Louis, Missouri, in 1904. But this took him by surprise. "Don't they have one this year?"

"In London, but I've missed that one. Stockholm, Sweden is the host in 1912." Her voice held excitement. "I know I can have him ready by then."

"That's four years away. A lot can happen between now and then, Hannah. And how do you propose getting to Sweden?"

"I haven't exactly figured that part out yet." Defiance snuck into her voice. "Grace says anything is possible if I work hard enough and believe. I really, really want this. I want it more than anything in the whole world. I'll find a way to get there somehow."

Never one to throw cold water on anyone's dream, Crockett aimed a smile his sister's way and tightened his arm around her. "You can count on me to help make it happen."

"Thanks, Crockett." She paused. "I'm not a silly girl with unrealistic expectations."

"I know."

"This won't be easy, but I'm certain me and Mister Pete can make a good showing and maybe bring home a medal. He's got what it takes. I've never seen a more intelligent horse anywhere. He works extremely hard."

Crockett laughed. "Hey, you don't have to sell me. I've seen him in action."

"Sorry, I get carried away." She slipped out of his arm. "Do you want me to show you back to your house?"

"You know, I think I'll steal a little of your independence and go see what Mama's doing." Besides, he had an idea clinking around in his head.

"She'll like that. See you at supper. Will your law clerks join us?"

"Yes, they won't go back to town until morning."

Parting ways, Crockett grabbed a walking stick and followed the worn footpath. He managed to reach his parents' home without falling on his face.

He scaled the porch steps without incident and went inside. "Mama? You busy?"

"She's gone." His younger brother, Ransom, strolled through the kitchen door, from the sound, chewing on something. The smell said it was a chicken leg.

"Gone where?"

"Said something about paying Paisley Mahone a visit. That's all I know."

A jolt of surprise rippled through Crockett. He and his mother had always had the same thoughts, but he'd expected to have to talk her into going. The one person who might get through to Paisley was another woman—one with no rooster in this fight. Just compassion.

He closed his eyes for a moment and sent the hope heavenward that his mother would succeed.

∽

A rider sounded outside the Mahone house. Paisley glanced out the window to see an elegant horsewoman in a blue riding skirt and leather jacket. The guest dismounted and patted the handsome chestnut mare before making her way to the porch.

Halfway to the door, Paisley recognized Lara Legend. Had Crockett sent his mother? What a low trick. Anger rose.

It wasn't going to work. Still, she'd hear Lara out. She'd always admired the strong woman who'd not hesitated to pull out a small handgun and fire it to stop the fight.

By the time Lara made it to the house, Paisley had opened the door. "I don't know what we have to discuss, Miss Lara."

"Please hear me out."

Paisley silently stepped aside and let Lara enter.

Lara wasted no time. "I hope your brother isn't home. This needs to be between us women."

"He's out but might not be gone long. You can speak your piece."

Lara peeled soft kid gloves from her fingers. "I'll make this short."

"Let's sit in the parlor." Paisley led the way and offered her a chair. "Did Crockett send you?"

"No, dear. He doesn't know I came. This was my idea alone. No one else need know."

Paisley nodded. "I'm glad. Your son is very headstrong and intent on having his way." She sighed. "That aside, he has his good points. I've never known a gentler, kinder man."

"Don't you want to marry and have a family?"

"It's impossible." Paisley gave a short laugh. "Besides, I wouldn't know how to live normally. Most everything I've ever known has been fighting and anger."

Which prompted the need for powerful, imaginary people.

"You can change that," Lara said softly. "We can fix what we don't like if we have the courage."

Paisley gave her a wan smile. "I ran out of that a long time ago."

"I don't believe that for a moment, dear. Crockett told me how you kept your wits about you during the train holdup, then tried your best to save the young boy. That's not the mark of a weak woman." Laura paused a moment. "But that's not what brought me. I came to beg you to listen to your heart and not believe everything your brother is putting in your head. Our family has never tried to cheat, kill, or engage in criminal activity to further ourselves. I think you know that."

"Sometimes I don't know what to believe. I'm so tired and heartsick."

"Honey, you've sat at our table, listened to the conversation, shared in so many happy times. Don't you think if we'd been doing bad things, you'd have heard us speak of them? At least somewhat."

The woman's quiet voice offered gentle comfort that was like a balm to her soul. No one had shown her more kindness and compassion. For a moment, it seemed as if her mother was sitting across from her. Paisley knew what Lara said to be true. The Legends were honest people. She couldn't let her father's and Farrel's ranting into her head. Her mother was right. She had to rise above that.

But her mother had betrayed her with Stoker.

"Think for yourself," Lara urged. "Wild accusations can destroy people's lives."

"My brother is eaten up with hate, and I stand as much chance of changing his mind as a zebra changing its stripes." Paisley jumped to her feet and began to pace. "He's dangerous. But I guess you already know that. I hate what he did to Crockett. And setting fire to your barn. For God's sake, his small son is already trying to find a way to escape his wrath. I know what Farrel is and what he's capable of, Miss Lara. But I can't help you."

"I didn't hold out any hope for that. I was only trying to make you see that we're not trying to kill you off or take your land." Lara stood. "I just came to see you, dear. Because I care and am concerned about your welfare."

Voices sounded outside, and Paisley froze. If Farrel found Lara here, no telling… "You have to go. Hurry. I'll see you out the back."

Lara's eyes widened. "My horse. I left it in front. He'll see."

A glance out the window had Farrel already checking out Lara's pretty chestnut.

"Paisley! Get out here!" he bellowed.

Her throat as dry as a piece of burned cornbread, Paisley wrung her hands. "Please, hurry out the back, Miss Lara. Then hide until I fetch you."

"Honey, I can handle myself. And Farrel. He won't harm me."

"Don't be crazy. Farrel has a vendetta against all Legends. That includes you." She would never forgive herself if her brother hurt Miss Lara, one of the kindest people she knew.

"Sister, don't make me come and find you!" Farrel barked. "You won't like it."

He said something to the two men and started for the door. Paisley's heart hammered against her ribs. They'd be lucky to escape his wrath without serious injury.

Seven

UNCHARACTERISTICALLY CALM, HILDA SUDDENLY APPEARED in the parlor doorway, wiping her hands on her apron. "Paisley, take Miss Lara out the back. I'll tell Farrel the horse wandered up or some such story."

"Are you sure?"

"Hurry, we have no time to waste. You know your brother's temper."

Studying Hilda's eyes, Paisley nodded. "All right, we'll do this your way."

Tye peeked around his mother's skirt, his eyes as large as silver dollars. Hilda pushed him toward Paisley. "Go with your aunt, son."

"I go with you, Mama."

"Paisley, take him, and don't let him come back until…" Hilda's voice broke. She raised her chin and stopped her trembling. "I'll come get all of you when it's safe."

"I have a gun, Hilda." Lara took it from her pocket. "Take it."

Hilda shook her head. "No, ma'am. The sight of that will only inflame my husband. Besides, he knows I'd never use it on him. Now go."

Paisley had never been prouder of her sister-in-law. She picked up Tye and ushered Lara toward the kitchen and outside. "Run for the barn, Miss Lara. We'll get behind it."

Ducking low to the ground, they sprinted for the dilapidated structure. Lucky thought it was a game and raced around them. Paisley didn't take a full breath until they made it to cover. Tye began to cry silent tears. She hugged him close. "It's all right, sweetheart. Don't be afraid. I won't let anything happen to you."

The boy bravely wiped his eyes with the back of his hand. He clung to her, his chin quivering. Lucky licked his free hand, drawing a pat on the head.

"Let's sit on those crates." Paisley hurried them over. Lucky laid down in front of them.

Lara patted Tye's shoulder. "You're such a good little soldier. I'm really scared though. Would you mind sitting in my lap to keep me calm?"

He nodded and moved over to her. At first, he was stiff, and it took a bit to relax. Bit by bit, he rested his head against her and didn't object when Lara folded her arms around him. "You're such a sweet boy, you know that?" she crooned. "I used to have two little boys, but they've gotten big."

"Where do them live?" he asked.

With one ear tuned to the faint voices outside, Paisley watched the trust build and knew she wouldn't go wrong in putting her faith in her mother's dearest friend. She listened to Lara's gentle voice answering Tye's questions. At last, the boy lapsed into silence. He was listening too, jumping at each noise. Getting ready to run.

Tears filled Paisley's eyes. This was so wrong. No four-year-old should be this frightened. Especially of his own father.

She stood and went to peer through a wide crack in the barn wall. Farrel suddenly came around the corner of the house, leading the pretty chestnut mare, with Hilda running behind.

"I told you the horse wandered up. I found her in front of the house," Hilda told him.

Farrel whirled. "Why should I believe you? A horse of this quality just don't wander up. Someone rode that mare. I'm betting it was Crockett." He put his hands around her throat. "Tell me."

Paisley gasped. She had to help her sister-in-law. But how? She gathered her strength and turned to Lara. "No matter what happens, stay here and keep Tye safe."

"Please, Farrel," Hilda begged, her voice straining with the lack of air.

Taking a deep breath, Paisley rushed out. "What are you doing? Stop it this instant."

"Ahhh, sis. Always coming to the rescue." Her brother released his hold on Hilda. He wore the most frightening expression. "Where are you hiding your friend, Crockett? Huh?"

"Have you lost your mind? Stop it. I'm not hiding anyone. Least of all Crockett Legend. In case you haven't noticed, we're not speaking."

Farrel narrowed his eyes. "Then where did this horse bearing the Legend brand come from?"

"I don't know, but you can bet they're looking for it. What are you going to do?"

"I think I'll keep it. Could come in handy." He barked a laugh. "This is my lucky day."

Paisley stared, her mouth dry, her heart racing. How would Lara get home? If the horse were to disappear, Farrel would fly into a rage and accuse her or Hilda.

"The smart thing would be for us to return the mare before they accuse us of stealing her," she suggested. "They'll bring the law out here, and I don't think you want that. You could go to jail." She jerked her head toward the house. "I don't know who those strange men are or what you have up your sleeve, but I know you're doing something underhanded."

Farrel's expression shifted, darkening. "That's my business. Stay out of it."

"Then there's the raid you made on Houston Legend and burning his horse barn," she pointed out. "Should they find evidence of that, you'll be in deep trouble."

Soft tendrils of dark hair curled around Hilda's face. She moved to Paisley's side. "I heard you and your buddies making those plans."

"Is that a threat, wife?" Farrel clenched his fists and took a step.

Paisley moved in front, shielding her sister-in-law. "I wouldn't."

Her brother's two persistent shadows rounded the side of the house. The taller man said, "We need a word, Mahone."

Farrel shot them a glance and nodded, then turned back to the women. "Take the horse. As you said, why jeopardize one far more important thing with something so small. I don't need this. But never cross me again. Either of you, or you'll have hell to pay." He dropped the reins and joined the men, then all three hurried from sight toward the place with the platform and tools she'd seen in the moonlight.

"Hilda, do you know what they're doing down there?" Paisley asked.

"I only know that Farrel thinks it'll make him rich." Hilda swung toward the barn. "We need to get Miss Lara out of here while we can."

"I agree."

Lara wasted no time in mounting her mare. "Both of you get Tye and come with me. Get away from Farrel. He's dangerous."

Paisley shook her head. "This is our home. I have to find out what's going on for all our sakes."

"Then listen. There's an old stump at the boundary between our two properties where we can pass notes back and forth. Keep me apprised of the situation here. I'll worry."

Having a way of communicating brought Paisley relief.

"I will, Miss Lara. Farrel likes to bark loud, but we've learned how to deal with him." She squeezed the woman's hand. "Thank you for caring."

Yet as Lara Legend rode away, Paisley shivered as though her heart had plunged into a bucket of ice water.

❧

Crockett rose from the porch the minute he heard his mother ride up. "Ransom said you went to visit Paisley Mahone."

"Yes, I did."

He heard worry in his mother's voice. "What happened?"

"Let me put Sandy away first."

"I'll go with you. This can't wait." He felt his way down the steps and his mother took his arm.

"Farrel almost caught me."

The blood slowed to a trickle in his veins. "Tell me all of it."

In the stroll to the barn they were using for the horses until the new one could be built, she related every detail about her trip to see Paisley.

Once she finished, Crockett was quiet for a long minute. "You came very close to losing your life, Mother. Promise you won't do that again. Farrel is unpredictable, and he's furious that we've thwarted him at every turn. He won't stop until...." Crockett's words trailed off.

Lara gripped his arm. "Until one of us dies. Isn't that what you were going to say?"

"No, Mother. Until we put him down like we do a mad dog."

But his thoughts went much deeper than that. When a rabid dog had to be put down, it usually called for a rifle. Farrel Mahone hadn't indicated that he was much different. Crockett feared for Paisley's life.

"You really told Paisley to leave messages in the old stump and we'd do the same?"

"Certainly. It's the safest way to keep the line of communication open."

"I agree." In fact, this was perfect and would suit Crockett's need to see her.

His mother shifted. "Here come your two clerks. Riding must've been good for them."

Dammit! He cursed being unable to see for himself.

"Why's that?"

"Julia's radiant cheeks for one thing. She's glowing, and Race Grant is laughing. I think they're in love."

Crockett chuckled. "You have such a habit of trying to get people married off, Miss Matchmaker. No, I don't think they have romantic designs on each other."

He sensed her smile. "Stop it."

Lara sniffed. "You're just a man. You can't see what's in front of you. You and your father are two of a kind."

"Believe what you will." Crockett kissed her cheek. "You're incorrigible."

"Your father says the same thing."

The lilt in his mother's voice made him happy. The danger had passed, and she had moved on, even if Crockett hadn't. He stewed about Farrel all during supper. He had to do something to help Paisley.

But what?

❧

The following day, Crockett received a telegram from Julia Bishop. He hurried to ranch headquarters, catching his grandfather, father, and Luke there. "This just came."

"Read what it says, Houston," Stoker urged.

The paper rustled, and Houston cleared his throat. "Caroline Mahone still appears to be the owner of the Jessup land."

"I guess that settles that," Luke said. "She did not change the deed."

Crockett breathed a sigh of relief. Paisley was still safe for the moment. As long as Farrel didn't learn about the existence of the land deed, things would be fine.

But if her brother somehow got wind of the section? Ice slid down Crockett's back.

A grunt came from Stoker. "We bide our time and move carefully. I promised not to interfere."

Crockett bit his tongue and listened as his grandfather and father went head-to-head.

Houston exploded. "Well, I didn't! Tell us what biding our time means."

Stoker bristled. "We don't do anything. Just watch and wait."

"For the world to crash down around us?" Houston countered. "Hell!"

"As long as Paisley harbors anger against us," Stoker said, "we can't breathe a word. Caroline stipulated that when she handed me the envelope to put in safekeeping."

"What envelope?" Luke hollered. "This is the first we've heard."

The air sizzled, and Crockett knew his grandpa was glaring. "You better start talking, Pa."

"You're both getting too big for your britches. Remember that I'm the father here." The desk chair creaked, indicating someone, Crockett assumed Stoker, sat. "Caroline knew she wasn't going to recover, so she gave me a sealed envelope to hold for Paisley. I don't know what's in it, and Caroline didn't say."

"For God's sake, open it!" Houston shouted.

"I gave my word I'd keep the seal intact."

"Well, we didn't!" Luke yelled. "Give it to us."

The loud voices were bouncing off the walls of headquarters like cannonballs. Crockett's head was about to bust open. He let out a shrill whistle. "Stop yelling and settle down."

"Like it or not, we're going to get to the bottom of this, Pa," Houston snapped.

A hand slapped the mahogany desk. "No one is going to open the envelope except Paisley. And until she proves her strength, it'll stay sealed. What good is it for her to get the deed only to hand it over to Farrel?" Typical of Stoker, a growl from deep inside sprang from his mouth. "She has to prove she has Jessup blood and is willing to fight for what she wants."

Crockett's ire rose. "Is she on trial here? Is that it?"

"I suppose in a manner of speaking, my boy."

"I can't believe this." Crockett ran his fingers through his hair. "In the meantime, she deserves our protection, and I'm going to see that she gets it."

"Of course, son. We'll try to keep her safe." The voice belonged to his dad. So did the hand on his shoulder.

"Thank God for that at least," Crockett mumbled.

"We won't stand by and see Farrel hurt her," Houston said. "But as far as the land goes, how do we know that Caroline Mahone didn't have a change of heart there at the end and intended the section to go to Farrel?" Anger tinged Houston's voice. "We don't know…and she can't say."

The words hung in the air like mist on top of water for what seemed several minutes. Finally, his grandfather cleared his throat. "Paisley Mahone will come around. She has a good head on her shoulders. When she comes to me, I'll hand her the envelope in my possession."

"And if she doesn't?" Crockett was tempted to tell her. She had a right to know.

"Then there is nothing we can do." The chair squeaked again. Heavy breathing told Crockett Stoker had risen. He could feel the old man's eyes on him. "Say one word to her, and I'll deny everything. You'll never prove any of what I've told you."

"You have my word, Grandpa." Even though it'd kill him, Crockett would keep silent.

He'd likely bite his tongue half off though.

❧

The next few days passed with no note in the old stump. Crockett counted each sunrise, anxious to get his bandages off. He had things to do and a murder to solve.

But all he really wanted was to hold Paisley in his arms and tell her everything would be all right, even though it might not be for a while.

His heart heavy, he stepped out of headquarters about dusk as footsteps sounded on the porch.

The male voice projected authority. "I was told I could find Judge Crockett Legend here."

"You've found him." Crockett angled his head toward the visitor. "I apologize for not being able to see. My dad's horse barn was set on fire, and smoke temporarily blinded me in the attempt to save them. I don't mean to be rude, but who are you?"

"I'm Special Agent Alex Lancer from the Cattle Raiser's Association."

Relief flooded over Crockett. "I've been waiting for you."

"Sorry. Another investigation kept me tied up."

"Come on inside. My family is here and should be with us to help keep the facts straight." Crockett held the door and ushered the man inside.

Now maybe they could get to the bottom of Joe Mahone's mysterious death, and Paisley would see beyond a doubt that the Legends had nothing to do with it.

Hope burst like a rosebud unfurling its petals.

Even if his firefly refused to renew their relationship, at least she wouldn't hate him.

Eight

CROCKETT AND THE OTHERS SPENT THE NEXT SEVERAL HOURS detailing everything they knew, including that Caroline Mahone died a year and a half ago after suffering broken bones following a fall. He'd often wondered about the circumstances of that accident.

"What's your next step?" He needed the water to be tested and for this feud to end as soon as possible.

A notebook snapped shut, and the special ranger spoke. "Judge, I think I have the facts. I'll pay the Mahones a visit and see what I can learn."

Grandpa Stoker's voice sounded on Crockett's right. "It's late, Lancer. I suggest you let us put you up for the night in one of the guest cottages and get an early start come morning."

Although he knew what the answer would be, Crockett couldn't help asking. "I'd like to accompany you."

The special ranger's voice was quiet, and Crockett imagined he wore a frown. "I can't let you do that, Judge. It would only add fuel to the fire that's already burning out of control."

The door opened, and Doc Thorp spoke, "I need you when you're finished, Crockett."

"We're through, Doc." Crockett got to his feet. "Your office or the study here?"

Houston's voice came from somewhere close. "What's going on?"

"I want to remove his bandages. Nothing can be gained by leaving them on longer. Either he can see or he can't." Doc Thorp released a sigh. "It'll be what it will. Wish I could say how this will go. But I can't."

Neither could Crockett. Nervous sweat rose on his forehead. He'd pushed the possibility of remaining blind to the back of his mind but no longer could. The time had come.

"What do you need, Thorp?" Stoker asked in his gruff way.

"Just a quiet room." Doc put a hand on Crockett's arm. "Let's go across the hall."

"His mother and I are coming." It was typical of Houston to state the fact instead of asking the question, thus brooking no word to the contrary.

"I'll get Special Ranger Lancer settled for the night," Stoker said, "but I expect a full report, Doc."

Crockett imagined his grandpa's piercing stare from beneath his shaggy eyebrows, the way Stoker had looked at him over the years. Or anyone he was trying to intimidate.

The rumbling in the doctor's throat said he was out of patience. "You'll get it, Legend."

They moved across the hall to the study.

"Dim the lamps, Miss Lara." Dr. Thorp led Crockett to a chair and began to remove the thick gauze from around Crockett's head. "Keep your eyes closed until I say to open them."

Slowly, light started to penetrate. Even with his lids lowered, Crockett could discern between light and darkness.

Hope rose. One more layer of gauze left.

When everything was gone, Crockett sucked in air between his teeth. This was it.

Doc's voice sounded by his ear. "Slowly open your eyes, son. Allow time to adjust."

His lids fluttered and watered as light began to hit them. Although Doc's face was blurry, he could make him out. He then blinked and moved to his parents. Lara's pretty features and Houston's dark hair with gray streaks came into focus. He blinked again, and they became clearer.

"I can see all of you. My vision improves each time I blink."

"That's wonderful. I'm so happy." Lara clutched her chest.

He couldn't see her tears, but he knew they were there because he had them in his own eyes. Now, he could see his beautiful firefly's face when she let him hold her again.

And one day she would. He believed that.

Most of all, he could protect her, and that was huge.

Doc Thorp looked in his eyes. "I want you to avoid bright lights for a while. There's more healing to do before you're normal."

"Thank you, Doctor." Crockett shook his hand. He hugged his parents and went out into the fresh air, needing to be alone. Darkness had settled over the land and was good for his eyes.

His steps led to the horses, where he quickly saddled his blue roan. "Let's go for a ride, Cato."

The gelding nickered and shook his black mane. Ransom rode him on a regular basis, which worked out well between Crockett's visits to the ranch. Occasionally, his cousin Elena Rose would ride him also, she being an expert horsewoman.

He led Cato from the barn and found Elena Rose dismounting. "Riding out late, Elena?"

She gave a throaty laugh and tossed her long black hair. "A habit I have, much to Papá's dismay. I fear he'd keep me locked inside the house if it weren't for Mamá."

That probably had to do with the fact that Luke Legend was once an outlaw and knew what lurked inside the hearts of men where a pretty woman was concerned.

"He just loves you and doesn't want to see you hurt."

Elena sighed. "I know. But I want to live. I want to do exciting things. Go places."

"Like where and do what? Do you have something specific in mind?"

A dreamy look came into Elena Rose's dark eyes. "I want to design and make beautiful clothes. I want to go to New York City, but I'd settle for Dallas."

Everyone had passion for something special. Maybe Crockett could help. If so, he would.

"How about riding with me? I could use the company."

"I'd love it." She stuck one booted foot into the stirrup and swung up. "I see you're not wearing your bandage. Are your eyes healed?"

"They're getting there." Crockett cast her a look. "Are you up for some adventure?"

"Always, Cousin. Where are we going?"

"The boundary separating us and the Mahones. I promise it won't be dangerous."

Her eyes danced. "I wouldn't mind if it is. I'm tired of being coddled. Papá can't see that I'm a grown woman."

A glance at his cousin and Crockett could see why Luke had set boundaries. Elena Rose's beauty was the kind to turn men into babbling idiots. Her flawless light-brown skin set her apart from other women, and her large, amber eyes added an air of mystery. For the life of him, he couldn't remember her age. Early twenties he thought, about five or six years younger than him and Gracie.

He laughed. "All the Legend men suffer from this malady. My dad tried his best to keep Grace in a box, and they butted heads over and over until she finally just did as she wanted anyway. I suspect you'll strike out on your own soon."

"I dream of a life beyond this ranch. One day I will escape."

They fell silent and rode across the ranch land under a million twinkling stars. Awash in thankfulness, Crockett had never felt so alive. He'd taken a great many things for granted.

Worse, he'd squandered his relationship with Paisley. And lost her.

A damn stubborn ego had gotten in the way. He'd thought his plans were all that mattered and hers seemed insignificant. Silly even.

A memory sparked in his head.

"Crockett, it's acceptable for women to have careers now, not just men," she'd said. "Ever since I was a little girl, I wanted to help people get well and fix their bodies."

He'd frowned and kissed her cheek, smoothing her hair. "You mean a doctor?"

"No, a nurse. I have an aptitude for it."

"What's wrong with marrying me and having our babies? Wouldn't that keep you busy? Wouldn't being a wife and mother be enough? I'll provide for you."

She'd jumped to her feet. "You sound just like Daddy and Farrel. I thought you'd be different. That you'd support me. I was so very wrong. You're like all the rest. I'm smart and I deserve a chance. Go on off to your law school." She had turned to leave and stopped. Tears clung to the lashes, framing her pale-green eyes, and a soft breeze toyed with her silky, blond hair. "This can't work. Forget about me and go your separate way."

His heart aching, he'd watched his beautiful firefly walk out of his life. He hadn't known then what he'd thrown away.

Though far too late, he did understand so much now.

If a man captured a firefly and put it in a jar, it died. It only lived when free to fly.

A shooting star shot above them in the sky and quickly faded, just like Paisley had from his life. It was impossible to go back, but if fate granted a second chance, he'd change many things and plan for the future he'd lost.

They trotted for about an hour, then slowed the horses. The old stump shone in the moonlight. The place was deserted.

Elena dismounted. "Funny, but Paisley and I used to write notes back and forth and put them in the hole in the middle of that stump."

Crockett had forgotten that the two women used to be really close friends despite the four-year age difference. "Have you seen her since her return?"

"No. I'm sure she's busy with her father just dying and everything. And there's the feud…" Her voice trailed off, followed by a shrug. "She probably doesn't want to see me anyway."

The supple leather creaked as Crockett swung from the saddle. "You should try."

"Maybe I will."

"Leave her a note. My mother went to see her and made Paisley promise to write notes occasionally. Do you have paper and pencil?"

"A journal. I wrote in it today while I rode."

"There you go." When Elena hesitated, he added softly, "I think she'd love hearing from a friend."

She nodded and got the journal out. While she wrote, he walked to the stump. In the dim light, he made out a scrap of white that he pulled out. His heart hammered as he opened it. Squinting, he tried to read the name at the bottom but was unable.

"Elena, see if you can make out who left this."

She glanced at it. "PM."

Paisley Mahone.

"Read what it says."

Miss Lara or Crockett, I may have some information regarding Farrel.

Elena's eyes met Crockett's. "What's going on?"

He quickly filled her in and said the special ranger with the Cattle Raiser's had arrived to investigate. "Not sure yet, but the Mahones' water might be bad."

"I see. I'd like to help if I can."

"Let me think on it. I'll probably know more after the special ranger goes out to their place in the morning. But you wouldn't be near as threatening to Farrel as us men."

She gave a throaty laugh. "You haven't seen me mad lately, Cousin."

"No, I haven't, but I imagine you're your father's daughter."

And that would be fierce. Luke Legend had certainly made many a man look for a hole to crawl into and pull it in after him. Crockett glanced toward the Mahone place. "At the moment, I need you to ride back to safety. I'm about to do something that may get me shot."

"You might need me. It'd be best if I tag along."

"Can't let you do that." He motioned to the page she'd torn from her journal. "Write your note and put it in the stump, then get going."

Pouting, she did as he requested, albeit with a great deal of reluctance. The note in place, she turned for home.

Only after she was out of sight did Crockett set his course with no clear agenda in mind. This was a reconnaissance mission only.

Unless certain opportunities presented themselves.

~❧~

Paisley sat on her bed, reading her mother's journal. It seemed she was moving along a dark path, trying to find her way with nothing making sense. There were so many garbled entries containing strange words that fit nothing. Her mother seemed to be talking about land with the mention of two hundred and fifty-eight hectares.

Wait. That equaled one section of land.

Was Caroline talking about the section she lost to the Legends? In the next sentence, she wrote, "Ask and you shall receive."

There was Stoker's name again with the word envelope next to it inside a square.

What on earth? Paisley rubbed her eyes and closed the book. Maybe Farrel was right, and their mother had been in some sort of delirium.

Drawn by the need for some fresh night air, she threw a shawl around her shoulders and stepped out the back door. The fragrant scent whispered against her face, and she inhaled the sweetness that reminded her of another time with Crockett. He'd thrown pebbles at her window to get her attention and talked her into taking a night ride with him.

He'd just returned from Fort Worth and the cattle broker job he'd had there for a short while. She'd been excited, hoping he'd settle down on the Lone Star where she could work with the ranch doctor.

Enthralled with the tall, handsome cowboy, she climbed on a mare he'd brought for her, and they rode to the bluff overlooking the Red River. For hours, they talked and kissed in the moonlight, and she'd felt so special. Love for him had beat inside her heart as she listened to his voice.

Until the blinders came off and she'd seen that he had more love and passion for his plans and his acceptance into law school than he'd ever had for her.

He'd only brought her along to listen to his plans, and it had crushed her.

That had been a hard lesson to learn, and now he no longer held the ability to hurt her. She'd grown into a woman with a career and goals of her own.

Still, she knew he'd be there in a moment if she should need him. A quiet promise came back to her. *If you ever find yourself in need of a friend, send word. I'll be there in a heartbeat.*

Yes, he would. She had no doubt about that at all. A few times she'd been tempted to send word. To lay her head on his broad shoulders, his arms around her, just having a friend to help would've been worth everything.

She stared up at the moon and wondered what her life might've been like had she married Crockett. Would he have gotten so carried away with court cases and only remembered her when hunger pangs had hit? Would she have existed at all? Maybe the nights would've been just as lonely as they were now.

But that wasn't quite fair to only think of one outcome.

Perhaps he'd have made an attentive, loving husband, driving her to distraction with hot kisses, his hard body filling her, murmuring sweet words in her ear.

Paisley gave herself a firm shake. *Stop it. That's not the way it turned out.*

Some things no amount of wishing could change. Life had moved on, and she wasn't that schoolgirl with stars in her eyes.

Nine

SILENCE ENVELOPED CROCKETT AS HE AND CATO MADE THEIR way toward the Mahone house. Every nerve had stretched to the breaking point. The smallest noise sounded like a gunshot. Danger, sharp and thick, crawled up his neck. Farrel could catch him and be within his rights to shoot him. A lantern up ahead wove through the brush. He dismounted and looped Cato's reins around a mesquite branch.

It never occurred to him to turn around. Paisley needed him, and he meant to get to her.

On foot was slower but far safer. Light from the lantern was coming closer. What were they looking for? Paisley? Maybe she'd struck out, determined to get help.

He knelt and took the gun from his boot. As he progressed, his heel dislodged a rock and sent it tumbling down an embankment. Dammit! He froze, listening.

"What was that?" a man asked from approximately thirty-five yards away.

A snarl came from his companion. "Probably a night animal. Quit jumping."

"It's spooky out here, and the Legends are a stone's throw away. Why did I let Farrel talk me into this? The man's a lunatic. I can't believe half of what he says. Do you really think we'll get rich by the time this is over?"

Crockett frowned. Rich? From what?

A grunt came from the second speaker. "I'm going to stick around and find out."

"All I'm saying is remember how him and his old man tricked us before with talk of taking everything the Legends have? Hell, they got more today than they ever had."

"And some of it has got to be from dirty dealings," the partner snapped.

"Remind me again why we're out here."

"Keeping an eye out for trespassers. We might get lucky and get us a Legend. Or that sister of Farrel's. I heard him say he'd just as soon she be deep in a grave." The speaker laughed. "But I'd sure like to get her naked and have some fun first. Whoo-ee!"

"That sister is sure a pretty little filly. I wouldn't mind finding out how wild she is."

Crockett's blood ran cold. If anyone tried to hurt Firefly, he'd make sure they regretted it.

The two moved on, their light bobbing with each step. He'd give them a wide berth. He moved slowly toward the house, taking each step slow and careful. There wasn't much cover to hide behind. Plus, the moon was too full. But living in darkness behind his bandages for a week had sharpened his night vision. He needed no lantern.

The back of the house came into view. Crockett ducked behind the corner of the saggy barn and studied it. Dim light shone in the kitchen and again in a room to his left.

Where was the dog? He distinctly remembered one. The pooch would give him away. He waited quietly for a while, and when a dog didn't appear, he stole forward.

Now that he was here, what was the next move? He couldn't very well stride up and knock.

One thing was clear though. He wasn't leaving without talking to Paisley.

Busy contemplating the problem, he almost missed a shadow that emerged from the house and walked toward him. He caught the flash of a skirt. Farrel's wife? He couldn't recall her name. Just then the moonlight tangled in a wealth of blond hair.

Paisley.

Crockett readied himself, and before she reached him, he stepped out, clapping his hand over her mouth. "I won't hurt you."

She gasped, her scream silenced by his palm. He led her behind the dilapidated barn. "It's me—Crockett."

At her nod, he removed his hand. "I read the note you left at the stump."

She pushed her hood back. "I thought your mother would get that." Paisley touched his face. "Your eyes. Are they well?"

"Getting there. Doc removed my bandages tonight."

"I'm so glad you can see. That's wonderful."

He lifted a strand of silky gold. "Makes two of us. I hope you don't mind that I came instead. It's too dangerous for my mother."

God, she looked even more beautiful than he remembered. Her light-green eyes had turned silvery gray in the dim light, and the freckle to the right of her mouth seemed to wink at him. But that was probably his imagination. In any event, the frost in her voice was gone, and for that he was extremely thankful.

"You shouldn't be here." She moistened her lips. "Farrel hates you."

"I know but I had to come." He drank in the sight of her and had heck remembering what to say. "In the note you left at the stump, you said you might have some information."

"Yes. I do think our water is poisoned, but not by your family. I think Farrel did it, but not on purpose. He's been drilling holes all over our land, and I think something leached into the groundwater. Not sure what though."

His thoughts raced. "A special ranger from the Cattle Raiser's Association arrived around suppertime. He'll come out in the morning to test your water."

She shook her head. "Farrel won't let him on the property."

"Why? This is crazy." He silently cussed a blue streak. "Doesn't he want to find out how your father died?"

"That's the thing, Crockett. I think he must know. He's been hauling water from upstream of the creek. But I'm worried about his son, Tye. The boy doesn't seem himself."

"How do you mean?"

"He's sluggish, and his eyes have sunk back in his head. I think it's the water." She moved closer. "Then I overheard a snippet of conversation between Farrel and this stranger that keeps showing up. They were talking about drilling."

"Where and for what?" Surprise rippled through him. The man must've lost his mind. Still, everything was starting to make sense. The conversation he'd heard between the two men on patrol of getting rich burst into his head.

Only one thing at the present came to his mind—oil.

"Have you heard him mention anything about oil?" Crockett scanned the dark landscape but had no idea what he was looking for.

"Not that I've heard. But strangers started showing up, and I've seen holes they leave in the ground and also some pieces of equipment that come to a point. To my untrained eye, they seem to be used for drilling." Paisley's face tightened. "Crockett, Farrel has become so angry, and he's focused on that section of land that once belonged to Mama. Now that my father is gone and no one to stop him, I'm afraid of what he'll do."

The strong urge to tell her that land was probably hers rose up. Damn that promise to his grandpa!

"Even if oil is there, how does he think he's going to get it?"

"I'm not sure." She bit her lip. "What's going on, Crockett?"

"You can bet I'll find out." The teasing freckle next to her mouth drew him. The powerful yearning to kiss her rocked him. He settled for running a knuckle across her cheek. "Right now, we have to concentrate on your water supply. I don't want you or the others getting sick. Make sure no one drinks of the well water."

"I only drank a little from the well before I started going

upstream of the creek. Now we haul water in." She lightly touched his arm. "Do you think Farrel's contaminated all of this?"

"It's a possibility. For sure something probably has." Crockett reached for her, only to have her back up. "I've missed you, Paisley. You're all I think about."

Her eyes blazed. "Stop right there. You and I are over. Remember?"

"I don't have a bad enough memory to forget. I was such a fool." The fragrance of her hair brushed his face. "Do you ever remember our time together? I wish I could go back."

Through the years, he was attracted to several women, but they didn't have Paisley's laughter, her smile, her intelligent mind. In the end, he walked away, unwilling to settle for less.

"We can't go back, and that's that. It does no good to remember what can never be."

Her stare held sadness and maybe some regret. He liked to think so. "Do you believe in second chances?"

"I can't afford to," she whispered. "It hurts too much."

"I was too young to know what I was throwing away. My idea of a wife was to take care of my needs and be there at night." He released a snort. "I was an arrogant bastard. It took losing you to see my stupidity."

"Don't be so hard on yourself. We were both to blame. I had my own flawed ideas of what marriage was."

The light touch of her fingertips on his jaw brought exquisite torture. He closed his eyes, savoring the soft caress. What he wouldn't give to erase the past, to love again with the passion and fire burning inside. Paisley Mahone deserved all that and more.

When he opened his eyes, he found her studying him, a ghost of a smile curving her lips. "What?"

"I used to imagine a life with you." The puff of a breeze carried her quiet words that seemed to accuse, but he didn't know of what.

"What are you saying exactly?"

"It never would've worked."

Silence fell between them, giving him a moment to shrug and digest that. "Who's to know?"

Again, they lapsed into silence.

"Too much has happened. I met someone else while I was away." Her low voice was sad. "He was kind and considerate to a fault with only a faint trace of obstinance."

"What happened, Paisley?"

"He wasn't you."

The whispered words barely reached him, and for a moment, he wondered if he'd heard them at all. He was about to ask her to repeat them when the sudden slamming of the back door froze their conversation.

Farrel called, "Sis, where are you? I thought I saw you come out here."

Paisley turned white. "If he finds you here, there'll be trouble."

"He won't." Crockett put his arm around her and drew her close, his lips on her temple. "You deserve so much more than this. So much more than me."

"Shhh! Quiet, he's coming."

Ominous footsteps crunched on the rocky ground, getting closer and closer. The sound was filled with foreboding.

Farrel called. "Paisley?"

"Let me go out there and create a diversion," she whispered and took a step.

Crockett tightened his grip on her. "I'll be fine."

Though she was trembling, he felt her backbone straighten. He was about to slip away into the blackness when men's voices reached them.

"Have you seen my sister?" Farrel sounded impatient and frustrated.

"Nope. Not tonight." The voice sounded like one of the two men guarding the back that Crockett had encountered.

Another man spoke up. "Are you sure she's not in the house?"

"Hell! If I wasn't sure, I wouldn't be asking, now would I?" Farrel snapped.

"She's only one woman, Farrel. Can't you control her?"

With that, the men moved away, their conversation becoming muffled.

Crockett chuckled quietly. They didn't know her very well.

"No one controls me, least of all my brother," Paisley muttered low and pressed her body against his chest. "Let him try."

She needed to get madder than a hornet because that might be what saved her. "If you go around to the front and slip inside, he'll never know that you weren't in the house all along."

Her pretty face tilted back, and her moist lips slightly parted. He could no more resist the impulse to kiss her than he could push away a thick, juicy steak.

"For the good times," he said low, his voice rough.

A palm anchored gently under her jaw, he settled his lips on hers and tasted the fragrance of her mouth. She stiffened at first then relaxed, clinging to his light coat. For a moment, the years melted away, and they were the same two people they once were.

Needing. Taking. Giving.

For a moment, he thought he saw a firefly blinking inside his line of vision. Crazy.

The beat of her wild heart sent a sudden, sweeping heat down his body. A shiver of wanting curled along his spine, promising no sleep for him this night.

"I need you, Paisley. Words can lie, but your body hasn't forgotten me," he whispered against her temple. "When this is over..."

"Nothing has changed. I've moved on. You should too." She pulled free, the ends of her silky blond hair feather-brushing his arm. "You need to go before they come back."

His nod was probably a little too abrupt to cover the awkward silence. But he wanted to say something more. Only what? He held her beautiful gaze. She seemed loath to go. He cleared his throat, but the quiet words still came out husky. "Thanks for giving me a few moments. Between us, we'll figure this out. Meanwhile, don't drink the well water."

"Be careful, Crockett. About the kiss…" Her words trailed off.

"I'm sorry." He sighed. "I couldn't help myself. Let's save this for another time, another place."

Sudden voices rent the breeze. *Farrel and the men.*

"Go, Crockett!" Her whisper held urgency. "Hurry."

"Good night, Paisley." Crockett melted back into the darkness and just in time.

Hunched down low, half-hidden by a barrel, he watched Farrel stomp around the corner of the house and draw up in surprise when he saw Paisley. The sharp breath hissing through her teeth reached him. Dammit! He should get going instead of hanging around, yet he had to make sure Farrel wouldn't hurt her.

If the man lifted a hand, Crockett would pounce on top of him in an instant, and to hell with his own welfare. She came first. Always would from now on.

The ill-tempered brother marched to her, with his friend John Barfield following behind. John was two years younger than Crockett, and he knew the Barfield family well. John had been in and out of trouble all his life.

"Where have you been?" Farrel asked.

Paisley seemed to take a moment to gather strength, but her angry words covered any fear. "I'm right here. What is your problem?"

Good for Paisley for standing her ground. Crockett couldn't have been prouder. She had more gumption than anyone he knew.

Light from the open back door illuminated Farrel's angry face. His bitter eyes narrowed, and his voice turned oily. "Where were you? I hollered your name."

"I told you I was coming out for a walk," she snapped. "I refuse to be at your beck and call, and if you think I am, you've lost your mind. What did you want?"

Crockett's attention shifted to Farrel's two companions. Their clothes bore dark stains.

"If you were to happen to fall into a hole, no one would find you in the dark."

"You're an idiot." She whirled and went into the house.

The lady knew how to end a conversation—and to pretend she wasn't trembling from head to toe.

He'd seen enough, but when he turned to go, his heel crunched on a rock. He froze.

"What was that?" John asked. "Someone's there."

Farrel reached for the gun he'd tucked into his waistband and stole toward Crockett. As sweat trickled down his back, Crockett gripped his gun and readied himself.

Seconds passed in tense anticipation. Now he was the trespasser, the one breaking the law. He could be disbarred, or censored at the very least, and everything he'd worked for gone.

He couldn't run, couldn't move. He couldn't do anything but wait and pray.

The rustle of air, a brush against his pant leg brought a quick, silent breath as a black shape ran past. The dog. Paisley must've let the dog out.

"It's just the boy's mutt," Farrel called. "There's no one here."

Crockett relaxed as he and the men moved away. The dog whined and came back. "Good dog." Crockett bent to ruffle the pooch's ears. "I'll bring you a treat next time."

As he moved away in the darkness, he paused and stared at the house. There was movement in a lighted window, and he liked to think that Paisley might be looking out, perhaps remembering the feel of his lips on hers.

Hope surged. This could be a new beginning.

Ten

Paisley's situation haunted Crockett the whole night through. The urge was strong to gather his uncles and cousins and go get her. But he knew she'd fight him. No one could force her to leave until she was ready, so he wouldn't make that mistake. And right now, she felt she had to stay.

She'd always had a strong sense of obligation, but now it could get her hurt—or killed.

If it were within his power, he'd have sent her far away until this mess with Farrel was finished. Still, having eyes and ears on her brother was a definite advantage. He tried to block the danger that presented.

He sighed and threw back the cover. His vision was even sharper with daylight. Relief wound its way through his body. Paisley's beautiful face as it looked in the moonlight hours ago filled his mind. Even in the dimness, he'd drank in every line and soft curve. To never be able to view her again was beyond anything he cared to think about.

After quickly dressing, he went to the kitchen and put coffee on to boil. The view of the ranch from the window sent gratitude to his heart. There was no place better than this. Upon turning twenty, he'd received fifteen sections of the Lone Star to do with as he wished, and he already ran five hundred head of the best Black Angus in North Texas. His clerks liked to tease that he'd soon quit law work and take to ranching full-time. Maybe one day. He did love to get out and work with the cattle, helping the cowboys with branding, moving the herds from pasture to pasture, and everyday operations. Even though he loved the law and being a judge, ranching was in his blood in a way nothing else was, and he longed to do it full-time.

His father had steered him toward the law, and Crockett had agreed to give it his best for six years. And it had engaged his mind like nothing else, yet he was drawn to the land and loved that it exercised both intellect and body.

He was getting ready to leave for breakfast at headquarters on Friday to meet up with Special Ranger Alex Lancer when he noticed a cloud of dust aiming straight for his home. Curious, he went out onto the porch. Surely the person would turn off. But no, he kept coming. As it came closer, he could see it was a motorcycle with a sidecar.

It sputtered to a stop in front of him, and the driver slid a pair of goggles down around his neck, leaving a clear ring of dirt around his eyes. Then he reached into the sidecar and pulled out something covered with a tarp. Loud squawking ensued.

"May I help you?" Crockett took the porch steps and, now that the dust had settled, saw that the contraption was an Indian Motorcycle.

The man peered at a slip of paper. "Looking for Crockett Legend."

"That's me, but I'm not expecting anything."

"I've noticed that a lot of these deliveries rarely are anticipated. Regardless, this is now yours." The man didn't crack a smile.

"Can you tell me who it's from?"

The deliveryman glanced at the form. "Beau Bedford."

Ah, good old Beau, a jokester he'd met in law school. Knowing him, there was little telling what was under the covering that hid what appeared to be a very large, very noisy birdcage.

"How much money would it take to get you to return that?"

"I'm afraid that's impossible."

"Name your price." Crockett was already thinking of the scathing letter he'd write his friend.

"Sir, the owner is dead. There is no one to return this to. He left it to you in his will."

Dead? Impossible. Beau couldn't be dead. He was too full of life.

The motorcycle rider cleared his throat. "Please take this off my hands, sir. I need to get back to town."

Crockett reached for the birdcage and removed the covering.

The large bird's brilliant green plumage was broken up with streaks of blue on the wings and a splash of red above its beak. It blinked, ruffled its feathers, and squawked, "Walk the plank, matey. Walk the plank."

The driver pulled an envelope from his pocket and thrust it at Crockett. "Instructions, sir. His name is Casanova." Then he hopped on the Indian Motorcycle and yelled, "Keep the cover handy!" With that, he roared off, leaving Crockett with his head spinning.

Casanova tilted his neck and stared, hollering, "Where's the whiskey?"

"I don't know, bird, but I tell you one thing, if I had some, I'd drink the whole damn bottle." Casanova his ass. He didn't even want to know where the name came from. Another one of Beau's jokes, no doubt.

Damn Beau Bedford. Crockett picked up the heavy cloth and marched into the house to the bird's singing, "Molly McBroom, for a dollar she lay naked and more. Whiskey and rye, rotgut and gin, and all the men they took turns having fun with the whore."

The bawdy song had to have come from Beau. It sounded just like him. Hell!

The feathered Lothario sang the same lines over and over until Crockett threw the cover over the cage so he could read whatever instructions had arrived. The morning had barely gotten a good start, and already he had a headache.

The envelope held a lengthy letter from an attorney down in

Austin. Beau had perished in a drowning accident when his boat capsized. Well, he'd always said he wouldn't live to see old age. Knowing Beau, he was probably three sheets to the wind. The friend had never seen a serious moment, so Casanova came as little surprise. Neither did the little ditty the naughty bird sang.

The attorney's instructions were simple. *Feed and water him every day.*

That sounded more like a plant, not a living, breathing bird. Feed him what exactly?

That reminded him. He was supposed to meet Alex Lancer for breakfast and try to talk the special ranger into letting him ride along to the Mahone place. When he jerked the birdcage up, the cover came off, and he didn't have time to put it back on. Therefore, Casanova sang the entire blessed way as they rode to headquarters. You'd think the bird was drunk. And this new song had Crockett blushing fit to beat all. Every cowboy he met snickered, shooting him funny looks.

"Bird, if you don't shut the hell up, you're going into a pot for supper."

"Dead bird, dead bird."

"That's exactly right." Crockett stomped up the steps of headquarters and jerked the door open to the surprise of his little brother, Ransom.

"What'cha got there?" Ransom asked.

Crockett held up the cage and growled, "Meet Casanova. He just arrived this morning, and I'm ready to wring his neck."

"I think Hannah would give you a fight, the way she loves animals."

"Probably right."

"Well, good luck. Your special ranger is in the breakfast room. I'm off to saddle his horse." Ransom bounded down the steps and headed for the corral.

Casanova squawked as Crockett hurried down the hall toward the kitchen. Two men were seated at the table.

Grandpa Stoker choked on his coffee. When he could speak, he thundered, "What in tarnation?"

"This was delivered just a few minutes ago." Crockett set the cage on a side table. "Seems his owner died, and lucky me, he's mine now, only I don't know what I'll do with him. He sure won't have any place in my courtroom."

Just then, the feathered delivery burst out, "Hang 'em. Hang 'em. Hang 'em."

On second thought, maybe this could be just what he needed.

"That's enough, bird!" Crockett pulled out a chair. "Good morning, Grandpa. Ranger Lancer. Sorry about the parrot. I apologize for being late."

Lancer laughed. "I think you have a good excuse. What's his name?"

"Casanova."

The ranger busted out laughing.

Grandpa wasn't amused. "Hell! Who would come up with such a godawful name?"

"Apparently my friend Beau Bedford. He had an odd sense of humor."

"Hmph!" Grandpa waved an impatient hand, clearly done with the subject.

As though sensing he was being dismissed, Casanova let out a shrill whistle that had everyone covering their ears.

"Get that damn bird out of here!" Stoker's face was a thundercloud.

"I'll be right back." Crockett grabbed the cage and carried it down the hall to a dark closet and shut the door. That should do it. He returned to the table and blessed quiet.

While he ate the eggs and bacon he'd scooped onto a plate, he told the two men about his night trip to the Mahone place. "The only thing that fits with the way Farrel is acting, the bad water, and the holes he's drilled is oil. I don't believe he's found any on his land, but he apparently thinks we have some on the Lone Star."

"Oil?" Stoker's faded blue gaze narrowed. "It makes sense. Maybe old Joe thought so too, only he didn't count on it leaching into the water. The joke may be on him—a deadly joke as it turned out."

Lancer picked up his coffee. "The only way to be sure that's what happened is by testing the water. I should probably head that way."

"I was hoping to go with you." Crockett shoved a forkful of egg into his mouth.

The special ranger shook his head. "I can't let you. From what I've heard, your presence would probably antagonize him. What we're needing is to get that water tested before others get sick, and I'm afraid you would probably delay that."

Disappointment wove through him. He would've liked to make sure Paisley was all right. "I understand, and you're right. Time is of the essence. Lives are at stake. Paisley shared that she's worried about her little nephew. He may be starting to show signs of poisoning."

"I'll give you a full report." Lancer studied him. "While I'm there, I'll insist on seeing everyone who lives in the household. I need to know their condition."

Relief swept over Crockett. "You don't know how much that means. Really."

"I think I might have some idea. It stands to reason you'd be worried about her."

"That's right." He still wanted to ride over there and whisk her away. But then she definitely would get her dander up.

"I'd best be going." Lancer stood and downed the last of his coffee. "Wish me luck."

He'd probably need a lot more than that, knowing Farrel. His heart heavy, Crockett's gaze followed him from the room. Now what? He needed something to take his mind off Paisley.

Retrieving Casanova from the closet, Crockett trudged home

with the parrot keeping up a nonstop line of chatter. When he reached his kitchen, he took a cold biscuit he'd mooched from Grandpa from his pocket.

"Parrot food," he muttered to himself. If the bird didn't like that, he could starve. Maybe doing without would keep Casanova from talking. Crockett was willing to try anything.

The feathered phonograph squawked when he opened the cage door wide enough to put the biscuit inside, then the bird hopped down to peck at it. "Bad. Bad," he said, sounding as though he was spitting it out. The bird coughed and squeezed out, "Water."

"That's a little dramatic, don't you think?"

Casanova flipped onto his back, closed his eyes, and tucked in his wings. For pity's sake.

"Get up from there! You're not dead."

"Dead bird."

"Stop this or I'll feed you to the ranch dog."

The mass of green feathers fluttered, and the parrot hopped up and went to chirping like a normal bird.

"That's better. See? Just be a bird. I'm going to work, so sleep or cuss or whatever it is you parrots do."

"Double, double, toil, and trouble," Casanova squawked, then started singing, "Swing low, sweet chariot. Coming for to carry me home."

Crockett let out a string of cusswords that blistered his tongue. He stuck a small dish with water inside, then threw the cover over the cage and went out, slamming the door.

A half hour later, he found himself helping with spring branding and being nothing more than a ranch owner. Although the noise level could compare to a dozen tugboats all blowing their horns at once, it was preferable to what was inside his head. He roped a calf and took it to the fire, where a man put Crockett's CL brand on it.

"Hey, boss, word is that you own a parrot." The speaker was a young cowboy named Jeremy with a mischievous twinkle in his eye.

The news had sure spread like lightning. Crockett removed the bandana around his throat and wiped his forehead. "That's right. Why?"

"Well, I wonder if me and the boys could teach it some words."

Another worker at the fire wiped the sweat from his brow and grinned. "We'd like to take it in to the saloon in Medicine Springs and make some money. We might win some free drinks."

It did sound like fun. "Sure, as long as I go along. I wouldn't want anything to happen to him. His former owner was a good friend of mine." But it would be right up Beau's alley. No doubt he'd done the same too many times to count.

The men asked what the parrot's name was, the songs he could sing, and the list went on. The laughter made the work go faster, and before Crockett knew it, quitting time had arrived and he turned his horse toward home.

Jeremy stopped him. "Mind if we drop by and look at Casanova, boss? I ain't seen any real parrots up close."

"If my door's open, you're welcome to stop." But depending on what Alex Lancer said, he might take a ride. Paisley had been on his mind all afternoon. He prayed everything had gone well at her place. Farrel was a stick of dynamite just waiting to go off and blow anyone around to smithereens.

 ∽

Footsteps sounded on the porch, and Paisley turned as her brother entered with the special ranger. That Farrel had allowed Alex Lancer on their property surprised her. Maybe it had been the subtle threat of reinforcements that had brought about Farrel's change of heart. They really had little choice in the matter.

Especially since Farrel had secrets to protect that a lot of strangers would've noticed in poking around.

Paisley had immediately liked the man from the Cattle Raiser's Association. Lancer had sharp eyes, but he didn't question things that were not his business—like Hilda about her bruises. And he also showed them the utmost respect. Even to Farrel, which had probably played a big part in him accepting the intrusion without too much fuss.

That Farrel had kept the special ranger away from the digging area had caught her notice.

However, the man's sole purpose in coming had been to test the water, for which she was glad. There was something wrong, and whatever they found, the Legend family wouldn't be at fault. That much she knew.

"Would you mind if I look in your eyes and at your fingernails, Miss Mahone?" Lancer addressed Paisley directly, and she liked that.

"I have no objection, but I have to tell you, I am a nurse and know the signs of poisoning. I don't think you'll find any on me. I've just returned from a year away."

"I see." He pulled her bottom lid down to look in each eye, then peered at her fingernails. "I don't see anything." Lancer turned to Farrel. "I need to see your wife and son."

Farrel released a cussword. "Look, I've been very patient, but I think it's time for you to leave. You'll have to take my word for it that my wife and son have been poisoned. The Legend family bears full responsibility. I swear on my father's grave."

"Have your wife and son been sick?"

"They're deathly ill."

Paisley glared. "Stop it, Farrel. They might be showing early signs, but that's all."

"Our water has the poison in it. You can't deny that."

"I have to see your wife and son for myself. You've made some serious accusations that I need to investigate. If the Legends poisoned your water as you claim, I need to know. And they have a right to know who else is sick."

Angered at Paisley for contradicting him, Farrel yelled for Hilda. She came from the kitchen with Tye, which told Paisley she'd overheard everything.

The special ranger smiled and made Hilda comfortable, then joked with Tye, drawing a shy grin. After looking them over, he jotted some notes in a book. "Both are exhibiting signs of poisoning."

Farrel erupted, "I knew it. The Legends are trying to kill us. I told everybody that!"

"Hold on, Mahone. I'm just saying it's happening, not where it's coming from. The soil and water samples will determine a good portion." Lancer narrowed his gaze. "Have you been drilling for water?"

"No, I have not been drilling for anything." Farrel's gaze shot to Paisley and Hilda. "If anyone says different, they're lying."

"No one's told me anything." Lancer picked up a case containing the samples. "Until I get the results of these, go upstream to get your water, Mr. Mahone. Good day."

"I'll walk you out," Paisley offered, hoping for a private word.

"Very good."

Once they reached the privacy of the porch, Paisley lowered her voice. "Thank you for coming. I'm not surprised that you confirmed poisoning in Hilda and Tye. Until I arrived, they were drinking from the well. And contrary to what he said, my brother has been drilling holes."

"I suspected as much. I've learned a lot about people in my twenty years of working this job."

Satisfied that Lancer knew the truth, Paisley waited until he got on his horse before she went inside.

Farrel was lounging against the parlor doorframe, picking his nails. "Before I'm done, I'm gonna make the Legends pay this time. Maybe not exactly all we're due, but we'll get Mama's land back. I'm riding over there in the next few days, and you're coming with me."

That should go over like curdled milk. Farrel didn't intimidate the Legend family. They were used to dealing with cheats, cutthroats, and scalawags.

Still, seeing Crockett again wouldn't be all that terrible. If he hadn't returned to Quanah. She didn't hate him. Not really. Hate was such a destructive thing that gnawed at a person.

That kiss hadn't changed the past. A few kisses wouldn't change her mind. He was going to have to prove himself before she trusted him with her heart again. She still bore scars that had barely scabbed over and would take very little to rip off. She'd never be hurt like that again.

Crockett Legend was just a friend. That was all, and it was enough.

For now, she'd watch and wait and protect her heart. Time would tell all things.

Eleven

THE FOLLOWING WEEK CRAWLED AS CROCKETT WAITED FOR test results from Alex Lancer's office in Wichita Falls. Crockett spent his time cursing Casanova and working cattle. The parrot cursed him right back in far more blistering words. Not a day went by that Crockett didn't threaten to kill the damn thing. At first, his sister Hannah had been an ardent defender of Casanova, but after a full day, she'd brought him back and said no more. The parrot seemed to know just how to get on a person's nerves.

But oddly enough, the bird never uttered a bad word when in the company of kids. In fact, he was on his best behavior, which further astounded Crockett. Maybe he brought out the worst in the parrot.

Damn Beau Bedford!

His friend should've known Crockett would make a terrible pet owner.

On Thursday, he caught the train and rode in to work in his office. His clerks were happy to see him and, even though he took a special joy in getting dirty and working the land, it felt good to get some law work done. He spent the night at his home in Quanah and rode back on Friday.

Paisley continued to be on Crockett's mind, fond memories at times arousing such a strong desire to see her. He couldn't help wondering how she was and had ridden to the stump every night in hopes of finding a note. Much to his disappointment, none had been there.

He arose Saturday morning, dressed, and went to eat breakfast with his grandpa and Noah.

Stoker glanced over his coffee cup. "If you brought that damn bird, you can leave the same way you came."

"A man would think you didn't care for Casanova." Crockett reached for a cup and filled it from the pot sitting on the table.

Noah grinned but went right on eating.

"Correct. Good Lord, annoying birds should live in a jungle somewhere, not made into pets! You can't make one lie down beside you or fetch a stick."

Crockett grinned, taking a seat. "I'm glad he's not here, or you'd hurt his feelings."

"Stop that. Birds don't have feelings."

"I don't know, Pa Stoker." Noah wiped his mouth with the napkin. "I knew an old sailor down in Galveston, and he had a parrot named Sinbad. When he died, that parrot went into mourning. It made crying sounds, wouldn't eat, and wouldn't sleep. A week later, it died."

"I guess I'd better watch it. I confess I haven't been very nice to Casanova." Crockett didn't know if Noah was serious or joking. It was hard to read his adopted uncle.

Stoker leaned forward, his elbows on the table. "We have a more pressing problem than that stupid parrot."

"What's happened?" Crockett took a sip of coffee.

Essie, the cook, opened the door to the breakfast room. "What do you want to eat, Mr. Crockett?"

"Three eggs, bacon, and two biscuits should do it. Thanks."

"Thorp fell and broke his leg is what's the matter." Stoker snatched his napkin off the floor. "I don't know how we'll get by while he's laid up. Two of our men's wives are due to have their babies any day, and who knows what accidents will happen."

"That's not good." An idea popped into Crockett's head. "Paisley is a nurse. Maybe we can ask her to fill in, and if there's something that calls for Thorp's expertise, he can hobble in and direct her on any procedures."

It was perfect really. And Farrel couldn't say much about her working and getting paid well. But then, he hated the Legends, so he'd likely pitch a wall-eyed fit anyway.

Hope sprang into his grandpa's blue gaze. "Do you think she would?"

"I think so, but we'd have to send the right person to ask."

"Who?"

"I was thinking about Elena Rose. They used to be close friends."

"By God, we'll do it. It's definitely worth a try."

"I have some news." Noah's quiet voice filled the room. "I hope you'll be happy for us." He cleared his throat. "Violet Colby has accepted my proposal. We're going to be married a month from now."

"That's wonderful, son!" Stoker jumped to his feet to hug Noah. "She's a pretty young woman with a good head on her. Of course, I'm happy. I'm as happy as a dog with two bones."

"Congratulations, Noah." Crockett shook Noah's hand. "This is great news."

He racked his brain before finally pulling up that Violet was the former outlaw Clay Colby's blind daughter. They lived in the Texas Panhandle.

"Now I know why you've been spending so much time in Hope's Crossing," Grandpa teased.

Noah chuckled. "Yes, sir. The distance makes it hard to court."

They wished him well, and Grandpa insisted on having the wedding on the Lone Star.

"I don't think it'll be a problem, sir. She's easy to get along with."

The two men talked ranching business, deciding how many cattle to sell to keep the herd manageable.

As soon as Crockett finished, he went to find Elena Rose. "Can you ride over and talk her into taking the job? I'd do it, but Farrel would shoot me on sight."

"Absolutely." Her smile was as wide as the Rio Grande. She kissed his cheek. "Thanks."

His beautiful cousin danced her way to the corral.

This was the chance Crockett had been praying for. He couldn't wait to have Paisley near each day. Maybe soon she'd start to imagine a life with him again—for real.

∽

Paisley squealed and embraced her old friend Elena Rose, then stood back. "Let me look at you. This is a wonderful surprise. Come in and catch up."

Truth to tell, she'd always been a little envious of Elena's straight, black hair, dark eyes, and curvy body. Crockett's cousin caught the attention of every boy in six counties without even trying. But of course, with Elena's father a former outlaw, no one had the guts to pursue her, much to Elena's frustration.

"It's been a while." Paisley led her friend into the parlor. "Have a seat."

Elena Rose squeezed Paisley's hand. "I'm so sorry about your father. If there's anything I can do, please don't hesitate to ask."

"His death was a shock, of course. Then when Farrel told me he'd been poisoned, it knocked my feet out from under me."

Elena sat down. "I hope you don't believe the rumors. My family would never be a party to murder. Not in any way."

"I did believe that at first, but not now. I think it was grief talking and Farrel's accusations night and day coloring my good sense." Paisley prayed Farrel would stay busy with his new friends and leave them alone. She'd really missed Elena and didn't want unpleasantness to spoil their rare visit.

"Sure. Grief does funny things to a person. I lost my best friend a year ago, and it left a big hole in my life that I still haven't filled."

"How is your pretty mama? I always loved Miss Josie's

laughter." Paisley had heard that the woman had gotten amnesia in her younger years, and Elena's father, Luke, had helped her regain her memory.

She often thought that losing her memory would be better than the pain of remembering certain parts of her life. Even so, she was glad nothing had erased Crockett from her head. She couldn't imagine that. Only the breakup had been bad. They'd had plenty of good times.

The kiss in the dark, his lips on hers, continued to burn like a fresh brand. She lifted her fingertips to her mouth, and memories of the way he'd held her, touched her, caressed her came flooding back. She'd worked all this time to forget him, and in one brief moment it had all been for naught. That kiss had sparked a flame inside her that she'd thought was long dead. It was crucial to go slow.

"Mama's doing fine. You look a million miles away, Paisley." Elena gave her a smile. "I've been rambling."

"No, no. I'm enjoying hearing about everything. Really."

"You must wonder why I've come."

"The question did cross my mind," Paisley confessed.

"Our ranch physician, Dr. Thorp, fell and broke his leg rather severely, which leaves us without medical care. We have some women due to give birth soon, not to mention the normal injuries a cowboy suffers on a daily basis. We're in desperate need." Elena paused before going on. "Will you consider helping out? Grandpa will pay you very well for your services."

Paisley got to her feet and stood looking out the window. Did Crockett have anything to do with this? Could she handle seeing him day in and day out?

Almost as though Elena read her mind, she said, "Crockett rides the train to Quanah to work several days a week, so he'll be gone part of the time. We really do need you."

"What if something arises beyond my capabilities?" Paisley didn't turn around.

"Dr. Thorp can instruct you on things of that nature."

"I assume you'd want me to start right away."

"The more time you have to familiarize yourself with the job, the patients, and the workings of the ranch, the better for everyone."

How could Elena Rose be so calm and self-assured? These were lives they were discussing—her life, Crockett's, the patients'.

Paisley really wanted to do this. It would give her something meaningful to occupy her time with and get her away from Farrel and nagging problems. She'd deliver babies, something she loved. There was nothing more rewarding than bringing new life into the world and giving it a good start.

The only part that really bothered her was leaving Hilda and Tye. The boy was getting sicker, his eyes more sunken. Maybe she could check on him and Hilda through the day.

Working with Dr. Thorp would give her a chance to see if charcoal would help the boy. Farrel wouldn't be happy, but then when had he ever? That concerned her little. The benefits far outweighed the negatives.

She turned from the window. "Tell them yes, I'll do it."

After Paisley agreed to start Monday morning, Elena rode off. For a split second, Paisley wanted to call her back and say she'd made a mistake. But when she really thought about it, peace filled her heart. This was something she'd trained for and loved.

❧

When Elena reported back, Crockett's smile couldn't get any wider. "This is good, real good."

"I thought you'd like it, cousin." Elena dismounted, her hair rippling down her back. "I'll take my horse to the barn."

"I'll tell your father you saved the day." Maybe that would get his uncle Luke out of his horn-tossing mood.

His gaze followed Elena Rose as she hurried toward the barn. He owed her, and just maybe he could repay her.

Crockett had supper with his grandpa and relayed the news that Paisley would start work Monday.

The old man's face lit up. "Best news I've heard. Now we'll have that girl where we can keep an eye on her. Her mother would be happy."

"Yes, she would." Or maybe she was. Crockett figured Caroline was watching over her daughter and guiding her along the way. From time to time, he felt the unseen hand of a descendant on his shoulder. After all, his dead relatives had to have something to do up there.

After saying good night, he saddled a horse and rode to Uncle Luke's home. His uncle was outside in the twilight, braiding a new rope, looking like a proud conquistador of old. In fact, Luke had descended from a long line of Spanish ancestors. Crockett didn't know a lot about the story of how Luke's mother fell in love with Stoker, but it had to be the stuff of legends.

A short while after Luke finally accepted that Stoker was his father and stepped into the fold, the bones of his mother were brought to the ranch to lie next to Stoker's wife. By all accounts, Elena Montoya had been a real beauty with a fire for living in her soul.

Some said Elena Rose was a spitting image of her grandmother, and Crockett was willing to bet she had the same fire.

Luke glanced up as Crockett dismounted. "*Hola, mi sobrino.* Such a fine day. Come and tell me about your parrot."

"Is there anyone on this ranch who doesn't know I was cursed with Casanova?"

"You, my nephew, are on the lips of everyone." Luke grinned. "It is not every day that a talking parrot comes to rugged North Texas. Sit." He motioned to an overturned barrel.

"Thanks." Crockett dropped onto the makeshift stool. "That

bird is about to drive me crazy. Talk, talk, talk. And about nothing. The worst thing is he's started repeating everything I say, and it's very irritating. It's like he's making fun of me."

Luke laughed. "Maybe he is."

"Well, I'm not going to stand for it. Not sure what I can do about it though."

"Nothing at all. These things he says, tell me more."

Crockett told his uncle about the overly dramatic bird, about the horrible curse words, and the singing. "It's day and night, and I can't get a wink of sleep. Hannah says to find someone else each time I suggest she take him, and Grandpa refuses to be in the same room with him."

"So why the visit? I do not think Josie would let Casanova stay here."

"No, I came about something else. It's Elena Rose. She's not happy and yearns to spread her wings and fly away." Crockett paused. "Everyone has dreams of something that fulfills them. For Elena, it's designing dresses and making them. That's something she can't do on the ranch."

Luke sighed. "*Si*. I have made many mistakes, but her happiness is everything to me. She knows nothing of the world, and I am afraid for her." His expression darkened. "I pity the poor soul who makes the attempt to hurt my daughter."

The words and his uncle's dark, glittering eyes shot a tendril of trepidation through Crockett. Though his father had rarely spoken of this subject and only in hushed tones, he knew Luke had sent more than one soul to hell.

"Uncle, you can't keep her in a cage." Crockett's words were soft. "Free her. What if Aunt Josie goes along and stays until she's settled? Or better yet, my sister Grace lives between Fort Worth and Dallas. She can help Elena Rose and would be happy to do so."

A long exhale escaped Luke's mouth. "I will think about it."

"That's all anyone can ask. There comes a time when you have to trust that your child has learned everything you tried to teach them. The rest is up to them. Elena Rose has a good head on her shoulders, and she's a Legend. You'll be surprised at her success."

"How did you get so smart, *mi sobrino*?"

"By making mistakes." Crockett had also paid dearly and would never repeat them.

They talked and laughed for a while, and Crockett rode back home with a sack of sunflower seeds, berries, and peaches for Casanova. According to his uncle, parrots didn't like biscuits.

Luke and he had had a good talk. Hopefully, Elena Rose would see some loosening of restrictions soon. Dreaming was a big part of living. Everyone needed something to work toward, or they had little reason to keep putting one foot in front of the other.

Paisley was Crockett's dream. If he could make that happen, life would be rosy.

It seemed a good omen that fate had intervened, and she was coming to work at the ranch.

After all this time, things were falling into place.

It must've been ordained.

Twelve

MONDAY MORNING, PAISLEY PULLED ON A DARK BLUE DRESS and put a crisp, white apron over it. Just looking the part brought pride in her accomplishments.

She was a nurse. She had a skill that many other women didn't, and that brought deep satisfaction.

With it came nervousness and that pesky voice in her head that sent doubt careening through her. What if the Legends and their men held Farrel's feud against her? They might refuse to let her treat them and cause scenes. A big gulp of air steadied her nerves. She could do this. Whatever came, she'd handle it, just like she always had.

Heavy footsteps in the hall told her Farrel was up or maybe just going to bed. She didn't know which. He'd been mad when she'd told him about the job and had brooded all through supper. That's why she'd deliberately waited to break the news. Listening to him rant for two days would've beaten her down. The cowardly part of her wished she could slip out the back door without anyone seeing her and saddle the horse a ranch hand had brought for her to ride.

But as much as she wanted, she couldn't do that. No matter how ugly or distasteful a thing was, she never tried to dodge it. She sighed and opened the door.

Farrel was at the kitchen table, drinking coffee, his shirt hanging open, a cigarette dangling from his mouth. "As long as you're going to work for Legend, you might as well be useful." He pointed a finger at her. "Keep your eyes and ears open. Especially where

Crockett is concerned. Find out what he knows and what he suspects. Remember what they did to our father and baby brother."

Busy making a cup of tea, Paisley didn't acknowledge that he'd spoken. Besides, she didn't want to listen to his rants today. Her mind was on her new job.

The screech of the chair scooting back warned of Farrel's anger. Before she could blink, he grabbed her by the throat and pinned her against the wall. "When I talk, you answer!"

"Let me go." She was struggling to get free when Hilda walked into the room.

Her sister-in-law's eyes widened. "What are you doing, Farrel? She has to go to work. Bruises will draw attention."

"Who cares?" he snarled. "I don't give a rat's hind leg what those Legends think."

"I heard what you said," Paisley managed through the narrow airway he'd left her. "Now let me go."

He released her, and his chuckle chilled her bones. "Did that help you decide which side you're on? The Mahones or the Legends, take your pick."

"You're crazy." Paisley rubbed her throat.

Hilda gave a cry, and Paisley turned to see Tye trembling in the doorway, his eyes terrified in his small face.

His mother lifted him into her arms. "It's okay, sweetheart."

"That's what's wrong with my son. You women have turned him into a spoiled titty baby." Farrel glared. "It's time he learned to be a man, learned how to be a Mahone."

He tried to yank Tye away from Hilda, and they scuffled, with Hilda evading him.

Tye's terrified scream filled the kitchen. "No! No!"

Paisley grabbed the butcher knife and stepped in front of her nephew. "It's a fine day for a gutting if that'll make you happy. And I can promise I will let you lie and not lift one finger until all your blood leaks out." Her voice held venom. "Choose, *brother*."

Farrel raised his hands and forced a laugh, backing up. "Not worth ruining my day over."

"Not so fast." Hilda lifted her chin, the bruise on her jaw dark and ugly. "I'm leaving, and I'm taking Tye."

"Watch who you're talking to, woman. You're my wife and if I say you stay, you ain't going nowhere."

"Think again," Paisley said low. "You've turned everyone's stomach with your threats and violence. We need a break from you and some peace and quiet." She turned to Hilda. "Go pack your things. I have a plan."

"Stay out of this, Paisley!" Farrel roared.

"Try to stop us. I think there are plenty of men over at the Lone Star willing to help. They have guns that shoot too and more bullets than you've ever seen. They can reduce this place to rubble in nothing flat."

"If anyone steps foot on this land, they're dead." Farrel's words had lost the roar, and his hand shook slightly when he put his cigarette out in the fruit jar lid he used for an ashtray.

"Go on, Hilda. Just take what you absolutely need for now." Paisley held the knife, ready to use it if Farrel made the slightest move. "When you finish, I'll grab my things."

Tye patted his mother's cheek. "Where are we going, Mama?"

"I don't know, but it'll be better than here." Hilda kissed him and hurried from the kitchen.

Farrel sat down at the table, a sickening grin plastered on his face. He was up to something. Then his eyes darted to the back of the chair where he'd draped his gun belt.

With the knife firmly in hand in front of her, she quickly yanked his gun from the holster, but before she could back from reach, he grabbed her arm. Swinging the knife, she caught the soft flesh of his belly. In disbelief, he dropped into the chair with a thud, clutching his stomach.

It was only a superficial wound, not serious. He knew she meant business though.

The sound of Paisley's breathing filled the room. "I wouldn't choose your side if there was none to be had. I have nothing but revulsion for you. You were rotten to me when we were younger, and that hasn't changed."

"I want my gun. Hand it over, and I won't hurt you."

"You must be crazy. All you speak are lies. I'll leave your gun down the road."

Throughout growing up, Farrel would catch her by herself and hit or push her down, then threaten to do worse if she told. But then he'd turn around and do something nice. Once he'd bought her some pretty ribbons and another time crawled up a tall tree to get her kite down. She never knew what to expect from him, and she suspected that's why he'd shown a nicer side. He wanted to keep her off balance.

Fifteen minutes had barely passed before Hilda and Tye rushed back. Though Hilda was scared, she had hope written on her face. Her sister-in-law showed more strength every day. Hilda wouldn't have any qualms about using Farrel's gun that Paisley handed her if she had to.

Paisley had never fully unpacked, so it took just a few minutes to shove the rest of her things into her bags. She grabbed her mother's journal as she left the room, and her father's pistol.

Farrel sat sullen and quiet as they left. Paisley kept the gun in her hand in case he tried to stop them. "I'm taking your horse to pull the buckboard, and I'll bring it back by noon."

"The hell you will!" He jumped to his feet. "You took my gun and now my horse."

"Sit down!" She waved the pistol. "You don't call the shots anymore. I'll bring your roan back."

"Dammit!" Silence filled the kitchen for a long moment. His eyes like twin flames, he bit out, "Make sure you do. I'll be waiting. And I want my gun."

She and Hilda made quick work of hitching the two horses to

the old buckboard in the barn and loaded up. Farrel stood in the kitchen door as they drove out.

"Good riddance!" he yelled. "Don't think you're safe with them Legends. I'll get you no matter where you go. You can't hide from me." He released a string of curses, then slammed the door.

Tye huddled close to his mother's side, crying. "Can he shoot us?"

"No, honey," Paisley assured him. "We took the power from him."

That was only a partial truth. She was smart enough to know nothing was over. Farrel would find a way to punish them, but for now they were out of his reach.

The minute they reached the narrow road, Hilda asked, "Where are we going? Who will take us in?"

"There are plenty of kind people on the Lone Star." Paisley patted her young sister-in-law's hand. "We'll find a safe place where Tye won't have to be terrified anymore."

"Thank you, Paisley. I don't know if I would've had the courage to face Farrel by myself."

"I know you would. I saw your face when Farrel tried to take Tye. You were ready to do whatever it called for to keep your child safe."

"You're right about that. I wasn't going to let him hurt Tye."

They lapsed into silence. A mile or two down the road, Paisley threw Farrel's gun into a bed of cactus. Two men guarding the gate at the Lone Star waved them through, and she headed toward Miss Lara's. Crockett's mother would tell them where to go from there.

But Crockett happened to be out front when they arrived and hurried over. "What's wrong?"

She climbed from the buckboard and searched his eyes. "You once said that if I needed a friend, you'd be here." She bit her trembling lip. "I need one now…if the offer still holds."

Almost immediately, his gaze went to her throat, where Farrel's fingers had probably left dark bruises. Anger flared in Crockett's eyes, and his jaw tightened. She prayed he'd not do anything fool-ish, though she knew he wanted to.

His touch was gentle, and the words came out a bit raspy. "I meant what I said. Tell me how I can help."

"I need a place to stay." Paisley gave the short version of the events that had transpired. "We have nowhere else to go."

"I'm glad you came here. Thank God Farrel didn't hurt you worse. You're safe now on the Lone Star. Come inside. You proba-bly haven't had breakfast."

"There was no time." She took Tye from him when he lifted her nephew down and stood while he gave Hilda a hand.

"Thank God you're here." Crockett didn't appear to know what to do with his hands. He started to reach for her and stopped, then ended up letting them hang by his side.

Miss Lara met them at the door with hugs. She seemed to need no explanation. "Come in. We'll take care of you."

Hilda began to sob. "I'm so sorry. So sorry."

Miss Lara put her arm around the woman. "Please, don't cry. None of this is your fault. You were doing the best you could. We're going to make you comfortable, and you'll be able to sleep without worry."

The overflowing kindness had Paisley tearing up as well. She blinked hard and walked at Crockett's side to the sunny breakfast room where luscious smells drifted in the air and lovely flowers lined the windows.

Tye pointed. "Look, Mama."

"I see, honey. It's so pretty." Forcing a smile, Hilda set him down.

Once they took a seat, Crockett excused himself, saying he had some telegrams to send and would see Paisley later.

Before she knew it, Miss Lara came wheeling out a cart laden with plates of food and various drinks. "Working people need a hearty breakfast. I brought a little of everything."

"It's delightful, Miss Lara." Paisley didn't have the heart to tell her that food didn't go down well when a stomach was tied in knots. She managed a wide smile, determined to show gratitude.

They didn't have to be nice, and after leveling accusations of murder at them, she had more than a little making up to do. She just prayed they'd not think too harshly of her.

The best part was watching Tye, his face becoming less pinched as he slowly relaxed. The boy ate more than she'd seen him eat and allowed an occasional smile. It bothered her why they'd waited this long to make the break.

She did manage to eat more than she thought. Her first stop would be at Dr. Thorp's to find out what he wanted her to do, but Hilda and Tye were a concern. How would they fill their time and where?

Miss Lara's gentle voice seemed to come from heaven. "Mrs. Mahone, when you're ready, I'll show you and Tye where you'll stay. There's also room for Paisley."

Paisley rested a hand on Miss Lara's arm. "Please, we don't want to be a bother."

"Don't fret about that, dear. You're not. The house is one Grace and Deacon stay in when they come to visit. It's complete with everything you'll need. I just have to add a few toys. It's all ready for you and Mrs. Mahone to unpack and settle into."

"Please, just call me Hilda like everyone else, and whatever you have will be perfect. We don't require much. Our needs are simple. I'll be happy to help any way I can."

"Perfect, Hilda. Tomorrow, we'll see about helping our two mothers-in-waiting. Both have other children to tend, and they're not quite feeling up to that." Miss Lara laid a hand on top of Tye's head. "I'm just so happy that you're all here, and I want to make you feel at home."

Paisley stood and smoothed the white apron covering her dress. "I need to head over to Dr. Thorp's and see what he wishes me to do."

Lara faced her and took her hands. "Promise that you'll stop every little bit and take some deep, cleansing breaths. People don't do that often enough."

A lump stuck in Paisley's throat. "I don't deserve your kindness after the hateful things I've said and done."

"Sure you do. I knew that wasn't the real you. Besides, you were hurting."

Overcome with emotion, Paisley kissed her cheek, feeling the remnants of Miss Lara's horrible scar. "You're the kindest woman I know. Thank you."

The doctor's house, next to headquarters, was at least a mile from Miss Lara's, but Paisley had already asked enough of their hostess, so she set off walking. She'd gone no more than a yard when Crockett appeared in a buggy.

"Would you be interested in a ride, fair damsel?" His wide smile made her heart flutter.

"Is it safe? I've been warned not to accept rides from strangers." She tilted her head and met his banter head-on. "There's rumors of big, bad wolves running loose looking for pretty young maids to abduct. Are you a big, bad wolf, kind sir?"

"I'll never tell, but I can assure you that there are no safer hands to be in." He jumped out and helped her onto the seat.

Once inside the buggy, she dropped the charade. "Thank you, Crockett."

"Now tell me exactly what happened. Details, lady."

Paisley started with going to the kitchen to make tea and finding Farrel lying in wait. "Things had been coming to a head, and even though Farrel's violence is nothing new, I didn't expect him to try to choke me to death. Thank goodness for Hilda. Then when he released me, all I could think to do was grab the butcher knife."

"I'm glad you did."

"He just kept at me to pick a side." She released a long sigh. "I guess this wasn't the side he expected, but we just couldn't stay there another minute."

"I agree. Your brother is too dangerous. Hate builds in him until he has to lash out. He's going to kill someone one of these days if he hasn't already."

"You know, I wouldn't be surprised if he has and got away with it."

"Well, you're safe from him now."

Paisley twisted to look at him. "Are we really? Your men can't guard every inch of the Lone Star's boundary line. Remember the barn fire that damaged your sight? That was Farrel's doing. I overheard him bragging about it."

He might slip across again some night, and she could find him standing over her bed. A shiver ran the length of her body. Farrel was right. He could get her and Hilda no matter where they went.

"I suspected your brother set that fire, but we had no proof." Crockett laid his palm over hers on the seat between them. "I'll make it my priority to watch over you, pretty Firefly."

"Stop it. I'm not your problem. Besides, you have your law work in Quanah. You aren't always here."

"I have people. And I like looking after you. It's no burden."

The direction of their conversation made her squirm. They still had a long way to go in straightening out their relationship.

"Crockett, thank you for wanting to protect me, but this time I have to save myself. I have my papa's gun, and I know how to use it. If…no, *when* Farrel comes, I will shoot to kill."

If not, she'd be dead in an instant. She'd only have one shot, so she'd have to make it count. To lose would mean Tye's future, and she wouldn't let Farrel take that.

"You've got that right. I just pray you get that one chance, Paisley." He removed his hand from hers and focused on handling the reins.

They rode in silence for a while before he spoke again. "I have a parrot now."

The words stunned her. She wasn't sure she heard correctly. "A parrot? You? What kind?"

"A talking one." He grinned. "I want you to come by the house and meet him. He's quite a jabberbox, and I never know what he's going to say."

"Does he have a name?"

"Get ready." He paused. "Casanova."

For the first time in a while, Paisley laughed, really laughed. "I have to see this."

"I'll take you by after you get through today." His grin faded. "Paisley, it's good to hear your laugh. I've missed that."

"I don't know when I last had a reason to."

They pulled up in front of the doc's and she got out before Crockett could come around. The little action was a reminder to herself not to get comfortable in depending on others. It was best to make her own way where possible.

Thirteen

HER THOUGHTS IN A TIZZY, PAISLEY WAVED AT CROCKETT, still seated in the buggy. "Thanks for the lift. And the talk. It was almost like old times."

"Remember we have a date this afternoon."

"I won't forget. I have to meet Casanova."

She went up the walk to the door. Before she could knock, a voice told her to come in.

Dr. Thorp, she presumed, sat in a chair with his splinted leg propped up, staring out the window. She hadn't been to the ranch since the old doctor had left and was shocked by the difference. Doc Jenkins had worn three-piece suits and carried a gold-tipped cane. This man was disheveled in wrinkled clothes that appeared to have been slept in and uncombed hair. A pair of crutches lay beside the chair.

Paisley approached, her hand extended. "Good morning, I'm Paisley Mahone."

"Nurse Mahone, you're right on time. I'm Dr. Thorp. Thank you for your willingness to help me out."

He looked more like a tousled bear than an educated man of medicine. The fact that he was sitting didn't hide that he was a tall man and big. Barrel-chested and young, no more than eight or nine years older than she. But to be fair, he probably hadn't slept too well with that broken leg. She wouldn't judge. He had to be an excellent doctor, or Stoker Legend wouldn't have hired him. The old patriarch got only the best.

Which brought up the question of why he chose her to fill in.

With his extensive contacts, he could've hired any number of professional people across the state.

She pushed the question aside for the moment. "Tell me what you want first, Doctor."

Thorp reached for a pad and pencil. "You might need to write this down."

"Of course." Heat flooded her face. She should've brought her notepad. Only she had no idea where that had ended up after the events of the morning.

"Check on the two pregnant women." He ran a hand across his bristly jaw. "Unless I miss my guess, Mrs. Fletcher will have a difficult breech birth. Mrs. Nolan's should be normal." He met her gaze. "Do you have any experience with breech babies, Miss Mahone?"

"Yes, sir. I worked for Dr. Marsh in Fort Worth for over a year, and I delivered two babies feet-first. Both times, the doctor was unavailable to assist. I didn't have any problems or complaints." In fact, she'd received glowing compliments from both mothers.

"Excellent. I also have two other patients I'd like you to check on. Gus is a crusty old cowboy with the gout. He's not happy to be idle, but don't let him scare you. I have a feeling you'll charm the pants off him."

"I'll do my best to keep him in a good humor." She wrote *crusty* beside his name.

"Dallam won't give you any trouble. He'll apologize at least fifty times for breaking his back, as though he did it on purpose to cause us extra work."

"What happened to him?"

"The young cowboy of twenty-two was bucked off a horse that wasn't quite broke, and the front hooves came down on his back." Dr. Thorp sighed. "By all rights, he should be dead, but he got a miracle. Or a curse. Depends on how you look at it. He's probably out of medication, so he'll need more to handle the constant pain.

You'll find a brown bottle of morphine in my office cabinet. Go get it."

How horrible. Her heart went out to the young cowboy. Often the people hurting the most complained the least.

She went into the doctor's office and brought back the medicine. "Is this it?"

"Yes."

"What is his prognosis, sir?" she asked quietly, putting the bottle in her satchel.

"Not sure he'll recover. His riding days are over, and that seems what he can't accept."

"That's sad. I look forward to meeting Dallam." She looked over her notes. "Anything else, Doctor?"

"Unless someone gets hurt today, that's all. Out here on the ranch, I never know what's going to happen, but it pays to be prepared and ready to dive in at a moment's notice." He studied her a long minute. "Your brother is causing this family a lot of grief. I've heard he may have set the barn fire that temporarily blinded Crockett. I don't know what brought you here, but if you share his viewpoints in any way, you won't find a warm welcome. These cowboys are a loyal bunch to the brand they ride for, and they won't stand for anyone speaking ill of their employer or causing him harm."

Paisley lifted her chin. "I understand, and you needn't worry. I left my brother's home this morning, along with his wife and son. We don't intend to go back. My brother stands alone in his vendetta."

Surprise crossed Dr. Thorp's face. "Then I see I was out of line, and I beg your pardon."

"You didn't know. I'm happy to be here in a more peaceful clime. I pray I can truly be of service. A broken leg isn't easy to manage."

"I'm always bumping the goldarn thing against the furniture or wall."

"Sir, have you heard of plaster of Paris being used on broken limbs?"

"I've heard of it, but don't exactly know the process. Do you?"

"I've applied a cast to broken bones many times while I was in Fort Worth. Would you like me to try it on you? That is, if you have plaster of paris."

A wide smile covered his face. "I do. I became curious after reading an article but haven't used it because the steps were a little vague. You'll be very beneficial to me. And I'd appreciate you putting my leg in a cast. It will allow me mobility, and it's less painful, I hear."

"Where exactly is the break?" she asked.

"The tibia, right below my knee."

"I think you'll find that you heal faster with the cast keeping your leg immobile."

"I'm sure you're right." He rubbed his hands together. "Where should I move?"

"I'll need you on an examining table if you have one."

"I do."

Paisley assisted him into the room that contained a narrow bed and an examining table. She helped him up onto the table. He told her where to find the plaster, and she mixed some up, then laid out long pieces of gauze.

"Would you have a roll of soft cotton to put next to your skin?"

"Second cabinet."

"You're well prepared." She took in the various brown and blue bottles, along with syringes, vials, and medical tools capable of fixing any type of injury or illness.

"Pays to be, Nurse Mahone. It's quite a ways to town."

Locating the roll of pressed cotton, she wrapped the broken leg. Then she began dipping the gauze strips in the thick plaster and applying them around Thorp's leg.

"Dr. Marsh liked to start at the foot, as will I."

"Does it make any difference?"

"I don't think so, sir."

"How long will it take to harden?"

"Two or three hours." She chuckled. "I hope you didn't plan to go anywhere, Doctor."

"You mean besides fishing, mountain climbing, and riding horseback?"

He did have a sense of humor. "Yes, besides all that."

"Just curious. I want to learn all I can about this procedure. I think it'll come in very handy." He was silent a moment, watching her. "Do you suppose it would work on a broken back? Have you heard of such?"

"I don't know if it's been tried, but I don't see why it wouldn't, as long as you leave the patient a way to do his business."

"Hmph! I might just try it if you'll help. I never asked, how do you remove the cast?"

"A saw, sir. That's one reason for the padding underneath. The other reason is comfort. The cast will rub. Oh, and I didn't tell you, we'll have to cut the seam of your trouser leg to fit over this bulk."

They talked while she worked, and she found Dr. Thorp to be a very bright doctor who had a thirst for learning. He asked a lot of questions about her work with Dr. Marsh.

Finally, she cut his pant leg up the seam and helped make him presentable. "As I said, you'll need to allow time for the plaster to dry. I'll help you to a comfortable chair."

"This has been exhilarating, Nurse Mahone."

"Please, call me Paisley. We'll be working closely together, and there's no need for the formality every time we turn around. I'll simply call you doctor."

"I agree." He put an arm around her neck and hobbled to the parlor and his chair where he could look out the window. "Thank you, Paisley."

"I'll return soon to check on you. Please don't put any weight on that leg."

"Gotcha."

She picked up her satchel and left. But instead of visiting the patients, she went across the street to the ranch headquarters. The tall Texas flag unfurling proudly in the sky at the corner of the dwelling brought a lump to her throat. It seemed to welcome her.

Next to that stood a heavy bronze star suspended between two iron poles. The lone star. The Legends celebrated the state's history with such splendor.

An old legend had it that a person could find their true worth by sleeping under the star. She didn't know if that was fact or rumor, but she'd like to test the theory.

Stoker was sitting on the wide, covered porch. She tried not to fidget as his sharp blue eyes took her in. Years hadn't stolen his mind. He knew everything that happened on the large ranch, and sometimes before anyone else. She remembered he'd always been a hands-on kind of man and doubted age had changed that.

"Can I have a word, Mr. Legend?"

"Of course, dear." He cocked his head to one side. "I have to say you look more like your mother every day."

"That's too kind." Her mother had been the beauty. Paisley only passable.

"How is your first day going?"

Paisley told him about casting the doctor's leg. "I think it'll heal much faster."

"Sounds interesting. Have a seat and keep an old man company."

"I can't stay long. I have patients to see." She sat next to him. "Thank you for giving me this opportunity. I don't know if you've heard, but there've been developments." She told him about the fight with Farrel, about Tye being sick with the poison, and the drilling. "I'm not going back to that place. Farrel is on his own."

"It's too dangerous for you there. You can stay as long as you wish."

"Mr. Legend, I have some questions concerning you and my mother."

"I figured you might, and I'll tell you everything you want to know. As much as I'm able anyway."

"Sorry for my bluntness, but were you and my mother having an affair?"

Stoker took her hand. His touch was gentle. "No, we were not. We had a deep, lasting friendship built on mutual respect and genuine caring. She was quite a woman, your mother. So beautiful and kind. Truthfully, I wanted more, but she drew a line, and I respected it."

Something inside softened, and worry eased. It shouldn't have mattered that much, but it did. Paisley guessed it was the fact that adultery was plain wrong. Not that her mother owed Joe Mahone much of anything. She'd given the man her best years, and he'd thrown them away. His bitterness and greed had killed every bit of love Caroline had felt for him.

"So, Mama came here?" She didn't think her mother visited headquarters that often.

"No, we'd meet halfway between our places, usually at dawn, and sit and talk." He patted Paisley's hand. "A lot of times she'd be upset, and I offered her comfort and a shoulder if she needed one. Sometimes she'd share something that Joe had said in anger." He raised his gaze to meet hers. "But never once in all that time did she allow more than friendship. Your mother was an elegant lady carrying a hurt that went bone deep. She was always, always a lady, and my best friend." His faded blue eyes filled with tears. "I'll miss her all the rest of my days."

Paisley stared at two cowboys riding past as she digested Stoker's words. She squeezed his large fingers. "I'm sorry I said those hateful things. I wanted you to hurt as much as I was."

"Water under the bridge." He wiped his eyes. "I'm glad you're here. Do you have your mother's journal?"

"Yes, I brought it."

"Read it and pay attention to what it's not saying. When you're ready, we'll talk again."

"It has a lot of confusing text that makes little sense. Is it a riddle? I almost feel as though it is."

"I wasn't privy to what she wrote, but I think she wanted you to work to get to the truth. One reason was that she couldn't be sure if you'd listen to your father and brother or form your own path. And she didn't want the journal to fall into the wrong hands. She had to protect her legacy."

"Her legacy?" Her mother had nothing, so why go to such lengths? "I don't understand."

"You will. You're a smart girl."

"I'm glad you think so, Mr. Legend."

He wagged a finger. "Nope. To my friends, I'm Stoker."

They both stood, and she kissed his cheek. "I have to earn my keep, so I'd best be going."

"Have a good day, dear. Let me know if you need anything."

Clutching her satchel, she hurried down the dirt street, her heart lighter. There were a few horses in front of the brick mercantile, and several women waved. It had always seemed odd that Stoker had built a small town on the ranch, complete with a telegraph, doctor, and school. Crockett had explained that in the early days, it was too far to travel to town, and his grandpa wanted to make things easy on his men and their families. But the icehouse and library were new.

Dallam was her first patient and lived at the end of the street. Mindful that he was out of medicine, she walked a bit faster.

The conversation with Stoker went around and around in her head. Now that she knew for sure that the strange journal entries were on purpose, she'd work harder to figure out what her mother had been saying. The idea to write down all the wrong words might be the way to go, and she couldn't wait to try it.

The little one-room house of Dallam's stood on the left. She went to the door and knocked.

A deep voice called, "Come on in."

Paisley stepped inside, and the man lying flat on the bed drew her attention. The smell of urine hit her. "Good morning, I'm Nurse Paisley. I'll be filling in for the doctor."

Happiness glowed on his face, and he hastily smoothed down his blond hair. "The judge stopped by to tell me you'd be coming, but he didn't say you'd be so pretty. I should've spruced up a bit."

The wrinkled bedsheet couldn't hide the large urine stain, but she tried not to look.

"I think you are a silver-tongue devil. Are you sure you're laid up and not just pretending?"

His wide grin spread. "I thought you might mistake me for someone hurt."

"You pulled the wool over my eyes." She sat in a wingback chair that was beside the bed and set her satchel on the floor. "Is Dallam your first name or last?"

"It's my only name. I was raised by wolves, and they couldn't speak." He laughed. "Mr. Legend hired me anyway." The laughter died and pain crept into his dark eyes. "Seriously, I never knew my parents. I was left on the church steps with a note that had Dallam scrawled on it."

Lying flat on his back with no reprieve, he probably made up wild stories to keep himself sane. However, she suspected the last part was true, and there were no words to say that would make it better.

"I see." Paisley retrieved the bottle of medicine from the satchel. "Doc said you're out of this, so I hurried." She reached for a spoon on the small bedside table and filled it.

Dallam needed no urging to open his mouth and swallow the

bitter medicine. He closed his eyes for a long moment. "Better," he murmured. "Thank you."

"I do this only for my most handsome patients." She got her stethoscope out and listened to his heart, then took his blood pressure. Except for it being high, everything was normal, but she knew pain could raise the level. "Your heart is strong. You're lucky you're young and in good shape. That helps."

"Guess so. I've started weaning myself off that medicine because I hate the way it makes me sleep all the time." Dallam scrubbed his face with his hands and ran his fingers through his blond hair, standing it on end. "I only take it when the pain gnaws at me like a starved badger."

"How long ago did you suffer this injury?"

His gaze went to a clock on a chest of drawers at the foot of his bed. "My mind's kinda fuzzy sometimes, but I remember that day like it just happened. It's been three months, twenty-seven days, and seven hours." He laid an arm across his forehead. "The sky was so beautiful that morning. So blue it hurt a little to look at it. I was bursting with happiness, because my girl met me at the corrals, and I kissed her. She smelled of cinnamon." He jarred himself. "Sorry, some things I can't forget."

So true. "Some things stay in a person's head forever, and there's nothing you can do." Her words were quiet, and she wasn't sure she meant Dallam or herself.

"No, ma'am."

Paisley put her stethoscope away. "Let's get you fresh sheets."

He winked and grinned. "After that, we'll run away and go live on love."

The soft, teasing words brought tears to her eyes, and she turned away for a moment to regain her composure. "Sure, but I have to be back by bedtime, or I'll turn into a nasty old crone with crooked fingers and a dastardly laugh."

Paisley pulled the sheet back and saw his thin, atrophied legs.

Dallam was wasting away, dying a little more each day. At only twenty-two, he'd already lived his best years. An ache formed around her heart. She couldn't let him go on like this without doing everything in her power to give him a more productive life. She'd discuss it with Dr. Thorp.

With clean sheets in hand, she rolled Dallam from side to side until she got them on and his nightshirt changed. At least someone had split the nightshirt up the back to make it easier. A wide-mouthed bottle three-fourths full of urine sat on the floor. She emptied it and set it within easy reach.

"There, that's better, don't you think?"

A smile formed. "You're an angel if I ever saw one." A sigh escaped. "I'm so sorry for making this hard on you. So very sorry. I wish I could change this."

"Hey, are you kidding? If you don't watch it, I'll climb into that bed with you, and we'll sleep the afternoon away."

That brought boisterous laughter. "I'm in love, Nurse Paisley."

A few more minutes of banter, and she left the medicine with a clean spoon on the small bedside table. "I have to check on some others, but I'll see you tomorrow. Don't go horseback riding in the moonlight."

"I go every night in my dreams," he said softly. "I'm always like I used to be before the accident. My favorite time. I had a girl back then, but she left. Said she needed a real man."

Anger washed over her. "It's her loss, Dallam. You're more man than a lot I've seen walking around. Now you can find a real woman, not one pretending to be." She bent to kiss his cheek. "Sleep well. I'll bring you coffee."

The soiled sheets lay next to the door, and she stopped to pick them up.

"Don't bother with those," Dallam said. "I have someone to collect them and clean a little." He grinned. "You never know when I'd want to do some entertaining. Maybe throw a big shindig."

"That's right. If you do, let me know. I love to dance." She dropped the sheets. "Do you have someone to bring food? Someone to bathe you?"

"Mr. Stoker sends food three times a day, and sometimes brings it himself. My best friend, Shep, washes me on the mornings when he can get up early enough before riding out to work."

"Tell Shep I'm taking over his job. I'll bathe you."

A red flush crept up his face. "I couldn't ask you to do that, ma'am."

"I'm volunteering. I'm a nurse, and that's part of my job. Ask anyone."

"Then I reckon it'll be okay to see me in my altogether."

"I won't look. I promise."

Saying goodbye, she threw the satchel over one shoulder and closed the door. No sadder case had she ever seen than cowboy Dallam. She would make getting him out of that bed a priority, somehow or another.

She'd bet her bottom dollar on that.

Fourteen

By lunchtime, Paisley had seen three of her patients. All that remained was the crusty cowboy Gus. He might prove difficult, so she'd saved him for last.

The two mothers-in-waiting had been a joy. Annabelle Fletcher voiced concerns about some back pain—little wonder with her huge stomach. She was small-boned to boot, with little room for such a big baby. Dr. Thorp had a right to fear a breech birth for her. It was not going to be easy. She wondered if the doctor had thought about trying to turn the baby. She'd ask.

Annabelle also had two small ones to look after. At nineteen, she was far too young to have two children with another on the way. Paisley had learned that Annabelle married at fifteen and had her son nine months later. But it was typical of half the young female population these days. They were in such a rush to grow up.

Paisley wanted to tell them to slow down. Things only became harder the older you got.

The other mother, Sally Nolan, had been the opposite of Annabelle. Robust and very hearty, she reminded Paisley of pioneer women of old, not thinking twice before setting off for California and walking half the distance behind a covered wagon. No worries there with her.

Miss Lara showed up in a buggy and took Paisley to the house where she'd stay with Hilda and Tye. "Hilda has made you some lunch." Miss Lara slowed for a group of cowhands on the dirt road leading back to her and Houston's part of the ranch.

The benefit of owning a million acres was that each family had their own section, with plenty left over. Even though Stoker's son Sam lived at Lost Point, Texas, where he served as sheriff, he shared in equal ownership of the land. Paisley liked how everything was divided equally among the brothers. That's how it should be.

In her family, Farrel had insisted on having it all and still wanted more. No wonder her younger brother, Braxton, had been so unhappy. He'd been left out of everything. She wished he were still alive so she could tell him how much she loved him. She doubted anyone but her and their mother had ever said those words to him.

While they rode, Paisley told Miss Lara about her conversation with Stoker that morning. "I'm glad Mama found some companionship during those last years of her life. She must've been so unhappy and lonely, and I was hundreds of miles away, not seeing what she was going through."

Miss Lara reached for her hand. "Don't beat yourself up, dear. Mothers hide a lot of things from their children. She didn't want you to know how bad life was with your father."

"If I'd just paid Mama more attention and come home more often."

"Wouldn't have helped. Caroline would still have kept everything from you and smoothed over the rough patches. That's what we mothers do."

Paisley turned in the seat. From all appearances, Houston adored his wife. She'd seen how they gazed at each other with such love.

The woman laughed. "I see the question in your eyes. I wasn't speaking about Houston and me."

"I'm glad. I've always thought of you two as a storybook couple."

"Hardly that, but we're in good shape. Our love is stronger than ever."

They pulled up in front of a cute little white house next door to Crockett's, with gingerbread trim and room at one end of the porch for three chairs. Spring flowers hung from large baskets and filled the flower box on the second-story balcony.

"This is too much," she whispered, tears in her eyes. "We can't accept this."

"You can and you will." Miss Lara set the brake. "Your lunch awaits."

Hilda opened the screen door and stepped out. "What do you think, Paisley?"

"It's unbelievable." Paisley climbed from the buggy. What a change in her sister-in-law. Worry had left Hilda's face, and she looked years younger. Why had they stayed so long with Farrel? He was as toxic as the water that killed their father.

Tye poked his head around his mama. "Hi, Auntie. Come on."

The change in the boy was as mind-boggling as that in his mother. Before this, he'd almost forgotten how to speak, and when he had, it had emerged in mere whispers.

"I'm coming." She turned to Lara. "Will you eat with us?"

Lara hesitated. "Are you sure?"

"We insist." Paisley linked her arm through Miss Lara's, and they went inside. She stood for a moment, taking in all the beautiful furniture and rugs. "This is stunning."

"Wait until you see your bedroom." Hilda's eyes sparkled. "But do you want to eat first?"

"Come." Tye pulled her toward the stairs.

"I guess it's been decided." She laughed and followed Tye.

Upstairs, the four-year-old opened a door, and Paisley truly was at a loss for words. The mint-green bed covering had large red roses embroidered in the center that immediately captured the eye. A white armoire and lady's dressing table of the same soft color set the feminine tone. In a corner stood a writing desk and chair. The dark wood flooring was beautiful and showed years of loving care.

She clasped her hand to her mouth. "Amazing."

Tye pulled her to the carpet bags she'd brought and opened them to show that they were empty.

"Did you and your mama unpack my things?"

He giggled. "Yes." Then tugged her toward the door. "See my room."

They went across the hall to his room, which also held beautiful furniture and lots of toys. The boy stood in the center with arms outstretched and whirled on his toes, joy on his little face.

His happiness was contagious. She stuck out her arms and mimicked him, laughing.

Dizziness got her, and she stopped. What a difference half a day had made. Gratitude bubbled over, and tears rolled down her face. In the middle of it all, she thought of Dallam with nothing, not even the ability to sit or stand. She dropped to the floor and wept big, sloppy tears.

Tye put his arms around her neck. "Don't cry, Auntie. It's real good."

That was where Hilda found them. She stooped and wrapped her arms around Paisley. "I know. I did the same thing. It was all too much to take in, and I felt so undeserving. Come and let's get you fed so you can go back to work." They stood and moved to the stairs with Tye rushing ahead in front of them. Halfway down, Hilda said, "I have a job too."

"Doing what?"

"Taking care of Mrs. Fletcher's two children every afternoon so she can nap."

"Good. Annabelle is extremely exhausted and faces a difficult birth. The more bed rest she gets, the easier it'll hopefully go."

Beaming, Miss Lara met them at the foot of the stairs. "If you two don't warm my heart, I don't know what does. You bring me so much happiness."

Paisley absorbed the feeling that she'd found a pot of gold at the base of a rainbow as they went into the kitchen. Hilda had made a pot of soup, and though she apologized for not having time to make more, lunch was the best food she'd had in a while.

The peaceful atmosphere made all the difference.

Miss Lara returned Paisley to the doctor's before heading off to Annabelle Fletcher's with a basket of goodies.

Before Paisley mentioned their patients, she checked the doctor's cast for hardness. "It feels firm, Doctor. Is it comfortable enough?" She chuckled. "I shouldn't ask that. Of course it's not comfortable. It can't be."

"You know, it's so much better than the splints. I'm not complaining."

"That's as good as we can hope." Paisley took a chair next to Dr. Thorp and caught him up on Dallam and the two pregnant mothers. "Doctor, are you certain Dallam's back is broken?"

Thorp rubbed his chin. "As positive as I can be without looking inside him. Paralysis from the waist down seemed to confirm it."

"You were unable to find any movement at all, even his toes?"

"Nothing. He had no reaction to a pin prick."

"Do you mind if I give him a thorough examination tomorrow? I don't mean to doubt your word. Please don't think that. It's just that sometimes swelling can obscure the truth."

"Miss Mahone, by all means check the young man out. I welcome your findings. Nothing in the world would make me happier than to know I'm wrong about him."

"One other thing. Have you considered turning Annabelle Fletcher's baby?"

"I tried, but the cord is too close, and I was afraid the movement would wrap it around the baby's neck."

"In that case, it's best to leave well enough alone." She stood and reached for her satchel. "I'm off to see how Gus's gout is doing."

"I feel I should give you some armor or something to protect yourself."

She laughed. "Surely he's not that bad."

"I'll let you be the judge." But he didn't sound optimistic. Not one bit.

The house was easy to find and, like Dallam's, consisted of only one room. The door stood ajar, so she rapped and stuck her head in. "Gus, I'm Nurse Mahone. Do you mind if I come in?"

A boot came barreling past her head and hit the wall. "I ain't home. Go away!"

She jumped back in alarm. Crusty her big toe. The man was a downright menace. It took her a second to regroup and for determination to build. He was not going to send her running. She had a job to do, and do it she would.

"Gus, Dr. Thorp sent me to check on your swollen knee. You, sir, have no choice in the matter. Do you understand?"

Silence met her. She didn't know if that was a good sign or bad.

Drawing a deep breath, she stood at the side and pushed the door open with one cautious foot. A plate hurtled through and broke on the stoop.

"Stop throwing things, Gus. I only want to help you."

When nothing more came flying, she reasoned he was searching for a new missile. She hurried in and found him half hanging from his chair, reaching for a heavy bootjack.

"Oh, no you don't." She moved everything from his reach and shoved a strand of fallen hair from her eyes. Her glare probably could've stripped the rattles from a coiled snake. "I've never met a more ill-tempered old coot! Give me two seconds and I'll be gone."

A female dog lying next to his chair raised her head and looked at Paisley. She had six nursing puppies on her that appeared near weaning age.

"Where's Thorp?" Gus roared. "I'll only let him near me."

"He broke his leg and is unable to tend to his patients right now. It's me or nothing."

"A woman's place is in the kitchen. Not looking at naked man parts."

Hands on her hips, she glared. "That's the most asinine thing I've ever heard. Us women see men from birth to death. Besides, you're not naked. Now, let's get on with it so I can gladly leave."

Gus muttered what sounded like curses. The years hadn't been kind to him, deep wrinkles leaving his face like drought cracks in the ground. And his cheeks were pockmarked. Looked as though someone had stomped on him with a pair of hobnailed boots. The few sprigs left of his sparse hair had grayed. But underneath the hostile resentment was a spark of something akin to affection in the way he gently patted the mother dog.

"Get it done then, Calamity. You're disturbing my dogs," Gus growled.

"Calamity?"

"Yep, you're a walking hazard."

"I am not. My name is Paisley, if you must know."

"Ain't nothing but Calamity."

After listening to his heart and checking his blood pressure, she asked him if she could look at his swollen knee. A nod was his only response, so she raised his trouser leg to reveal angry, red flesh that had swelled over twice the normal size.

"I'm having hell walking," Gus murmured. "And I need to see to this mama dog."

"She's sure a pretty thing. Looks like she has some blue heeler blood in her."

"Yep, some. Not sure what the daddy looked like. Around here, no telling. Hope I can find homes for the pups."

"Do you mind if I take two? I just met a young man with a back injury and unable to get out of bed. I think a puppy would give him good company."

"Dallam. Yep, that boy's sure got a long road ahead of him. I reckon he'd like a pup."

"The other one would be for my four-year-old nephew. Would you mind if I bring him over to pick out the one he wants?"

"I reckon he can."

She fixed him with a narrowed gaze. "You won't throw things or be mean to him?"

"I don't rightly think I can be mean to a little tyke."

"Good. Do you think another week for them to be weaned?"

"Sounds about right."

"What have you been doing for your knee, Gus?"

"I rub it with castor oil and sleep with garlic tied around it. Ain't helping much, but that's what Felix told me to do."

No wonder it hadn't worked. In her opinion, the cure smacked of superstition.

"Who's Felix?"

"My sister's husband. He thinks he's a witch doctor or one of those shamans."

"Did Dr. Thorp ever tell you about wild cherries or to bathe your leg in cold water?"

"Yep, he told me. I guess I'd try it if I had some cherries." He snorted. "They ain't in season yet."

But home-canned cherries were.

"If I can get you some, will you try them for two weeks?"

Gus ran a hand across his grizzled jaw. "I might."

"I'll see what I can do." She packed her satchel. "Are you going to show off your pitching arm again tomorrow when I come?"

"Sorry about that. I thought you were that old crow that brings me eggs from time to time and tries to kiss me. Her mouth puckers up like an old sow, and she snorts. I'm too old and hurting too bad for sparking."

"But I told you who I was, and you kept throwing."

"I thought she was tricking me on account of she claimed to be a census taker before."

"Aww, I see. Makes perfect sense."

"You're a pretty little filly, Calamity. And you haven't snorted a bit."

"Why thank you." She saw through his effort to smooth things over and appreciated it. "Bathe your knee in cold water, Gus, and I'll see you tomorrow."

She was glad that was over. And doubly glad that all her patients weren't as difficult as Gus. Calamity her hind leg.

Crockett was waiting with Dr. Thorp and stood when she entered. Her pulse beat faster at the sight of his powerful, well-muscled body. He carried himself with an air of self-confidence as a judge who held the fate of people's lives in his hands should.

There was something different about him that she'd never noticed before. Or maybe she'd changed. Dropping the mantle of hurt and self-righteousness had opened her heart. Whichever, she was acutely conscious of the gleam in his quick, brown eyes, and she wondered if he remembered their unexpected talk in the moonlight behind her house.

The kiss that neither had planned.

"I'm told you're free for the day once you returned from Gus's so I waited." Crockett shifted his stance, his lips twitching at one corner. "Is it safe to ask how Gus took your visit?"

"He threw a boot and then a plate at me! Thank heavens I have good reflexes."

The men laughed.

"I'm sorry." Dr. Thorp lifted his casted leg onto a footstool with his hands, wincing just a little. "I was afraid of something like that. Gus has very definite ideas about women."

"Which he freely shared." She released a frustrated breath. "But those puppies of his gave me an idea. I want to take one to Dallam, and Gus agreed that it might provide company for him. And the irritable man said I could also have one for my nephew."

Crockett nodded. "A dog should bring Tye out of some of his shyness. That'll be good."

"I think so too," Paisley agreed and asked the men, "Do you perhaps know of anyone in possession of canned cherries or a way of getting some? Gus said he'd try them for his gout if I could deliver."

"Check with the mercantile," Crockett suggested. "They may have some cans on the shelf. And I'll ask my mother, of course."

"I'll ask around too." Dr. Thorp looked pleased. "You've made a big difference here, Paisley. You're quite an asset."

Crockett shot her a look of admiration and moved to her side. "There is no one better, and I'd stake my life on that."

Satisfaction and happiness wove through her. Helping people was her calling, and she knew things could only get better as she worked with the folks of the Lone Star. They needed her, and she for sure needed them.

Dallam and the two ladies in waiting had captured her heart. Gus, not so much.

Paisley missed the doctor in Fort Worth and their patients. It had been a joy working for him, and she'd felt an immense loss when he told her he was closing his practice and moving back east. The news had come on the heels of her father's death and shaken her to the core. Then the shock of running into Crockett on the train after all this time only added to that. She'd felt as though her entire world was crumbling.

Her harsh words still echoed in her ears. Despite that, Crockett had shown incredible kindness when she'd arrived with Hilda and Tye, seeking refuge.

She cast him a glance. His profile, from his determined jaw to sculpted cheekbones and generous mouth, revealed the strength of his character. He stood out even in a crowd.

At one time they could've been very happy.

But now?

A soft sigh escaped. Who knew where this would lead? She turned toward the door. "I believe we have a date with a parrot, Mr. Legend."

Fifteen

Outside Dr. Thorp's, Crockett took Paisley's satchel and helped her into a buggy similar to Miss Lara's. "Putting Gus aside, I'm glad you had such a productive day." He tucked the hem of her dress inside the carriage.

"It's been very emotional from start to finish. I feel I've lived two lifetimes in this one day."

"You always did give a hundred percent in everything you do." He took his place on the seat beside her and set the buggy in motion. "Even when we were kids, you never halfheartedly tried anything. I remember you swinging off the high cliff overlooking the river and jumping into it, landing farther than I ever dared. You beat me like a drum, no matter what challenge I threw down."

"How could I ever let you beat me? I'd never have heard the end of it from the mighty Crockett Legend." A laugh floated up her throat, as light as the breeze that danced in her hair.

God, how he loved her. But he had to get this right this time, and that terrified him.

A sudden cry sprang from her, and she clapped her hands over her mouth. Color drained from her face. "I told Farrel I'd return his roan, but I got too busy and forgot. I have to get it back. He'll be furious and accuse me of stealing it."

"It's all right. You don't have to." He put an arm across the back of her seat. "Hilda told me about that arrangement, so I sent a couple of our hands over with the horse. I told them to get within seeing distance of the house and whip the roan on the rump to send it on."

That Farrel had emptied his gun at them was a fact Crockett wouldn't share. She would only blame herself for putting the men at risk. Not that they were ever close enough for her brother to hit them. Crockett's men were smart enough to keep out of range.

She slumped on the seat. "You saved me again. How can I thank you?"

"By having supper with me."

Paisley studied him. "Are you sure? Did you learn to cook?"

"Don't stare at me like I have horns sprouting out of my ears. Of course I can. I'm very proficient in many, many things, Firefly." He didn't want to confess that the things he could cook were limited to steaks, eggs, bacon, and sometimes rattlesnake and rabbit. "Tonight, I'll cook you the perfect steak on the firepit in back of my house."

"Mmm, I love anything cooked over an open flame. What can I bring?"

"What more do you need other than steak and beans? I already have both."

"Dessert? If Hilda bought apples from the mercantile, I'll make some fried apples."

"Make them with lots of cinnamon, and we have a deal." He savored the feel of Paisley against his side, and she'd seemed to scoot closer on the seat as she talked. But maybe that was wishful thinking.

The distance between the doctor's place and Crockett's melted away as Paisley told him about her patients. Dallam's plight touched him. He'd meant to ask Grandpa information about the young man. Maybe they could do something more to help, although he didn't know what it could be. And it sounded like Dallam still had a lot of pride and would worry about putting people out. If Crockett could just rig up some kind of contraption to get him from the bed. Maybe he could build a device they could strap him into that supported him. He'd think on it.

But tonight, the only thing on his mind was his lady.

He shot her a look from the corner of his eye. The breeze had loosened little sprigs of hair that curled on her forehead and around her delicate, shell-like ear. Black lashes framed her beautiful eyes the color of seafoam. She reminded him of an exotic beauty more suited to a canvas hanging in some king's castle.

"We're just about there. Are you excited?" Crockett lifted his arm from her shoulders. "After all, this isn't some ordinary bird."

"How can I not be absolutely beside myself?" Her droll voice made him chuckle.

"Don't go overboard with enthusiasm." He pulled up in front of his home and jumped out. It made him happy that she waited for him to come around, but then he discovered she'd merely been gathering her satchel.

The house was silent when they entered. Maybe Casanova was asleep. Crockett led her into the kitchen and removed the cover from the birdcage. The parrot blinked and fluttered his wings.

"Hello, Casanova." Paisley's soft words evoked a loud wolf whistle. She cringed and stepped back.

"Kiss me, baby," the bird squawked. "Kiss me."

The stupid bird! Heat rose to Crockett's face. "I'm sorry, Paisley."

"Sorry, Paisley," Casanova mimicked. "Sorry. Sorry."

Riotous laughter burst from her mouth. "I love you, silly bird."

"Love you! Love you!"

Paisley swung to Crockett. "Does he repeat everything you say?"

He rubbed the back of his neck. "Not always. He spends half the day arguing with me. Seems to get a kick out of proving me wrong."

She giggled. "Who wins?"

"Not sure but I think *he* does." Crockett knew he probably looked a tad sheepish, letting a bird get the best of him, but she didn't know how irritating the parrot was. "If you'd been there, you'd understand. Casanova is mean. Sometimes he sings these naughty little ditties that just about make me blush."

The parrot blinked and rubbed his head on the side of the cage. "Pretty girl. Kiss me."

"You taught him to say that. I know you did." Paisley shook a finger. "You're hopeless."

"When did I have time?" Crockett crooked an eyebrow. "He's only been here three days. Hardly time to teach Casanova anything. I assure you he's parroting what he learned long before arriving here." He tilted his head and stared. "Do you honestly think I'd tell the bird to say that about kissing?"

Paisley's lips turned up at the corners. "Yes, I do. I wouldn't put anything past you."

Mock horror filled his voice. "I never thought I'd hear you accuse me so unfairly." He grabbed her and nuzzled behind her ear.

Giggles erupted as Paisley pushed him away. "What are you doing?"

"You've driven me crazy all day, knowing you were a stone's throw away," he growled. "You should be ashamed for taking the parrot's word over mine."

Wild giggles told him she was enjoying the playful banter.

"Is this the way you treat all your supper guests?" she asked.

He lifted his head and let her go. "Aren't we dear friends?"

Casanova flew to his perch and let loose. "Let's be friends. Be friends." An instant later the feathered lothario sang, "Old Dan Tucker was a fine old man, washed his face in a frying pan, combed his hair with a wagon wheel, died of a toothache in his heel."

Paisley extracted herself from Crockett and sang along, adding another verse that the bird didn't know. He listened with rapt attention then repeated the verse word for word.

"Good Lord!" Crockett used his driest tone. "I don't know who's the worst—you or the bird."

Hands on her hips, Paisley turned. "You're just jealous of my boyfriend. Admit it."

The sight of her flushed cheeks, disheveled hair, and dancing eyes sent heat surging from his belly. He'd never seen her so alive and happy. At least not in a long while. The sudden urge to sweep her into his arms and carry her to bed shook him.

Laughter was gone, and somberness washed over him. "Yeah, you guessed the truth."

Sensing the change of mood, Paisley put more space between them. "I need to run over to change clothes and talk to Hilda a minute. I'll bring back a light dessert." She touched Casanova's cage with her fingertips. "Goodbye, boyfriend, I'll see you later."

"Goodbye. Goodbye." The parrot ended with another whistle.

Still melancholy, Crockett walked her out. "All kidding aside, thank you for taking supper with me. It means a lot."

"To me too." Saying she'd be back in an hour, she strolled toward the house next door that she shared with Hilda and Tye.

He stood, unable to bring himself to go inside. Paisley's hips moved in a seductive way with her gait. He didn't think he'd ever paid attention before. In fact, there seemed to be a lot he'd never noticed. Had he been so shallow back then?

No, that wasn't it. He'd been self-absorbed with his plans, his life, his dreams. And young. No wonder she'd left without a backward glance. Served him right.

Even then, losing her hadn't shaken him up at first. Not in the way it should have. Truth was, in the first year of law school, he'd been too busy to spare her much thought. She'd been right about a lot of things. He wouldn't blame her if she never spoke to him again. But if she did quit talking, that would be the end of him. In the twilight, he remembered the softness of her skin, the fragrance of her hair, and the taste of her lips. He couldn't bear to think of an entire life without her in it.

Paisley Mahone was the beginning and end. She held his happiness in her hands.

⤠

True to her word, Paisley returned promptly, toting a hot pan of fried apples soaked with butter and cinnamon.

Crockett met her at the door. "Let me take that. I'm almost tempted to grab a fork and dive in."

"What's stopping you?" She threw down the challenge. "It took little time to make." She smiled up at him. "Hilda was going to buy apples, but instead your mother shared these from her root cellar. She's been a godsend to us."

"Mama's greatest joy comes from helping others." He set the cast-iron skillet on the counter and took out two forks. "I meet your challenge and raise the stakes. Do you dare?"

"Absolutely." She grabbed a fork. "Choose your side."

He plunged his fork into the hot apples. "This one." He took a bite and moaned. "This is heavenly. What did you do with that nurse? She was worn to a frazzle, but here you are with not a tired line around your eyes. You look ravishing."

"Why thank you, sir." Paisley bowed low, removed her shawl, and draped it on the back of a chair before digging into the dessert.

The beautiful rose-hued fabric of her dress brought soft color to her skin and complemented her golden hair. A pendant hung from her neck on a gold chain and rested between the deep valley of her breasts. Crockett wondered if the necklace had been a gift. Perhaps from the gentleman she'd mentioned meeting while she was away.

A twinge of jealousy pricked him. What kind of man had she met?

"I didn't hear Casanova when I came in."

"Hannah has him for a few hours. My sister thinks she can

teach him some tricks. I'm perfectly fine with those he already knows. He doesn't need more." He hoped she didn't see through his fib. Truth was, he didn't want a bird or another human vying for her attention on their first meal together after so long apart.

"Good heavens, I think you have a grudge against that bird."

"No grudge. I'm just really not a parrot person. Give me a dog. Now that's a pet."

They finished the fried apples off, and he picked up the steaks that he'd already seasoned. "Let's go outside, and I'll put these on."

At her nod, he held the door for her, and they went out into the fragrant night air. The canopy of stars presented a breathtaking display, rivaling the dancing sparkles of Paisley's green eyes.

He set the steaks down, noticing her attention on the small table he'd brought out with a few special things on it.

"Oh, Crockett." Her hands went to her mouth. "This is incredibly beautiful. The roses, the wine, the candles. Just lovely."

"This is our first meal together in years, and I wanted to go all out." He moved behind her and rested his hands lightly on her shoulders. "Did I wow you?"

"Most certainly." Paisley turned to face him. "When did you have time to light the candles?"

"I spied on you between the hedgerow, and when you started this way, I ran and lit them." He brushed a kiss behind her ear, inhaling the faint fragrance of something like lemons. "For you." He cleared his throat. "I'd walk five hundred miles just to see this light in your eyes."

Worry crossed her face. "Slow down. Let's see where this leads first."

"I didn't mean to overwhelm you. We'll go at whatever speed you wish." He dropped his hands to his side and went to check on the meat. "Tell me your fragrance. It eludes me...although I think I detect lemons."

"It's bergamot with a slight touch of lemon. I developed a fancy for it while I was in Fort Worth."

"Ahh, that's why I didn't recognize it. Bergamot is an old scent and used in many things, but not so much around here. On the Lone Star, we specialize in cow fragrance." He loved her perfume though and made a note for future reference.

She glanced up at the sky and inhaled the night air. "It's really beautiful tonight."

"If memory serves, this is your favorite time of the day."

A look of surprise crossed her eyes. "You remember."

"I have everything about you stored in my head," he said quietly. Including the fact that she liked her steak juicy but cooked through and that she found pleasure in swimming bare. The memory of her slim body slicing through the water was one he took out each night before he went to sleep. His hands knew the feel of her satin skin, he knew the taste of her lips, and the hunger darkening her eyes. He'd just forgotten everything for a while until he'd seen her on the train.

Pushing the heated recollection aside for the moment, he cleared his throat. "If I might interrupt your stargazing, how about a glass of wine?"

"I'd love some." Soft laughter sprang up. "You aren't trying to get me drunk, are you?"

Crockett lifted a sarcastic eyebrow. "You've become quite suspicious of me."

"With good reason, I think. You can be pretty devious, and who knows what new tricks you learned at law school and in your courtroom."

"You wound me, fair lady." He uncorked the bottle and filled their glasses, raising his high. "To a beautiful woman whose light burns brighter than ever. Here's to new beginnings."

"New beginnings," she murmured, clinking her glass to his.

"Paisley, I've been trying to keep things from getting too serious, but I have this to say, and I'll be done." He met the questions in her eyes. "I'm sorry for being an ass. For causing you hurt and for failing to support your wishes and goals. I was very wrong. I hope you can forgive me. I'm most sorry for Braxton's death."

"Thank you for that. But my brother did wrong. I apologize for blaming you. You were doing your job."

He studied her face and watched sorrow fill her sensitive eyes. "If you're able, can we start over with a clean slate?"

She was silent for a long moment, sipping from her glass. He held his breath for fear she'd spurn the olive branch. And if she did, he didn't know how long it would take to try again. He just knew he wouldn't give up.

Not on her. Not on them. Not again.

Finally, she spoke, her voice quiet. "I'd like that, Crockett. We've both made mistakes, not just you. I'm relieved that the anger I felt is gone, because it was eating me alive. I never want to feel that way again." She paused and ran her tongue around the lip of the wineglass. "That being said, we shared a lot of good times, happy times that I never want to forget. I think our relationship went too fast, and then for you it became comfortable. We both had some growing up to do."

"You are a very wise woman." He brushed her soft cheek with his thumb.

"But, Crockett, this doesn't mean I'm ready to resume what we had. That's gone. You hurt me badly. How do I know you won't again? One open conversation won't fix us."

He swallowed hard. "I understand, but it's a start. I will win your trust back. Just don't shut me out."

"I won't." Paisley glanced down, her dark lashes fanning across her cheeks. "If we find we can go forward, we'll make new memories because we're different people now." She raised her eyes that glittered with unshed tears. "I'm at a crossroads, both with you and my work. I don't know where I'll go once Thorp recovers. My life is uncertain."

"Let's take this one day at a time. Nothing has to be settled right now." He put an arm around her shoulders. "I hate the reason that brought you back, but I'm glad you came."

"Me too. I think I'm meant to be here. It just feels right."

A strange spell seemed to weave around them like a golden thread, and he didn't want to break the perfect moment. He appreciated her honesty and to know the direction of her thoughts. There was a certain release that came after clearing the air.

Finally, he moved. "I think our steaks are ready, Firefly." He pulled out her chair.

Paisley tilted her head. "When did you first start calling me that?"

"Let's see. I think it was the summer you turned sixteen. You loved fireflies and used to chase their blinking lights. You always said if you could be reincarnated, you'd want to come back as one."

The bright light shining inside her was bringing joy to so many.

"I still love them. I want to teach Tye about them, and I want him to meet Casanova. He'll be enthralled with the parrot."

"Bring him anytime. He's a cute kid. Too bad he couldn't pick a father he could look up to and admire."

"I agree." Paisley sliced into her steak. "There's been such a change in him already since we've been here. He's opening up now that he doesn't have to be afraid all the time." She closed her mouth around the bite on her fork.

"Feeling safe is a wonderful thing." Crockett waved his fork. "How's the steak?"

"Perfection. I'd forgotten what a Lone Star steak tasted like. Melts in my mouth."

"Holler when you want your memory jarred again." He cut into his and plopped a good-sized bite into his mouth. "Damn, this is good."

They talked of old times as they ate but steered clear of more soul-searching. Crockett was glad for the earlier chance to clear the air though. He'd needed the sorry-saying. That Paisley had let go of things she'd been holding on to had been welcome news.

With luck, they could forge a new path. And maybe, just maybe, if the gods favored them, somewhere along the way they could find a future.

Sixteen

A telegram arrived from Special Ranger Lancer the next morning. Crockett lost no time in opening it. The message read: *Tests confirm suspicions. Poison not arsenic. Water shows dynamite particles. Be there soon.*

He hurried across the street to headquarters to relay the news to his grandpa.

"Well, I'll be damned." Stoker slapped the telegram against his leg. "I'm not too surprised though. Farrel seems desperate for money and will try everything in his power to get it."

"He's driven all right," Crockett agreed. "This clears us."

"Maybe. Until he tries another way. They never stop coming." Stoker let out a long sigh and dropped into the leather chair behind his desk. "In the early days, we battled outlaws, rustlers, and shysters trying to take our land. The methods have gotten more sophisticated."

"Doesn't matter, we have what it takes to hold on, Grandpa. This is our land, and we're keeping it. Maybe one day Farrel will give up."

Stoker snorted. "Don't bet on it. He's a Mahone."

"We wait long enough, he may end up killing himself like his father apparently did." What a waste of a life. Plotting and scheming must keep people like Farrel awake at night.

He looked out the window in time to see Paisley going into Dr. Thorp's house. My, she looked pretty in a dress the color of a ripe peach. Maybe he'd show up at lunchtime and see if he could spirit her away for a bite to eat here at headquarters.

On second thought, a picnic sounded better. And they wouldn't have Grandpa to contend with.

She'd kept busy with her patients and patching up the cowboys' cuts, scrapes, and sprains. If he didn't rescue her, she probably wouldn't eat.

Yes, a private spot under a shade tree would be just the thing. He whistled all the way out the door.

✿

Paisley juggled a container of coffee and opened Dallam's door. "I'm coming in. Are you decent?"

The young man laughed. "I'm never decent. Especially my thoughts. You'd blush if you knew what I think about."

She set her satchel on the wingback chair next to the bed and handed him the coffee, noting his neatly combed blond hair. "And what on earth would that be?"

"That juicy steak you had last night." Dallam made a tsking sound with his tongue. "I heard all about it. Crockett Legend brought me a piece and stayed until midnight." He took a drink of coffee and smiled with the pure joy of having a simple thing he loved.

"Oh, he did, did he?" It pleased her that Crockett paid the lonely man a late-night visit.

"And I think he likes you."

What had he said? She couldn't imagine Crockett being loose with his words.

"Oh? I wouldn't know. Did he tell you?"

"Not in so many words, but little things gave him away. The softness of his voice when he spoke your name and the fact that he couldn't go very long without bringing you up. He admires you." Dallam released a long sigh. "He stole my girlfriend."

"No one can steal what they don't have." Still, she'd lain awake for quite a while thinking about the warmth of his arms and his lips nuzzling the skin behind her ear.

"Thank you for the coffee. I didn't know if you'd remember."

"How can I forget? You're my favorite patient."

All of a sudden, Dallam's mood changed. "Judge Crockett told me his plan to build a contraption that'll let me stand up, and he took some measurements. What do you think?"

"Are you asking me if this thing he wants to build will work?"

"Yeah."

"I think it's possible. I've seen one that did. But you have to want to get out of that bed, Dallam." She paused. "Do you?"

"Miss Paisley, sometimes I think my backside has grown to the mattress. I'd give anything to just be able to sit in a chair, but I don't want to get my hopes too high. Disappointment would kill me. I'm sorry." He rolled away from her.

Yesterday his mood was jovial, nothing like this. Then it hit her. He was more afraid of failure than to keep living as he was. In fact, he was terrified to pin his hopes on an unknown.

"Let's not even think about it. You are in charge of your life, and only you can decide how you wish to live it." She removed her shawl. "I want to examine you this morning unless you have an objection. Then I'll bathe you and change your sheets."

"Sounds like a deal." He cradled his cup, staring through the window. "It looks like a pretty day out."

"It's gorgeous." She pumped water in the small kitchen for his bath.

"Sometimes I can imagine the breeze against my face and the smell of rain. There's nothing to compare to rain in the air."

"I agree." The water was tepid and suited to the warm temperatures, so she had no need to heat it. Paisley carried the pail and set it on the floor next to the bed. She pulled back the sheet. "Can you lay on your stomach if I roll you?"

"Yes."

In a matter of seconds, Dallam lay facedown. "The last time it rained, Shep came and opened the window, and in a way, it felt like I was outside in it. Course, it hardly ever rains here."

"No, it doesn't, and that's a pity."

Paisley ran her hands over Dallam's back and tapped on his muscles. They responded until she reached his waist, and there they stopped. She proceeded down each leg, kneading and tapping with no sign of movement.

"Do you feel my hands?"

"No."

She moved to his feet, that were ice cold, and pressed harder. "How about now?"

He shook his head. "Sorry."

"Me too." Disappointment washed over her. If there was just something to bring hope.

"I didn't tell you the best news," she continued. "How would you like to have a puppy to keep you company?"

Light filled his eyes. "For real?"

"Absolutely for real. They're blue heelers. Would you like a boy or girl?"

"I don't care. I'll love either. Your hands feel so good."

"I'm glad. Just relax and take deep breaths."

They discussed names as she worked her way down his body, washing every bit of sweat and urine away.

"Okay, let's get you turned over." Paisley was about to help him roll when Dallam's toe jerked. "Wait a minute."

She tried everything to get it to jerk again but nothing happened. When he asked what was wrong, she said his toe had gotten tangled in the sheet. She couldn't tell him she was imagining things.

By midmorning, she'd finished with Dallam and had him situated with the window right at his bed open and a gentle breeze cooling him.

"I'll return this afternoon and shut the window."

"No need. Shep will be by, and I'll get him to."

"It's good to have a loyal friend." Paisley glanced around for anything she forgot.

"Shep and I grew up together. He's like a brother to me." Dallam waved. "Now go on. I want to take a nap and dream about you and me riding across the pasture."

"That sounds lovely." An ache in her chest, Paisley blinked back tears and left.

At Gus's, she'd come prepared with a couple of gourds she'd picked up. She opened the door a bit cautiously, ready to swing the gourds. "Hi, Gus, it's Nurse Mahone."

"Calamity, you mean. Well, git on in here."

"Are you going to throw anything?"

"Not today, Calamity. Now that I know who you are, I don't need to."

"That's a relief." Paisley dropped the gourds and went in. "How are you doing?"

"Hurt like hell. I thought of slicing my throat, but I didn't want anyone to have to clean up the blood. It's a nasty job."

"That was very considerate of you. I, for one, am happy that you showed restraint." She suppressed a laugh as she rolled up his pant leg. "Did you bathe your knee in cold water?"

"Nope. Didn't want to deprive you of the pleasure."

"You're a hoot. I'll think you're flirting with me. You'll become human if you don't watch it."

He snorted. "Me? Not likely, Calamity."

"That's what I told myself."

The knee looked no better and had more fluid in it than the day before. He sure needed the cherries. She'd go by the mercantile at lunch to check their canned fruit.

"Mama dog is sure getting anxious to stop nursing her pups. Won't be long."

Paisley rolled Gus's pant leg down. "I told Dallam, and he's excited. Says he doesn't care if it's a boy or girl."

"Girls are easier to train. Some think they're smarter."

Easier to train? Did he mean that remark for her? She wouldn't doubt it.

"I've heard that." She knelt down next to the mama and stroked her head. "Pretty girl. You're a sweetheart." One of pups jumped on her. Paisley turned it over and saw it was a girl. It was the only one of the litter with definite blue heeler coloring. "Gus, if this one isn't promised, I'll take it when you say the word. She's perfect for Dallam."

"Yes, ma'am. I reckon he can have her."

"Gus, did you see Dallam's accident?"

"Sure did. Thought that boy was a goner. Feel real bad for him. Got his whole life in front of him and can't even walk, much less sit a horse." Gus reached for a pipe and lit it. "Me, I've lived a long time and did pretty much everything I set out to do. Was even married for a time before she ran off with a Bible salesman. Figured he needed her worse than I did. I didn't like her much nohow."

"You've got a funny outlook on life." Paisley stood and picked up her satchel. "See you tomorrow and will hopefully have some cherries."

"Don't work yourself into a tizzy, Calamity. This'll pass one of these blessed days."

She said goodbye and let herself out, returning to Dr. Thorp's. Crockett waved from headquarters and came toward her, carrying a basket, shirtsleeves rolled up showing rippling forearms.

When he reached her, he asked, "Are you hungry?"

"I was thinking about eating." She squinted up at him and lifted a hand to shield her eyes. "What do you have in mind?"

"A picnic. With me." His grin showed a row of white teeth. "Where I can see that tempting freckle next to your mouth. It has always teased me, dared me to kiss you."

Her pulse raced as she laughed. "My freckle?"

"That's right. You didn't know that?"

"All this time I thought you were staring at the raised bump of my nose."

"Silly goose." He pointed. "Over there under that large tree looks like a perfect spot for a picnic."

The old elm had to have been there probably before Stoker was given the land by General Sam Houston during the Texas War for Independence. Some of the lower limbs almost touched the ground, forming a shield against prying eyes. Her pulse raced despite a stern lecture. Crockett was the sort of man who made women feel special. He certainly did her, much to her frustration when she was angry.

Even-tempered to a fault except with Farrel, he drew people to him like bees to honey. He loved animals and children, people who couldn't defend themselves. Maybe that was what she liked best about him.

Though she'd dug in her heels, she could feel herself falling for him again. Darn it!

It was too soon, and she wasn't ready to trust him fully with her heart.

Paisley heard herself saying, "You know, a picnic sounds like fun. I would love it. It's such a beautiful day."

"Eating some fried chicken with such a lovely lady would be no hardship for me at all." He offered a gallant elbow and they moved to the tree.

"This is perfect." Paisley took the basket and opened it to find everything they'd need. Reaching for the tablecloth, she spread it on the ground. "Whoever packed this thought of everything, right down to jars of lemonade."

"I told Grandpa's cook, Essie, what I needed, and she took care of it."

The chocolate pie caught her eye. "All of it and then some. I can't wait to dive into that dessert."

Crockett straightened the tablecloth's edge and plopped down. "Pie is my weakness. However, those fried apples last night hit the spot too. You did good, Firefly."

"They're easy to make." She passed him a jar of lemonade and set the dishtowel-wrapped fried chicken out. "This looks scrumptious, though it doesn't beat your steaks. By the way, Dallam told me you visited him last night and took him a portion of the meat."

He took a drumstick from the dishtowel. "I feel sorry for the kid, laid up that way through no fault of his own and with no hope. Has to be depressing."

"You lifted his spirits," she said softly. "That was a nice thing to do."

Paisley reached for the wishbone part of the chicken and bit into it. "This is perfect. So moist. What a nice change from the usual."

"Food always tastes better outdoors. Don't know why that is." He waved the drumstick. "Remember how I used to swing you from this tree?"

"I do. And I recall how high you pushed me. I got scared a time or two."

"You scared? That's a first. You've never been afraid of anything. You were a daredevil."

"Farrel terrorized me. I never told you this, but he used to get me going high in the swing at my house and push me out. One time I thought I broke my arm. I couldn't use it for a few days. Regardless of injury, the fall would always knock the breath out of me."

"Why didn't you tell me?"

"Because you would've gotten into a fight with him, and he'd treat me a lot worse just to punish me. It was safer to keep quiet." She thought of her brother and wondered what he'd try next. He wasn't finished. There would be lots of repercussions for packing up and coming to the Lone Star. He'd see that as a thrown gauntlet.

His yelled words that they wouldn't be safe from him any-where rolled around in her head. No, he'd not fade quietly into the background.

She shivered. He'd come. The question was when, not if.

"Are you chilled?" Crockett asked.

"No, I'm good. Just thinking about Farrel. One time he got angry at a horse that wouldn't follow commands. He made it gallop, then roped its front legs, the sudden stop making it fall. Of course, it broke one leg and we had to shoot it. Farrel was uncon-cerned and said the animal should've minded him." Her hand trembling, Paisley laid her chicken down and tried to smother a cry but didn't quite succeed. "That's what he'll do to me and to Hilda too. We're not minding him, and we'll pay."

Crockett moved behind her and held her against him with his arms folded across her chest. "You're safe. I'm not going to let him hurt you or Hilda. I'll kill him if I have to before I let him cause you more pain."

"You can't stop him, Crockett. He has the most devious mind I've ever seen."

"A bullet can halt him in his tracks."

He said the words so calmly, as though they were discussing the weather. Yet she knew he was right. One day, someone would have to meet Farrel with deadly force. There'd be no other way.

She swiveled around to face Crockett, and he brushed her hair back. She loved the gentle way his hands moved on her. "Let's talk about something else."

"How are Dallam and Gus?"

"I'm a little disheartened over Dallam." She told how she'd examined him and thought she saw toe movement, only to have imagined it. "I desperately want him to have a better quality of life. How he can be so upbeat about his condition is beyond me."

"I noticed that also during my visit last night. We joked around quite a bit, then he became wistful about riding his horse. I think the memories of riding and being vital are what's keeping Dallam sane." He ran a fingertip over her cheek. "It's a shame you couldn't see anything to bring hope. That young man desperately needs something to keep him going."

"Crockett, I love talking to you about my patients. We seem like a team, you know?"

"I feel that also." He tweaked her nose. "You'll be delighted to know that my mother has one jar of home canned cherries."

Paisley threw her arms around his neck. "Thank you. This is great news. Gus's knee looked even worse today. It has so much fever in it."

"I brought it with me in my saddlebag."

"You're my savior! Name your price, cowboy."

"A kiss. That's all."

She held his face between her hands and placed her lips gently on his. Heat raced through her, leaving a scorched path. The faint rustle of leaves and the flutter of the Texas flag high overhead barely registered. The hammering of her heart sounded loud in her ears, blocking everything.

One palm slid to rest on his broad chest, and the muscles underneath quivered as though in response to her touch. With the scent of lilacs close by, she let the velvet warmth of the kiss wash away the pain of the past.

Crockett laid her back, mumbling against her mouth, "Firefly, you have no idea what you do to me."

Tingles curled along her spine. Was it wrong to let her feelings for him show? He wasn't the same man who'd failed to support her dream. Maybe fate had delivered this second chance so they could get it right.

"Did I settle my debt?" she asked.

"All that and more." His voice was husky. "You have change left over."

"Then I'll save it for a rainy day."

When her spirits needed lifting. Or to know she mattered.

Seventeen

SAFE FROM CURIOUS EYES BENEATH THE SPRAWLING ELM tree, Paisley stared up into Crockett's face. The smoldering passion in his brown eyes made her heart race.

As a young girl, she'd cared for this man, and now as an adult, she still did, but in a different way. She had to go slow and let trust build. Let her heart tell her what to do.

A rider passed by headquarters, calling to someone. Guilt made her jerk before she reminded herself they were mostly hidden by the low branch.

"No one can see us." Crockett's words reassured.

She reached for her jar of lemonade. "Thank you for this. And for not pressuring me. I've become far too careful."

"As you should, and me too." He picked up another drumstick and bit into it.

Her lashes lowered, and her breath hitched as he leaned to gently brush crumbs from her skirt. The tart lemonade lingered on her tongue as she fought to swallow.

A swift intake of air left her trembling. *Careful.*

Crockett spoke softly, "Ah, Firefly. We're flirting with danger." His breath was ragged as he touched her hair. "I've been trying to be good, but this is making it very, very difficult."

"I should be going. This isn't fair to either of us. You want far more than I can give right now." She finished her lemonade and put the jar in the basket.

"You're right. Your touch makes me remember things."

"Me too. Even what I've vowed to forget."

"If we continue on this path, my promise to go slow won't be worth a tinker's dam," he growled.

She knew he was right. Where was her wall? "What happened to the old Crockett?"

"He matured and took a job that calls for a good bit of wisdom."

"Yes, he did." Paisley kept her thoughts away from what could've happened if she'd let herself. "I like the new you. Thank goodness for work—both yours and mine." Her laugh was a bit shaky. She stuck a loose strand of hair back into place, praying he didn't know the extent of what he'd started inside her.

Crockett stretched out his long legs in front of him. "I think this has been the most pleasurable lunch I've ever had." He picked a leaf from her hair and winked. "Evidence."

"Only a person in law would think of such an innocent leaf that way."

"That's right." He gathered up the eating utensils. "Paisley, I got a telegram from Ranger Lancer this morning. Tests confirm your water isn't fit to drink. I'm glad you got out of there." He peered through the branch at a person walking past. "The tests also picked up traces of blasting material. Did Farrel use dynamite or blasting powder?"

"Not while I was there. Are you sure?"

"Positive. Maybe your father and Farrel did."

"Honestly, nothing would surprise me. They dug lots of holes. If they stuck dynamite into a hole, would I be able to hear it?"

"One stick would likely not make too much noise."

"Wait a minute." She recalled the walk in the moonlight in the area containing the holes. "I found a charred piece of wood right after I got back and went out for a stroll. I was curious but could find no sign of a fire."

"Yeah. Maybe Hilda will remember. I'll ask her."

Paisley eyed the chocolate pie, still uncut. "You took my fork. What did you do with it?"

"Sorry. I thought you wanted to leave." He handed her an extra.

"I have to have a bite or two of this pie." She sat down.

He followed with a fork in hand. "No way will I let you have it all. Unless you beg."

"Nope. You're welcome to dig in."

After eating their fill of the dessert, she helped him repack everything. "Tell your cook it was delicious."

"I will. Essie will prop her hands on her ample hips and beam like a light on a lighthouse."

The wind ruffled his dark brown hair, and his eyes had a roguish look. He reminded her of a pirate, with his sleeves rolled up, showing muscled forearms. She swallowed hard and let him pull her up. She hadn't known many men as handsome as he. And none with kisses that made her forget time and space. Her thoughts swirling in her head, she started to walk away.

"Wait. Let me get those cherries from my saddlebag."

"Thanks for reminding me."

A moment later with the cherries in hand, she headed back toward Gus's place, a smile on her lips and her head in the clouds.

Gus was napping and didn't even try to throw anything at her. She got a spoon and gave him a dose of laudanum, then a big spoonful of cherries. "This should help, but it'll take a few weeks to note a difference." Paisley shook her finger at him. "You have to eat them twice a day."

He mumbled under his breath, "There ain't much here so it won't take long to go through 'em."

"I'll try to get you more."

"Next time I'm sleeping, don't wake me." He glared and turned away. "Close the door on your way out."

Gus offered no thank you, not even a hint of one. He might as well have told her to kiss his butt. She tried not to let it bother her but just couldn't let it go.

She swung back. "I know I'm not your favorite person, and

we don't see eye-to-eye, but you are the most gripey, most ill-tempered man I've ever met. You're ungrateful even when people go out of their way to try to help you."

"I didn't ask for your help or theirs. I didn't ask anyone for anything!"

"I wish you could spend one day, one hour with Dallam. But then even that probably would have no effect on you." She slammed the door and leaned against the side of the one-room house, shaking.

Soon guilt set in. She should be ashamed. Gus was a patient. Dr. Thorp would probably fire her for unprofessionalism. The urge hit her to go back and apologize, but instead, she moved on to her pregnant ladies.

Hilda, dark hair curling around her shoulders, let her into Annabelle Fletcher's. She smiled and motioned silently to Tye sitting on the floor playing with Annabelle's two children and their dog.

He looked up, "Hi, Auntie. We're having fun. This is Biscuit."

"Oh, good." She knelt beside them. "What a cute dog. It looks like someone socked him with that one black eye."

"It wasn't me," Tye said. "I like Biscuit."

"I know, honey. I wasn't accusing anyone." She kissed his cheek.

"I wish I had Lucky. Do you think my papa is feeding him?"

"Oh sure. I wouldn't worry about it. Your father will take care of Lucky."

That seemed to satisfy Tye. "This is Charley and Jane. They're my friends."

"How wonderful. Hi, kids."

"You're the nurse," Jane said.

Paisley figured the girl had to be about four, and her brown hair lay in long braids. Charley had a mess of freckles and a bad cowlick in front. He was somewhere around three. The kids were good for her nephew. She got to her feet.

Hilda grinned. "Tye will talk your arm off if you'll let him. Don't know where he found all these words."

"I think they got unlocked inside his head. It's a refreshing change." Paisley took Hilda aside. "Crockett was asking me about explosions at our Mahone place, and I told him I hadn't heard any. Did you ever hear loud blasts?"

"Yes, I heard quite a lot of them when Joe was alive."

"Tests found traces of dynamite in the water samples." Paisley hushed when Annabelle waddled from the bedroom, her blond hair in braids wound around her head.

"How nice of you to drop by, Nurse."

"How are you feeling today?"

Annabelle gave her a wan smile. "Tired, of course, even though my Richard has taken on all the work here. I feel really bad, because he works hard all day then has to work nonstop until bedtime." Annabelle placed a loving hand on her swollen belly. "He'll have even more to do once the new baby comes."

"Just for a while until you get back on your feet." Paisley helped her to a chair. "I'm sure he doesn't complain."

"No, ma'am. Richard is the salt of the earth. I love him so much."

"How long did you say you've been married?" Paisley checked Annabelle's feet, that were twice their size.

"Four years. Honestly, I don't know where they've gone. It's like I blinked and here we are, with a houseful of kids."

"I'm sure Dr. Thorp asked you this…did you have any trouble with childbirth?"

"Some with Jane."

The little girl glanced up with concern on her face.

"That's fine. We'll talk later." Best to get the information in private or from the doctor.

Annabelle nodded. "My back has been hurting more than normal."

"Let's examine you." She and Hilda got the woman into the bedroom and on the bed.

"I hope nothing's wrong," Annabelle murmured. "I can't remember feeling the baby move."

Paisley patted her hand. "I'm sure everything is probably fine. Try not to worry."

Hilda moved a pillow under the mother's head. "Are you comfortable, Annabelle?"

"Yes. Thank you, Hilda. You've been such a godsend."

"I'm happy to help." Hilda stood back, one ear probably listening to the kids.

After feeling the size and position of the baby, Paisley was anything but relieved. However, she pasted a smile on her face. "The heartbeat is strong, and the baby is kicking. I guarantee it'll come very soon. Do you and your husband have a plan for when it happens?"

"Yes, ma'am. Richard will run to the doctor's house." As Annabelle said the words, her expression changed to one of near panic when she realized the doctor couldn't help them. "I don't know where you live, Nurse Mahone. What if the doctor can't get word to you? What if something happens to the baby before you can get here?"

"Annabelle, take a deep breath. I'll leave written instructions for your husband on how to find me. It'll be fine. Really."

Hilda patted her hand, adding, "You can count on me too. Paisley and I share a house, so I can tell your husband exactly how to find us."

That seemed to calm the woman, and she breathed easier.

Paisley put everything back into her satchel. "That's right. Between all of us, I assure you we'll get this babe safely into your arms."

"Thank you. Panic took over for a moment." Annabelle smiled and folded her hands over her stomach. "If not for it coming feet-first, I could birth it by myself."

"You won't have to. I want you to keep your feet elevated. With

Hilda here, you won't have to chase after your children. Drink cups of chamomile tea and take lots of cleansing breaths to help you relax. Keeping calm and in a positive frame of mind will help tremendously."

The young woman vowed to do all she could. Satisfied, Paisley wrote out the directions to her home as promised and went on to her last patient.

Mrs. Sally Nolan met her at the door. "Come in, Nurse."

The robust woman led her to the parlor that was as neat as a pin. If a speck of dirt had the audacity to get in her house, Sally would reprimand it severely and boot it out.

Paisley took a seat. "You look the perfect picture of health, Sally. I hope you feel that way."

"Yes, ma'am." The big-boned woman sat in a rocker and picked up her knitting. She'd pulled her auburn hair back in a knot on her neck and wore a serene expression. "I get tired a lot, but I've been taking afternoon naps as you suggested."

"Good. Any back pain?"

"Only when I'm on my feet too long." Her knitting needles clacked as her fingers flew.

"That's a pretty shade of yellow. What are you making?"

"A blanket for the wee one."

"It'll be nice and warm. What are you hoping for?"

"A little girl. But my husband wants a son. I guess it doesn't matter."

Paisley took the stethoscope from her satchel and listened to Sally's heart. "You're lucky you don't have any children underfoot. Poor Annabelle Fletcher has two, and she gets very little rest. I hope my sister-in-law will help in that respect. Hilda started working over there today."

Sally's chin trembled, and her quiet voice seemed strained. "I guess Dr. Thorp didn't tell you I had one stillborn. It was a boy, and I never got to hold him."

Which was probably why Sally wanted a girl.

"I'm so sorry." Paisley knelt down. Thorp should've told her. Losing a baby had a definite impact mentally on the mother's next pregnancy. "Are you worried it'll happen again?"

"It's there in the back of my mind, but I try not to dwell on it. My husband doesn't like me thinking about Billy lying in the cold ground because it makes me weepy. So I try to pretend that Billy's only sleeping for a while. I can't stand—" Her voice broke. "I can't bear to think of bugs and worms crawling on my precious boy."

Paisley rose and put tender arms around the woman. "Whatever gets you through the day, Sally," she said softly. "I can't imagine your pain."

The woman wiped her eyes and put her tears away like they were a toy. "I'm not being fair to this child inside me now to pine for Billy. My mother would tell me to buck up and get on with living."

She sounded like a cruel woman to Paisley. "No one gives us a book of instructions when we come into the world. It's up to us to figure things out for ourselves. We do the best we can. Sometimes we manage just fine and then something comes along that knocks us down and forces us to muddle through." Paisley patted Sally's hand. "This is only my opinion, but I think there's more than one right way to handle a problem, and it's the one that's best for us."

They talked some more, then Paisley examined her. "You're doing very well. I see no difficulties with this birth. You're a healthy woman. I wish all my patients were like you."

"I guess it was the way I was raised. Self-pity had no place in my family's life."

Sally's mother and father must've been hard people, who took no joy in anything. Paisley said goodbye and headed back to the doctor's house.

On the way, she noticed Crockett's sister, Hannah, jumping hurdles with her horse and stopped to watch. The girl and the horse were amazing. Then, Elena Rose joined her, and the pair practiced hitting a target with bow and arrow as they galloped past. Paisley didn't know how they did it so smoothly, but she imagined they'd had hours and hours of practice.

When she reached Thorp's, he was hobbling around in the kitchen on crutches, making coffee. "Did you finish?"

"Mrs. Nolan was my last patient. She told me about the stillbirth of her first child." Paisley fixed him with a stare. "Why didn't you mention it?"

The doctor propped himself on the crutches, looking more unkempt than ever. "There were extenuating circumstances with Sally's first. Just weeks from delivering, she slipped on some ice and took a bad fall, landing on her stomach, and that is probably what killed the baby. Now, she's in good health, and her spirits are up. There is no medical reason why she can't have a perfect delivery this time." He studied her. "I apologize for not telling you everything. You need to know all the details about a patient even if it doesn't always apply. I promise to do better."

He did look contrite. Paisley patted his arm. "Sometimes communication breaks down, and that's a simple fact. You're doing the best you can. That brings us to Annabelle Fletcher. She went into a panic when it registered that you won't be the point of contact when she goes into labor. She's concerned that she might not be able to quickly get word to me. You and I have never discussed that."

"If her husband comes here, I'll send someone for you. In any event, I'll be there if at all possible. This one might take both of us."

"I agree. I'll be relieved to have you." Paisley reported Sally's swollen feet and back pain, then gathered her things. "Now, I'm off to take my four-year-old nephew to see a talking parrot before supper."

Thorp laughed. "That sounds exciting. Little boys love things like that."

"Indeed they do." And Paisley might find a private moment with the bird's owner if she played her cards right. He was doing that thing again of drawing her to him. Only this time she had her eyes open wide.

Eighteen

"Shake, Pardner," Casanova said, his green head tilted. "Wanna be friends?"

Tye giggled and leaned forward. "Yes, bird. Be my friend."

Crockett had given the parrot a stern talking to before the boy arrived, and he was happy to see the bird on his best behavior. It often struck him that Casanova and kids were a lot alike. The only thing was you could reason with kids—at least somewhat. Although just seeing Tye once on the day he arrived with an ashen face and sad eyes, Crockett could see the immense change in the boy. He had color, didn't look as sickly, and laughed now.

Hilda was staying with Annabelle Fletcher until her husband got home, so Paisley had dropped by and picked Tye up.

Paisley met Crockett's gaze and mouthed a thank-you. He squeezed her hand.

Casanova hopped down and stood as close to Tye as he could get. "Let's shake on it."

"You can't, bird." Tye giggled so much he lost his breath. When he could speak, he turned to his aunt. "He don't have a hand." And the giggles started fresh.

"Have you ever taken Casanova out of the cage?" Paisley asked Crockett.

"Briefly to change the paper in the bottom."

"What did you do with him while you accomplished that?"

"Hannah held him. She doesn't seem to care if she gets bird poop on her."

"Do you mind if I get him out?"

"Let me shut the door first, and you can be my guest." Crockett shut the back door. Why on earth she wanted to play with that parrot was beyond him, but if it made her happy, he'd do anything.

With anxiousness on his face, Tye backed up next to Crockett when Paisley unlatched the little door to the cage and reached inside.

"Come to me, my darling Casanova," she crooned. He hopped on her finger, and she lifted him out.

The bird jumped to her shoulder and rubbed his beak against her neck. "Kiss me, baby."

"Parrots can't kiss!" Tye erupted in fits of laughter again. "He thinks he's a person."

"We don't know all of what that bird thinks." Crockett gave his feathered buddy the evil eye. He'd better watch it. "You won't think he's so cute after he leaves bird droppings on you, Paisley."

"You're just jealous."

She had a perfect right to say that, because he was. The crazy bird was saying and doing things Crockett wanted to but wouldn't get away with.

"Can he sit on my shoulder, Auntie?" Tye moved closer.

"Don't be afraid." She transferred the parrot to the boy. "See? He likes you."

Tye stood very still, as though afraid to move. "Can I have a bird like this, Auntie?"

"Honey, your mama will have to answer that, not me."

Crockett draped an arm around her and murmured in her ear. "She'll probably try to find one after she sees the big smile Casanova puts on his face."

"Probably. Where do they sell talking parrots?" she asked.

"Hell if I know." He inhaled the fragrance of her hair and zeroed in on the teasing freckle next to the corner of her mouth. "Have supper with me."

"Stop it," she whispered. "I need to eat at home for a change.

I've been so busy, I haven't given much thought to my mother's journal and solving that riddle. I know she's trying to tell me something, and Stoker confirmed it. He told me to keep working toward the truth."

"I could help decipher." Pointing her to the right path wouldn't be the same as telling her. "Besides, I'd like to see what Caroline Mahone says."

Her light-green eyes studied him. "If you're sure, I guess I could come back after we finish supper."

"Good. I'll sharpen my pencils as well as my wits."

Thank God Grandpa hadn't made him promise not to assist her. She needed to get at the truth before Farrel figured it out and started drilling on the land.

"Let's be friends. Friends. Friends." Casanova waddled down Tye's arm. "Walk the plank, matey. One, two, hup."

"Are you getting tired, Tye?" Crockett asked.

"Not much. Wait'll I tell Charley and Jane. They'll wanna come see."

Paisley stepped away from Crockett. "Your mama's proba-bly home by now, Tye. She'll wonder where we are. Let me take Casanova."

"Okay, Auntie." He stayed still while she lifted the parrot off him.

Casanova snuggled against her neck. "Kiss me, baby. Kiss me."

Tye giggled. "That silly bird thinks he loves you."

"How about that?" Paisley put the bird back in the cage and added some seeds from her pocket, which he started eating.

"This has been fun. What do you tell Mr. Legend, Tye?"

"Thank you for letting me see your bird." The boy stuck out his small palm, and Crockett shook it.

"Come back when you want to laugh, young man. Paisley, I'll see you later."

Her eyes sparkled. "Maybe I'll bring some more fried apples."

"Ah, you do know the way to this man's heart, Firefly." He followed them out onto the porch, his hand lingering on hers.

Knowing how the hours would drag until she returned, he saddled Cato and went for a ride. Before realizing where he'd headed, he arrived at the swimming hole where he and Paisley spent their summers so long ago. He dismounted and let Cato nibble at the grass.

Memories and images flooded his mind of a time and place he could never return.

Where he'd found the girl of his dreams and foolishly let her go. If he could get her back, he wouldn't ask anything else. The silly bird might be the key.

And one day if things went right, Crockett would be the one saying, "Kiss me, baby."

❧

At the sound of the light tap on his door, Crockett hurried to let Paisley in. "Right on time."

The journal under one arm and a pan of fried apples in her hand, she stepped inside. "I thought you might've taken supper with your folks or Stoker, so I didn't rush."

He brushed a light kiss to her cheek and took the pan from her. "Actually, I saddled up and took a ride out to the swimming hole. I hadn't been out there in ages."

"Me either. Wouldn't be surprised if there's ghosts."

"Nah. Just the wind whistling through that tree we used to jump from into the water. You were something, Firefly. Both then and now. You haven't lost your fire."

"Gus would vouch for that. I'm afraid I let him have it when I took the cherries by. I've never met a more ungrateful man in all my life. It was difficult enough to get the cherries, then he never said thanks."

"Sounds like he deserved the blowup." Crockett motioned with his head. "Follow me."

She fell in behind him, and they went to the kitchen. "I feel bad though. He's a patient, and I should've been more understanding." She sighed. "I'll have to apologize next time I visit him. I'll skip tomorrow though."

"That's good. Let him wonder if you're coming back." He set the apples down, stood behind her, and massaged her neck.

"My, that feels good. I could get used to this."

Casanova's voice came from the other room. "Kiss me, baby! Kiss me."

Paisley laughed. "I don't know why he says that only to me."

"That's easy to figure out. He's in love, Firefly."

"You're pulling my leg. Birds can't feel love. I don't believe that. He repeats things."

"Trust me. This parrot is in love."

Casanova piped up again, "Love Firefly. Hello, Firefly."

"For heaven's sake." Paisley went toward the voice, pulling up in the parlor. "Now you get this straight, Casanova. You're a bird and I'm a lady."

The parrot hopped from his perch and lay on his back on the paper. Then he folded his wings over his chest. A tiny tear leaked from one eye.

"Now look what you've done. You've crushed him. You got through to him all right." Crockett thumped the cage. "Get up from there. Be a respectable bird, not a worm."

Casanova flew to his perch and released the loudest wolf whistle Crockett had ever heard.

"All right. I'm fixing you." Crockett threw the cover over the cage. "Good night."

"Swing low, sweet chariot. Coming for to carry me home."

Paisley laughed. "Of all things. Let's take the journal to the kitchen table."

"And get forks for the fried apples." Crockett wagged his eyebrows.

"You're hopeless." She accepted a fork, and they both dug into the sweet treat.

"I think this might be better than the other one. It has a tad more cinnamon."

She laughed. "Oh please. I made them both the same."

After finishing off the apples, they settled down with paper and pencils, and she showed him several of the most confusing entries.

As he read, he could see how Caroline laid things out. Crockett glanced up. "How do you want to proceed?"

"I want to write down the oddest words that stand out. If I'm right, they'll be a message."

"That's pretty clever of you to come up with that idea." He meant that. She was one of the brightest women he'd ever met.

"Save your admiration." She tapped her pencil on the table. "I could be totally wrong. Mama didn't know much about hidden codes and stuff like that."

Grandpa would have his hide if he didn't proceed carefully. The last place Crockett wanted to be was on the receiving end of one of Stoker's blistering tirades. And this Mahone land in the middle of the Lone Star with no clear ownership had gotten the old man up in arms like nothing else.

Crockett picked up a pencil and poised it over the open pad. "Why don't you go through the journal and tell me which words to write down? Then we'll try to make sense of them."

"Okay. I've marked the some of the parts so I could go back and read them again." She started at the first and began to thumb through. "It seems to begin with the word *lost*." She turned the pages, scanning each entry. "*Stoker* and *section* are sort of mentioned together, so I think that's important."

She was on the right track. Crockett wrote and underlined each word. She was going to get it.

"Mama talks about two hundred fifty-eight hectares, and I

think she did that so I'd understand she was talking about land, so write that down. Then this is odd. She says to ask and you shall receive."

"Maybe that all needs to go on our list, don't you think?"

"I certainly do." Paisley bent over the journal. "Here's another odd one. *Sometimes an envelope can hold important information. Look inside.*"

"Have you found any envelopes among your mother's things?"

"No, but Farrel could've. If he did, Lord knows what he would've done with it." She read the passage over. "List the words *envelope* and *information.*"

"Yes, ma'am." Crockett shot her a look of admiration. "I have to say, you're really determined to find the message. If, in fact, there is one."

Paisley's eyes met his. "This is so unlike Mama, and I don't share Farrel's opinion that she was crazy. She wrote these things deliberately in hopes of someone finding whatever it is. Since she didn't trust my father or Farrel, that leaves me. She mentions me in one entry, warning me to be careful. Let me find it." She flipped back to the first. "Here it is. *I pray Paisley listens to her heart. War and anger breed hate. Joe and Farrel will stop at nothing to distort the truth and turn her to their way of thinking.*"

Crockett's voice was quiet. "Your mother lived with that hate. I'm sorry, but that's the truth."

"We both did. I got out, but she couldn't. Her only reprieves were the mornings when she'd meet Stoker. He told me they were only friends and nothing more. He was just her safe harbor."

"We all need one at times. I'm glad Stoker helped her."

"Me too. Okay, I don't see anything else. Let's put all that together."

"*Lost section Stoker two hundred fifty-eight hectares ask envelope information.*"

"I don't see that the hectares add anything except to clarify. Let's take those words out," Paisley suggested. "That leaves…*Lost section Stoker ask envelope information.*"

A thread of excitement wound through Crockett.

"That's it." Paisley clutched his arm. "I have to ask Stoker about the lost section which would mean the Mahone land that the Lone Star swallowed up. I think he's the key, and he's holding an envelope that possibly my mother left in his keeping. There's information in it that I need."

"That seems exactly what I'm getting also." And Crockett never helped one iota. His conscience was clear.

"I never told you that I had a talk with Stoker the day Hilda and I came running. We needed to clear the air, which we did." She closed the journal and laid down her pencil. "He told me to read this and pay attention to what it's not saying. I told him I thought Mama left a message, and he said she'd protected her legacy."

"She must've been really afraid that your father or Farrel would take it and you'd get nothing." Crockett leaned back. "Caroline had a very valid point."

"You're right. So the legacy is the Jessup land that had been Mama's? But she didn't own that anymore."

"I don't know, Paisley. You should talk to Grandpa first thing tomorrow."

All of a sudden, a horrendous blast shook the house and rattled the windows. Crockett jumped out of his chair as Paisley rushed into his arms.

After that died down, there was a moment's lull, then another stronger quake that broke a near window.

She leaned back, panic on her face. "Farrel. Oh God, Farrel's done something terrible."

"We don't know that, and jumping to wild conclusions won't help us. I'll see you home. We need to check on Hilda and Tye. Then I have to check on what the hell happened."

Yet he knew in his heart she was probably right. They had never had an earthquake in North Texas that he'd heard of.

Nineteen

PAISLEY CLUTCHED CROCKETT'S ARM. ALL HELL HAD BROKEN loose. People ran this way and that, yelling fit to wake the dead. A second later, a group of cowboys galloped toward headquarters to get their orders.

Fear raced through her, chilling her bones as they hurried toward her house. "This is madness. But Farrel thrives on that."

"Agreed, but we don't know this is him." Crockett helped her over a hole in the ground.

"I do know," she insisted.

Hilda and Tye came out onto the porch, the boy clinging to her dress. Paisley raced to them. "Are you all right?"

"Shaken up is all." Hilda put a hand to her forehead. "Do you think Farrel did this?"

"I hate myself for thinking this, but yes. My brother is very capable of sowing chaos and fear."

Crockett gave her a hurried hug. "I need to see what's happened. We'll talk later." Houston careened toward them in a wagon, and it seemed unusual not to see him on a horse. Crockett jumped in with his father as the wagon slowed a bit and they sped off.

Paisley's heart plummeted to the pit of her stomach as she watched them hurtle toward danger. She wanted to call them back and keep them safe, but she knew nothing she said would make any difference. She clutched her hands to her heart. The Legends thought they could win. They thought Farrel was a little nastier than most yet mortal all the same.

They didn't know he was the devil incarnate.

The porch shook beneath their feet as she caught a flash far in the distance. The explosion reverberated through the ground. God help them! Was he going to keep this up until he blew up the entire county?

"Come, let's get inside." She put an arm across Tye's shoulders and opened the door.

Tye looked up at her. "Do you think Casanova is okay?"

"Yes, honey. I think he's fine. Why, I'll bet he's sleeping and hasn't felt a thing."

Her face pinched, Hilda came in behind them and shut the door, pasting on a smile. "I went to the mercantile today and bought some popcorn. Would anyone want some?"

"Yea! I do, Mama!" Tye jumped up and down. "Popcorn's good."

"I agree." Paisley considered the kitchen area the safest place to be at the moment. "And what if your mama and I read from that book you like?"

"Oh boy! I like *Arabian Nights*. Aladdin uses magic in it."

Remembering the fantasy werewolf Tye pulled from the air when he was so distraught, Paisley lovingly touched his head. "I often thought I'd like to ride a magic carpet and go anywhere in the world I wanted. Wouldn't that be fun?"

"And you could get away from bad people real easy."

Although Farrel's name didn't come up a lot around Tye, the boy glanced up with worry lining his face. He was very smart, and it wasn't any stretch to imagine he was probably thinking about his father and that he was responsible for the explosions. Tye knew what Farrel was capable of.

"Furthermore," Paisley continued as Hilda lit the stove and got out a pan, "you could make the magic carpet drop on top of their head where they couldn't see."

"I wish I could do that." His wistful words brought a lump to her throat. "And Casanova could scare them. Casanova's my friend."

"Yes, he is."

"I'm going to have to go see this parrot." Hilda's smile showed her pretty dimples. "He sounds amazing."

"You'll see. He's in love with Auntie." Tye scampered off to get the book from his room.

"The parrot is in love with you?" Hilda asked.

"He learned this phrase, 'Kiss me, baby,' and repeats it when he sees me. So Tye thinks he's my boyfriend or something. But it's nothing more than something he was taught."

"I hope I don't have to worry."

"Nope." Paisley turned the conversation to something they needed to discuss. "Hilda, we should bar the doors tonight and make sure the windows are shut."

"I know. Farrel's words that we won't be safe anywhere have been going around and around in my head. I can't imagine what he's doing setting off these explosions. Do you have any idea?"

"Not sure, but maybe he's blasting the ground in hopes of finding oil. He's so obsessed with getting rich. In his mind, that would put him on a level playing field with the Legends." Paisley ran a hand over her eyes. "Or maybe he's trying to blow the Legends off the face of the earth."

"There's no telling. He's crazy." Hilda's troubled dark eyes shifted down. "I can't believe I married him. Had his child. I feel so foolish, and I know I can never go back to him. The love I once felt is gone. It left the first time he hit me."

"Women aren't meant to be beat on." Paisley put her arm around her sister-in-law. "We have each other, and we're among friends."

"That makes me feel better. Thank you." Hilda patted Paisley's back.

The only way they'd get through this was by sticking together. Two were stronger than one.

"When we get some privacy, I'll tell you what I found out

tonight. There was a surprising message in my mother's journal. How she thought to put it there, I'll never know."

"I'll be interested in hearing what you discovered."

Tye clomped back down the stairs, and they turned their attention to making popcorn and reading about a magic carpet.

Paisley thought of Crockett and said a prayer that he'd be safe.

❧

The wagon bumped across the rough dirt road, and Crockett felt sure his teeth were about to be jarred from his mouth. He grabbed the lantern before it tipped over. "Why did you bring this thing? Why not your horse?"

"There may be injured people we have to haul back, and it was already hitched. Ransom had just returned from mending fence in it."

"Yeah, makes sense." Crockett took the gun from his boot and checked the chamber. "Dad, we'd best be ready for anything. Paisley thinks these explosions are Farrel's doing, and seeing we're heading in the direction of the Mahone land, I tend to agree, although I didn't tell her that. Don't we need a plan?"

Houston flashed a glance. "It's the same one we've always had. Ride through hell until we come out the other side and take care of what we find as we go. There are no rules when you're dealing with scum."

"Pretty much what I thought." They rode in silence, catching up with others on horseback. Everyone racing to find the trouble. "Dad, Paisley went through Caroline's journal tonight and figured out that her mother left an envelope for her. She's going to speak to Grandpa tomorrow. I didn't help her even though I wanted to. She did it on her own. She's very clever."

"I always knew she had a good head. I liked it when she used to hang around."

"Me too." A whole lot.

Houston caught the group of cowboys and pulled alongside. They all held lanterns. "Have you seen where the explosions are coming from?"

"I thought it must be Mahone again, sir. But the blasts came from Lone Star land. Leastways that's what Shorty told me. He said it's on that section we used to call Jessup land."

The Jessup land. That figured.

"Your name's Jeremy, isn't it?" Crockett asked. "I can't see too good in the dark."

"That's right."

"Thanks for the information. You men be careful."

Houston urged the team faster, and they pulled ahead of the cowboys. Crockett hung on.

"Do you suppose Farrel somehow found out that maybe the Jessup land belongs to Paisley?" Crockett asked. "If, in fact, it turns out that way."

Nothing was for certain, although Caroline's journal had sure seemed to suggest she meant to leave the land to her daughter. But Caroline had no idea she'd die so suddenly, which was why things were left in such a state. Why hadn't she just told Paisley? Why go to such extremes to hide the ownership unless she was trying to protect Paisley from her brother? Maybe Caroline knew her daughter wasn't strong enough to fight Farrel. They should get clarity come morning, and it couldn't come too soon.

"Anything's possible I suppose, but I don't see how Farrel would have gotten hold of the deed unless he found out the name of the lawyer and broke into his office." Houston shook the reins harder.

"Maybe the lawyer is unscrupulous and told Farrel," Crockett mused. "Wouldn't be the first time."

They fell into silence and rode through the night, Crockett wondering what they'd find. Could even be a trap. That thought crossed his mind. The darkness was an excellent cover for most anything nefarious, and Farrel was the best at that.

"I don't know that we'll be able to see much of anything when we get there. But I'm glad we have the lantern." Crockett didn't know if he'd said the words aloud or kept them in his head.

"Doesn't do any good to speculate. We'll see soon enough," Houston replied.

They caught up with more riders, and a half mile later, they reached the Jessup land. The homestead was gone. Nothing was left but a pile of rubble and a big hole in the ground. Men were milling around. Grandpa was there with Luke, and both held guns pointed at three men.

His hand gripping the lantern, Crockett beat his father out of the wagon by several seconds. "What's going on?"

"We caught Farrel red-handed," Grandpa growled. "He blew up the old Jessup home and left this crater plus several others."

"I did no such a damn thing!" Farrel yelled. "You Legends did this. You're trying to erase us and our gentle mama's roots off the face of the earth."

"You're a lying sack of horse shit!" a cowboy yelled.

"Hold on." Crockett stood between the two sides with arms outstretched. "Farrel, who do you have with you?"

"These are some friends just trying to make sure we get a fair shake. And we're not!" Farrel spat on the ground. "We was over at my place playing cards when we heard the explosions and rode here as fast as we could."

"You didn't find anyone. Did you?" Houston barked.

"No, because you was smart enough to get the hell out of here."

"Why would we run?" Luke asked. "This is our property. It's no one's business what we do on it."

"I don't know why you Legends do any of the stuff you do," Farrel shot back. "You cheat and you lie."

Crockett narrowed his gaze. It was pretty clever of Mahone to try to shift the blame, only it wasn't working. "I don't suppose we'd find any dynamite on you."

"Not one stick." Farrel spat again.

"You two with Mahone. Can you back him up?" Crockett asked.

One man wearing what looked like a two-dollar suit shifted. "Well, it's pretty much like Farrel said. We were playing cards, and suddenly the house shook."

The other one in a Stetson picked up the story. "We ran out in the yard and looked this way and another explosion dropped us to our knees. We saw an orange glow and a bunch of dirt in the air. Jumped on our horses and rode over. Never saw the like in all my born days. I don't know why you folks are taking all Farrel has. His wife and kid left with his sister, and he's all alone."

"I wouldn't be surprised if you don't blow up the house he's living in and put him out in the open," said the first.

Stoker glared and shook his fist. "That's a crock of horseshit, and you know it! I'll call in the Texas Rangers at daybreak to investigate. Now, get off my land before I shoot you."

"Ain't this just like the Legends?" Farrel yelled, waving his arms. "You think you're big and powerful, but let me tell you something. We ain't done with our business. You'll pay for taking my wife and son, killing my father and brother. You'll pay for every bit of the wrongs. You ain't heard the last from me."

Anger shot through Crockett. Farrel had always blamed everyone else for his problems, and it had started way back in his youth. Due to the man's volatility, Crockett had never wanted anything to do with him. Houston once called him a loose cannon, and that said it all pretty plainly.

Illuminating the ground with what light the lanterns put out, Stoker, his sons, and Crockett carefully walked over the piles of dirt and destruction, then huddled together. "Dynamite didn't do this." Stoker opened his palm to reveal a blasting cap. "They used nitroglycerin."

"Yep. I found another one." Crockett showed them his. "We have to call in the Texas Rangers."

Houston dropped down on his haunches. "We didn't have enough to warrant the telegram before, but we do now."

"The thing is, Farrel has become a thousand times more dangerous." Crockett's gaze followed the trio trotting away. "As his friend pointed out, he's lost dearly. His wife and child, mother, father, brother, his sister. He's left with nothing. Men with their backs against the wall have little to fear. I shudder to think what he'll try next."

Luke muttered something in Spanish. "We must be on alert for anything."

"We should leave some men here to guard things until daylight so nothing is disturbed. I can't wait to see it clearer." Houston's words settled over Crockett, and he knew his dad was right. Farrel could try to come back.

The ranch hands stood in their own group, and four broke off, striding toward them. The lead one, named Shep, spoke. "Me and the boys think we should stand guard until morning."

"Good idea. Are you volunteering, Shep?" Crockett asked.

"Reckon I am. Don't feel right to ride off. Jeremy, Barker, and Smith share my feelings."

"Then you all have my gratitude." Stoker shook their hands. "When I get back to headquarters, I'll have someone bring you a coffeepot and cups."

"Thank you, sir." Shep's expression was somber as he turned back to his friends. Most days the young cowboy wore a ready grin, but not tonight.

"We have no better group of hands, Pa." Houston patted his father's back.

"I'm proud of them all."

Crockett silently agreed. The ranch hands were loyal to a fault and would stand a fight in the blink of an eye if anyone threatened their boss. "There's not much more we can do right now. I suggest we get some sleep. We'll have a full day tomorrow."

"That is true. Josie will be worried, so I'll go on." Luke moved toward his horse, his Colt hanging in his worn gun belt.

"I'll wake up Jonesy and get that telegram sent to the Texas Rangers tonight. This can't wait. We need the big boys, and the sooner the better."

Crockett nodded. "Excellent idea, Grandpa. I'll meet you at the telegraph office. I need to send one to Alex Lancer and apprise him of the latest."

They made their way back to headquarters. Crockett imagined Paisley would be parked on his doorstep, wanting word of what happened. He didn't want to tell her she was right.

Their world had become far more dangerous, and it would take all their strength to emerge in one piece.

Twenty

PAISLEY STOOD AT THE WINDOW WHEN CROCKETT RODE IN with his dad. She quietly let herself out so as not to disturb the sleepers and went toward the light shining in the small barn behind his house.

He must've heard her. He shut the barn door and turned. "You were right."

"I didn't want to be." She folded her arms across her middle and tried to breathe. "How bad?"

Crockett closed the space and pulled her against him. "No one was hurt. He blew up your mama's old homestead that stood on the Jessup land."

"Why? What did that accomplish?"

"Not sure, but he's trying to blame it on us. He said we did it to wipe all trace of the Mahones off the land."

"But it's not Mahone land and never will be again. That's crazy." She clutched the front of his shirt, staring up at him. "When will all this stop?"

"Wish I knew. And how many have to die before it ends." He kissed her temple. "A big part of it might've been to rattle us or to see if oil truly lies under the surface. Maybe he thinks an explosion would bring the oil up."

"Possibly. It's exhausting to try to get into my brother's head. He doesn't think like we do." And he never did, which was the sad thing. Fear raced through her, and she trembled. "I'm so afraid of what he'll do next. I have a very bad feeling in the pit of my stomach that he's going to hurt someone. Or try to take Tye."

He smoothed her hair back from her face. "It's impossible to predict Farrel Mahone. Try not to dwell on it. Just stay alert and watchful. I'll keep an eye out as well. If I have to, I'll post some men outside your house."

"Thank you. I'm probably being silly."

"Not at all. We need to get some sleep. If you want, I'll bed down in your parlor. Would that make you feel better?"

Paisley smiled and laid a hand on the side of his face. "You'd be miserable, and I'd worry about the crick in your neck come morning. Sleep in your own bed. I'll lock the doors. You and I have a busy day lined up tomorrow. I mean to talk to Stoker about the message in the diary at some point. I know he'll be busy though."

Still, she wanted to talk to him. Could she be right about her mother leaving an envelope? What could be in it?

"Yes, he's going back out to the explosion site." Crockett paused. "You should know Stoker wired the Texas Rangers when we got back tonight. Your brother is treading on dangerous ground, and it's no longer just a feud between our two families. He's going to wind up either dead or in prison."

That had been coming for a long while, and Farrel had lost their father's protection.

"Somehow, I always knew it would come to this." Paisley shuddered. "I'm so glad Hilda, Tye, and I got out of there when we did."

"Lady, if you hadn't, I would've come and gotten you tonight."

Despite the serious nature of their talk, a smile curved her lips. "I like it when you get all Legend on me."

"Get ready for more of that. I won't stand for anyone hurting you."

The rough pad of his thumb brushed her cheek. She knew without a doubt that if anyone did harm her, he'd go after them with a vengeance. He was a Legend, and Legend men took care of their ladies like no other.

Weary to her bones, she rested her head on his broad shoulder.

His arms came around her, and it was like he'd wrapped her in a warm cocoon, protected and safe. She needed this man and his strength for a few moments until she could find her own.

"Ah, my beautiful Firefly."

He claimed her mouth hungrily but with such sweet gentleness, sweeping her to a place of peace and calm. Her knees gave way, and had he not held her, she'd have fallen. She slipped her arms around his waist, clinging to him, trying not to think of what would come next.

Right now, this moment, was all that mattered.

With the deepening kiss, his mouth softened, and she held on. Tomorrow, she'd find her courage and be brave.

This was what she'd longed for, dreamed of for so long, but part of her warned that it was dangerous to trust and even more risky to love. Yet, though she'd tried to deny it, the love she'd once had for him had never left but continued to live inside her, at times emerging as a small sigh of hope.

Paisley trembled as he murmured her name against her mouth. This thing they'd found on a sweltering summer day burned through her blood. Her heart fluttered wildly as her breath became ragged.

She pulled back, searching the strong lines of his face, the brown depths of his eyes. Anguish twisted inside her. "Crockett, what are we doing? This didn't work before. How can it now?"

"It can if we both want this. I've learned how to protect the feelings I have for you, and I think you have too. Relationships are fragile things that require loving care to flourish and grow. I didn't do that before, but I'm ready to give ours another try. We deserve a second chance. Don't you think?" He released his hold. "I don't know if I can find the strength to ask many more times."

"I'm afraid of failing again." Her voice dropped to a whisper. "To fail once more will destroy me."

He lifted her chin with a finger. "When everything is right, you won't be scared. I just ask that you not shut me out. Let me court you, let me woo you over. One chance is all I'm asking. If it doesn't work, I'll walk away and never bother you again."

The sincerity of his words, his gentleness, told her she'd regret not trusting him. He was different now. So was she. Older. Wiser. Their landscape was littered with craters. But she couldn't miss the love on his face. She had to trust him.

"Yes. Yes, I will try again. I feel things for you that I've never felt for anyone else."

"That's all I need," he said softly, kissing her forehead. "Good night."

"Good night, Crockett." She stepped away, her heart lighter. She'd let go of a little more of the past.

"Wait," he called. "Let me see you home just to be on the safe side. Who knows what the shadows hold."

They spoke little on the short walk. He brushed a light kiss to her lips and told her to lock the door when she got inside, then he was gone.

Paisley bolted the lock and leaned against the door, her fingers to her mouth. His kiss burned on her lips, his soft breath fluttering across her face. Of all the men in all the world, he was the one she wanted.

She finally moved, glad for the dim lights they'd left on in the kitchen and hallway. Quietly, she crept up the stairs to her room and eased the door shut. Instead of getting ready for bed, she went to the desk in the corner and thought about her brother. The escalation of the fight was something he could never win. Now the Legends would be the least of his problem. He should worry about the Texas Rangers and the hell they would rain down on him.

Still, knowing Farrel, he would foolishly believe he'd come out on top. And what would he do in the meantime until the law squashed him?

It took no thought. He'd come after her and Hilda. And try to take his son.

Paisley's stomach twisted. This would not end well. For any of them.

They had locks, but when had those ever kept Farrel from what he wanted? Outside, the wind got up and banged a shutter. She strained for other noises, sounds of an intruder, jumping at every jangle, bark, and thud. At last, she gave up and went to bed. To do her job, she needed sleep.

Before she knew it, dawn was stealing into the room. Her thoughts on talking to Stoker, she hurriedly dressed and made herself presentable. The best time to catch him would be at breakfast.

Hilda was already downstairs, looking pretty in a pink dress Paisley had never seen her wear. "You look real nice in that dress, Hilda."

The smile brought Hilda's dimples out. "Thank you. Miss Lara gave it to me. She said it was one of Grace's that she could no longer wear since having her baby."

"That was nice. I haven't heard anything of Grace and Deacon in a long while. How are they doing?"

"Apparently very well. According to Miss Lara, they've added another fifteen sections to their ranch outside of Fort Worth."

"I wish Grace all the best. She was always kind to me," Paisley said softly. But Crockett wanted to strangle his headstrong sister a time or two. "I have to hurry out, so don't fix any breakfast for me. I need to catch Stoker while I can. Then I'll head to Dr. Thorp's. Please be careful, Hilda, and don't let Tye out of your sight."

"You can count on it. Have a good day."

Paisley gathered her things and set out for headquarters. She found Stoker having coffee with Crockett. Her gaze flashed to Crockett for a moment, and a smile crinkled the corners of his eyes. "Good morning, gentlemen."

They both rose, and Crockett pulled out a chair. "Sit down. Have you had breakfast?"

"Not yet. I was wanting to catch Stoker before he heads out." She sat across from Crockett and wondered if he was remembering last night's kiss. He poured her some coffee. "Thank you."

"How did you sleep?" he asked.

"In spite of jangled nerves and wondering what Farrel is up to, I slept surprisingly well."

"That's good. You're looking very pretty today, isn't she, Grandpa?"

"She certainly is. It's awfully rare that I get to eat my eggs and bacon with such a beauty." Stoker's blue eyes had a determined flash in them. Despite his age, he seemed ready to take on Farrel.

"Thank you. Now stop. You're making me blush." She lifted her cup and took a sip of coffee. "I wonder if I can bother you a moment, Stoker? I read my mother's journal, and if I'm right, and I hope I am, you have an envelope or something for me, possibly that Mama left in your care."

"You are correct. She did. I'm rather relieved that you figured the message out. Your mother worked herself into a tizzy trying to make sure no one would override her wishes. Then she ended up dying too soon, before she got everything into place."

Essie brought set down his and Crockett's plates, and they dove in.

"Of course. I understand that. She had to be careful. I know full well about my father's and Farrel's greed."

"Furthermore," Stoker went on, "she had to make sure you would have the strength needed to hold on to it. It wouldn't do you much good if you crumbled under your father or brother and let them snatch it from you." He shoveled a big bite into his mouth and chewed.

"If Farrel takes anything from me, it'll be after I'm dead." She took her plate of food from the smiling cook. "Thank you, Miss Essie."

"You're welcome, dear. It does my heart proud to see you in

this house again." Essie patted her shoulder and disappeared into the kitchen.

"You'll never hear me complain." Crockett winked at her.

Paisley shook her head at him and turned to his grandfather. "Stoker, would you happen to know what is in this envelope?"

"I have a pretty good guess, but I don't know for sure. Caroline only had one thing of value, so I believe it's information about that."

"You must be mistaken, sir. Mama had nothing to her name."

"Then, we'll just have to see. Let me finish breakfast, and the mystery will be solved." Stoker turned back to his food.

Crockett nudged Paisley's foot under the table and lifted an eyebrow. She tried her best to ignore him, so he nudged it again.

"When will you have to go back to your courtroom, Crockett?" she asked sweetly. "I heard from Elena Rose that you have to make the trip to Quanah at least once a week. But she must be mistaken, because you've not left since I've been here."

He propped his elbow on the table, his brown eyes full of mischief. "I didn't know my comings and goings caught your notice to such an extent, Paisley."

"It's just that I'm concerned about Casanova. The parrot needs food and water."

"All I hear about is that damn parrot," Stoker growled. "It's the most irritating bird I've ever seen, and I've forbidden anyone to bring it into this house."

"I think he's sweet." Paisley hid a smile behind her cup. "And my nephew is quite taken with him."

"I guess kids tend to like those things," Stoker admitted.

Crockett waved his fork, chewing. "All I have to say is that damn parrot had better watch it or he'll find himself in a pot. Grandpa, you never heard the things he says to Paisley as he rubs up against her neck. It's disgusting to watch."

"You're just jealous," Paisley threw back.

Stoker raised his hand. "I've heard just about enough of that stupid bird."

The men talked a little about going back to the site of the explosion, speculating what they might find, and wondered how soon the Texas Rangers would arrive.

Then Stoker pushed back from the table. "Let's go get that envelope."

Excitement washed over Paisley. "I can't wait."

With Crockett following, they went into Stoker's office, and he retrieved the ordinary envelope from his safe, handing it to her.

Her name was on the outside in her mother's flowing script. Using Stoker's letter opener, she slit it open with trembling fingers. Inside was a single sheet of stationery and a lawyer's calling card. She read the letter aloud.

Dear Daughter,

If you're reading this, you've been strong enough to be your own counsel and not that of your father or brother. I'm proud of you because it's not easy to stand up against such an overwhelming force. I apologize for the hoops I made you jump through, but I needed to be sure my legacy wouldn't fall into the wrong hands. My dear, you are the owner of the Jessup land which Stoker secretly returned to me. To claim it, you need to see Mr. Caleb Seymour in Medicine Springs. He's been holding the deed for you. I'm sorry I won't be with you. It's always been you and me. It's going to require even more strength and determination to hold on to this. You know your father's and brother's greed well, so don't let them steal it.

I love you dearly,
Mother

Paisley glanced up with tears in her eyes. "I never knew. Thank you for giving back her birthright, Stoker. It meant everything to her."

"I know, and I was happy to return what was hers." He patted Paisley's shoulder. "And it meant even more in her last days."

Crockett, standing silently beside her, shifted his stance. "When you get ready, I'll be happy to take you to Seymour's office. Just say the word. Besides, it wouldn't hurt to have an armed escort. Just in case Farrel might try something. Your life might not be worth much when he hears about this, which is why I think we should keep it between us and Hilda."

"I agree. No one will hear about this from me except Hilda. I trust her." When the full implication of Crockett's words sank in, fear crawled up the back of Paisley's throat. "Oh God, Farrel will be furious," she whispered, clutching Crockett's hand. His squeeze let her know he stood behind her, and that brought comfort.

"Hopefully, he won't learn of it, but we have a few things on our side. The Texas Rangers will be here soon, and you're surrounded by hundreds of people on the ranch, all of whom will protect you in a heartbeat. Besides, he'll have to go through me to ever get to you."

She smiled up at him. "I know, and I'm very grateful. I hate being a lot of trouble."

"You're not." Stoker closed his safe. "I think of you as the daughter I never had."

The statement sparked some thought. What would it have been like to have had a father like Stoker? Someone who believed in her instead of trying to tear her down.

Tears in her eyes, she went and put her arms around him. "I would've loved belonging to you. Life would've been so different." But that would've messed up her and Crockett, and she wouldn't have wanted that.

"I've had fun thinking about it over the years." He cleared his throat. "You're everything I would've wished for."

Crockett moved closer. "Grandpa, I hate to break this up, but we're running behind."

Just then, boots sounded on the wooden floor, and Houston stuck his head into the office. "Here you are. Ready to go, Pa? Noah's ridden ahead."

"I was born ready." Stoker winked at Paisley. "Guess I'd best get a move on."

She laughed. "Looks that way. Thank you." She kissed his cheek.

"I was happy to give that envelope to you at last."

Houston raised a questioning brow, and Stoker explained that she'd gotten the message in the journal. "That's good. All that's left is getting the actual deed. Do you know when you'll go?"

"Not sure, but soon." She hugged Crockett. "I hope you find the evidence you need. I have to get to work myself. Dr. Thorp will be wondering what happened to me."

They walked out together to find Luke waiting. Waving, they parted ways. Paisley stuck the precious envelope inside her satchel and hurried across the street. She paused, her hand on the door-knob, and glanced at the five Legend men sitting tall in the saddle. A lump formed in her throat. Seeing this many together was a sight she wouldn't soon forget.

Stoker shouted, "Let's ride!"

Their legacy was a proud, honorable one, and she had to have been crazy to have ever thought for a second that they could be guilty of killing her father.

A flick of the reins, and they galloped away as they'd done countless times.

Only this time they were after her brother.

She shivered and pushed the door open, looking forward to diving into work. Best to keep her mind occupied. "Good morning, Doctor."

Thorp hobbled from the examining room with a brown bag. "Thank goodness you're here. I was about to send someone for you. There's been an accident over in the west pasture. The ranch hands got into a snake den, and one got bit."

There was no time to waste, depending where on the body the injury occurred.

"How long ago?"

"Probably an hour, I'd say. All Justin did was apply a tourniquet and ride like hell."

The window was closing.

"I'll need to take a wagon to haul him back in." Her thoughts whirled as she listed in her head everything she might need. "How will I find the patient? This is a big ranch."

"The young man's friend hurried out to hitch up the wagon. He'll take you." Thorp handed her the brown bag. "I think this will have everything you need."

"Thank you." She opened it and made a quick inventory of the contents. "Yes, I think this will cover everything." A wagon pulled up in front. "I assume that's Justin."

"Yes. Paisley, be careful."

"I will, Doctor." She rushed out and waved Justin off when he started to get out and help her. "I can manage." She tossed her satchel and the bag with its lifesaving contents onto the seat and climbed up next to a very serious cowboy who likely had a few years yet to see thirty.

His hat pulled low hid most of his face, but with the turn of his head, she could see that he had deep crow's-feet etched at the corners of his eyes. His skin bore a dark tan, evidence of too many hours in the sun. What she could see of his hair wasn't much, but it appeared the color of a bay horse.

She shook the man's hand. "Justin, I'm Nurse Mahone. Thank you for taking me out there to your friend."

"Yes, ma'am. He sure was in poor shape. I hope we get back in time."

"That makes two of us. How long to get there?"

"Probably forty-five minutes or so, I figure."

The blue sky was so pale it was almost white, and the sun shone brightly, full of promise. Looking at the beautiful morning, she would never have guessed that death loomed for someone.

"What is your friend's name?"

"Kirk, ma'am. He knows everything about this country. We thought a snake den could be in those rocks, and he went up top to look. His feet slipped, and he fell right in with the snakes. They covered him real quick. I managed to pull him to safety without getting bit and rode to headquarters."

"It was a miracle they didn't bite you too."

"I ain't exactly sure how they missed me, but I'm glad they did. Three of 'em got Kirk."

"He's lucky you were with him and could go for help." Ranch accidents could be deadly, and snakebites especially, as remote as many of the Texas ranches were.

But for now, all she could do was pray that she could swing the pendulum in Kirk's favor.

Twenty-one

THE WIND KICKED DIRT IN CROCKETT'S FACE. THEY'D BEEN OUT at the explosion site all morning, and even though they'd scoured every inch of the debris, they found little evidence that pointed a finger at anyone. He was hot, tired, and frustrated. They needed some definite proof that Farrel had set the blasts, or he'd get away with it one more time.

The noon hour was approaching when a Texas Ranger arrived and introduced himself as R.R. Callahan.

It said volumes about Stoker's stature in Texas that when he reached out for help, no one hesitated. It appeared Callahan had ridden the train for the better part of the night to get there. He resembled a vagrant of some sort with wrinkled clothes and a beat-up, sweat-stained Stetson. Grit layered his voice, and Crockett could tell he was used to not repeating his words. Callahan was the once-said-and-done kind of man.

Stoker finished relating the explosion. "We found these blasting caps last night."

Callahan examined them. "With the current oil boom, lots of folks have these. Everyone's trying to get rich."

Crockett nodded. "Our suspect has dug and blasted all over his land without finding any oil and now seems convinced that it's here. Although, his family has been feuding with us for several years, so it may just be that he hates us."

"Either way, it's led to this," Houston added.

Luke and Noah had walked off, searching the ground, and Luke stooped to pick up an item from the dirt. "Got something!"

Callahan hurried over along with the rest. "What is it?"

"An engraved pocket watch with the name Joe Mahone." Luke handed it to the ranger.

The timepiece wasn't crusted with dirt or rusty, which meant it hadn't been exposed to the elements long.

Crockett wanted to say that proved Farrel was guilty, but he knew it was far from being a smoking gun. Whoever set off the explosions could've stolen the watch, or it might've been lost by anyone riding across the land and just now coming to light. Still, it seemed important.

The Texas Ranger said as much. "This gives me more of a reason to talk to the man."

"You should know Farrel has a sister who recently split from him and is living on our ranch along with the man's wife and son," Crockett added. "Farrel has threatened to kill Paisley. She still feels her life is in danger."

"Ho! This case has more twists and turns than a sausage roll." Callahan laughed. "Lots of work ahead for me. At least I won't be bored."

"I hope you leave some time for a card game." Stoker's eyes held a gleam. Everyone knew his love for poker. "I haven't taken any ranger's money in a blue moon."

"All work and no play would make me a very boring man, Stoker. I'm looking forward to the challenge." Callahan turned back to Luke. "Nice find. I'll hang on to this for a while."

They scoured the ground twice more with nothing to show for it. Crockett turned toward his horse, his mind on getting back in time to eat lunch with Paisley again.

Spending time with her, kissing her, could become a new, very enjoyable pastime.

◞◟

Justin pulled the wagon to a stop near a large rock outcropping and set the brake. Paisley lost no time in climbing down and reaching back inside for the brown bag.

"I'll get your satchel," Justin barked, jerking it up. "Kirk is over here."

He led the way to a makeshift shade he'd built over his friend out of a blanket stretched across some brush. "Hey, buddy. I brought help."

A man, somewhere in his twenties, opened his eyes, but Paisley could see it took effort. His breathing was shallow, his face ashen. The arm and hand lying across his belly were triple the normal size.

She took his good hand. "Hi, Kirk, I'm Nurse Mahone. I'm going to fix you up and get you back to town where Dr. Thorp's waiting."

Kirk didn't, or couldn't, answer. He just squeezed her hand to acknowledge he'd heard.

Time worked against him, and she didn't know if she could save him, but she had to try. She tightened the tourniquet that Justin had tied around his friend's arm and elevated Kirk's chest so it was higher than the wounds before slicing the bite sites open. Then she reached for the suction cup Dr. Thorp had put into the bag and began the slow process of drawing the venom out.

She knew some people swore by pouring ammonia into the wounds to neutralize the venom, but she'd never bought into that. However, she noted the bottle in the bag.

Justin hovered. "Don't you think we should get Kirk into the wagon and head for town?"

Paisley wanted to take him aside, out of Kirk's range, but she had to keep pumping. "It would be difficult to work on him in a jostling wagon, and we have no time to waste." She didn't add that he would most likely die on the way. If they could've gotten to Kirk sooner, he probably would've had a better chance.

A moment passed as her mind worked. "Justin, can you pump while I bathe his forehead and make him more comfortable?"

After Justin got into place, she took out her stethoscope. The slow beats didn't surprise her. Neither did his blood pressure. They were losing him. She untied the kerchief from Kirk's neck, wet it, and laid it on his forehead. The soft sounds of the pump filled the quiet.

Kirk opened his feverish eyes, his voice so weak, she could barely hear him. "Let me die."

Her reply held raw emotion and emerged too loud, as though the primal tone alone could make him live. "No. I'm going to fight for you and fight hard. I'm not giving up." She would work to the very end, doing everything in her power.

But despite her heroic efforts, his heart began to beat slower and slower. Anger filled her. Why could she not give Kirk back his life? He had barely begun to make his way. She wondered if he had a wife. Children. Like Dallam, a favorite horse. What did he enjoy?

Her hand lost the ability to feel herself squeezing the pump, but she kept on. With each rise and fall of the young cowboy's chest, she prayed for another.

Justin knelt down. "Kirk, buddy, you have to live. Don't you die on me. I'll never forgive you."

A smile curved Kirk's lips as he lifted his good hand to Justin's face. He released a soft gasp, and the breath left his body. Paisley gently closed his eyes, then rose and walked away. Only then did she allow herself the heart-wrenching sobs. Why? Why? Why?

Anger shook her. Medicine was such a waste if it couldn't stave back death. She knelt on the rocks and didn't feel their sharp edges cutting into her knees.

A touch on her shoulder reminded her she wasn't alone and had practical things to do.

Justin's voice was soft. "You did the best you could, ma'am. It was just too bad."

Paisley didn't turn to face him until she'd wiped her eyes. "Thank you. It just makes me so mad to lose a patient."

He handed her a faded kerchief, and she blew her nose. "Kirk came up here from San Antone and said he wanted to work with the best. He was the hardest worker I've ever seen." His voice broke, and he took some deep breaths. "He was going to be married in two weeks. His bride, Becky, is the mercantile owner's daughter."

"Thank you. I was wondering." She patted his back. "I'll speak to Becky and tell her how sorry I am."

"I don't know what I'm going to do with his horse." Justin swung around to the sorrel gelding nibbling on bits of grass around the brush. "I reckon one of the Legends will take care of that part. I'd kinda like to have it though." He coughed. "It would feel a little like having Kirk with me."

"I'm sure no one would care. You should take it." She glanced at the sky that had been almost white that morning and was now a grayish blue. Clouds were moving in. "We'd best get Kirk loaded in the wagon and head back. Maybe we can beat the rain." She didn't care though. If it poured, no one could see her tears.

It didn't take long to get on the road. Justin was silent, and from time to time he glanced back at Kirk's blanket-wrapped body and the sorrel tied to the wagon. Paisley rode quietly. Numbness and the feeling she'd failed sank into every corner of her being.

That she'd thought she could save the world, indeed even one cowboy, had been ludicrous.

⚜

Lunch had come and gone with no word from Paisley. Crockett sat on the porch at headquarters, staring across at the doctor's place. He'd heard that she'd gone to treat an injured cowboy, but that was almost five hours ago. She should've been back.

When Thorp hobbled outside on his crutches, Crockett went over.

The doctor had begun the painstaking process of navigating the steps of his porch by the time Crockett reached him. "Looks like you could use some help."

"I can probably make it, but I wouldn't mind a hand." Thorp laughed. "I'd like to throw these crutches into the nearest ditch. They're more of a hazard than something useful."

"I wouldn't know, and I pray I never have to find out." Crockett took the crutches. "Hold on to my shoulder, and I'll get you on solid ground. I wouldn't want you to break the other leg."

They reached a wicker chair at the bottom without incident. Thorp collapsed onto the seat. "Thanks, Judge. When I stood at the top, I was certain I could make it. Halfway down, I was calling myself a fool."

"That's pretty typical of us humans." Crockett brought a second chair down from the porch and sat. "Have you heard anything from Miss Mahone?"

"I'm sorry but no, and I'm growing a little concerned."

"If I knew where they were, I'd ride out there." Crockett slapped at a fly. "But without knowing precisely, I'd stand a snowball's chance in hell of finding them. Who is the cowboy who came to fetch her?"

"He said his name was Justin. I'm no good with last names."

"If it's Justin Baker, there's none better. He's as seasoned as they come." A noise drew Crockett's attention to a wagon moving slowly toward them. There were two on the seat and one was a woman. A lone horse trailed behind. "Do you think that's them?"

Thorp strained to see. "Could be. Guess we'll find out."

Crockett waited at the white picket fence until they were ten yards away. Something was wrong. Paisley's long face, her eyes staring straight ahead, wasn't normal. She was fighting for self-control. He opened the gate and hurried around to her side before

Justin set the brake. He saw the blanket-wrapped body in the back. Now it made sense.

Without a word, he offered his hand and helped her down, then opened his arms, and she walked into them. No words were necessary. She laid her head on his shoulder. The professional she was didn't allow herself tears in public. No, those would wait until she reached the privacy of her room.

Justin rested a hand on his friend's chest before turning to the doctor, who'd risen and stood at the fence. "We couldn't save him. Kirk was in very bad shape, and it took too long for me to get help."

"I'm sorry." Dr. Thorp touched Justin's shoulder. "Doesn't make it hurt less though. Snakebite is terrible no matter how you look at it."

"Yep." Justin let out a long breath. "I should've ridden harder, maybe found a place to cut through to shorten the distance."

"Stop. Second-guessing yourself will keep you torn up inside. Let it go. You did your best."

"Can't help it." Justin wiped his eyes. "I just want you to know… that nurse tried her hardest."

"I'm sure she did."

Crockett's chest swelled with pride. If the young cowboy could've stood a chance, Paisley would've found it. There was no doubt about that. He recalled how desperately she'd worked to save the young train robber after he was shot.

She stirred and stepped out of his arms, her face set in long lines. Two deep breaths bolstered her, and she was ready to carry on. "Doctor, where should we take Kirk's body?"

The ranch had a small stone morgue, with walls three feet thick, but Crockett waited for the doctor's answer.

"Let's wrap him in thick canvas and put him in the icehouse for now, until we can get a coffin made."

"I'll take care of that." Crockett turned to Justin. "See to his horse and get some rest."

"Thank you, sir. I'll collect my mount from the doctor's barn and take it too." The cowboy went to the sorrel and untied it, rubbing its nose, talking gently.

Paisley looked up through red-rimmed eyes. "Kirk was due to marry in two weeks. I need to go see his girl and tell her what happened." She swung her gaze to Thorp. "I'll give you my report after that."

"It can wait until tomorrow," Thorp replied. "Go do what you need to do."

Crockett ended up dropping her off at the mercantile on the way to the icehouse. She didn't say much, just stared straight ahead, not stirring until he pulled up in front. "Would you like me to come in with you?"

"No, you need to get Kirk on ice as soon as possible."

He waited until she went inside before he drove on. At the icehouse, he told the proprietor what he wanted and soon had Kirk wrapped and cooling in a separate room away from the ice for sale. It didn't take long before he returned to the mercantile. There was no sign of Paisley, so he went in. Sobs came from a room at the back.

A young man approached. "Can I help you?"

"I'm just waiting for Miss Mahone."

"She's in with the family at the back." The clerk's round spectacles gave him an owl-like appearance, and his red hair parted neatly in the middle seemed to suggest he was very studious. "It's a shame what happened to Kirk. I still can't believe it."

"It's hard to take in." Crockett glanced out the window. A person never knew when they'd breathe their last. It seemed a message to him not to waste a single minute.

A door at the back opened and Paisley emerged. Though stoic, she was trembling when she reached him. "I'm ready."

They got in the wagon, and she sat there. "What am I supposed to do now? I don't know."

"I have to take this rig back to the doctor's barn and put his horse up." Crockett patted her hand. "Maybe you want to talk to Thorp while I do that, then let me take you home. It's been a long, trying day."

She faced him directly for the first time since that morning. "I think it would help if I went to see Dallam for a bit. He didn't get a bath today, and I could get him cleaned up. Would you mind helping?"

"Firefly, not only would I not mind, I'd love spending time there with you." Or anywhere else she wanted to be. His days were only brighter when she was near.

He drove slowly to the young cowboy's place, content with the silence if that was what she needed.

"I did everything right, Crockett." Her voice came quiet as she tried to make sense of it. "I elevated his upper body, tightened the tourniquet Justin had applied, and was suctioning out the poison. If it just hadn't taken so long to get there. Time is what killed Kirk. Or if Justin had known to raise his friend to a sitting position before he left for help. But he didn't know to keep the heart higher than the wounds. I don't fault him for that."

Crockett put an arm around her. "It's good to talk it out. Sounds like there was nothing you could've done differently."

"I keep going over it and there really wasn't anything I would've changed once I got there."

"Then let it go and accept that some things simply are meant to happen."

"I guess so. Yet I hate this feeling that I somehow failed."

"Well, you didn't, so get that out of your head." They neared Dallam's and he needed to catch her up before they arrived. "We found something at the explosion site this morning."

Paisley faced him, curiosity on her face. "What?"

"A silver pocket watch with your father's name engraved on it. Do you know anything about that?"

"I bought it for him in Fort Worth, a gift on the last time I came home. Usually, he complained that my gifts weren't good enough or fancy enough, but he truly seemed happy with the watch. How do you suppose it got there?"

"We're still trying to figure that out. Maybe it fell out of a pocket. Maybe the person who blew everything up."

"Farrel took everything belonging to my father after his passing. It's possible he could've given the timepiece to someone as payment for something. I'm sure those two men hanging around our place, digging holes and everything, aren't doing it for free."

"Absolutely. You've given me a new avenue to explore. I'll pass it on to Ranger Callahan."

But a large part of him wanted the watch to have come from Farrel's pocket. His old enemy needed to pay for trying to kill Paisley. Oh yeah. Justice couldn't come soon enough.

Twenty-two

"THERE'S MY GIRLFRIEND." DALLAM GRINNED WIDE. "I thought you'd decided I was too much trouble." He shot an uncertain look at Crockett but didn't apologize.

"Never." Paisley sat in the wingback chair next to the bed, wishing for some easy way to break this. "I have something to tell you."

The blond cowboy's gaze flicked to Crockett standing behind her. His smile faded. "Tell me straight out. No beating around the bush."

"Since ranch hands are like a big family, I assume you know Kirk Black."

"Sure. Kirk and I are good friends."

She took a deep breath to steady herself. With Crockett's touch on her shoulder, she told him what had happened. "I couldn't save him. I tried, but I couldn't."

Dallam's face crumpled, and tears sprang into his eyes. He put a hand over his mouth, but no sound came out.

Crockett reached around her to touch Dallam's chest. "I wish there was something I could say or do."

"Thanks." Dallam blinked hard.

Paisley knew it would take a while to process, so she rose and put some water on to heat while Crockett emptied Dallam's widemouthed urine bottle. Quietly, she took her stethoscope out of her satchel and listened to the cowboy's heart, then took his blood pressure.

"Kirk and I were the same age, so I reckon that's why we seemed like brothers." Dallam worried the sheet between his long fingers. "Him and Shep were the first ones to me after my accident."

"You must've shared a lot of fun times." She put the stethoscope away.

"He played a trick on me once." Dallam's laugh erased the sorrow and brought a sparkle back to his eyes. "Kirk coiled a rope up in the corner of the bunkhouse next to my bed and dimmed the lights. When I stomped in, he shook a pair of rattlers and yelled, 'Snake!' I thought for sure I was gonna get bit."

"Oh my goodness, that prank would've given me a heart attack!" Paisley found the clean sheets and laid them out. "Memories are the best way to remember a friend."

Dallam grew quiet. "I wish those snakes that bit him had been ropes."

"Me too," Paisley agreed. "Would you like to sit up a bit? Crockett can lift you into the chair while I make the bed. You could get out of it for a little while."

His eyes grew round. "What about my back?"

"Moving you won't do any more damage than it already has." That was if his spine was truly broken. If it was just badly bruised, as she suspected, the change in position could be good for it. Lying for so long would've limited the blood and oxygen supply.

The unexpected hope brought another smile to Dallam's face. She could tell he loved the idea of sitting up.

"Then let's do it. I have to warn you though. My head feels like it weighs a ton. It might fall clean off."

"We'll go slow." If she could find one sparkle in this crappy day, she'd dance for joy.

Crockett returned from outside, and she told him the plan. "Just ease him into the chair. But be ready to catch him if he faints." She covered the wingback chair with a soft blanket.

"I'll be careful." He scooped Dallam up. "Put your arm around my neck. Are you okay?"

"So far so good. Nurse, now don't you go to looking at my bare backside. It might get you all excited."

"I'll try my best to hold myself back." She laughed, wondering how on earth he could manage to joke after just losing a close friend who was like a brother.

Crockett lowered the cowboy onto the chair and held him steady when his head started to wobble.

"I'm a little woozy," Dallam warned. "It'll pass. Just give me a minute."

"Take as long as you need." Crockett met her gaze and smiled. "I think we did it."

"Man, this feels really good." Dallam leaned his head back against the chair and closed his eyes. A tear inched its way down his face.

Her own vision blurred. She squeezed his hand. "You're up. I'm so proud of you. Has the room stopped spinning?"

"Yep." He opened his eyes. "This…" He swallowed hard, his Adam's apple bobbing as he tried to get control of his emotions. "This is a miracle."

"I want to see something." Crockett stared at the ceiling above the bed.

"What are you looking at?"

"I just had an idea. When horses are hurt or die and we have to move them, we use a pulley system. What if I can do the same thing here by attaching the pulleys to the ceiling?"

"That would be wonderful! We could probably teach Dallam how to use it himself and be able to get up when he wants. You're a genius, Crockett." She threw her arms around him. "This will make such a difference."

Dallam grinned big. "To get out of bed will change my life. Wait 'til I tell Kirk and Shep."

When he realized what he'd said, the light in his eyes dimmed. "It'll take a while to remember Kirk's no longer here. He'll never walk through my door again. Never laugh with me. Never ride across the pasture."

"It takes time for reality to set in." Crockett sat on the bed and talked to Dallam for a while about friendships and death and the importance to keep living.

Having a man to voice things to seemed to help Dallam, and soon his smile was back.

Paisley nudged Crockett. "How soon can you put the pulleys in?"

"Shouldn't take long. I might get them in tomorrow."

A smoldering fire darkened his brown eyes, and she knew if they hadn't had an audience, he'd have reached for her. Quivers danced their way through her. Desperate to hide the response in her gaze, she grabbed one end of the dirty sheet and yanked it off the bed.

In no time she had the fresh ones on, but Dallam wasn't ready to get back in, so they sat talking until he finally called enough. Paisley changed out the nightshirt, and Crockett did the honors of moving Dallam back to bed.

Paisley pulled a sheet over the cowboy. "Do you mind if I massage your legs? Or are you too tired?"

"Nah, I don't have to pay *you* to do it." Dallam glanced up at Crockett. "Uh, I mean—"

Crockett laughed. "I know what you mean. It's okay. I'm not the jealous kind."

"Ha!" Paisley glanced up. "It wouldn't do you a nickel's worth of good if you were because I'm my own boss and do what I want." She poured some oil from her satchel onto her hands and began rubbing each of Dallam's legs.

A muscle jerked beneath her palm, and she ran her hand over it again.

Another jerk.

"Do you feel anything, Dallam?"

"I don't think so."

She moved to his feet and rubbed them with oil. The big toe moved. Excitement rushed through her. This was not her imagination or wishful thinking. "Did you feel your toe just now?"

"I might've. Do it again."

Crockett moved closer to watch. Paisley massaged the tendons and two toes jerked. "There. Did you see that, Crockett?"

"No mistaking."

Paisley raised to meet Dallam's searching eyes. "Your lower body is waking up."

"What do you mean?" he asked.

"I suspect you had a tremendous amount of bruising and swelling that kept Dr. Thorp from fully seeing your injury." She paused for a moment as the implication of what she was about to say sunk in. No nurse should override a doctor's prognosis. But—"Dallam, your back is not broken. You are not paralyzed."

"But the doctor said."

"I know. It's just that when you have swelling such as yours that involves such a large area of muscle and tendons, it's easy to mistake a diagnosis. Dr. Thorp admitted to me that he could be wrong and prayed he was."

"Why couldn't I feel my legs and feet if I'm not paralyzed?"

"Again, the swelling and bruising. The morphine that blocked feeling really hampered you, even though you required that for the pain."

"A week ago I cut back, deciding I'd rather take the pain than being dead inside."

"That's been a good thing for you and allowed you to feel your legs and feet."

"Are you sure? This isn't a mistake?"

"I'm positive. Your back is not broken."

Dallam raised a shaky hand to his eyes. "This has been both the worst and best day of my life."

"For me too." Her hand sought Crockett's and he squeezed her fingers. She had salvaged something wonderful out of a day that had taken her to rock bottom.

"Tomorrow, I'm going to begin exercising your legs to get more feeling into them. Do you think you're up to that?"

"You betcha."

His grin was like a bright ray of sunshine on a cloudy day. She hadn't saved Kirk, but she could darn sure give Dallam back part of his life…if not all eventually.

The weight gone from her shoulders, she winked. "Prepare to work hard, because I'm not going easy on you just because you're my boyfriend."

Satisfied that they'd made his day a little sunnier and full of hope, they left. Outside, the afternoon rays blinded her. "I'm so happy I'm about to burst, Crockett."

"We need to take the wagon back to Thorp's and we can tell him about Dallam's progress."

"I'd like that. I need to tell someone. If not, I'll grab the first stranger riding by."

"I think you would." He gave her a hand onto the seat and went around the wagon.

"Do you blame me?"

"Nope." He climbed up and leaned to brush a kiss to her lips. "I had to do that."

"I understand. Do you really think you can rig a pulley system in there?"

"Positive. It'll be easy, and I can't believe I didn't think about that before now."

They drove the few blocks to Thorp's and found him out in the yard, leaning on his crutches, watching some birds build a nest in a sheltered recess outside the attic.

"Are you finding your feathered friends of interest, Doctor?" Paisley asked.

"It's entertaining. I don't know which is the female, but one is working harder than the other. I suspect that's the mama bird. The other is just flying around and occasionally goes off and comes back with a twig, not seeming all that enthused. Kinda like some people."

"While I put the horses back in the barn, Paisley has some great news to share." Crockett went out the back door.

"We went by Dallam's to check on him and do a few things." She told Thorp about getting him out of bed. "After I changed his sheets and got him back in, I massaged his legs." She paused as another surge of excitement sped through her in the retelling. "Doctor, he moved his toes. He's not paralyzed. I'm sorry for contradicting your diagnosis. A nurse should never do that."

Thorp balanced himself on the crutches and reached out to touch her arm. "Some doctors with a God complex might throw a hissy, but not me. I'm fully aware of my limitations, and I'm only concerned with the best for my patients."

Crockett returned from his chore.

"I'm happy I didn't overstep my bounds, Doctor. We have something else." She met Crockett's eyes and took his hand. "Tell him about your idea."

For the next several minutes, Crockett explained the complexities of the pulley system. Pride for him burst inside her. He was so much more than a judge. He cared for people, really cared. Once more, shame washed over her for blaming him for Braxton's death. Crockett had had no hand in that. He couldn't control the prison environment, and Brax had done wrong. She just hadn't wanted to face that.

"This news indeed calls for a celebration." Thorp frowned. "I don't exactly know what we'll find to drink, but this is such a milestone and deserves to be marked."

They went inside, Crockett helping Thorp up the steps. Soon they had a toast—her with hot tea and the men with a little bourbon—basking in one small victory.

On the best of days, all she could hope for was a single moment when chaos subsided and the world briefly settled.

Crockett Legend seemed to understand. He leaned back, sipping from his glass, and reached for her hand. When the doctor dragged himself to his feet and went into the next room, Crockett kissed her. Warmth flooded over her like a rushing river. She parted her lips slightly, and he slipped his tongue inside to dance with hers.

This Legend was ready to be at her side through happy times and sad, always finding the right words to say.

He ended the kiss and smiled. "Ah, Firefly, life with you is darn right exhilarating, and I wouldn't miss it for anything."

That seemed to put it all in perspective. She enjoyed reconnecting with him and learning this new relationship. It seemed made up of a combination of old memories but with fresh maturity lending beautiful, earth-shattering sparks underneath.

∽

It had certainly been a day of ups and downs, and Paisley was exhausted. Bedtime couldn't come too soon. A knock sounded as they were finishing with supper. Now what?

She went to the door. "May I help you?"

The man wore an air of authority about him as well as a heavy gun on his right hip. "Sorry to bother you so late, ma'am. I'm Texas Ranger R.R. Callahan. I'm looking for Paisley and Hilda Mahone."

"You've found us." She opened the screened door. "Please come in."

Callahan removed his hat and stepped inside.

Hilda appeared. "Let's go to the parlor." She led the way and offered him a seat. "I suspect this is about my husband. I don't wish my son upset, so I need to make sure he's busy with something upstairs."

"I understand, ma'am." Callahan smiled and settled into a chair, laying his hat on a small table at his elbow.

With a swish of her dress, Hilda bustled from the room. Paisley made herself comfortable on the sofa. "I know you're here investigating last night's explosions. Crockett Legend shared that his uncle found a watch with my father's name engraved on the inside."

"That is true." He pulled the silver timepiece from a vest pocket and handed it to her. "Do you recognize it?"

Memories swirled as she held it. She hadn't inscribed the word *Father* on it, choosing *Joe Mahone* instead, because in truth, he'd never shown her the love of a parent. And his name had pleased him more anyway, stroking his fragile ego.

She flipped the lid open. "I bought this in Fort Worth for my father last Christmas."

"I understand you were away for a couple of years."

"That's right. I never saw him or this watch again following that Christmas."

"Even after he passed and you came back? Maybe you ran across it when you and your brother were going through his things," Callahan pressed.

"I'm sorry, but no. Farrel had already disposed of my father's belongings by the time I arrived. I asked him what he'd done with everything, and he told me not to worry about it. That was a very typical response for him as well as his callous actions."

Hilda returned, and Paisley showed her the watch. Callahan asked her the same questions.

"After Joe died, I saw Farrel going through his pockets and drawers, but I didn't specifically notice the watch," Hilda said. "Farrel was very…secretive and became so angry if I questioned him about anything. I learned to see nothing, say nothing, be nothing. It kept some bit of peace." She passed the watch back to Callahan.

Paisley didn't know why she felt the need to explain. "My brother is very difficult on the best of days. You don't want to know him on the worst."

"I did go out to speak with him," Callahan said. "And, Miss

Paisley, he claims that this watch has been in your possession since the day you arrived back for the funeral."

She gasped. "That's a lie!"

But again, typical of Farrel to cast blame on her. The fault lay with everyone except him.

"Don't worry." Callahan wore a somber expression that hid what he was thinking, but she liked his steely gray eyes. "I'm not easily taken in. Your brother seems to think he's smarter than everyone and safe from suspicion. I've seen a lot of men with that same mentality, so I'm not fooled."

That was a relief. Paisley relaxed. "Farrel has problems from way back."

Callahan stood. "I need to go and let you folks enjoy your evening." He reached for his hat. "I'll be in touch, and if you happen to think of anything, I'd appreciate it if you'd get word to me."

Paisley sat discussing the turn of events with Hilda for a moment, then rose to wash dishes. Bedtime came early, and Paisley went to sleep the second her head touched the pillow. In her dreams, Dallam was walking as good as new and riding his horse across a lush meadow.

The morning dawned too quickly, but she rose and dressed. She was making her bed when a scrap of paper slid to the floor.

A chill shot through her at the scrawled words.

I told you there's no place safe enough from me.

Twenty-three

FRANTIC POUNDING ON THE DOOR BROUGHT CROCKETT IN A run. He yanked it open to see Paisley standing in the early dawn. "What's going on?"

She burst past him and shoved a scrap of paper at him, her fingers trembling. "I found this on my bed this morning. Farrel was in my bedroom! He was inside our house." She paced back and forth while he quickly read it. "He probably stood over my bed, watching me sleep."

While she was walking through peaceful dreams, unaware of evil so near.

He could've killed her.

"And you're sure nothing was there last night? You couldn't have overlooked it?"

"Not a snowball's chance in hell." Her fingers still shook as she pushed her hair back. "I immediately ran to Tye's room, expecting to find the boy gone, but he was there. Hilda had a similar note in her room, warning her about keeping Farrel's son from him."

Crockett's thoughts whirled. It seemed odd that he didn't take Tye when he clearly had a chance. So what was Farrel's motive? Was he toying with the women? Was this a mind game of some sort that would keep them on edge?

Crockett pulled Paisley's quivering body against him, her heart hammering through the layers of fabric. "I won't let him hurt you."

"Stop. Don't promise something you can't do." She glanced up with worried green eyes. "If he'd wanted to hurt me, he could easily have done it. Nothing was stopping him, not you, not a bolted door, not the hand of God."

"How did he get in?"

"A window. He broke the glass. And I never heard him. Not one blessed sound." She released an angry cry. "What's wrong with me?"

"Don't go blaming yourself. You were totally exhausted after the events of the day, and besides, Farrel wouldn't have made any noise. He would've muffled the sound of the breaking glass and probably removed his shoes."

"I did find a dirty piece of canvas on the ground under the window."

He led her to a chair in the kitchen and got her a glass of water. "Did you notice if he took anything?"

"I haven't made a thorough search yet, but I don't think so. We didn't bring anything much except our clothing, and Mama's diary is still over here with you, where I left it when the explosions happened. Did he simply want to terrorize us?"

"I believe so. Maybe his ultimate goal for revenge is to spook you and Hilda so badly, you won't find a moment's peace. You'll be afraid to go to sleep."

"So true." Paisley nodded. "That's Farrel's brand of fear, and he's excellent at terrorizing."

"I'll speak to some men about guarding your place at night. That should ease your mind a bit."

"It will. Thank you, Crockett." She stood and slipped her arms around his waist. "When I found the note, I came instinctively here. You were the only person I thought of." She pressed a kiss to the hollow of his throat.

The feel of her warm lips on his skin, the fragrance of citrus teasing his senses, made him wish for a day locked inside with nothing better to do than show her how much she meant to him. If Farrel ever did anything to hurt her, Crockett would tear the man limb from limb. A strong desire shook him to hunt her brother down for giving her such a shock.

Paisley shifted and lifted her lips to his, her breasts straining against his chest.

His voice was hoarse. "Lady, I'm tempted to forget all my plans for the day."

"We can't do this now," she mumbled against his mouth.

"I agree. This isn't the time." But it didn't stop him from lifting her up onto the table, standing between her legs. "The good doctor would send out a search party."

"You're right." She sighed and ran a fingernail down his chest. "One day maybe."

"It's a promise." He wouldn't take advantage of her vulnerable state. She was clearly not herself. The note alone had brought her fear. Immense fright did funny things to a person.

Damn the timing. Yet he didn't want her to regret her actions, and she would.

Her breasts were too close, and he itched to bare them like she'd done a number of times in their skinny-dipping days. It took little to remember how they'd looked, so full and round in the water.

Crockett swallowed hard and forced out the words he needed to say. "I don't want to rush you, but I think you should finish getting ready to go to work. By the way, we're having a service for Kirk later this afternoon at the ranch cemetery in case you want to go."

"Yes, I do. Thanks for telling me." She slid off the table and straightened her dress. "Before then, I have a ton of work ahead. I'll start exercising Dallam's legs, and I need to check on my little mothers." She retrieved Farrel's note from the floor. "Will you show this to Callahan? I'm tempted to grind it under my heel and toss it into the fire."

"I'll take care of it. The ranger needs to see it."

Casanova was moving around in the next room, making grumbling sounds and scratching on the bottom of the cage.

"Sounds like your feathered friend's awake." She motioned with her head.

"Yep. He'll be squawking for his breakfast." An idea hit Crockett. "You know, I wonder if that bird wouldn't make a better night guard for you?"

Paisley laughed. "He'd certainly work cheaper. And he'd sure raise a ruckus if Farrel broke in again. I'd like to see my brother's face."

The more Crockett thought about it, the better he liked the idea. "We'll talk more later. I'll get someone to fix your broken windowpane."

"Thanks. I appreciate that."

They said goodbye, and he went to headquarters, waving to Hannah as she put Mister Pete through his paces jumping hurdles. Preparing for the Olympics was hard work, but his sister was dedicated and determined. Pride in her swelled his chest. She was going to make it.

It surprised him to see Elena Rose out indulging in her latest passion—target practice with bow and arrows. His cousin appeared a lot happier following his visit with Luke.

Ranger Callahan was eating with Grandpa. Crockett poured himself some coffee and took a seat. "Good, I'm glad you're here, Callahan. There have been developments." He told the men about Paisley's note, and the fact that Farrel had gotten not only onto the ranch but in the women's bedrooms. "They're scared and rightly so. Farrel Mahone is very unpredictable. I fear, at some point, he'll try to steal his son, and I'm not about to let that happen."

Grandpa buttered a biscuit and asked, "What are you going to do to stop him?"

"Not sure yet, but if it comes down to it, I'll sleep in front of their door."

"Hell." Grandpa shook his butter knife. "Then he'd just come in the back way."

Callahan had been quiet until now. He took a drink of coffee and set the cup down. "This is deeply concerning all right. I had a bad feeling when I went to question Mahone yesterday. He has no respect for authority or other people for that matter. If I didn't know, I would swear that the brother and sister are no relation at all."

"But of course they are, which is a real pity. Paisley doesn't need this." Crockett leaned back in his chair. "I'm taking her to see that lawyer in Medicine Springs on Saturday. Hopefully, that'll produce a deed to the land."

"I shudder to think what Farrel will do when he finds out," Grandpa muttered.

Callahan nodded. "One thing I saw yesterday at Mahone's is his short fuse. I think he might try to kill her."

"He's already attacked her, Ranger. It happened the morning she started work here." Crockett straightened in his chair as Essie set a full plate in front of him. "And now this note. My question is…why didn't he just kill her and Hilda while he had a chance? Instead, he threatened."

"Did you ever watch a cat after it caught a mouse?" Callahan asked. "It almost never eats its prey right away. It toys with it first. That's what Mahone's doing. Invoking terror and making sure these ladies pay. It's a power thing, and he first wants them to know he holds their lives in his hand."

That made perfect sense. Yet each time Farrel snuck onto their land to satisfy that craving inside him, he ran a greater risk of being caught.

Thank goodness the man thought he was far too smart.

❧

Paisley went by Gus's first on her rounds and wasn't sure what kind of reception she'd get after her outburst the last time, but she was prepared for scathing anger. She knocked on the partially open door. "Gus, this is Nurse Paisley."

"Well, don't stand out there all the blessed day, Calamity."

"I think I'm in the wrong house. Are you sure this is Gus's?"

He sat in his usual spot, puppies crawling all over him. "I hoped you'd come by and take the dogs you wanted. Mama pooch has had enough and me too."

"Oh, good. I can't wait to give Dallam his. Yesterday he made remarkable progress, and you should've seen the joy on his face. This puppy will give him something to work toward." She didn't mention anything about the wonderful turn of events. It wasn't her place. "I'll bring my nephew by tomorrow and let him pick out the one he wants. I doubt he'll be particular."

"Likely not." Gus pulled up his pant leg. "I heard about Kirk. He was my sister's boy and came here in part because it was where I worked. I told my sister I'd watch out for him. Now—"

"I'm so sorry, Gus." She set her satchel down and gave the old grouch a hug.

He slapped at her. "Ain't no need to go slobbering on me. Living and dying is part of being here. Cain't have one without the other." His voice softened. "Heard the snakes got him."

"Yes, they did. I tried to save him, but he was too far gone. He seemed so sweet. They're having a service this afternoon, and I'll take you if you want to go."

He looked up through one squinched eye. "I reckon I would so I can tell his ma."

"Then I'll come back for you." She turned her attention to his knee, pressing gently on it.

"I done ate all those cherries you left," he said. "They was pretty tasty, and maybe my pain ain't as bad."

"I was going to say that I can see slight improvement in the swelling." Guilt rushed over her for not checking for the fruit at the mercantile. Everything got in her way. She'd head over as soon as she left.

Paisley finished her examination. "Do you mind if I leave Dallam's pup here while I run to the mercantile?"

"I reckon that'll be fine."

The change in the man had her head dizzy. Maybe Kirk's death played a part. Or maybe it was the fact that Gus wasn't in as much pain. Whatever the reason, she was glad for it.

Saying she'd be right back, she hurried off and found a can of cherries on the mercantile shelf. Paisley bought it but was informed by the owner he didn't know when he'd get more.

Discouraged, she took the one can to Gus. "Hopefully, I'll locate more in a few days."

"Nothing you can do about that." He ducked his head. "I'm sorry for the words between us last time. I'll try to do better."

"Thank you, Gus. All's forgotten. I'll be back this afternoon for you."

"I appreciate it."

She gathered the pup and went to Dallam's, poking her head in. "Knock, knock."

"I've been waiting for you."

"I went by Gus's, and he said I could take this pup off his hands."

His bright smile erased the bad start to her day. She set the pup on his chest, and it immediately began licking his face. His deep laughter filled the one-room house while she heated water for his bath.

"You're in a mighty fine mood today," she called.

"I have good reason. You just missed Crockett. He was here to look at the ceiling again. I think he'll have the pulleys and sling in here by this afternoon." Dallam was quiet a minute. "I heard there's a service for Kirk later. Sure wish I could tell him about this. He'd be happy."

"Indeed, he would." She carried the water to the bed.

For the next hour, she washed and dried him, then went to work exercising and massaging his legs. She had almost decided that was enough for one day when Crockett arrived with everything he needed. He transferred Dallam to the chair until he got the ropes and pulley attached.

Paisley put clean sheets on the bed, then sat with the young cowboy, scratching the pup behind the ears and running her hand over the short gray fur that had a blue cast to it. "Have you decided on what to call her?"

"Yep." He held it up. "See the spots on her nose? I'll name her Freckles. She's real smart."

"I'm sure she is. Gus is giving one to my nephew also, so I'll be Tye's hero for a little while. It's not as good as a parrot, but I think Tye will love his dog."

Crockett grinned. "I'd trade the parrot for the dog any day."

"I don't know if Tye would go for that or not. But he might." Paisley held a hammer for him.

"As Grandpa pointed out, you can't take a parrot for a walk or play catch with it."

"True. But you can't with a goldfish either. Or a few other pets."

Dallam looked on in silence, Freckles asleep in the crook of his arm. It was as peaceful a scene as she'd ever seen, and it did her heart good. Some things money couldn't buy.

"I need to find a way for Freckles to do her business." Paisley glanced around and spied an old newspaper. She spread it out on the floor beside the bed. "Here you go. I'll change it each day when I come."

"You're so kind to me. Thank you." Dallam gripped her hand. "I don't know what I'd have done if you hadn't come."

"You'd have managed. I'm happy to help."

"Well, let's see if this works." Crockett climbed down from a ladder.

"I'll hold the pup," Paisley volunteered. This was an anxious moment, and she wanted it to go off without a hitch.

Crockett held out the wide strap that made a seat to Dallam. "Put this under your bottom."

It took some fumbling, but Dallam got it in place with a little help.

"This will go easier the more you use it." Crockett handed him the pulley ropes. "Now swing yourself into the bed."

It worked like a charm, and Paisley clapped. "You did it! You have some independence back."

"I sure do." Dallam couldn't stop grinning. "Thanks to both of you."

"Hey, we're not stopping there, buster." Paisley pushed a lock of blond hair from his eyes. "You are going to walk one of these days."

"Do you really think so?"

"I know so. You're going to be the talk of the Lone Star." She just prayed she'd be there to see him bask in the glory.

Crockett put an arm around her. "Believe it, buddy. Half the battle is knowing it'll happen. And now that you can get out of bed, you'll get stronger."

"That's true," Paisley agreed. "I'm going to give you some easy exercises to do when I'm not here that'll build up your muscles faster."

"I'll work hard, Miss Paisley."

"I know you will. And Freckles will keep you entertained. She's going to be a good dog."

"That's right." Dallam ruffled his new companion's ears and kissed her head.

Immense satisfaction rushed over her. Dallam was going to walk. She was still having trouble believing that. To go from no hope to a spark was huge. As long as a person moved forward and they could actually see a future, they stood a big chance of reaching the thing they strived for. It was when they came to a dead stop that the glimmer of light dimmed and went out. She'd seen that in her own life and vowed to remember what she'd learned.

Before they reached the door, Dallam called them back. "You've done so much for me I feel bad asking for one more thing, but can you please put something in Kirk's grave?" He asked Crockett to open a drawer and get a large eagle's feather. "Kirk found it one day in a pasture, and I think he might want it as he's flying above the ranch."

Crockett nodded. "I'll put it in the grave."

The struggle to hold back tears proved too much for Paisley. She wiped an escaping one away while the men were talking. Although knowing Kirk for only a few hours, she thought he'd love the eagle's feather.

They said goodbye and left to the sound of laughter and yippy barks.

"He's going to be all right." Crockett helped her onto the loaned horse they'd given her while she filled in for Dr. Thorp and handed her satchel up. Then he climbed into his saddle.

Paisley bit her lip. "I have a slight problem."

"I'm a good problem solver. What can I help you with?"

"I promised Gus I'd pick him up and take him to the service. Kirk was his nephew. Only I have no way to do that."

Crockett grinned. "It so happens that I have access to a surrey. Will that work?"

"Perfect. How far away is it?"

"Headquarters. We can leave our horses there and pick them up afterward. Sound okay?"

"It's an excellent plan." She got lost in the depths of his brown eyes that were making promises and almost dropped her satchel.

In short order, Crockett pulled the surrey into a spot at the ranch cemetery where employees and their families were buried. Kirk's family was unable to make the trip, and was absent from the mourners, but the large group told how popular Kirk had been.

Leaning heavily on a crude walking stick, Gus hobbled over to the group of cowboys.

Paisley noticed Kirk's Becky in a dark veil, with her parents. They never got that life they'd planned or brought any children into the world. Never got to celebrate a first Christmas. Paisley took Crockett's arm and went to stand at the front with Stoker. Crockett whispered in Stoker's ear, then laid the feather on top the rough-hewn coffin.

Houston and Lara arrived, and Paisley spoke to them. News of Farrel's note had gotten around, and they offered support and anything she and Hilda might need.

"Just name it." Lara laid a comforting hand on Paisley's arm. "We want to help. Would you like to move into our home with us?"

"That's very generous, but we can't. I refuse to let Farrel win."

"Well, if you change your mind, you know where we are."

Just then the preacher began the service with a prayer, stopping conversation. Then the reverend spoke of Kirk's kindness and how he'd gone out of his way to make someone's life better. Paisley had seen kindness in Kirk's anguished eyes as she'd knelt beside him and held his hand. Why the good Lord couldn't have taken someone mean, she didn't know. It wasn't fair.

Amid hymns and tears, they laid Kirk to rest, and the crowd began to depart.

Gus's eyes were red. The ill-tempered man crawled into the surrey and didn't speak until they pulled up in front of his house. "Thank you for taking me. I ain't much of a churchgoer, but I think I might listen in on occasion. Just to see if it helps a rough old cob like me."

Paisley patted his hand. "Every person has to decide that for themselves. But remember...you get out of anything what you put in."

"Reckon that's right." Gus climbed down and said good night, then went inside.

"Now there's a positive man." Crockett laughed and set the surrey in motion. "You weren't exaggerating one bit." He patted the seat. "Would you like to move closer to me?"

She measured the distance on the seat, and probably two

people could've fit between them. "I might." She scooted a little. "Is this better?"

"Not to speak of. Closer."

Her heart hammering, Paisley moved a bit more. "How's this?"

"I think you might need some help." His voice teased, but heat had darkened his eyes.

She closed the space, and he put his arm around her. Laying her head on his shoulder, she snuggled against his side.

This was where she belonged. This was home.

Twenty-four

THE WARMTH OF PAISLEY'S BODY NEXT TO HIM AND SUNSHINE on his skin gave Crockett hope. The day was beautiful as he tightened his arm around her and guided the surrey down the street. He closed his eyes for a moment and let emotion wash over him. Grandpa had always told him that you never fully knew what you had until you lost it, and that spoke to him now.

He knew exactly everything he'd lost but now had gained back.

Over the last few weeks, they'd made progress, and the wide chasm between them had closed a little. Maybe with more time, he'd ask her to marry him. He didn't want to rush that though. It was okay to enjoy their newfound love awhile.

She wiggled, burrowing like some animal into a hole and sighed happily.

"Are you a blind squirrel looking for a morsel?" he teased.

"Am I bothering you? I can move back to my side of the seat."

"Absolutely not. This spot has your name on it."

"I was just thinking about how happy we made Dallam." She glanced up at him. "Thank you for getting the pulley system installed so quickly."

"No thanks needed. I would've done it eventually. Between my office and short time here on the ranch, it would've taken me a while to hear of his need, and without you telling me, I don't know when it would've come to my attention."

A sudden horn blared from behind, and one of the newfangled Model T Fords blew past. Startled, the horses tried to bolt and would have if not for Crockett's strong hand on the reins.

Paisley sat up, all ideas of romance seeming to leave her head. "Fool!"

"Don't get too upset. This is the way the world is heading." By the time he got the team settled down, they'd arrived at headquarters. He silently cussed a blue streak. Just when he had things with Paisley to his liking, the automobile had ruined it.

"Do you think you'll ever buy one of those?" Paisley asked as she took his hand to step down.

"Never say never I guess, but I have no plans at the moment. I think I'll stick with horses awhile longer." He enjoyed the slower pace that allowed conversation and a bit of romance. "What about you?"

Laughter sprang from her mouth. "Not a chance. They look very dangerous. I wouldn't have a clue how to stop one. I'd probably kill someone. Who do you think that was?"

"I'm not sure, but he'd best watch it, or Grandpa will give him an earful he won't soon forget." It was the first automobile he'd seen on the ranch, so it was likely someone who wasn't familiar with the workings of the Lone Star.

They thanked Grandpa, who was sitting on the wide porch with Ranger Callahan, for the use of the surrey. Sure enough, he was livid over that fast Model T. "I'm going to have Houston or Luke post a sign that those contraptions aren't allowed on this ranch. We use horses. Always have and always will." He slammed a fist down on his knee. "That's final."

Ranger Callahan was smart enough to let his wide grin speak for him. No one knew how long the ranger would stay, but they hoped until the trouble ended.

Exchanging glances, Crockett and Paisley got their horses and were soon home.

"Want to stop in and see your boyfriend?" Crockett waggled his eyebrows.

"Oh, you mean Casanova. My goodness, it's tempting, but another time. I think I'll relax for a bit, then have supper ready for

Hilda and Tye for a change. When my pregnant mamas have their babies, I won't have a lot of extra time." She flashed him a smile. "I should take advantage of this."

"Indeed, you should."

Paisley had seemed to manage to keep worry at bay as she went through her day, but now Crockett noticed dark shadows creeping into her pretty eyes. "I'll have some men keep watch as I promised, but tell me your plans for securing the house."

"Bolt the doors of course and check all the windows. I'll sleep downstairs in the parlor with my father's loaded gun. Between both of us, I think that'll send Farrel a message."

Crockett dislodged a small rock with the toe of his boot. "I was serious about letting you keep Casanova at night."

"Do you really think he'd raise a ruckus or simply sleep through an intruder?"

"Of course, the bird is unpredictable, and seeing as how I've not had anyone break in, I can't be sure how he'd react." He touched her shoulder. "It's worth a shot I think."

"Sure, we can try it, but I still intend to stick to my plan as well."

"I'll bring him over after a while."

"Please hold off until we eat, or Tye won't put a bite of supper into his stomach. He'll want to play with that parrot."

"Gotcha."

That settled, they each went their separate ways. Crockett felt better with her agreeing to keep Casanova. However, he didn't think Farrel would come two nights in a row. The man was smarter than that.

No, Mahone would wait until everyone let their guard down. Then he'd strike again.

Another thing that might work was shuffling houses. Crockett filed that away for a later conversation with Paisley, but he already knew she'd fight him on that. The lady already felt they were too much of a burden.

After taking his supper with the family, he sat in his backyard, happy to see the two guards outside Paisley's house, and watched the sunset, then the first stars.

Movement in her bedroom window drew his gaze, and he blew a kiss, hoping she was looking out. He loved living next to her and being able to protect her. That eased his mind greatly. After dark, he'd take a walk around.

Every moment of that morning in the kitchen filled his thoughts. Her kiss had rocked him back on his heels, and it had taken all his willpower not to take advantage of her. Farrel's note had greatly upset her, and she hadn't been thinking clearly.

But next time…next time he'd not be such a gentleman.

❧

"Pretty bird. Pretty bird," Casanova squawked in Paisley's parlor. He perched on a little swing Tye had made for him. "Be my friend."

Tye giggled and put his hands on his head. "I already am. Why does he keep saying that?"

Paisley laughed. "He's only saying what he's learned. Try to teach him something new."

"Like what?"

Hilda put her knitting aside. "Tell him to reach for the sky."

For the next hour, Tye worked with parrot, but the bird seemed rather unconcerned. In fact, he appeared to doze on his new swing. But then when Tye said good night, the ornery bird squawked, "Reach for the sky!"

Tye looked at them. "He said it!"

"Yes, he did, honey." Paisley was amazed at how quickly the parrot had learned something new.

But then they couldn't shut him up. He kept repeating the phrase, and she found out how irritating Casanova could be. She finally hollered, "Good night! Go to sleep."

"Good night. Kiss me, baby."

"Nope. You're on guard duty." She shook her finger. "Scare the pants off burglars. That's your only job." Too bad they couldn't put the cover on the cage, but if they did, Casanova couldn't see any intruders. Still, it was tempting.

"Walk the plank, matey."

"No planks tonight. The ship is docked." She left a dim light in the kitchen, checked the doors and windows a second time to make sure they were secured. After making sure the two guards were outside keeping watch, she climbed the stairs. Hilda was putting Tye to bed, and Paisley went in to say good night.

All seemed peaceful, but how long would it last?

The quiet hours passed uninterrupted, and morning came with no sign of a break-in.

Before she saddled her horse and rode to work, she carried the bird to Crockett and gave him the news.

"That's good. I'm glad you got a pleasant night's sleep. Care to have a cup of coffee?"

Paisley's cheeks grew warm at the invitation in his eyes. "Do you have tea?"

"You're in luck."

For a little while, they sat at the table, discussing the day's work, just like a married couple. She wondered if the thought occurred to him too and prayed not. But they did have a comfortable relationship, and sometimes it seemed the coldness that had once been between them had never happened.

How could she have moved past that so quickly?

The question had barely entered her head than an answer followed. Oddly enough, Farrel had been the reason. She and Crockett had been forced to work together.

Little things caught her notice about him. The way the edges of his hair curled around his collar. The smell of his shaving soap. The crinkled lines at the corner of his eyes when he laughed. His large hands cradling his coffee cup. The soft sound of his voice when he said her name.

Paisley's breath hitched in her chest. *She loved him.*

That fact rocked her. But she realized it was true. Maybe she'd never stopped. Else why couldn't she have given Reese Donovan in Fort Worth a chance? The reason was simple, and the same as she'd told Crockett. Reese wasn't him. She wouldn't marry just anyone.

Crockett set his cup down and laid his hand over hers. "This is nice, you being here."

"Yes, it is."

Someone knocked on the door. "Paisley, come quick."

"That's Hilda." She hurried to let her sister-in-law in. "What's wrong?"

Before Hilda could get the words out, she saw Annabelle's wild-eyed husband on the porch.

"It's Annabelle." Mr. Fletcher jerked off his hat, crushing it between his hands. "Her water broke."

Concern rushed through her. Time could change the outcome as it had with Kirk.

"I have to get my satchel." She turned to Crockett. "It's the breech baby. Sorry."

"I'll saddle your horse while you gather your things."

They rushed back to her house and Paisley spoke with Fletcher. "Get back to Annabelle and keep her calm until I get there. This is a natural part of life, and the doctor and I are not going to let anything happen to her or the baby."

"Thank you, ma'am." Fletcher climbed on his horse and raced away.

With everyone helping, she arrived at the Fletcher house quickly. Hilda came on her heels and took charge of the children. Crockett went to give Dr. Thorp the news and to assist in getting him there.

Paisley turned her focus to the mother and got the bed ready. Since this was her third pregnancy, the birth would likely go pretty fast, but anything could happen. Her contractions were already coming close together.

In an effort to keep Annabelle calm, Paisley walked her around the house with her husband on one side and kept up a stream of conversation. Still, panic crept in.

"Will my baby be all right, Nurse?" Annabelle asked for the third time.

"Your baby is going to be just fine. Stop worrying."

"Where's the doctor? You said he'd be here."

"It takes time to navigate with a cast on his leg. He'll be here."

Her husband stopped and took her hands. "Try to relax as the nurse says. You're not doing yourself or us any good. Take some deep breaths and think about holding our baby when it gets here, all healthy and safe. Can you do that?"

"Yes."

And she did for a few minutes before she started all over again. Finally, Paisley got her into bed and checked her progress. "It won't be long now." She turned to the husband and asked him to get her a straight-back chair. He left and returned with one. "Thank you, Mr. Fletcher."

Paisley stepped aside and went over everything she'd been taught in her mind. Men's voices filled the next room, and she recognized Crockett's and Thorp's. Thank God the doctor had made it.

He hobbled in on crutches. "Crockett had something to do and said he'd be back later." He sat in a second chair. "Mrs. Fletcher, you have to relax and follow our instructions. Push only when we tell you."

"Yes, Doctor."

"I'm going to check on the kids." Annabelle's husband seemed relieved to be able to disappear.

"You're going to be fine." Paisley bathed Annabelle's face with a wet cloth and listened to the baby's heartbeat. "Everything's good, Doctor."

Not long after, strong contractions began in earnest, and Paisley said, "It's time."

Thorp nodded. "Okay, Mrs. Fletcher, I want you to go to the chair and lower yourself into a squat, facing us."

Paisley laid some towels within easy reach, helped get her into position, and sat beside Annabelle on the floor. They had to get this baby out fast if they stood a chance of saving it. She said a prayer that the cord would stay out of the way and a leg didn't get hung up. So much could go wrong. "On the next contraction, we want you to push hard and long. It's very important."

"I can't."

"If you want this baby to live, you'll find the strength. Come on now. You're almost there," Paisley urged.

Dr. Thorp moved where he could see. "Mrs. Fletcher, just think about holding this babe in your arms. You can do this."

When the contraction gripped her, Annabelle let out a blood-curdling scream and pushed as hard as she could. As the baby began to slide down, Paisley went to work clearing the legs to the buttocks. So far so good.

"Okay, you did great, little mama. Now pant like a dog and get ready for the next contraction. The next one should push the baby out." Paisley's mouth was dry with fear. Now came the most crucial part, and if she didn't get this right, none of the other mattered. As the next contraction began, she murmured a quick prayer.

"I can't stand this!" Annabelle screamed. "It's ripping me apart."

"Push and push hard!"

Dr. Thorp leaned close to Paisley. "Try to turn the head to face the spine as the baby descends. Do you feel the cord? Is it around the neck?"

She squeezed her hand inside and followed the doctor's

instructions. "The cord was around the neck, but I moved it. I think it's fine now. I've turned the head."

She caught the baby as it came out. "It's a girl, Annabelle. You have a daughter."

The infant's skin was as blue as a robin's egg. "She's not breathing, Doctor."

"Massage its back." He handed her a soft towel, and she wrapped the child.

Turning the little fragile body over, Paisley gently rubbed the baby's back, willing it to take a breath. To cry. To live.

A clock ticked loudly in the room as the seconds dragged. The precious new life was running out of time.

Twenty-five

KIRK'S ANGUISHED FACE SWAM BEFORE PAISLEY'S EYES. WAS she doomed to repeat the same outcome?

Something had to work. It had to. Fear and hopelessness made her hands tremble. Her tongue worked in her dry mouth.

Desperate for some sign of life, Paisley rushed the baby to the kitchen and grabbed a straw from the broom. Using that, she cleared the baby's nose. "Come on. Breathe."

But nothing happened.

Desperate, she put her finger inside the small mouth to clear any mucus. Still nothing.

Dr. Thorp hobbled to the doorway. "Hold its nose and breathe gently into the mouth. Hurry!"

"Here, lay the baby on this towel on the table." The voice belonged to Hilda.

Paisley hadn't even noticed her sister-in-law in the kitchen. She laid the baby down and followed the doctor's orders, blowing gentle breaths into the mouth. After two or three puffs, she stopped, then delivered another set.

Despite the last-ditch effort, the baby lay lifeless.

Defeated, Paisley picked the tiny girl up and held her close to her chest, rubbing the small back. She dropped her head, closing her eyes. How could she tell Annabelle?

She'd failed again. The loud tick of the clock measured each empty second.

Then came a very weak cry. It was the most beautiful sound she'd ever heard.

Her eyes flew open, and she met the doctor's. "We did it."

"No, *you* did." Thorp's smile stretched across his face. "You were my hands."

Now that the baby was getting oxygen, her color was beginning to pinken. Paisley took the tiny bundle to the doctor. "I don't know about you, but I'm exhausted."

"I couldn't have asked for a better assistant." He kissed the infant's red cheek. "Welcome to the world, sweet girl."

Hilda got a peek, and Mr. Fletcher came into the kitchen with his children and Tye. Then Paisley took the newborn in and placed her in her mother's arms. Happy tears flowed.

After Paisley cleaned up Annabelle and the baby, she made the room presentable for company. Then Crockett arrived to take Thorp back to his place, saying he'd see her later.

Hilda made tea for them all, and the women sat talking. Paisley still had so much to do, but she seemed to be too tired to move. However, the tea and a bit of rest revitalized her. "What will you name her, Annabelle?"

Annabelle's husband entered. The couple looked at each other, and Annabelle didn't hesitate. "Miracle. That's what we got today. Miracle Fletcher."

"It's perfect."

Sometimes you won some and sometimes lost. And sometimes, if a person was lucky, they got a little miracle.

⤞❦⤝

Although Paisley had little energy left after Annabelle, she went by Dallam's and massaged his legs, then changed his sheets and switched out the newspaper for the puppy. She was encouraged, especially seeing that Dallam had religiously done his exercises. And he loved being able to get himself out of bed and into the chair. She hadn't stayed long but knew he appreciated every second.

That night, Crockett invited Paisley over for steaks again, and she had no willpower to refuse, even though she was dead on her feet. A relaxing evening with him and his mouthwatering steaks promised to be just what she needed after such a demanding day. With tomorrow being Saturday, she was nervous about going to see the lawyer in Medicine Springs. All the what-ifs were circling in her mind like a merry-go-round.

The biggest worry was that Farrel would somehow find out. Her brother seemed to have eyes and ears everywhere. She pushed all that out of her mind, determined to enjoy the evening.

With Casanova over at the other house with Tye, they didn't even have that distraction.

"Guess who was behind the wheel of that Model T?" Crockett sat on a chair and pulled her into his lap.

"I haven't a clue."

"My brother Ransom, and I can tell you he got an earful." He chuckled. "First my dad, then Grandpa lit into him."

"Poor Ransom. What was the outcome?"

"They made him park it in the barn until he gets some kind of lessons. Even then, I'm not sure he'll ever be allowed to drive the vehicle on the ranch. Not while Grandpa is alive."

"That's too bad."

A rider came down the dirt path and stopped at Houston and Lara's. Ranger Callahan waved at them and went inside. Maybe he'd turned up new information. Paisley wondered about that for a moment before deciding she didn't have the energy to worry about it tonight.

Her attention went to the man making her pulse race. He'd rolled his sleeves up, and the corded muscles of his arms sent quivers through her.

The steak was superb and the conversation delightful. Of course, Crockett had grown up with some pretty good experts when it came to putting guests at ease and making them feel at home. The Legend men and women excelled at this.

Tonight, he'd brought the settee from his parlor outside so she'd be comfortable. She sank down on it.

With purple twilight around them, he stood behind her and massaged her shoulders, his large hands fitting the shape of her muscles. "Just relax. You have no place to be right now except here, and nothing to do other than engage in a bit of conversation."

His deep voice lulled her. His capable hands were getting rid of each knot and kink. "Watch it, cowboy, or I'll go to sleep on you."

He chuckled. "If you do, I'll carry you up to my bed and show you all the advantages of a boyfriend *without* green feathers."

Paisley laughed. "I don't know, I might like the feathers."

This playful banter was fun. She and Crockett were alike in so many ways and often had the same thoughts a lot of the time.

"Hold it right there, lady. I'm not letting you near Casanova again." He gave her shoulders another squeeze. "Does that feel better?"

"Immensely." She stood facing him and couldn't resist. "Of course, it's not the same as Casanova's soft green feathers on my neck."

"You just had to shake my self-confidence."

"You? Ha!" She shook a finger at him. "You're one of the most confident men in the state of Texas, and one of the most successful too, I might add, so don't give me that song-and-dance routine."

His brown eyes darkened in the lengthening shadows, and he lost the teasing look. "You're extra beautiful tonight, standing there even after such a demanding day. That freckle near your mouth is winking at me. I think I might have to kiss you. And I have to say, your green eyes rival the deepest ocean. You don't know how much you mean to me." He lifted a lock of hair to his lips. "My dad once said that a beautiful woman is simply that, but one with brains...now that's a rare combination. You have both, Firefly."

Paisley glanced down and picked at some lint on her skirt. Put the scrutiny on someone who enjoyed it. A lesson learned in the past: when she heard a compliment, it usually meant she was about to be the object of her father's or Farrel's scorn.

"Thank you, but please, let's talk about something else."

Crockett studied her for a long moment. "Done. What would you like to discuss?"

"Cherries."

"What?"

"I need more cherries for Gus, and the mercantile won't have a shipment anytime soon."

"Will anything else work for his gout?"

"Lemon tea maybe, but where would we find lemons here in North Texas?" She'd heard a doctor in Fort Worth mention the root of devil's claw. It was worth a try. "Have you seen any patches of devil's claw close by?"

"I don't exactly know. I'll ask Grandpa and Dad." He rubbed his forehead. "If it were summer, I could get you some lemons. Folks in southern Texas grow them. I think devil's claw will be your best bet though. It's late enough in the spring."

"Probably. Let me know what you find out." Dogs barking, cattle lowing, and horses whinnying vied for dominance in the approaching darkness, with the dogs coming out on top. Paisley cast Crockett a glance. "I thought you had to work in Quanah several days a week, but you haven't gone since I've been here."

"I took a month's leave when I injured my eyes in that fire." He grinned and sat down, spreading his arms across the back of the settee. "Are you trying to get rid of me?"

"Why is it that so often you answer a question with a question? Is that a law tactic?"

"My but your thoughts are hopping around like a bunch of magician's rabbits. All we need is a hat." He patted the cushion beside him. "Come here and sit down. Relax."

"I'm sorry if I'm making you nervous." That lazy grin, the gleam in his eyes, made her heart race. All that brawn and muscle next to her stimulated thoughts of "what if" and set off a happy hum beneath her skin.

A delicious shiver curled in her stomach at the idea of finding out if what she was feeling could lead to a future.

Paisley settled beside him on the short settee, their thighs touching. "I'm afraid I'm crowding you," she murmured.

"You'll never hear me complain." As natural as breathing, he dropped an arm around her shoulders.

Memories of those days when they swam naked circled in her head. Crockett's body had been perfectly formed back then, lean and tanned. He hadn't been shy about showing it off either. And she'd looked. Plenty. But never touched. Now, ten years later, he'd filled out, though he was still lean. She couldn't help but wonder what he looked like beneath those butt-clinging denims and shirts that stretched tight across those broad shoulders.

Was it just yesterday she'd boldly flirted with him in his kitchen while sitting on his table? Seemed so long ago.

"Crockett, did you look at me when we used to skinny-dip?"

His deep voice came out husky. "I couldn't take my eyes off you."

"You never let it show." She swiveled. "When we first met, I didn't think you were interested in me. That you thought of me as your sister."

"You've got to be kidding. I was then, and still am, very interested, and not as a sister. Make no mistake about that." He paused. "Did you watch me?"

"Most definitely. I was very curious about your anatomy. I knew about mating from watching the horses, and I wondered how it would feel to have you inside me." She released a low laugh. "Now you know what young girls think about."

"About the same as boys." His eyes crinkled at the corners when he chuckled.

"Why do you suppose we never found out? We had a lot of opportunities before our paths split."

"I was scared. I knew if I got you in the family way, it would ruin the future I had laid out, and everyone had a lot invested in me. Dad noticed how close we were and took me aside for the man talk." He released a heavy sigh. "You'll never know how hard it was to keep my hands off you. To look but not touch below your waist." He paused. "Shortly after that, I moved to Fort Worth."

"Oh yes, that's when you tried your hand as a cattle broker, and you and Grace got that house." Paisley had almost forgotten that short period in his life. Actually, the shattering events that followed had overshadowed everything.

"That's when Grace met Deacon Brannock, and I came home, then went on to law school."

She rose and held out her hand. "Nothing's stopping us now, and I want you."

Crockett silently pushed to his feet, and together they went up to his bedroom, not bothering with the gas light. Enough came from the hallway, where a wall fixture burned. Sliding his hands around her waist, he nibbled along the seam of her mouth before capturing her lips.

The first touch sent waves of heat rushing through her. She'd wanted this for so long, and to have his hands, his lips on her made her knees weak.

With a soft cry, she leaned into him, pressing herself against his chest. Driven by hunger like she'd never felt, Paisley worked at his belt and undid the buckle.

Crockett released his hold for a moment to unbutton her dress. Piece by piece, their clothing came off until they stood skin to skin.

She ran her palms across his wide chest. "You don't have to worry about getting me pregnant. I'm wearing a pessary."

His voice held surprise. "I've heard of those. Must be quite an invention."

"They are—for women. You won't feel it."

"I trust you. But it wouldn't matter." He nuzzled behind her ear and inhaled a deep breath. "You smell so good. Your hair, your body. I want to eat you."

His hands moved over her, making every nerve ending come alive. He touched her breasts, then held them. Her nipples hardened, straining for his lingering caress. This felt so right—familiar yet different. The years had changed them both and brought a new awareness of their bodies.

Paisley cupped his jaw and left a shuddering kiss on his lips, moving closer until his swollen need poked her belly.

"I want you, Firefly. Oh God, how I've dreamed of this," he murmured against her mouth. "I've loved you for so long."

Tears filled her eyes. Her heart fluttered wildly in her chest. "I love you, Crockett. It's the kind of feeling that shakes me to my very soul."

She broke the kiss and laid her cheek against his chest. "I want to make love slowly, inch by inch, and soak up every bit of feeling."

"Will you stay 'til morning? Please."

"Of course. I doubt I'll be able to leave you."

Crockett swept her up and carried her to the bed. He lay next to her, running his fingers along her curves. Paisley faced him in the dim light and slid her hand between them. Her palm curled around him, sending anticipation careening through her.

Soon but not yet.

Burying her face in his neck, she breathed a kiss there. Then moved along the hard wall of his chest. The firm muscles and sinew running along his body amplified the assurance that she was every inch a woman. Lifting her gaze, she found a smoldering flame in his beautiful brown eyes.

A delicious shiver raced up her spine and sent a wild swirl to the pit of her stomach. How had she resisted this for all these years? A giddy happiness rushed over her, spreading heat in its wake.

He caressed her hair, letting the strands fall through his fingers like spring runoff. "Ah, pretty lady, I hope you know how to put out this raging fire."

"Take heart, cowboy." Her breasts tight against his chest, she kissed her way down his throat to the pulsing hollow.

He quivered. "I have to have you."

"Soon."

Paisley took her time exploring the fascinating anatomy that had long ago aroused a young girl's curiosity. She had almost caressed and kissed her way down every inch of him when he flipped her over onto her back.

"My turn. You've teased me long enough. You've twisted me up seven ways to Sunday." He left a heated kiss on her lips and down her throat while his hands paid homage to every dip and swell of her body, fondling and squeezing. Then he raised over her. "You are so beautiful. Men, old and young alike, stare when you walk past. Did you know that?"

"They do not." She didn't believe that for a moment.

"Oh, but they do." He stared into her eyes, smoothing her brow with his fingers. "You make them dream of impossible things. It's nothing bad. Everyone needs dreams to feel alive."

The way he studied her sent her heart racing. As his soft breath fanned her face, she wound her arms around him. "I've never wanted anyone the way I hunger for you."

"I've longed to hear you say that." His gentle touch seared a path down her belly to her thighs and had her gasping with sweet agony. When it seemed she couldn't bear another minute, he shifted and started a new delicious assault on a different area.

And his tongue…

Oh God, his tongue on her skin sent an insistent desire cartwheeling along her body.

He traced the curve of each leg with his fingertips, then slid back up to the hot center of her being, to the throbbing pulse that begged for more.

There. Right there. She held her breath. That felt so good.

Trembling, she parted her legs in invitation, which he lost no time in taking. His mouth on her soon had her breath coming out as harsh gasps that she barely recognized. On every level, she knew she needed what he alone could give. Her chest heaved as though she'd run a mile.

"Now." She tugged on him. "Please."

Paisley inhaled, anticipation gripping her as he got into position. His eyes staring into hers, he slowly lowered himself into her.

Fire exploded in a breathtaking shower of sparks as her muscles clenched, tightening around him. This was what she'd longed for and fantasized about as a young girl. She met him stroke for exquisite stroke, a man and woman seeking fulfillment and love.

She cried out and arched her back, rising to meet him as she held on and rode each clenching wave that grew higher and higher, carrying her along a river of molten passion.

When the shuddering climax came, she rushed headlong into a place of utter beauty and contentment where no one could hurt her. In that same instant, Crockett's body tightened as he took his pleasure. Wrapped in love, they floated together beyond the earth's plane.

She was finally complete.

❦

Crockett awoke a little later and pulled Paisley against him, covering them with a light blanket. Her heartbeat kept up a steady pace as she lay in the curve of his arm. Love for her whispered through his veins and made him tremble. He kissed her hair, and she stirred.

"I must've gone to sleep." Her eyes opened, and she touched his face. "You wore me out, cowboy."

He snorted softly. "You're a wild woman. I can't keep up with you."

"I think I hear a but coming."

Passion made his voice husky. "But you're *my* wild woman, and I'm not giving you up. I found you, and I'm keeping you."

"Thank God for a determined man." Her laugh was light. "I think I'll give up my feathered boyfriend. You're a much better kisser."

"At last you come to your senses." His teasing smile faded. "I love you."

"That's good, since I adore you. I've heard it said that there is one true match for every person. I think you're mine."

"Lucky me." He outlined her lips with a lazy finger, then lifted her chin and gave her a kiss that hopefully left no doubt about his feelings.

Hunger for her curled inside him and raced through his veins with a fierceness he couldn't ignore. He pushed the blanket aside and ran his palms over her smooth skin. Soon, they were panting like young pups with their first love.

He rephrased that. Paisley would always be his last love, no matter how long they lived.

Twenty-six

Sleep-drugged, Crockett woke to find Paisley dressing. "Going somewhere?"

"This is Saturday. I'm riding over to Attorney Seymour's office in Medicine Springs."

Dammit, he'd forgotten!

It was her fault for keeping him up half the night making love. He grinned. No, that was his fault. He couldn't get enough of her.

"I'm coming with you." He threw back the covers and jumped out of bed. He didn't miss her appreciative glance at his body, and it stroked his ego just a bit as he pulled on his denims. "I know a nice little café over there where we can have lunch. We'll make a day of it. You've earned time off."

"I feel terrible about having just a few minutes for Dallam yesterday, so I'm going to take him some coffee and get his day started before breakfast." She reached for her dress. "I also want to check on Sally Fleming. She'll have her baby any day."

Crockett moved behind her and nuzzled her neck. Untying the ribbon holding her chemise closed, he slipped his large hands inside the thin garment to cup her breasts. "I love to watch you work and witness the loving care of your patients firsthand. These people are lucky you agreed to fill in. You're amazing, and you see things others miss, including the good doctor." He rolled a nipple between his finger and thumb. "I'll go so far as to say that baby Miracle, and possibly her mother as well, would not be alive if not for you."

"Guess we'll never know. But I'm getting as much as I'm giving."

She extricated his hands from inside her chemise and turned to face him. "I needed to get away from Farrel for all the reasons we know, and so did Hilda and Tye."

"I can see that." He lowered his mouth, and the sudden depth of the kiss shook him. A burning hunger rushed through him, threatening to scorch everything in its path.

Locked in the kiss, he caressed the soft lines of her back and waist before his palms rested on the flare of her hips. Overpowering love for her lodged in his belly. He didn't think he'd ever get enough of this amazing woman.

A faint moan escaped from Paisley, and she slid her arms around his neck, winding her fingers in his hair.

His breath became ragged as a fire raced through him. He cursed the clock and the fact that they had no time to put out the flame.

Finally, they broke apart, and Crockett stepped back. His voice sounded hoarse in the quiet room. "We should finish getting ready to leave."

She nodded and picked up her blouse. In no time, she was dressed. "I'm going to check on Hilda and Tye. I'm sure they're fine though, or Hilda would've been over here pounding on the door."

"I'm glad our houses are so close." Crockett buttoned his shirt. "You go ahead. I'll catch up."

Paisley brushed a light kiss to his lips and dodged his seeking hands. "No, you don't."

"You're stingy! You know that!" he yelled, grinning. As she clattered down the stairs, he grabbed his boots.

He caught up with her next door as she was feeding Casanova. The parrot twisted his head to the side. "You're late. You're late."

"Don't test me, bird." Crockett filled his little water dish and set it inside.

Tye watched it all. "When I get big, I'm gonna get me a parrot. I'll name it Aladdin an' we'll fly on a magic carpet."

"You don't say." Crockett squatted to put himself on eye level. "What if your carpet loses its magic? I've heard of them sometimes doing that, you know."

Tye rolled his eyes as though wondering how dumb Crockett could be. "The magic stays an' it's gotta do whatever you say." He turned his palms up. "'Cause that's the way it is."

"Okay. I'm glad you're here to straighten me out." When Crockett put up his fists, the boy did too. They play fought until Crockett played dead.

"I won." Tye rolled on the floor, giggling.

The boy needed a man to play with like this. Too bad he didn't have one. Crockett reached for him and drew the boy into a hug. "Promise to never get too old for this."

"I won't." Tye threw his arms around Crockett's neck and kissed his cheek.

Not long after, Crockett left with Paisley, and they rode to check on Sally, Annabelle, and the new baby, then it was on to exercise Dallam's legs and get him ready for his day.

They had coffee and a biscuit with Grandpa, then saddled two horses and, as it neared 9:00 am, rode out side by side for Medicine Springs. The morning was perfect, with only a few white, fluffy clouds overhead.

Paisley chewed her lip and kept scanning the sides of the road as though expecting Farrel to leap out of thick brush with gun drawn.

"Relax." Crockett moved his horse closer and put his hand on top of hers. "Your brother doesn't know about the deed."

"Farrel has eyes and ears everywhere. Somehow, he unearths everything. And with the recent explosions, it sure seems to suggest he knows about this."

"Not necessarily. That could've been a crazy attempt to see if that land did have oil on it. He probably doesn't know that drilling down is usually the way to find the crude."

"Maybe. Farrel is dumb enough to believe anything."

"Please don't let worry ruin your day. Whatever happens, we'll deal with it, but don't borrow trouble. It'll come soon enough. And always know that you're not alone." His words were gentle and free of judgment. "Let's just enjoy our day together."

"You're right. No more gloomy thoughts." She pointed to a slight rise ahead. "I'll race you to that high ground."

They spurred the horses and were neck and neck almost all the way, until Crockett pulled slightly ahead.

Paisley laughed. "I just about had you."

He stared at her, mesmerized by the sight. The sun framed her face, casting a golden glow around her head as the breeze danced in the blond strands of her hair like playful children. Her plump lips parted just a little as though in invitation. But his eyes were drawn to the buttons open on the swell of her chest. He knew the delights that lay hidden beneath the layer of fabric.

Crockett grew hot. How was he going to last until tonight?

"I guess I left you speechless," she teased. "Just think if I'd have beaten you."

"That'll be the day." He stood in the stirrups to loosen his trousers.

They took the rest of the hour trip at a more leisurely pace and arrived in the growing town. The constant echo of hammers spoke of the furious pace of expansion. Paisley pointed to a new dress shop and said she might go in later. Crockett's gaze flew to a recent hardware store.

Attorney Caleb Seymour's office was in the second block, between a saloon and a hotel. They tied up at the hitching rail and dismounted.

Paisley shook out her dress and readjusted the sides of her hair. "How do I look?"

"If you were any more beautiful, I wouldn't be able to stand it."

"I guess I'll do then."

He removed his hat and held the door for her. No one sat at the desk inside. He cleared his throat. "Anyone here?"

A door opened, and a short, dapper man with slightly graying hair strode toward them. "Can I help you?"

Paisley introduced herself. "I believe you're holding something for me that my mother put in your care before she died. Her name was Caroline Mahone."

Caleb Seymour took his chin between a thumb and his fingers. "It must've been some time ago."

"Yes, sir. She passed about a year and a half ago," Crockett explained.

"Mahone. Mahone." Seymour raised his eyes to the ceiling. Finally, something sparked his memory. "I do recall her." He opened a filing cabinet, thumbed through, and removed a file. Inside was a large envelope, which he handed her. "This is for you, young lady."

Her fingers shook as she broke the seal and pulled out an official document. Crockett watched her face and the emotion coming in waves. Ever since she was a young girl, she'd never owned anything to speak of. What little they'd manage to get, her father and brother had taken.

"It's true." Paisley lifted her sparkling green gaze to Crockett's face. "All I have to do is change the ownership, and the Jessup land is mine. All this time, I thought it was gone for good."

"Nothing is forever—except my love for you."

Seymour cleared his throat. "I advise you to get the ownership changed right away. There's a rash of greed overrunning this town."

"I intend to, sir." She moved toward the door.

"Don't you want to know what else is in the file, Miss Mahone?" Seymour asked.

"Yes, of course, I would."

The lawyer pulled out a smaller envelope. She took it from him and stood at Crockett's side. "I have no idea what's in this. My hands are shaking so badly. Will you open it?"

"I'd be happy to." He removed a letter that was in the same flowing script as the journal. "This looks like your mother's handwriting."

"Read it aloud please."

"Dearest Paisley, what you're about to discover is shocking, so maybe you should sit down. Farrel is not your brother."

Paisley gasped and grabbed his arm. He helped her to a chair, and Seymour got her some water.

Crockett lowered beside her. When she had recovered somewhat, he asked, "Do you want me to go on?"

"Yes please."

"He was born to an unmarried woman I came to know, and she was unable to care for the boy, so we took him and raised him as our son. We were always honest and told Farrel from the start that he was not our real son. Trouble followed him, and as time passed, I discovered he thrived on chaos and dissension. Yet my hands were tied. Your father wouldn't allow me to discipline him, and I always suspected that Farrel was actually his child, although he denied it. I know Farrel will cause you pain. He certainly caused me a lot. I only wish I could be there to help you. Lean on the Legends. They're good, caring people. And let love into your heart. There's no better man than Crockett. I watched your friendship grow into more over the years and was saddened when you went your separate ways. My fondest wish is that you'll find your way back to each other. Again, I'm horribly sorry for bringing Farrel into our family." Crockett folded the letter. "She signed it 'Love, Mother.'"

Paisley sat in stunned silence. He put his arm around her shoulders. "I wish I had something comforting to offer. On the bright side, you have no family bond holding you."

Finally, she spoke. "This explains everything. I always wondered why he was so mean to me and Brax, and now I know. He was jealous because we had everything he wanted. I kind of feel sorry for him in a way. He had no one, not even a real mother."

Crockett took her hand. "I think you're right. Belonging to no one would put a man in a strange mindset. He was a throwaway. How sad to grow up with that."

"Yes." Her eyes held unshed tears. "I just realize I owe Farrel nothing, not loyalty or trust. In fact, he owes our family a debt of gratitude."

"You've wrestled with guilt a lot longer than even I knew. It's time to let that go."

She nodded.

Caleb Seymour closed the file in his hands. "That's all that I have for you, Miss Mahone."

"Thank you, Mr. Seymour." Clutching the deed, Paisley rose and shook his hand. "You've been most helpful."

"It's been a pleasure to serve, Miss Mahone." The lawyer held the door for them.

Out on the boardwalk, Crockett put a supportive arm around her. "That was a surprising turn of events." He wondered if Grandpa knew about this but immediately decided Caroline had never shared that with him or he'd have let something slip. But then again, maybe not.

Who knew how many skeletons were in Grandpa's closet?

"I can't believe this." Paisley's features still reflected shock, and she moved in a daze.

"There's a little café across the street. Let's go over and let this soak in," Crockett suggested. If not, Crockett feared she'd collapse on the boardwalk. "Even if you don't want to eat lunch, something to drink might be nice." He removed a silver timepiece from his watch pocket and flipped it open. "It's only a little after 11:00, so a little early for lunch, but then we didn't get breakfast. I'll leave that up to you."

"No food yet. I need to let this news settle. It was certainly a surprise."

"I would imagine. You grew up thinking one way all your life, only to discover it was a lie." He offered his elbow, and they crossed the street.

The café was almost deserted, save for couples at two tables. He glanced around at the pretty flowers in pots sitting everywhere and decided a table at the back would offer the most privacy. He escorted Paisley back there and pulled out her chair.

A young waiter in a vest and bow tie appeared before they got seated. "Welcome, Judge. I haven't seen you around lately."

Crockett glanced into his face and found him familiar. "George, isn't it?"

"Yes, sir. I usually see you when you're catching the train for Quanah."

"I haven't gone to my office in a few weeks." Crockett slid into the chair. "George, I think we're just having something to drink. I'd like coffee please. Paisley?"

"Hot tea for me."

The waiter smiled. "Coming right up."

"And, George, please see that we're not disturbed." Crockett passed him a dollar and hung his hat on a decorative nail above the table expressly for that purpose.

"Gotcha, Judge." The waiter hurried away.

Crockett took Paisley's hand. "I know your parents took Farrel in out of the goodness of their hearts, but why they never told you and Braxton is beyond me."

"I think Mama really tried hard to treat us kids all the same. It was Father who treated him as a favorite over us. I wish we'd have known this." She released a heavy sigh. "This has opened my eyes. I understand now, his meanness to me in particular. He must always have hated me for having Mahone blood and tried every way he knew to make me pay." She paused, glancing at the envelope holding the deed. "And when he discovers I have the land, he'll be absolutely furious. He's convinced there's oil either there or around it."

"We'll protect you." He squeezed her hand. "But I think the fewer people knowing about Farrel the better. As far as us, we'll limit it to the immediate family."

"I have no one to tell except Hilda. She needs to know."

If Farrel did get wind of this, he'd kill Paisley without batting an eye and steal the deed.

George brought their tea and coffee. They talked a little more, sipping from their cups, then Crockett turned the conversation to the dress shop she'd seen. "Would you like to head over when we finish here? I'll buy you something new."

She flashed a beautiful smile that lit her green eyes, and he knew she was back. "I haven't had a new dress in so long. But I won't let you buy it. I have money of my own." She leaned closer. "I work as a nurse, you know. And they pay me quite handsomely."

"Is that right? I might see if old man Legend will give me a job."

"He might. I have an inside connection with the family, in case you need a recommendation."

Her plump lips enticed him, poised only two inches away. The blood rushed in his veins. He glanced around. Seeing no one watching, he kissed her. It was just a brief brush of their lips, but he imagined Paisley found his boldness very scandalous. Maybe it was. But he'd long decided to grab every moment with her and let nothing pass him by again.

Paisley leaned back, tender passion brimming in her eyes. "You, sir, like to play with danger."

"If it involves a golden-haired beauty with fire in her soul, yes I do."

He was happy to see her return to herself. It scared him when someone had the ability to steal the light shining from her heart. Farrel had done that very often but hopefully no more. Especially if Crockett had any say in the matter.

"Are we ready?" He covered her hand.

She nodded. "But I want to go to the land office before we do anything else."

"I agree. Business before pleasure." He stood and retrieved his hat from the decorative nail, then pulled out her chair.

"Would you please carry the deed?" Paisley asked. "I'm afraid of losing it."

Crockett stared into her eyes and brushed a flawless cheek with a finger. "Whatever makes you feel better." He folded the envelope in half and stuck it inside his vest.

The street was filled with people who'd gotten off the train. Maybe they should've waited a few more minutes in the café. He kept a grip on Paisley's arms and guided her three doors down to the Wilbarger County land office and opened the door.

Men were two deep along the counter, and all were hollering and waving papers at once.

Crockett caught a man leaving. "What's going on?"

"An oil discovery." The man's eyes sparkled. "Black gold. I just filed my plot of land."

He rushed out, and Paisley leaned close. "This is what's gotten hold of Farrel, and he'll stop at nothing to get it."

"Appears so."

Just then, a fistfight broke out between two fellows desperate for the same piece of land. The blows knocked the men sideways and created havoc among those waiting.

"Paisley, we'll have to come back." He took her outside. "Let me go back inside and see what time they close."

At her nod, he went in and was told they'd close at five sharp. When he returned to her, his glance happened to catch an insolent man lounging against a post across the street.

Farrel.

Twenty-seven

THANK GOODNESS FOR A BUSY STREET AND BUSTLING PEOPLE. Crockett quickly moved in front of her to block Farrel's view. "Don't get upset, but Farrel is watching us."

She gasped. "What do we do?"

"Pretend you don't see him, and we'll go next door to the mercantile and head out the back way."

"I'm so thankful you're here."

Keeping her on the far side of him, they went into the general store. "He hasn't moved," Crockett whispered. Just then, Farrel pushed away from the post. "Sorry, he's now crossing the street. Come on."

With a grip on her hand, they wove around shoppers to the back door. Crockett peered out, then seeing no sign of Farrel, they exited the store. Bright sunlight blinded him for a moment. They moved along the side of the building, and as his eyes adjusted, he got his bearings. Although he knew the town well, he had no reason to be familiar with the back alleys.

"Where are we going?" Paisley asked. "Our horses are in front of the lawyer's."

"That's not a worry. I can pay any kid some money to get them for us. I want to stick around here until the land office clears—somewhat at least. I'm heading for the dress shop. Farrel won't look for you there."

"Good idea."

"While you're busy with that, I'll figure out where Farrel is."

Her voice shook. "With him across from the land office, I think he knows why I was there. Or at least suspects. He has to. No one can say he's dull-witted."

"No matter if it was a coincidence or not, Farrel sure knows we had business at the land office now." Hell! Crockett wanted to cuss. Paisley appeared to be right about the man having eyes and ears everywhere. Still, there was no way in hell Farrel could've known they would be in town or at the land office.

Unless someone on the ranch was helping him.

Crockett pushed the thought away. It wasn't possible. They had a loyal bunch of men. He'd put good money on that bet.

They came up on the back side of Miss Felicity's Fine Women's Apparel, and Crockett quickly opened the door to a tinkling bell.

A woman with dark, wavy hair stepped from a curtained area. "May I interest you in something?"

Worry vanished from Paisley's face with her smile. "I noticed your shop when we rode in, and I want to look around. I don't remember this being here the last time I visited Medicine Springs."

Crockett kissed Paisley's cheek. "I'll be back in a little while. I'm sure you ladies have much to talk about."

"Thank you, Crockett. I'll be fine."

With a last glance to reassure himself that she was safe amid the dresses of high fashion, he turned to the business of locating Farrel.

What he'd do when he found him—Crockett left that up to circumstance.

⁂

The door closed behind Crockett, and Paisley let herself relax. Having seen her with Crockett, and the fact he wouldn't be caught dead in a women's clothing establishment, this was probably the last place her…Farrel would search. It still seemed odd not to refer to him as her brother, but she'd gladly get used to that. Thank goodness he was no kin.

She had never been a huge shopper, and when she did, she searched for cheaper places, not fancy dress shops with higher prices. That was a well-known fact, and Farrel knew that about her, which was why she put money on him walking by.

"I'm Miss Felicity, and I'll be happy to show you whatever you wish." The woman was about Paisley's age and had striking blue eyes that seemed to be laughing.

The shop was airy with potted plants here and there. A beige satin sofa set in the middle on a red Oriental rug. The colors and furnishings blended together in such harmony.

"Would you have something light for spring?" Paisley asked. "I haven't had anything new in a while."

"Does your husband have a particular color he likes on you?"

Paisley started to correct her but stopped herself. It might be fun to pretend for a moment. But a favorite color? She thought of his hands sliding into her chemise and fondling her that morning and heat climbed into her face. The color of preference was skin tone. She smothered a laugh.

"Light green. Something the color of sage, I think."

Miss Felicity brought out a dress that was more of a mossy green. It was pretty but not what Paisley had in mind.

"That's a bit too olive."

They went through what the woman had, and nothing really caught her eye. "I'm sorry, miss. Your fashions are lovely, but not what I'm looking for."

A glance through the window, and her heart stopped. Farrel was crossing the street and coming this way.

"Oh dear." Miss Felicity wrinkled her forehead. "I might have something in the back. I'll go check."

"I hate to be a bother. I'm sorry. May I just sit here a minute?" She chose a chair protected from view by a beautiful screen.

"Let's not give up. I'll go check the new arrivals."

Before Paisley could say a word, the dress shop owner

disappeared. Once she was out of sight, Paisley hurried to the door, turned the "Closed" sign around, and lowered the shade.

Farrel frowned but didn't try the knob, thank goodness. A second later, he sauntered on.

Left in the silence of the shop, Paisley raised the shade, leaving the closed sign showing, and returned to her chair.

She prayed Crockett wouldn't do anything he'd regret. Farrel wasn't worth ruining a life over.

Miss Felicity came rushing back. Her face was flushed with excitement. "Look what just came in. I think it's a romantic color, and I think your husband will love it."

Paisley gasped as the dress drifted onto the beige sofa. With a soft neckline and pearl buttons, it was the most beautiful dress she'd ever seen. "This is so lovely, and the color is perfect. How much?"

"It's on sale for half price. Just a low five dollars. You have to take this. It matches your eyes."

"I don't think I've ever seen anything quite this pretty." Paisley fingered the fabric of the skirt. Five dollars was a lot, but she couldn't leave without it. "Consider it sold, Miss Felicity."

"Excellent." The woman clapped. "I don't think you'll regret your decision."

Paisley doled out the money, and the woman arranged the folds of the dress in a box.

"Would you like to have some tea with me while we wait for your husband?" Miss Felicity asked.

"Yes, I do think I'd love that. I thought he'd return by now." She couldn't just leave after promising to wait. Hopefully nothing had happened to Crockett. What if Farrel had killed him? Given the chance, her despicable adopted brother would in a heartbeat. That much was sure.

She sat with her delightful hostess and learned that Miss Felicity had come to Texas all the way from New Orleans, brought on the arm of a man who'd ultimately betrayed her.

"Antoine was handsome with a heart of stone. He deserted me in Fort Worth and left me penniless." She made a wry face and took a sip of tea. "My skill as a seamstress came in handy and kept me from starving."

"That was fortunate." Paisley ran a fingertip around her teacup. "I worked as a nurse in Fort Worth and I loved it. Are you new to Medicine Springs?"

"I arrived a month ago, and I really like it here."

They talked a little more and had just finished their tea when Crockett entered.

Paisley took him aside. "Is everything all right?"

"For now. I followed Farrel all over town." His face darkened. "Your adopted brother has a lot of unsavory friends. He's at the Lucky Lady Saloon right now, so it'd be a good time to conclude our business."

"I'll get my dress." Paisley went back to Miss Felicity. "Thank you for such a lovely time and for finding me the green perfection."

The woman waved a hand. "I enjoyed it. You'll have to stop in next time, and we'll do it again." She smiled at Crockett. "Your wife has such excellent taste. You'll love her in this dress."

Crockett quirked an eyebrow and chuckled. "I know I will." Outside, he took the box from her and stuck it under his arm. "Wife?"

"Our relationship is too complicated to explain, so I let her think what she would." Paisley met the humor in his eyes. "Somehow I didn't think you'd mind."

"Not at all." He put an arm around her waist. "Say the word and we'll make it so."

"What are you talking about? Today?"

"Yep. Or tomorrow. Or the next day."

She laughed. "You're not in any rush, are you?"

They sidestepped a puddle of water. It was amazing how the boardwalk had cleared.

"We've wasted too much time already. Don't you think?"

"Crockett, I have Hilda and Tye to consider. I don't want to rush this." Yet a part of her yearned to grab him and head for a church. He was right about a lot of things.

"Just remember, you were the one playing married back there, my darling Firefly."

All while they'd been walking, he'd scanned the street. Suddenly, he pulled her into a doorway and covered her with his body. "I see one of Farrel's buddies. Let's wait a moment in case he shows up."

In the teasing exchange, she'd forgotten the danger. She wished Farrel would leave town.

Finally, Crockett moved. "I think it's safe. Let's hurry back to the land office."

Without any further conversation, they lengthened their stride until the land office came into view. Farrel had ruined another fun moment. He always had to steal her sunshine.

Crockett didn't stop to scan the street; he just hurried her inside. It wasn't as busy as before, but the wait would take a while. However, to her surprise, a man signaled to them to follow him. They went into a small office.

The older land officer dusted off a chair. "Have a seat, Miss Mahone. Judge, I'm sorry I just have the one."

"That's fine. I'll stand." Crockett shifted the box containing her new dress and shook the man's hand. "Thank you for taking care of this little matter for Miss Mahone."

"Happy to do it." The gentleman, who had to be in his fifties, smiled at her and sat at a desk.

Crockett pulled the deed out of his vest and laid it in front of him. "She just got this from Caleb Seymour down the street a few hours ago and needs to register it in her name as soon as possible. I fear her adopted brother will try to take it from her."

"I understand."

Paisley watched the two men, who appeared to have mutual respect for each other. She was safe enough in here, but what about on the road home? Her foot began to tap. When the land officer glanced her way with what seemed a look of annoyance, she quelled her foot's nervousness. "Sorry."

"I don't think this will take long," he said. "Do you have anything that proves who you are?"

Oh no! She didn't think about that.

She moistened her dry lips with the tip of her tongue. "I'm afraid not with me. I'm a nurse and have my certificate, but it's at home."

"I can vouch for her if that'll work." Crockett's confident voice filled the small area. "She's an old acquaintance."

"Of course, Judge. Having you vouch for her will speed this along." The man pulled a form from a drawer. "Your full name, miss."

"Paisley Ann Mahone." From there, she told him her date of birth and birthplace, then her parents' names.

Before she knew it, they were finished and were shaking hands. A weight seemed to lift from her shoulders. Crockett ushered her outside, where she glanced up at the sky and inhaled a deep gulp of air. Only then did she remember Farrel and looked across the street. He wasn't there.

Crockett put a hand on her elbow. "We need to hurry to the horses and get back to the Lone Star."

"I agree." She breathed a sigh of relief when she and Crockett mounted up and trotted to the edge of town, the dress box tied to her saddle.

They set the horses at a gallop, anxious to reach the safety of the ranch. The thick brush at the sides of the road caused concern, and Paisley didn't miss Crockett's intense scrutiny of the vegetation.

Five miles outside of Medicine Springs, shots rang out, one barely missing Paisley.

As she let out a yell, Crockett dove for her horse's headstall and yanked the animal into the brush, where they took cover behind a group of trees. She leaped off her mount and pressed herself flat on the ground as a volley of shots filled the air.

She had no question about the identity of the shooter. It had to be Farrel.

Crockett jerked a gun from his boot.

"Stay down and don't make a sound." He crawled silently through the high grass and thorny brush, and she wondered how many people would guess that he was an esteemed man of the court.

He disappeared from sight, and she lay still, waiting, listening, barely breathing.

Minutes passed before two more shots rang out and a horse galloped away. Still, she didn't move.

Crockett's voice called at last. "It's safe to get up now." He came through the thicket.

Paisley rose and hugged him. "Are you hurt?"

"Nope. You're shaking."

"I was worried." She leaned back. "Did you get a look at him?"

"I did. A close one. It was Farrel."

He'd never looked so good, and the dirt and leaves added even more to his rugged handsomeness.

Concern lodged in his eyes. "Are you all right, Paisley? I was pretty rough in my hurry to get you behind cover. If I hurt you, I apologize." He picked a twig from her hair.

"I couldn't be better. On second thought, I could use a bath and some clean clothes." She released a nervous laugh. "Not enough to mention. We're both alive and well, and I'm counting my blessings. Do you think he'll lie in wait for us farther down the road?"

"He's too busy nursing a wound I put in his shoulder. He's bleeding pretty bad."

"I won't waste a moment's sympathy. He deserves what he gets. And then some."

They went toward the horses, and Paisley gave a sharp cry. Her dress box had fallen onto the ground, and her beautiful new dress was partially in the dirt.

"The first new dress I've splurged on in a while and look at it." Paisley rushed to pick it up. "Miss Felicity gave me a half-price discount and everything."

"What can I do? I'm really sorry." He hunkered down beside her and stuck the gun back into his boot.

"It's not your fault. For now, you can hold the box and let me put the folds back inside. It appears just a small part of it touched the dirt. I was lucky." Her eyes met his. "We were both lucky. Farrel could've killed us."

"I agree. Thank goodness Ranger Callahan hasn't left. He has plenty to arrest Farrel on now."

After tying the box securely onto her horse again, Crockett gave Paisley a hand up into the saddle, and they arrived at Lone Star headquarters without further incident.

She dismounted, her thoughts on the deed. Like it had to her mother, that land meant her own independence. That was very important for a woman in this day and age. She didn't have to rely on Crockett or anyone to provide for her. That 640 acres was her future—her birthright.

And she would fight like a wild animal to keep it.

Twenty-eight

"WITH LUCK, I'LL HAVE FARREL MAHONE IN CUSTODY BY sundown, Miss Paisley." Ranger Callahan reached for his hat. "If everything goes right, he won't bother you again."

"I confess I'll be relieved to have him behind bars." She glanced at the sun. Only about an hour of light remained. To accomplish it by sundown, he'd have to hurry. But she wouldn't mind if it was full dark when he hauled Farrel to jail.

The tall ranger stood. "I'd best be going."

Her gaze followed him to the door of headquarters. A big man, he cut an impressive figure, and she was glad to be on his good side. He wore authority like a coat of iron with the full force of Texas behind him.

She got to her feet, turning to Crockett. "I'm going to stop by Dallam's for a bit before I go on home. I'll pick up my dress at your place."

"You might want to try it on for me. Don't you think?"

Hope underlying his tone made her laugh. "You're pitiful. I'll wear it for you sometime, but tonight, I'll take it home with me."

"Can't blame a guy for trying. Wait, and I'll come with you. I'd like to see how the pulleys are working."

"I promise." She strode out and rode down the street.

Dallam was sitting in his wingback chair playing with Freckles. The change was tremendous from the first time she'd seen him. He had new life, and that was a joy to behold.

"Miss Paisley, I taught Freckles a trick. Watch."

The little pup's sharp eyes never left her master, alert to his every movement. He raised his hand above her head, and the little fur ball stood on her hind legs.

"Bravo!" Paisley clapped. "It's amazing how quickly she learns."

"I don't think I've ever seen such an intelligent animal." Crockett leaned to pat Freckles's head.

Dallam's dark eyes held pride. "I told you she was smart."

"Yes, you did." Paisley ran a loving hand over the short fur. She'd forgotten all about taking Tye over to Gus's to pick out his puppy. Things had been happening too fast. "Are you ready to exercise?"

"Yes, ma'am. I've set myself a goal. I'll be walking in two weeks. Maybe not totally on my own, but at least taking a few steps."

That might be a tad ambitious, but she wouldn't tell him that. He needed something to work toward. Crockett met her gaze but said nothing.

"Then we'd best get busy. I wouldn't want to hold you back. Move onto the bed."

He adjusted himself on the seat in one smooth motion and grabbed the pulleys. Paisley helped lower him.

"You're almost an expert at this." She moved his pillow aside for now. "I'm impressed."

"I move myself back and forth a lot during the day. Now that I can get up, I don't lie in bed much. I've been exercising my legs like you taught me because I can't wait to stand up."

"You're going to get there." She'd never seen anyone so committed.

Crockett watched them with interest. "Even I can see the progress. You're amazing."

It was clear from the first moment how much stronger his legs had gotten. Even though she worked him hard, he didn't voice one complaint. Sweat broke out on his forehead and soaked his nightshirt, and still he wanted more. She worked his legs for an extra twenty minutes and finally told him no more.

"You have to rest and give your muscles time to soak up what we did." She shook a finger. "And no more exercising after I leave."

"I promise." He sat up and wiped his face on a towel.

For the first time since she'd been coming, his sheets had no urine stain. Dallam was getting up to use the bottle. She smiled as she straightened his bed and fluffed his pillows, then emptied his bottle and set it next to the wingback chair. Freckles playfully nipped at her ankles as she worked. She really was a sweet little dog.

"Miss Paisley?"

"Yes, Dallam?"

"I want to get real clothes on tomorrow. Do you think you can help me?"

"I'll be happy to." Her heart soared. He was feeling human again and wanted to look the part. Praise be.

She left with Crockett humming a happy tune. In a world filled with so many ups and downs, this was a day she'd remember for a long time to come. She owned land. Dallam had a purpose. And Farrel was going to be arrested.

That night, with her new dress hanging in her room and the hem that had touched the dirt washed, Paisley looked out the parlor window at the two cowboy guards at their post. It was nice to feel protected.

But Farrel wouldn't be concerned with guards. A cold shiver ran through her. Something told her that Ranger Callahan wouldn't find him at the Mahone house.

There were a million hiding places, and Farrel knew them all.

Paisley carried Casanova up to Tye's room and closed the door, then went to her bedroom.

Turning back the covers, she slid between the sheets. In no time, she was asleep and having terrifying dreams of Farrel. She tried to run, but her legs wouldn't move, tried to scream but no sound emerged. She tossed and turned.

"Fire! Fire! Fire!" Casanova squawked like a banshee.

Her heart pounding, she sprang from bed and reached the dim

hallway in three strides as a dim figure clattered down the stairs. Toward the bottom, the black-clad man tripped, falling against the wall with a loud crash and a string of curses.

She fired her pistol at the fleeing form. The sound of breaking glass reached her, and more shots came from outside.

"Tye!" She and Hilda reached the boy's room at the same time. Tye was sitting up, clutching his blanket, terrified. "Someone was in here. Was it my daddy?"

Hilda met Paisley's look. "I'm sure it wasn't. He can't find us, remember?"

Tye climbed into his mother's lap, and Paisley went downstairs. She opened the door. "Guards?"

Gripping a gun, Crockett appeared with one of the cowboys, both breathing hard. "We chased the intruder, but he got away in the darkness. Are you all right?"

"A little shaken, but I'm fine. He didn't get Tye thanks to Casanova." She told him about the parrot yelling *fire*. "Farrel ran like a wild thing was chasing him."

"That was a darn good thing to say. That bird might earn his keep yet." Crockett slid the pistol into his boot. "I'm going to saddle my horse and take a good look around. We don't want him waiting until things settle down and coming again."

"I thought Callahan was going to arrest him."

"The ranger couldn't find hide nor hair of Farrel at the house."

That's exactly what Paisley had figured. She ran a hand over her eyes. "Will this ever be over?"

He pulled her into the circle of his arms. "Don't worry. He can't hide forever. The law has long arms and an excellent memory."

Paisley took the comfort he offered for a moment, then pushed him away. "Go. I'm fine."

With a nod, he headed for his barn. She stared after his tall figure, praying he would see trouble coming.

Though the men searched the remainder of the night, they

were unable to find Farrel. Crockett stopped in for coffee at daybreak, and she talked about Dallam wanting to get into his clothes.

"Maybe not today, but wouldn't it be something if we could get him into a wagon to take a short ride?" Crockett asked. "Would that be too much for him?"

"I don't think it would hurt him. His legs are getting stronger every day."

"It's something we can think about." He pulled her close for a kiss and went home to sleep for an hour or two.

Tye was a mess of nerves for such a little boy until Paisley dropped Hilda off at Annabelle's and rode to Gus's.

She called from the outside of the door. "Gus, it's Nurse Paisley, and I have my nephew with me, so you'd best be on good behavior."

"Well, bring the little tyke on in here."

Inside, Gus was in his chair with his leg propped up. He was freshly shaven, and his hair was wet.

"Good morning. You look pretty chipper today." Paisley drew Tye over to the old cowboy. "This is Gus, and he's going to give you a cute puppy. What do you say?"

"Thank you. I like puppies, but I had to leave mine with my daddy."

"It's nice to know you, little feller." Gus shook his hand, and Tye dropped down to the blanket full of squirming pups.

"How's your knee, Gus?" Paisley rolled up his pant leg and gently pressed around.

"Most of the time the darn thing hurts like a sonofagun." He winced at her touch. "I'm out of cherries."

"I'll try to find you more." Paisley noticed Tye cuddling a mottled gray pup to his chest.

Out of all the litter, this was the homeliest.

Tye grinned up at her. "Can I have this one, Auntie?"

"Ask Gus, dear."

"Mr. Gus, do you need to keep this one?"

The sourpuss died laughing at the way the boy put it. "You can have it, son. I certainly don't need it."

Paisley finished and put her things back into her satchel. With Tye hugging the pup and promising to love the little thing forever, they left. She dropped him and the dog off with Hilda. Yelling that Charley and Jane would help him name it, Tye rushed to get inside.

Next on her patient list was Dallam. He was waiting in the chair, eager to get into real clothes.

"Have you been up all night?" Smiling, she set her satchel on the small table.

"Me and Freckles slept for a little while." The pup glanced up from Dallam's lap and yawned. "But I didn't want to miss you and thought you'd go on by if I wasn't awake."

An ache shot through her heart. He had so little to look forward to, and this was a huge day for him.

"Well, then we'd best get to it. How about I bathe you first, so you'll be nice and clean?"

"Yes, ma'am. I reckon I'd like that."

She heated some water on the stove and handed him a wash-cloth. "You probably want to do this yourself."

"I was going to ask, but I didn't want to hurt your feelings since it's your job and all."

"Nope. Point me to your clothes, and I'll lay them out."

He told her where to find a shirt and denim trousers. "I think I'd like to put my long johns on too. They're in the top drawer I think."

"You're going all the way I see."

"I am. I want to feel like my old self again." He gave her a wistful glance, shoving a lock of hair out of his eyes. "You know?"

"Yes, I think I do. It's been a long time." She laid the clothes on the two-chair kitchen table. "Why don't we do your exercises first? I think it might be best."

"It'll probably be easier."

He finished his bath and swung onto the bed. She gave him a workout and massaged the kinks out of the muscles. Then she helped him dress and move back into the chair.

Paisley stood back, her chin trembling and stared for a long moment. Dallam looked so different. Like a real cowhand. If he had his boots on, she'd expect him to get up and go out the door.

While he played with Freckles, she straightened up, changing his sheets and putting down clean newspaper for the pup.

A wagon pulled up outside, and Crockett came in. "You look like you're ready for work. What do you say about going for a short ride around the ranch?"

Hope sprang into Dallam's dark eyes. "Do you mean it?"

"I sure do." Crockett slid an arm around Paisley's waist.

Warmth and love seeped down into her bones. It deeply touched her that he took time from his day to make Dallam's one he'd remember forever.

She pulled away. "Let's get your boots on, cowboy. You've got things to do and places to be."

"Do you hear that, Freckles? I'm going for a ride." Tears bubbled in Dallam's eyes, and Paisley blinked hard, stumbling over the end of the bed to get to the young man's boots.

With Crockett's help, she got them on his feet. "There. Are you ready to stand up?"

Dallam's slow nod held doubts, but she suspected it sprang from worry about falling. He set Freckles on the floor and told her to stay out of the way.

With Paisley on one side and Crockett the other, they lifted him up, supporting his weight.

"How does that feel?" she asked.

"You don't know what this means. I never thought I'd ever wear real clothes, never thought I'd stand—" Dallam's voice broke, and tears rolled down his cheeks. "I can't believe this. Thank you, both."

"Put your arms around our necks and try to move your legs as we go." Paisley gripped him securely. "Are you okay?"

"More than okay," Dallam answered.

With a gentle nudge of his boot, Crockett scooted the frisky puppy aside. "We'll come back for Freckles so she can ride too. Let us do the bulk of the work, and when we get outside, I have some men standing by to lift you into the wagon."

"My legs feel strange with weight on them again but they're trying to remember what to do."

"That's good. Personally, I think you're ready to run a foot race." Crockett chuckled. He glanced over at Paisley and winked. "Or maybe you're thinking of dancing with your nurse."

"Right now, I'm just focused on making it to the wagon."

"Good answer, Dallam." Paisley willed him to take step after step, to make it to the door.

It was painstaking and took forever, with him mostly dragging his feet, but she was so proud of his strong will. The next time she felt like giving up on anything, she'd remember Dallam and how precious the smallest things were to him.

At the door, four of Dallam's friends lifted him over the threshold and up into the wagon. Shep couldn't hold back his tears and had to turn away in sobs once they got Dallam seated.

Paisley touched Shep's back and spoke low. "It's all right to cry. You've waited by Dallam's side a long time for this moment."

"Yes, ma'am."

She ran back into the house for Freckles and delivered the pup to Dallam's waiting arms. Then they all piled into the back and rode around the town area of the ranch. They passed by headquarters, and Stoker waved, calling encouragement to Dallam.

Dr. Thorp was in his yard and hobbled to the gate. They stopped to let him talk to Dallam. Paisley could see happy surprise in the doctor's eyes.

Then they rode on, and when they came to the mercantile,

the owner flagged them down and lifted a whole box of cherries into the back of the wagon. When they passed Gus's place, they dropped them off.

It didn't take a genius to know Crockett had used some pull to get the fruit. Paisley would be sure to give him a proper thank-you later.

Dallam waved and called to everyone they passed, apparently anxious to let them know he was on the way back.

Watching him, Paisley felt energized. Doubts had filled her before, but now she knew Dallam could do this. He had a will of iron with her and Crockett behind him. They couldn't fail.

Life was what you made it, both good and bad. Her gaze met Crockett's, and he winked again. That second chance had come. For all of them.

Twenty-nine

CROCKETT DIDN'T KNOW WHO THE DAY MEANT MORE TO— Dallam or Paisley. After the men carried Dallam back inside, Crockett put his arm around her. "I have a surprise of my own."

She glanced up with questioning eyes. "For Dallam?"

"See for yourself." He pulled back a tarp covering some metal poles tucked along the side of the wagon bed. "He's going to need these if he's going to walk. Me and those boys in there are going to put these up along a wall." He kissed the tip of her nose. "All you have to do is teach him to move between them and practice walking."

"This is...you're amazing!" She threw her arms around his neck. "You seem to read my mind. I was thinking this morning how much he needed something like this."

A burst of happiness stabbed his chest. He stared into her pretty face and brushed her cheek with a finger. "My goal when I wake each day is to make things easier for you in some way. Your joy is mine, and I want to put a smile on your face every chance I get."

Tears misted her eyes. "That's so beautiful. I love you, Crockett Legend, and I'm never letting you go."

Noise from inside filtered through the door. The young cowboys were celebrating Dallam's milestone with a lot of good-natured ribbing. They'd all earned it.

Crockett tucked a strand of hair behind her ear. "I guess I'd better put those guys to work in there."

"I have to check on Sally Nolan, but I'll be back a little later.

Thank you for taking Dallam for a ride. It meant so much to him. But these rails will give him back his life. Make them sturdy."

"Yep. Don't want them falling with him." He gave her a kiss and watched her stride toward the Nolan home, her hips swaying to music as old as time. He was such a lucky man.

He meant what he'd said about making her happiness a priority. He'd seen what life without her was like, and he wanted no more of that.

∽

Sally Nolan let Paisley in. "It's nice to see you, Nurse."

"How have you been?"

The woman's large belly looked about to bust. Paisley wondered how she'd gained so much in just the time since she'd last seen her. The good-natured woman was gone.

"I'm so tired of not being able to see my feet." Sally clutched her back. "And I haven't been sleeping much. My husband has to get up so early that it seems I barely get comfortable enough to sleep and it's time to get up and make his breakfast."

"Do you nap during the day?"

"I try, but I can't."

"Let's see what's going on." Paisley helped her to the bed.

While she examined Sally, she told her the good news about Dallam. "His grin covered his whole face."

"I'm so happy for him. I'll have to tell my husband. It was so sad when Dallam got hurt."

The baby's heartbeat was strong, and measuring the size by pressing on Sally's stomach showed it to be at least a ten-pounder. Maybe more. That concerned her. She'd have to speak to Dr. Thorp about this.

"The head is in position, Sally. I don't think you have much longer." Paisley smiled as she adjusted the woman's dress. "Another week at most, then you'll get rid of your stomach."

"It can't come too soon for me." Sally sat up and reached for a small, wrapped package on the bedside table. "This is for you. My thanks for taking care of me."

Deep gratitude washed over Paisley. "Sally, you didn't have to do this."

"I needed to keep my hands busy. It's just a small token. Open it."

Paisley unwrapped the gift and gasped at the white, crocheted choker with a pink rosebud in front. "Oh, my goodness! It's so pretty. Thank you." She gave Sally a hug. "I bought a new dress in Medicine Springs and this will set it off perfectly."

"I'm glad you like it."

"I do. I really do." It was delicate and just what she needed.

The women talked over tea, and Sally didn't look as frazzled by the time Paisley went to the door. "Get more rest. You're going to need it. And again, thank you for the choker necklace."

Paisley went down the street to Dr. Thorp's and found him in his office reading a medical journal. "I'm concerned for Sally Nolan. She's suddenly gotten very large, and I fear her baby will be in the ten-pound range."

Thorp frowned. "That's a little surprising."

"For me too. And she's not sleeping because she can't get comfortable." She took a seat on his settee. "The heartbeat is strong, and I could find no distress in the baby, so that was good."

"A big baby has the strength to push itself out, but it can tear the mother up. How close are we?"

"Soon. I'd say no more than a week. I'll check on her every day."

They talked some more, and Thorp congratulated her on Dallam's surprising progress. "You've done an excellent job in such a short time."

"I'd like to take the credit, but I can't. Dallam is driven to walk again, so he exercises even when I'm not there. At the rate he's going, I'd give him three weeks to take his first steps unassisted, and it might even be sooner than that. Crockett and the boys are installing parallel bars in his house, and those will speed everything up."

Surprise lit the doctor's eyes. "Good Lord. I don't know if I'd have thought to do that."

"Of course you would've. You're a good doctor. Don't let doubts creep into your head."

He sighed and rubbed his face. "I feel so useless with this leg. How long before we can take the cast off?"

"It must be getting so tiresome." She patted his hand. "You have a long way to go yet."

Thorp groaned. "I'll never make it."

"You will because you don't have much choice."

"You're right."

"Maybe you need a distraction. I could get Crockett to bring his parrot over." She laughed. "Now that would keep you entertained."

"No thanks. I'm watching the birds build nests in my tree outside. That's excitement enough. There's a couple of blue jays, and yesterday, one was squawking to beat all. I think it must've been his wife laying down the law to the husband. He acted unconcerned and flew off in the middle of the tirade."

"You lead such a full, rewarding life these days, Doctor."

"Don't I?"

A knock sounded, and Paisley went to answer.

Ranger Callahan stood holding his hat. "Can I come in, Miss Paisley?"

"Of course."

Thorp hobbled from the parlor. "Come in, Ranger."

"I just need a word with your nurse, and I'll get out of here."

Questions circled in Paisley's head. "I have a feeling this concerns Farrel."

"Ma'am, it appears he's fled the country. Do you know where he could've gone? Or friends who might be hiding him?"

"Let's go to the parlor, Mr. Callahan, and I'll provide you with a list of friends."

They went into the next room, and Paisley took paper and pencil from her satchel, writing down the names of Farrel's friends. She handed it to the ranger. "The first name on there is Digger Patrick. He and Farrel had a falling out, so if Digger knows anything, he'll talk. The rest are thicker than thieves and will button their lips."

"Thank you." Callahan stuck the paper in his pocket. "Does Farrel have a favorite fishing or hunting place?"

"He has a little fishing shack near Medicine Springs on the Pease River. Maybe he went there. Digger can tell you how to find it. As far as hunting, it's all over this county."

"I appreciate this. Don't worry, I'll find him."

Until now, Dr. Thorp had sat silently. "Ranger, how about a cup of coffee? My nurse just reminded me I could use the company and suggested a parrot."

Callahan laughed. "That parrot is the talk of the ranch. I guess I can spare a minute."

"I'll make some. Won't take long." Paisley stood and hurried to the kitchen with the murmur of the men's voices trailing. She put the coffee on and stood looking out the back door at the beautiful spring afternoon bursting with so much promise.

Where could Farrel be? If she knew he was far away, she'd go after more of Tye's and Hilda's belongings.

But it was too dangerous. She couldn't risk it.

She made the coffee and had just taken it to the men when someone pounded on the door. She opened it to two bloody cowboys holding each other up. She recognized Shep.

"Need the doctor's help," the second man gritted out.

"Come in." She held the door. "I'm Nurse Mahone. What happened?"

"Trampled by a horse, ma'am."

Chills raced up her back. She couldn't imagine.

"Come with me." She got on one side of Shep and helped the men into the examining room. "Both of you have a seat on the table and remove your shirts."

From the other room, she heard the ranger say he'd come back another time and a door closing.

Thorp hobbled in. "Any broken bones?"

"I think some ribs." The cowboy hissed through his teeth as the doctor pressed on a badly bruised area.

"I'd say three." Thorp swung to Paisley. "If you'll take this one, I'll look at the other."

"Yes, Doctor." She tightly bound the man's chest and doctored his cut arms, face, and chest. "It looks like you've been dragged."

He tried to grin but found it too painful. "I'd grabbed the halter, trying to settle the horse down, and the rope wrapped around my hand. The stallion took off at a gallop, and I couldn't get loose. Shep got hurt trying to stop it. How is he?"

Paisley glanced over at the familiar face. "We don't know yet."

If something happened to Shep, she didn't know how she'd tell Dallam. How much more could the young cowboy take?

Blood was streaming down Shep's face. Dr. Thorp wiped it away and peered into his eyes. "Do you know who I am, son?"

"No."

The doctor held up two fingers. "How many fingers am I holding up?"

"Four."

"Is your head hurting?"

Shep gripped the edge of the table. "It's pounding and I'm real dizzy. Gotta lay down." His voice was faint.

His friend moved off, and Shep stretched out, his feet hanging off the end. He'd no more than lain down when he threw up.

"Will he be all right, Doctor?" the friend asked.

Paisley ran for water and a rag. After bathing Shep's face, she wiped up the floor.

"Shep has a head injury," Thorp explained. "Did the horse's hooves strike his head?"

"It looked like it, but I was busy trying to get free of the stallion. I hope he'll be okay."

"He will in time." Thorp took Paisley aside. "Can you make the bed in the other room? I want him to stay here overnight where I can watch him."

She nodded. "I think that's very wise. I'll get it made, and we'll move him."

Soon they had Shep into bed and gave him something for his headache. With Thorp insistent on watching over him, she left as the sun was going down.

Crockett seemed to know how tired she was and was waiting outside with a buggy. "I'm taking you home. You look beat. I heard about the accident with the horse and imagined it would be bad."

She rested her head on his shoulders, and his arms went around her. For a long moment, she stayed there in the warmth, listening to his heartbeat.

"You don't know how much I thank you." She lifted her head to meet his eyes. "It was Shep. The doctor is keeping him. He has a head injury." Her voice trembled. "I can't tell Dallam another friend is hurt."

"Then don't." He smoothed back a lock of hair. His touch was so gentle, it brought tears to her eyes. "By tomorrow, everything could be lots better. We should spare him what could be needless worry."

"You're right. We'll sleep on it." She got into the buggy while Crockett tied her horse to the back. He was taking such tender care of her.

While they drove to the house, she told him about Callahan

coming to see her. "I wish I knew where Farrel went, but I don't. Do you think there's a chance he's hiding somewhere on the Lone Star?"

"Of course, there's a chance he's on some remote section. This is an enormous piece of land. But I don't think so. We sent men out looking in all directions today and they'll keep looking." He put an arm around her, and she scooted close, loving that he wasn't off in Quanah working. "Try not to worry. We'll keep guarding the house, and we have a secret weapon—Casanova." He laughed. "I don't know how that bird knew the best way to get help, but yelling *fire* was pure genius."

"I told you he was smart. See?"

He kissed her hair. "I'll never doubt you again."

They talked about Dallam's parallel bars and how happy that had made the young cowboy.

"He couldn't wait to pull himself up." Crockett eased over to the side to let a group of men ride past.

"Oh dear. I wish he'd wait for me or someone else to be there in case he falls."

"He can't. Now that he can see a future again, he's charging ahead, and I can understand that. The more he works those muscles, the stronger and steadier he'll become." He shook the reins at the horses and got the buggy back on the road. "What else is worrying you besides Shep, Dallam, and Farrel? I can see that little wrinkle on your forehead."

"You shouldn't be able to see me so well."

"I notice every little detail about you. Especially that freckle by the corner of your mouth."

The suggestion in his low voice set her pulse speeding through her veins. It was true though. He let nothing get by him where she was concerned.

"It's Sally Nolan. Something's wrong, and I don't know what. She's far bigger than she should be. But the doctor assures me it'll be a single birth."

"It beats me how you can tell what's going on inside a person by listening to the outside."

"We can hear a lot."

"Can you put it aside for tonight? Come over, and I'll cook supper again."

"That sounds wonderful. I'll wear that new dress I bought in Medicine Springs." She sat up straighter and opened her satchel, taking out her gift. "The dress reminds me...Sally crocheted me a pretty choker necklace."

Crockett reached for it. "It's so delicate. Will you wear this tonight with the dress?"

"I certainly will."

"I'm looking forward to taking both the dress and this off you."

Happy tingles danced through her. "Oh, you are, Mr. Legend? And what else do you have in mind?"

He whispered in her ear, and heat rose up her neck.

"Oh my. I think you'd best get this rig moving faster."

Thirty

NIGHT GATHERED AROUND, ENCLOSING CROCKETT AND Paisley in a warm vacuum. Love for her whispered along the length of his body. He'd never felt this for any other woman. Ever since Paisley boarded that train in Fort Worth, coming to her father's funeral, he couldn't sleep, didn't eat a full meal, and couldn't think a clear thought.

He turned the steaks and looked at her now sitting on the outdoor settee, grateful for this time away from work. "I've never known a princess, either real or in a fairy tale, but I think she'd be the spitting image of you. That dress was made for you, and the neck thing really sets it off."

"You're very handsome tonight yourself."

She rose and moved to his side, her dress whispering with each step. The scent of lemons wafted in the breeze, reminding him of soft sheets and her bared body lying next to him.

A light palm on her shoulder drew her to him. He dipped his head, his lips pressing hungrily to hers. The kiss was full of raw need and aching passion.

His free hand followed the lines of her back, moving slowly down her spine to her fascinating bottom that curved so enticingly. Crockett felt as though he'd gambled and won a pot of gold.

He broke the kiss and nibbled along her lips and down her throat.

Paisley leaned back, her arms still around his neck. "You were always a good kisser, but you've become quite the expert."

"I try to please."

"You'll hear no complaints from me."

"Good to know. You bring out the best in me." And that was no idle observation. He worked a little harder to please when it came to her.

"It feels a little odd to be all dressed up and no place to go, but it's nice to feel pretty."

He slid an arm around her trim waist and breathed into her hair. "You're always pretty, even in your nurse's apron. I've said this before, but it bears repeating. I love watching you work. You're always confident and sure of your abilities."

"Thank you." She ran a finger lightly up his arm. "Tell me about your job. I don't know what being a judge entails."

He laughed. "It's boring, really. It calls for lots and lots of reading."

"Like what?"

"Case precedents that set deciding factors for current laws mostly. Witness statements, attorneys' filings. Things that affect what I hear in my courtroom." He gazed at the clouds drifting across the moon. "I strive to always be fair, to listen to both sides, and render the correct verdict."

Paisley glanced up. "It must be horrible having that weight on your shoulders."

"It's definitely not easy. Your brother Braxton's was the hardest case I've ever had. I had the dead guy's wife and kids on one side and Brax on the other. Your brother never meant to kill that man, but he was wrong in not stopping when the man went down. His anger blinded him."

"I don't want to make excuses for him because there is none for taking that life. But Brax was furious with Farrel and hurt. They'd fought over Farrel stealing a prized gun that Brax had won in a shooting tournament. My brother caught Farrel red-handed. You couldn't have known about that."

"No, I didn't. I doubt it would've made much difference

though. The dead man was a bystander with no part in the theft. Brax could've stopped himself."

"I'm glad we can talk about this now. I should've heard you out."

Her hand resting on his arm left a heated imprint—and drew explicit pictures in his head that dried the spit in his mouth and sent hunger tumbling into his belly.

Behind his lowered eyes, he had no trouble seeing her luscious curves begging for his touch.

Her lips hungry for his kisses.

Dammit! Why did they need to eat first? He itched to get to the important part, but she needed the sustenance. She didn't eat near enough.

"I think those steaks are done." He released her and put the meat on plates.

They sat at the small outdoor table already containing potatoes and glasses of wine. Crockett was telling Paisley about a funny incident in his courtroom when Hannah and Elena Rose came over.

Crockett groaned inwardly but welcomed them. "I notice you two practicing your bow-and-arrow techniques and shooting skills from the back of a horse, and I have to say you're getting to be quite expert."

Elena Rose laughed. "Let's say we're getting better. We only miss fifty percent of the time."

Hannah gave her cousin a playful push. "Speak for yourself. I think we're very good."

"It's fun, and that's what it's all about." Elena Rose swung to Paisley. "I'm glad I could talk you into taking the job over here. It's wonderful seeing you all the time. How are you liking it? Uh…I mean the job. I know how much you like Crockett."

"I love my job. And Crockett is a side benefit. It's great getting old hurts out."

"I'm glad, because I got tired of seeing my cousin mope

around." Elena cut a bite of the steak from Crockett's plate. "You two belong together."

Hannah glanced at the house. "I brought Elena over to meet Casanova."

"Help yourself, but don't stay long." Crockett covered Paisley's hand with his. "We have plans."

The girls started for the back door. Elena turned back. "Thank you for speaking to my father, Crockett. I don't know what you said to him, but he's letting me go to Dallas to pursue my dress-designing career."

"That's cause for celebration, Elena. Glad I could help."

The two girls had left by the time Crockett and Paisley finished eating. They carried everything into the house, then Crockett took her hand, and they climbed the stairs.

They hurriedly undressed, then Paisley lay facedown on the bed, her head on her arms. Crockett knelt over her, running his hands across her shoulders and down her spine.

"That feels so good. Don't stop."

He chuckled, his hand resting on her very pretty bottom. "No worries there. Did you know you have a remarkably fine derriere? It's the perfect size and shape, and the way it moves reminds me of ocean waves. I can watch you all day."

"You're not supposed to notice things like that. You're a judge."

"Hey, I'm not dead." He kissed his way down the curve of her spine and watched the skin prickle. "And I'm no saint. I'm a man who appreciates a woman's body." He pressed kisses along the swell of her hips. "You taught me that, Firefly."

"How?" She rolled over, her lazy, sensual gaze meeting his. "I don't recall any lessons."

"You have no inhibitions when it comes to your body. But you aren't showing it off either. You simply accept yourself as you are and offer no apologies for any perceived lack, as so many women do. I love that. So yes, you taught me to see differently. Even myself."

"People get too obsessed with things like that. I like the way the wind feels against my bare skin. I say be proud of what you have. Come here, my darling. I have something for you." She curled a hand around his neck and pulled his mouth to hers.

The kiss held fiery promise that exploded along the edges of Crockett's sanity. It seemed a contract of sorts between them. From now on they would treat each other respect and kindness and always let love lead the way.

Paisley's hand slid between their bodies, tightened around him, and squeezed. Heated anticipation rushed through him, leaving him achingly hard.

He had to have her or go out of his mind.

Once he was certain she was ready, he climbed on top. She tugged on his back, pulling him down. Unable to hold back, he plunged into her hot center. With her muscles clenching around him, he began the climb to the top of the world, where he could see a glimmering forever.

Pleasure, so deep and excruciating, swept him to the pinnacle.

As he released inside her, he captured her lips. Locked in the kiss, they reached a place where love reigned and blocked out all the bad. Where peace and harmony would always live. If hard work alone would ensure it, he'd make it happen. Paisley was his life, and he meant to keep her happy.

He struggled to get his breath and rolled off, trembling and limp. Every bone had turned to a quivering mass of jelly.

"Crockett, do you think we'll ever take this for granted?"

"Nope." He turned to look at her. "At least not for me." He pulled her next to him. "I cherish every moment of our time together. I see this as a bank, and each time we make love, it'll be a deposit. When we're old and gray, we can count it all and be rich." He smoothed her wealth of hair. "I cherish every moment with you and take nothing for granted."

"I love you, Crockett."

She raised up and pressed her lips to his with a fierce hunger, and he responded in kind, crushing her to him. The satiny fringe of her long, blond hair brushed his arm like a whispering sigh.

Finally, lying back, her hand on his chest, Paisley spoke softly. "I'll always remember this moment, just as we are now."

"Me too."

Her eyes were like green glass in the dim light. He'd never felt this close to anyone in his life. She snuggled against his chest.

"Let's get some sleep, pretty lady. You might get awakened to go deliver that baby or Lord knows what else."

"Thank you for making me feel every inch a lady. There have been times when I seemed far from that."

"You've always been a lady." He kissed the teasing freckle at the side of her mouth. "My beautiful lady."

∽

Shep was much better and sitting up by the time Paisley got to Dr. Thorp's. "How did you sleep?" She noted the blood on the pillow that had to be left from his head wound.

"I think I'm going to make it." Shep gave her a half smile. "Yesterday, I wasn't sure."

Dr. Thorp hobbled in. He appeared to have freshly shaved, and his hair was wet. "Our patient got his best sleep after three o'clock. I'm pleased with his progress, and will let him go around noon."

"Excellent news." Relief flooded over Paisley that she wouldn't have to say anything to Dallam.

After fixing coffee and straightening up, she collected her satchel and went to check on Sally Nolan. The woman's hair was uncombed, and dark circles rimmed her eyes.

"If I don't have this baby soon, I'm going to lose my mind." Sally waved her inside.

"I was hoping things were better. Let's see what's going on."

They went into the bedroom, and Paisley started her examination. Nothing had changed.

"I'll make us some tea, and we can talk for a bit."

"I always feel better when you're here. I've never been one who needed a lot of companionship, but these days, it helps to talk to another woman."

They sat over several cups of tea, and Sally had relaxed and was laughing by the time Paisley left and went down the dirt street.

Dallam sat in his chair in his nightshirt. Sweat bathed him, and he was exercising his legs with a vengeance. "Morning, pretty girlfriend."

"Are you trying to kill yourself? Is that what you're doing?"

"No, I'm trying to live."

"You can slow down a little bit."

He grinned. "I waited for you before I used the rails. What more do you want?"

"Just you to get well. We both want the same things," she said softly. "Did you sleep at all? The bed looks untouched."

"Freckles and I laid down for a little while, then it felt like I was wasting time."

"It's important for your muscles to rest."

"I know, but I can't."

Freckles whined at her feet, and she picked the little dog up. "Is your master neglecting you, pretty girl?" Paisley cooed, holding the wiggling body to her chest. "Has he fed you today?"

Dallam leaned back in the chair. "Of course. I do that first thing. When will you help me walk?"

"Hold your horses, cowboy. You have to rest a bit. Let's get your bath and the day started. Do you want to put your clothes on again?"

"Absolutely. In fact, I want to wear real clothes every day. I want to feel like a man."

"Then you shall."

She massaged his muscles, then warmed some water for his bath. While he washed, she emptied his bottle of urine and changed the dog's newspaper.

Brown eyes twinkling, Crockett dropped by, and she fumbled, almost dropping the pail of water. The heated look he gave her showered her with remembrance of their lovemaking the previous night and all the ways he'd made her feel beautiful and cherished.

"I thought I'd stop in and see if I can help." He scooped up Freckles, holding her small body close.

Dallam's nightshirt hung on him. "Do you have a magic wand, Mr. Crockett? I can use one."

"Afraid not. Wish I did though."

Paisley pointed to the clothes on the bed. "You can put those on him. I'm glad you came. You can help get him to the rails to walk."

Crockett's wide grin stretched. "At least I'm good for something."

Her cheeks heated. "You're good for a lot actually."

For a moment, it was just the two of them and the second chance they'd found when everything seemed impossible.

She searched for the warmth of his hand and found it. He squeezed her fingers as though to say he'd always be there in rain or shine—constant and true. She gazed up at him, her heart full of love.

Thirty-one

FOUR NIGHTS LATER, A BANGING ON THE DOOR WOKE PAISLEY. At first, she thought it was thunder from the rainstorm, but when it became more insistent, she grabbed her wrapper and hurried downstairs.

Sally's husband stood there, dripping wet. "The baby's coming."

"Give me a minute to dress. Make yourself at home in the parlor."

Hilda appeared on the landing, and Paisley filled her in.

"I'll come to help after I get breakfast for Tye," Hilda said.

"Thank you. I can probably use you." Paisley gave her a quick hug and hurried to dress. She left shortly after with Sally's tall cowboy.

"Thank God you're here." Sally grabbed Paisley's hand when she entered. She was drenched with sweat, her hair in ringlets around her face. "Tell me everything will be all right."

"It's going to be perfectly fine, Sally." Paisley moved her to the bedroom. "Let's get you comfortable, and I'll see where we're at." She never would've believed her most hearty mother would resort to panic. But then, birthing pains could melt a person's strong resolve. "I'm going to speak to your husband, and I'll be right back."

Mr. Nolan stopped pacing and looked up. "Is Sally okay?"

"She's just a little harried, but I'll help her through this. Can you go to Dr. Thorp's and let him know? Tell him it's crucial that he not get his cast wet, and I can handle things here."

"Yes, ma'am. I'm happy you're available, ma'am."

"Me too." She rested a hand on his arm. "It'll be all right. Try not to worry."

Paisley refused to voice her nagging fears. Sally had grown too large for just one baby. Sheer will alone would push her and Sally to a successful birth. Sally *would* hold her new baby in her arms. Paisley would accept no other outcome. She stilled her trembling hand, lifted her chin, and let hope take root.

For the next several hours, as lightning and thunder crashed around the house, she walked Sally around and around the rooms. Mr. Nolan came back and took over for a while.

Finally, during the last examination, Paisley saw the head. Sally released a long, painful cry, gripping the head of the iron bedstead.

The baby slid into Paisley's waiting hands. It was quite small—a boy. She tied the cord and cut it.

How could Sally be so large and the baby this tiny? Something didn't add up.

Before she could call to Mr. Nolan that he had a son, the light flickered and went out, plunging them in darkness. Paisley felt for the towel and wrapped it around the infant. "You have a son, Sally. A beautiful, healthy son."

"What happened to the light?" Sally asked.

"I don't know."

Mr. Nolan appeared in the doorway, holding half a candle, which he set on the bedside table. "I'm not sure why the light went out, but I found some partially burned candles."

Weak light bathed the baby's sweet face. Despite the low birth weight, the little tyke had strong lungs. Paisley passed him the baby.

Just then Sally let out a bloodcurdling scream. "Something's wrong!"

Paisley's mouth dried, and she hurried back. Putting her hand on Sally's stomach, she felt the gripping contractions. "Hold on, you're giving birth to another one."

"I can't believe this," Sally wailed. "I'm just supposed to have one. Doc said so."

"We can get things wrong sometimes. I could've sworn there was just one heartbeat. Get ready for twins. Mr. Nolan, can you get me another towel?"

"Yes, nurse." He hurried for it and returned.

With only the flickering flame of the low candle, the second one arrived pretty quickly.

"It's a girl, Sally. A beautiful baby girl." After tying off the cord and cutting it, she wrapped the infant in the second towel.

Mr. Nolan held out an arm, and she placed the baby in it. He chuckled. "That better be all, because I'm running out of places to put 'em."

"I'd take one dear, but I'm not feeling very well." Sally's face twisted, and she let out a yell, gripping the iron bedstead. "Here we go again."

Good Lord! This was one for the Lone Star record books.

"Mr. Nolan, get another towel, please."

"We're about to run flat out," he answered, juggling the babies. "Then I'll have to use horse blankets or something."

A big flash of lightning lit up the room, and thunder shook the house.

"Maybe so, Mr. Nolan. It's been a wild night, both inside and out." She turned her attention to Sally. "You're having triplets, it appears. I know you're exhausted, but you can't give out now."

"I can't push anymore. I can't."

Paisley grabbed the woman's nightgown. "Yes, you can. Now bear down as hard as you can with the next contraction."

A second later, Sally gave a loud yell and put everything she had into it. The baby slid out.

"It's another boy." Paisley wrapped the third child in a towel that Mr. Nolan handed her. With his arms full, she laid the infant on Sally's stomach, praying that was all.

"Are you finished, Sally?" Paisley pressed on her stomach.

"I hope so. I can't take another moment."

Just then, the candle went out. It had burned to nothing.

"Where are your candles, Mr. Nolan?"

"Kitchen table."

She felt her way through the doorway and located a taller one. Soon, dim light helped her make her way back to the bedroom and three squalling babies.

Hilda was coming after breakfast, but they wouldn't need her then. The nighttime had yielded all the births.

Mr. Nolan sat on the side of the bed and put the other two babies in Sally's arms. "I think I'm going to have to work night and day both to feed all these kids. I don't know what we're gonna do."

Sally kissed their babies' heads. "We're going to love them, dear."

The love shining between them brought a mist to Paisley's eyes. This was what she wanted someday with Crockett.

The storm had passed by the time the sun came up. Paisley made coffee and cooked breakfast. She took Sally a plate with some milk. Just as she and Mr. Nolan sat down to eat, Crockett appeared at the door.

"Come in. I made enough for an army."

A smile lit his brown eyes. "I believe I will. Hilda told me about Sally and said she'd be here after she feeds Tye."

"The worst is over. Sit down. Do we have an unbelievable tale for you." She got him a plate and moved her chair closer to his. Mr. Nolan wouldn't notice a bull running through the kitchen.

Wrapped in the warmth of love, she slid a hand under the table and rested it on Crockett's leg.

❧

The next two weeks passed fairly quietly. Farrel had gone underground, but Callahan was hard on his trail.

Crockett knew he'd turn up sooner or later, and when he did, they had to be ready.

Right now, things were much too hot for him.

Paisley's nerves were on edge with all the waiting. "Crockett, I feel him. He's around here somewhere. Watching. Waiting. He'll strike again soon."

"Darling, try not to let him get under your skin, because once he does, he's won."

"I'm not going to let him win. I've got to have my due."

But hard as Crockett knew she tried, she couldn't help watching the shadows and jumping at every sound.

This had to end soon.

Meanwhile, she went about her duties with a smile. She exercised Dallam's legs each day, and Gus had improved so much he resumed work with the other ranch hands. The new mothers were enjoying their new little ones, praising Paisley at every turn.

She'd made a great difference in everyone's lives.

One morning, after a night of lovemaking, Crockett draped an arm around Paisley's neck and nibbled behind her ear. "Want to ride out to our old swimming hole?"

"I'd love to. The weather has been so nice and warm. I might dip my toes in the water."

"Is that all?" He couldn't help his crestfallen look. "Just your toes?"

"Funny you'd ask that. What else would you suggest, my distinguished Judge Legend?" She placed a finger on his lips.

He nipped at her finger. "How about all of you, every single luscious inch? Some skinny-dipping. It'd be like old times."

She barely breathed. "And then what?"

"I'm sure we'll figure it out."

A knock on the door interrupted the hot kiss.

Crockett opened it to find his brother Ransom. "Is something wrong?"

"Grandpa is a little puny, and Dad sent me to get Paisley to come and check him out."

She nodded. "I'll get my satchel."

"We'll saddle the horses." Crockett reached for his hat. "Come on, little brother."

"I sure wish Grandpa would let me drive that Model T Ford," Ransom griped. "It's a lot easier than saddling horses. Saves on feed too. He's stuck in the Dark Ages."

"Maybe so, but we have to respect his wishes. None of this ranch or anything else would be here if not for Grandpa."

Ransom sighed. "I know, and you're right. I just wish he could see my side."

They saddled the horses, and Crockett rode at Paisley's side. Headquarters was quiet. Inside was a different story. As soon as they stepped through the doors, they encountered chaos, with everyone hollering.

The loudest voice belonged to Stoker, lying prone on the sofa, waving his arms. "I tell you, I'm fine. Everyone get away from me. I'm getting up, and there's not a soul can stop me."

Paisley parked herself in front of him, blocking his attempt to throw his legs on the floor. "I may not be as big as you, but I can pack a mean wallop. Now lie back and let me check you. Then if I find you healthy enough, you can get up."

Crockett chuckled. She had plenty of experience handling unruly patients. Gus and his pitching arm came to mind. He'd never seen his grandpa this flustered.

Stoker glared. "Miss Mahone, I'll have you know I'm as healthy as a horse."

"I have no intention of arguing with you." She calmly lifted a stethoscope from her satchel and listened to his heart.

Her expression revealed troubling concerns, and Crockett knew his grandpa wouldn't accept that he had to slow down and let the rest of them run the ranch. He was eighty-nine years old, for

God's sake. He didn't have many more years left. Crockett's eyes misted. He couldn't imagine the Lone Star without Stoker galloping across the wild country.

At last, Paisley raised and removed the stethoscope. "Stoker, your heart is getting weak. All this fast living and the adventures piling up are wearing it out. You need rest. You're going to have to start taking it easier."

"See, Pa." Houston crossed his arms across his leather vest. "Now will you listen to reason?"

Stoker was quiet. Paisley stepped aside and let him sit.

Luke pushed away from the wall. "Papá, let us run things. You taught us well, and I do not know if we are ready to step into your shoes, but we will try. Just give us a chance." His voice broke. "You have earned a rest."

Stoker pulled to his feet and drew Luke into a hug. "My son."

Houston's boots struck the floor as he went to his father's side and joined them.

"My boys." Stoker's eyes filled with tears. "You make me proud. Sam too. Sorry he missed this."

Crockett cleared the lump in his throat.

Houston pulled back. "So are you going to make things difficult?"

"No," Stoker answered. "I always knew this day was coming. Just didn't know it would arrive so fast. The reins are in your hands. I want to call a meeting though and discuss some things. We'll get Sam here for that."

"*Muy bueno*. I will send him a telegram." Luke put on his hat and left.

Paisley moved to Crockett and put an arm around his waist. He glanced down. "You can be pretty fearsome, lady."

"Nothing to fear as long as you mind your p's and q's."

"You are grinning. Aren't you?"

They went arm in arm onto the porch, and she told him

Stoker's days were numbered. "He can prolong things if he slows down. But you and I both know that's not possible after running full bore all his life."

"The day's beautiful. Let's go for that ride," Crockett suggested. "Might do us both some good."

They climbed on their horses and rode to the old watering hole. Perching on the bank, they reminisced about carefree times of their youth with plenty of kissing thrown in.

Crockett's voice dropped low. "I dare you to strip down and dive in the water."

"Oh, you do?"

"Frankly, I don't think you have it in you. You're not sixteen anymore." He held his breath, waiting to see if she'd take the bait.

"Buster, I'll take your dare and raise it. You have to do the same." She began yanking off her clothes, her eyes never leaving Crockett's face.

When both were as bare as the day they were born, Crockett took her hand, and they leaped.

The water was refreshing on his warm skin. They came up for air, and her eyes promised an eternity of love.

"I will always love you, Firefly." And he meant every word.

As they bobbed in the water, he captured her lips in a kiss that seared down to his toes.

Thirty-two

CROCKETT'S LAW CLERKS, RACE GRANT AND JULIA BISHOP, arrived the following week. Paisley had a bad feeling when they locked themselves into the office inside his house. Something big was going on, that much she knew.

She sat outside in front of the house with Casanova and Tye, enjoying the glorious fresh air. They had a good view of Crockett's, as well as Houston and Lara's across the dirt street.

Tye threw a ball for his puppy that he'd named Magic. "Go get it, Magic."

The parrot piped up, "Get it! Get it!" He let out a long whistle. "Kiss me, baby."

Magic stopped, turned his head from side to side, and whimpered. He ran back to Tye.

"Stop it, Casanova," Paisley scolded. "You're confusing Magic. Bad parrot."

"Bad. Bad. Bad."

"Auntie, he's not nice to Magic." Tye shook his finger at Casanova. "Be good."

The bird dipped his head to his chest, hopped down from his swing, and flopped onto his back, playing dead, which seemed his favorite thing to do. Paisley laughed. She turned her attention to Hannah and Elena Rose, who galloped from the corral area and down the street that ran between her house and Houston and Lara's. She and Tye had an excellent view.

Both girls stood in the stirrups, the reins clenched between their teeth, clutching bows. She released a sharp gasp. As the women rode past a large, red target, each shot an arrow into it. One hit the circle, the other landing just outside the middle.

It was most amazing thing Paisley had ever seen. They were very expert horsewomen and target shooters.

Tye stopped to watch as well. "How do they do that?"

"I don't know, but it's sure something."

They sat there for quite a while, and the two women rode over to them.

"You're both so talented!" Paisley stroked Hannah's horse, Mister Pete. "I've never seen anything like that."

"Thank you, Paisley. We've been practicing for some time."

Elena Rose dismounted. "It gives us something to do, and besides, we love it." She handed Tye an arrow to look over. "I'm sorry we haven't had much time to talk. But I think you've been too busy anyway. Every time I look up, you're rushing somewhere."

"Over to my brother's too," Hannah added with a twinkle. "I'm glad. He needs someone. All he does is work."

Paisley laughed. "That's all any of us do, seems like. But I enjoy his company."

They chatted some more, and the two horsewomen rode off.

Crockett finally emerged from his place with his clerks. All three were grim-faced.

"Is something wrong?" Paisley's stomach made a dizzying whirl as she stood. "Is it Farrel?"

"No." He strode to her side. "Someone burned my house and law office in Quanah. I'll board the train at daylight."

"That's horrible. I'm glad that you don't have to leave tonight." Her hand fumbled for his. "We have this time at least."

His brown gaze spoke of soft sheets and dim light. "We'll make the most of it. Let me get Race and Julia some horses, and I'll be back."

At her nod, he moved away.

Tye looked up. "What's wrong, Auntie?"

She put a smile on her face. "The only thing wrong is that I haven't gotten to tickle you enough." She grabbed him and tickled his stomach, that had filled out since their arrival, and soon his giggles made Casanova squawk up a storm.

That night, she changed into an older dress, but one Crockett had never seen. She wanted to look her best. No telling how long he'd be gone. Sorting through the fire would take days.

Her fingers shook as she fixed her hair. She'd been a bundle of nerves the last few days, and each time she turned a corner, she expected to come face-to-face with Farrel.

A knot formed in her stomach. He wasn't about to go away quietly. He wanted that land, and when he discovered she had the deed…Heaven help her!

Paisley patted a loose hair into place, gave herself one last look in the mirror, and went to spend some time with Hilda and Tye. The antics of Magic and Casanova had her in stitches and helped to settle her nerves. But as pleasant as that time was, she couldn't wait to go next door.

Her pulse raced when Crockett let her in. He was such a handsome man and seemed even more tanned and broad-shouldered than usual. He had the height of his father and the sensitive features of his mother. If truth be told, he had his grandpa's stubbornness. One thing no one could deny—he was a Legend through and through.

"I've been counting the minutes. You look good enough to eat in that pink dress." He brushed a kiss to her cheek. "I'm missing you already."

"I wish you didn't have to go."

"Me too. Let's move to the parlor for a minute before we eat."

She led the way and took a seat on the sofa. He got comfortable beside her, putting an arm around her shoulders. She rested her head on his chest.

"I couldn't say much outside, but in addition to destroying

my house and office, the culprit stole some valuables." He took a deep breath. "Even worse, they took files containing the names and addresses of men we were trying to convince to testify against Farrel in a murder case. We just about had them ready."

Shock swept through her. "Oh no! He'll kill them."

"He'll try. Right now, Texas Rangers have placed them in protective custody. Paisley, a friend of Farrel's has been arrested."

She put a hand over her mouth. "I'm not surprised. This is crazy. Why would anyone think they could get away with this? Farrel hasn't got a lick of sense and neither do his friends."

"You'd be surprised what people think. Some never believe they can get caught."

"Like Farrel."

"Yes." Crockett lifted her hand and wove their fingers together. "Let's talk about something else. What are your plans when Farrel is caught and you don't have to be afraid anymore?"

"I don't know." She glanced up at him. "I haven't thought about it."

"Marry me. Be my wife."

Stunned silence filled the room. She didn't know what to say. It hadn't been right the first time he'd asked. But now?

She started slowly. "I do love you, and you're everything I want in a man, Crockett. But can we hold off until Farrel is caught?"

He kissed her fingertips. "I can wait for however long it takes."

They ate and talked some more, then made their way up to the bedroom. Lovemaking was satisfying. Paisley didn't know how she'd stand being apart from Crockett. He filled her days with joy and the nights with unadulterated pleasure. She'd never been loved so completely.

Paisley lay in his arms, listening to his soft breathing. Her palm lay on his chest. "Do you know how long you'll be gone?"

"I hope not over a week, or I'll go crazy." His quiet voice filled the dim room. "With a day seeming like an eternity, a week will be unbearable."

"At least we have our work to keep us busy." She drew lazy circles on his arm. "I wish I could go to the train station with you, but I don't dare, and I curse Farrel for that."

His mouth moved on her temple. "I'm glad you recognize the danger. Stay close to the people here on the ranch."

"Make love to me once more before I go home. Fill this burning need inside me."

He covered her lips in a searing kiss, then climbed on top. She clung to him, tears wetting her face as she plunged into the waves, riding them to the peaceful shore.

Afterward, they dressed, and he walked her home. "Will you look after Casanova?"

She adjusted the collar of his shirt. "You don't even have to ask. At this point, I think he's spending more time with us than you anyway."

"Don't forget to bolt the doors and windows. The men had to go out to round up the cattle. Dad said he'll keep an eye on things."

"Stop. Everyone has more to do than hold Hilda's and my hands. There's a large ranch to run, and it needs to make a profit."

"We can do it all, so quit feeling guilty." He slid an arm around her waist and drew her closer. "I don't know how I'll stand the torture of being away from you."

His kiss took her breath. She wound her fingers in his hair, inhaling the scent of the wild Texas land on him. As the kiss deepened, she let her hand slip down to his nice, firm backside.

She clung to him, memorizing the solid feel of him under her touch. They fit together so perfectly, her curves molding into the shape of his hard body.

When they broke the kiss, he turned and strode silently away.

For some strange reason, it felt like more than goodbye. She wanted to call him back, to beg him not to go. To kiss her one more time. Tears blurred her vision as the night swallowed up his tall, lean form.

What was wrong with her?

He'd be back. Marrying him would have its benefits. They could make love every night and talk about their days. He'd help her make decisions, and she wouldn't have to do things by herself. She wiped her tears with an impatient hand and took a deep, shuddering breath. Whatever this feeling was, it would pass.

Sighing, she turned the bolt and went up to bed, careful not to wake the others or, heaven forbid, the parrot.

Dreams of being chased and shot at plagued her through the night. Finally, an apricot dawn broke, and she got up. The thought leaped into her head that Crockett and his clerks had already left for Medicine Springs. She prayed this feeling of foreboding had nothing to do with him.

She took coffee to Dallam, and they sat and talked. Then she massaged and exercised his legs, after which she helped him walk by holding to the rails Crockett had installed.

"I plan on dancing with you when I can walk again," Dallam warned, laughing. "Just get ready."

"I'll dance with you anywhere, anytime, cowboy. How can you be so cheerful this early in the morning?"

"Easy. I can see my life's not over. Even if I don't completely recover, I'm so much better than I was." He got overconfident and almost fell, grabbing hold of the bar. "Hope is a beautiful thing."

She tightened her grip on him. "Indeed it is."

"Where's Mr. Crockett?"

"He rode the train to his office in Quanah. He has a big case. Why?"

"I wanted to know if the coast is clear for us to run off together," he joked.

She laughed. "I think you're worse than his parrot, Casanova."

The noon hour was approaching by the time she finished giving the young cowboy a good workout. "I want you and Freckles to take a nap and let those muscles rest."

"I promise." He turned serious. "I don't know what I would've done if you hadn't come. You changed my life."

She laid a hand on his arm. "I'm glad I could make a difference."

That stayed with her as she went to have lunch with Hilda.

Lunch consisted of warmed-up soup and juicy wild berries.

"Tye, honey, put Magic down and eat so you can go play with your friends," Hilda said gently.

"But he's lonely on the floor. He needs me."

Paisley silenced a laugh. This was the first time he'd ever argued with his mother, and it had to mean the poison had fully left his body. That was something to celebrate.

After he left the table, the women talked in low voices.

Hilda poured them more tea. "I've been so jittery. I know Farrel is hanging around. I feel his ugliness spreading over me like a thick sludge."

"I've felt him too. We need to really be on our toes and take every precaution." Paisley ran a finger around her cup. "I dream of someone chasing me, and I either can't get my feet to move or I can't run fast enough."

"Me too. When will Crockett return?"

"In about a week, maybe longer. Hilda, we can't depend on anyone to help us. We have to save ourselves."

Hilda gripped her hand. "We will. We don't have a choice, and I'm not rolling over and playing dead."

Those words went through Paisley's head as she visited her patients that afternoon. She was coming from Gus's in the long afternoon shadows when Hilda ran toward her with an ashen face. "I can't find Tye."

Before full-blown panic could take hold, Paisley calmed herself. "Did you look at Annabelle Fletcher's? He loves playing with Charley and Jane."

"That's where I left him while I went to the mercantile. But the children said Magic scampered off, and he went chasing after him." Hilda's voice was strained with worry. "We have to find him."

"We will." Paisley gripped Hilda's hand. "Tye'll turn up."

Hilda nodded. They split up and went separate ways so they could cover more ground. Miss Lara and several dozen cowboys joined them. Even though they found Magic whimpering and bloody in thick brush behind the Fletchers' house, there was no sign of the little boy with an infectious giggle.

Thirty-three

THE NINE A.M. HOUR HAD SNUCK PAST BY THE TIME CROCKETT nodded to the Texas Rangers outside the door of a temporary office at the courthouse in Quanah and hurried in. A prisoner was shackled to a chair with a ranger standing behind him.

The man's sullen expression spoke of his character. "Shoulda known they'd bring you in."

"I thought you had better sense. Out of all of Farrel's friends, you seemed to have more than a speck of decency." He recognized John Barfield. "Why did you burn and loot my house and office?"

"Who said I did? Don't you have to prove that? I'm innocent."

Crockett snorted. "About as much as the coyote caught with a hen in his mouth." He pulled out the chair at his desk and took a seat. "My question is why take the risk?"

John glanced down at the floor. "I need a lawyer."

"Not sure there's a lawyer around who'll take your case. At least not one around here." Crockett opened the file on his desk and read the report.

John had been caught with Crockett's valuables as he was attempting to pass them off to an accomplice. Who knew where the stolen files were, and that concerned Crockett most.

This wasn't making sense. Why had John done something so stupid?

Crockett narrowed his eyes at the acquaintance. "What's going on, John? I know your family. They didn't raise you to break the law. What about your wife? Your children? Did you think about them when you stole my files, coin collection, and money from my safe?"

A quick mental inventory put the cash at a little over ten thousand, but the value of the rare coins was a sight more than that.

John Barfield shook back a long strand of hair that had fallen in his face. "Leave them out of this. What do you care? You have more money and land than God allows. You've never had to worry about anything in your whole life."

"So this is about money? Did someone pay you?"

"I ain't saying another word. Go to hell, high and mighty Crockett Legend."

The dark-haired ranger spoke. "We found a note in his pocket that said, 'Nine. Ten. A big fat hen.' It should be in that file, sir."

"Interesting." Crockett turned some of the papers and there it lay. The writing was in block print and very uneven, seeming to have come from an uneducated person.

The words were familiar. But from where? He mulled them over in his head.

Then it hit him. A nursery rhyme from long ago.

> *One. Two. Buckle my shoe.*
> *Three. Four. Shut the door.*
> *Five. Six. Pick up sticks.*
> *Seven. Eight. Lay them straight.*
> *Nine. Ten. A Big fat hen.*

What kind of message was that last line? It meant something. A reminder. Or a promise. You do this for me, and I'll take care of you and your family.

Crockett glanced up into John's laughing eyes. The only person the man would do a favor like this for was Farrel Mahone. His gut twisted, and he broke out in a cold sweat. Suddenly, it all made sense. John was supposed to get Crockett off the ranch.

Farrel was going to make good on his promise to kill either Paisley or Hilda or both.

Or maybe he intended to abduct Tye. Maybe all three.

The man had already tried that once, and Casanova had prevented it.

"Ranger, take him to his cell." Crockett stood so fast, he knocked his chair over. He had to get to a telegraph.

He hurried out and collided with a woman in the hall. "Pardon me, ma'am. This is life and death."

Cursing the fact that Stoker had yet to install a telephone at headquarters, Crockett rushed down the street and sent a message to the Lone Star.

"I'll wait for a reply," he told the operator.

Ten minutes passed. Crockett paced, praying for a miracle. Then the machine began to tap while the man scribbled it down.

"Here you go." The operator handed the paper to him.

Too late. Boy has disappeared, and women riding to get him back.

A moment later, Crockett fired off another, asking about his dad. The return message said he and Stoker had gone to Medicine Springs to pick up a shipment.

He sagged. Too late. He read the first message again. What women? Paisley and Hilda? Where were the men? Had they all left the ranch? He thrust a hand through his hair. He had to get home.

"Isn't there a noon train to Medicine Springs?" he asked the operator.

"Not today."

"That's right." The noon train was only three days a week.

"There's the seven o'clock tonight," the telegraph operator added helpfully.

"Thank you." Crockett's thoughts whirled. He couldn't wait that long. He was eighty miles away. If he bought a horse and rode it hard, he still wouldn't make it by dark. He'd have to wait on the train. That would get him to Medicine Springs by eight, then forty-five minutes to the ranch.

That was it. All the air went out of him. Whatever was going on, the women were on their own. He dropped into the nearest seat and put his head in his hands.

&

The blood didn't belong to the little dog, which meant Tye must have been hurt. Paisley's stomach knotted with the reality that Tye was gone and Farrel had to have taken him.

Oh God, why did Crockett have to leave?

The women rushed to headquarters but were told Stoker and Houston had ridden out for Medicine Springs. Fear turned the blood in her veins to ice. Why had the men left at once?

This was Farrel's plan. She knew it as sure as the sun was shining.

Paisley stared at Essie the cook. "Where is Ranger Callahan? We need to speak to him."

"Miss Paisley, he done left too, after he got a telegram. Mr. Luke went with him."

Gone. All the men were gone except for a few cowboys, and at the moment, she couldn't see any of them either. They couldn't wait, because there was no telling when they'd be back.

Hilda gripped her arm. "What are we going to do? Tye is so terrified of Farrel. And…"

The words trailed, and Paisley had some idea of the unspoken part because the thought was in her head as well. Farrel had a short fuse and might kill his son if he cried too much. Or… Her heart froze.

Farrel might kill Tye just to hurt Hilda and teach her a lesson.

"I know. Push that out of your head, Hilda. We're not helpless. We've got to saddle up and ride."

Some unseen strength seemed to bolster Hilda. She lifted her chin, and Paisley didn't recognize the guttural voice. "Tye is my son, and he needs me. Let's go get him."

Doubts plagued Paisley each step of the way to the small barn that sheltered their horses. They alone weren't enough. They had to have help. Hannah and Elena Rose trotted by and slowed as they came alongside. Both had taken part in the search, as well as Miss Lara.

"I see you marching with determination." Elena Rose rested an arm on the pommel. "Whatever you're planning to do, Hannah and I would like to help."

Paisley stopped, hoping against all odds. "Hannah, is your father around? I didn't see him when we were looking for Tye."

"I'm sorry, Miss Paisley. He and Uncle Luke went to Medicine Springs to pick up a large delivery arriving on the train." Hannah glanced at her cousin. "Let me and Elena Rose help."

"It'll be very dangerous. I don't know what your parents would say."

"They taught us to have compassion and to help whenever we can," Elena replied. "They'll understand. You need our skills. You can't do this alone."

Hilda touched Paisley's arm with a trembling hand. "She's right."

"Okay. You can ride along, but stay out of range if there's shooting." Still, four of them might not be enough either, but they would have to do. "We'll saddle our horses. Meet us at our house."

They parted ways and met in front of the dwelling a short time later. The women had Miss Lara with them.

"I'm coming, and I don't want to hear any argument; that'll only waste time." Miss Lara's chin was raised. "I know how to shoot, and you might need me. That little boy is like my own grandson, and I love him."

"Welcome aboard. Thank you." Paisley stuck her father's pistol in her waistband and gave the woman a quick hug.

She scanned her skirted army. They wore determined expressions, each rider outfitted with weapons. Hannah and Elena Rose had their bows and quivers of arrows on their backs.

Warrior women all. They might be the fairer sex, but they looked awfully impressive.

Satisfied, she stuck a booted foot in the stirrup and threw her leg over the horse's back. "Let's ride."

The five drew stares as they galloped past headquarters and on toward Mahone land. The afternoon was quickly fading. Worry crawled up her spine. It would be dark in two hours. And Farrel might not even be at the house. He could be anywhere. Farrel could have them chasing their tails in the darkness.

She could only imagine what was going through Hilda's head. She maneuvered her horse close to Hilda's and gripped her hand, willing some strength into her sister-in-law's icy fingers.

Words wouldn't carry above the pounding of the hooves, so Paisley didn't try. Instead, she concentrated on the fight ahead. Farrel wouldn't count on the women riding to rescue Tye, so they'd have the element of surprise on their side, which would help. He also wouldn't count on their resolve and a mother's wrath that burned so strong, something he would never understand.

Given his ego, he would think himself safe at the house.

Suddenly it hit her that he'd somehow had something to do with Crockett having to leave. And that shipment for Houston coming in on the train? Something told her it wouldn't be there. All of it was Farrel's diabolical planning to get them out of the way. A shiver of fear crept through her.

How could they win against someone like that?

Yet she didn't slow. Finally, they reached the Mahone boundary. About five hundred yards or so from the house, they stopped in a grove of mesquites.

Paisley dismounted and scanned their faces. "Hilda and I will go see if Tye is here. Once we confirm that, we can plan how best to proceed."

Miss Lara touched her arm. "Be careful. You know the danger."

"Yes, I do." The most uncertain element was Tye's dog Lucky.

He could bark and alert Farrel. There was nothing they could do about that though. She prayed Lucky was in the house.

She and Hilda crept through the brush, trying to make as little noise as possible. With the house in sight, they stopped to study it thoroughly. Outside, all was quiet. Paisley saw no movement in the windows, but with the light the way it was, they couldn't really see inside. Lucky was nowhere in sight—if the pooch was still alive. Anything or anyone that made too much trouble for Farrel usually wound up dead.

"What do you think, Hilda?"

"We need to move closer."

"I agree. Don't make a sound."

The women moved silently through the weeds and tall grass, ready to fall to the ground if anyone came from the house. Paisley's ears pricked at every sound.

The root cellar was on their left. The house on the right.

Knowing Farrel as she did, the cellar seemed a logical place to stash Tye. She motioned to Hilda, and they moved to the pad-locked door. Paisley couldn't budge it. She thought about trying to bust it open with a rock but decided it would make too much noise.

Hilda put her mouth to the door. "Tye, honey, can you hear me?"

There was no sound.

"Tye, are you down there?" Paisley asked.

No voice answered back.

With tears in her eyes, Hilda tried again, speaking low, but she got the same result.

"I don't think he's here." Paisley glanced toward the house that appeared deserted. "Maybe Farrel's at that fishing cabin of his." She gripped Hilda's hand to give her strength. "I'm going to peek in the windows of the house just to make sure there's no one here. Keep a lookout. Whistle if you see anyone coming."

At Hilda's nod, Paisley moved away. Hunching low to the ground, she ran to the side of the house. The first window was the kitchen. Nothing. Methodically, she moved from room to room and had to conclude the place was empty.

As she went all the way around the house a second time without seeing the boy, she didn't know what to think. Had they been wrong in thinking Farrel had taken him?

Was it possible it'd been someone else?

Paisley returned to Hilda and told her.

The news hit Hilda hard. "Where could he be?"

"I don't know. You stay here and watch. I'm going to get the others."

A few minutes later, she reached them and saw that the women had tied burlap around each of the horses' hooves to muffle the sound. "That was smart."

Miss Lara shrugged. "We had time. What did you find out?"

"I couldn't find Tye or Farrel here."

"Where else could they be?" Miss Lara asked.

"Let me think." Paisley scanned the area. Where did Farrel like to go when things got too hot? He'd know the Texas Rangers were still looking for him. It wouldn't be the fishing shack. It would probably be somewhere close.

She glanced at the ball of orange sitting low on the horizon. Time was speeding by.

Hilda shifted in the saddle. "His friend John Barfield has a place just around the bend, where they go to get drunk. I know about it because I followed Farrel one time when he was drinking. He might be there."

Miss Lara leaned over to pat her hand. "Good idea. Lead the way, Hilda."

The four women followed Hilda a short distance before they cut onto a narrow trail that wound through heavy brush. Swarms of flying insects attacked them. Paisley and the other women swatted them right and left.

With nothing yet in sight, Hilda stopped and spoke low. "If memory serves, the trail opens up into a wide meadow. That's where the house is. I think we should get off and lead the horses. If Tye's here, he's scared to death."

"Try not to think about that, dear." Miss Lara slapped at a winged insect on her arm.

Hilda nodded and proceeded. Just as she said, the pig trail opened up into a wide compound. Four horses were tied at the side of a ramshackle house. Paisley stared hard, relegating every detail to memory while a little light remained. In another thirty minutes, darkness would fall.

"I'm going to weave through the brush and come out on the side of the dwelling nearest to the thicket," Paisley said just above a whisper. "I want to see inside and hopefully locate Tye. They think they're safe here, so they won't be expecting anyone."

All murmured in agreement, and Paisley set off on foot. Arriving at the point she'd aimed for, she crept to the nearest window and peered inside. It was an empty room with a small bed and little else. She moved to the next one. It looked like a parlor, with four men playing cards. So this was where the skunk was hiding.

They were laughing and kidding each other, having a good old time. Thinking they were safe. Paisley stepped into a hole and grabbed the side of the house to keep from falling.

"What was that?" Farrel asked.

"Probably an animal. Stop being so skittish. No one knows about this place."

"And that's just the way us men like it," said a third.

"Your neck ain't the one the rangers are wanting to stretch," Farrel snapped.

A different voice spoke, "I never knew you to be a bellyacher, Mahone."

"Yeah, well. Whose deal is it anyhow?"

"What do you suppose is keeping John? He should've been here hours ago."

"Reckon they caught him?"

"If so, his butt's gonna be in a sling," Farrel ground out. "I told him he'd better not let anyone catch him."

Paisley moved on around the secret abode, looking for Tye, but came up empty. She returned to the women and told them what she'd learned. "We'll have to draw the men out of the house. Suggestions?"

Hannah spoke first. "A noise of some kind."

"Let's pepper the windows with small rocks," Miss Lara suggested.

"Then when they come out, Hannah and I will release our arrows while you and Aunt Lara can shoot them." Elena Rose pointed to a coiled rope on her horse. "We can also use that if we have to."

"Sounds as good a plan as any. I doubt if they'll hear us. They seem awfully confident of themselves." Paisley picked up some small pebbles and climbed into the saddle. She liked the shooting part. Especially if Farrel got belligerent. He didn't know any other way to be, so she checked the ammunition in her pistol again, cursing her nerves.

The group moved out, and she and Hilda parked themselves on their horses in front and began to throw rocks at the window. It didn't take long for Farrel to throw the door open and stomp out, surrounded by his three friends.

Surprise lit his face. "What the hell are you doing here? How did you find me?"

"I got ways. What have you done with Tye?" Hilda's voice shook with anger. And a helping of fear. "I want my son."

Farrel recovered quickly. "He's mine. What makes you think I got him? The titty baby chose his dear old mama."

Paisley pointed her pistol and pulled the trigger. The projectile landed at Farrel's foot. She shot again and again as he danced. "Tell us where he is, and we'll leave you to rot in this little paradise you got here. I'm surprised a rat hasn't gnawed one of your legs off... *brother*. Maybe you sleep with one eye open."

"Dammit, woman! Stop shooting! Christ almighty." Farrel resembled a chicken, with his arms flopping and legs dancing.

One of the men reached inside the door and brought out a rifle, ratcheting a bullet into the chamber.

She fired before he could get them in his sights. The bullet tore a chunk out of the man's leg. He yelled and dove inside, but not quick enough to escape Hannah's and Elena Rose's arrows. He caught them in both legs.

The other three made a mad scramble, getting through the door with arrows landing all around them. But Miss Lara's piece of hot lead caught the last one in the backside.

An arrow also protruded from the last one's arm before he managed to pull himself to safety.

Yells and curses blistered the air. The sound of breaking glass filled the compound, and guns poked from every window.

"We're not leaving until you give us Tye!" Paisley yelled.

"We don't want you jackanapes." Hilda's voice shook. "But know one thing...we'll get Tye or see your blood run into the ground."

Farrel laughed and answered, "You'll have hell finding him. That boy has to pay for turning against his father!"

Breath froze in her chest. So he did take his son. She didn't think Tye was here though. And they wouldn't leave until making Farrel talk.

Night was settling in like an old woman into her rocking chair with her knitting. Somewhere, a four-year-old little boy was alone, hungry, and frightened.

Thirty-four

DEFEATED, CROCKETT WENT BACK TO THE TEMPORARY OFFICE in Quanah. He sat down at the desk and put his head in his hands. He'd been outwitted.

Farrel had thought of everything.

A young ranger entered with a tray. "I took the liberty of getting you some breakfast from the café, Judge Legend."

"I appreciate that." Crockett reached for the cup of coffee and a piece of bacon. "I don't think I've seen you around here."

"Just got assigned to this area." The blond-haired man smiled. "Still unpacking."

"Sit down. Were you the arresting ranger?"

"Yes, sir. Name's Paul Preston." The lawman took a seat, and they talked about the curious nature of the case.

Crockett's chair squeaked as he leaned back, munching on a biscuit. "I can't understand why John Barfield did this, Paul."

"He mumbled something about a blood oath, and that he doesn't owe Mahone anything anymore."

A blood oath. Something must've happened, and Farrel saved John's life.

Still, John Barfield was paying a hefty price.

They talked a little more while Crockett ate, and he told Preston about the abduction on the ranch. "I really need to get home, but the train doesn't run until seven."

"I may have a solution. My brother owns a Model T and will be delivering some auto parts to Medicine Springs later today. I'll ask about you hitching a ride."

Hope soared inside Crockett. "I'll be forever in your debt, Ranger."

"The only thing is he can't leave until he closes the shop at six."

That would be a whole hour earlier and might make all the difference. Crockett got to his feet and pumped Preston's hand. "It's a deal. Tell him I'll be waiting. Thank you."

Now, how to fill the time until six o'clock.

❧

Dark shadows fell about the ramshackle hideout. The group of reprobates hadn't lit a lantern or even one candle, choosing to nurse their wounds in inky blackness. Paisley stared through narrowed eyes. Being unable to see the blood, maybe they didn't know any was leaking out.

She called from cover, "Tell us where Tye is!"

"Find him yourself...*sis*." Farrel had lost a little of his bluster.

"We're no kin. I learned the truth about you and the fact that you had no father. My parents took you in and gave you everything, right down to a last name."

"I always hated you, you know. If it hadn't been for you, I would've had it all when Braxton died."

"Yet here I am to stop you, and here I'll remain long after your bones are rotting in a field."

"Maybe, but so will Tye's," Farrel shot back. "I didn't leave him any food."

A chill swept through Paisley. She stared a hole toward the door her adopted brother hid behind. His statement made her blood run cold. "I think you had a hand in Brax's death. You did, didn't you?"

"It took some doing, but I managed. I had to get him out of the way."

"You're despicable." What else had he done? Maybe somehow

killed their mother? She huddled with the other women. "We're going to have to hit them with everything we have and not let up."

Hilda's jaw had become hard and determined. "We could set the shack on fire. Would only take one match, and it'll go up like a bonfire."

"That's a good idea." Miss Lara leaned in. "I'll go through the brush to their horses. Let's turn them down the trail to keep the men from sneaking out in the darkness and getting to them."

Elena Rose's black eyes went around the circle of faces. "Hannah and I want to try something first that might get their attention in a hurry—flaming arrows."

"I like that, but it's dangerous. You could get shot." Still, Paisley would do it herself if she had the skill.

"Not really." Hannah glanced toward the wooden structure. "Have you ever tried hitting a rider on a galloping horse at night after you've spent hours drinking?"

Paisley laughed. "I get your point. Okay, but wait until Miss Lara sets their horses loose."

"Ladies, did you decide to go home and wash dishes and tend to your knitting? I can't hear you." The voice belonged to one of the other men.

They didn't bother with a reply. Paisley hoped they'd step out.

Shortly after, the horses ran past and galloped down the trail. The men's hollering and cussing raised the roof, but they didn't come out. Now that the horses were gone, the women could get down to business.

She and Lara reloaded, and Paisley gave the girls a signal. With each lighting an arrow, they galloped from one side of the clearing, releasing the flaming projectiles as they rode past. Making sure the girls were clear, Paisley and Lara let loose with a blistering volley of bullets.

Different areas of the shack had burst into flames. They could hear the men stomping to put out the fires. But no sooner had they extinguished one than the girls rode by and started another. The smoke inside the dilapidated structure started the men coughing.

Hannah and Elena Rose made their fourth pass when a white handkerchief fluttered from the door.

"For the love of God! Enough!" someone shouted hoarsely. "Can we talk?"

"No one's stopping you," Paisley answered. "Tell us where Tye is or die. Your choice."

"I ain't gonna tell you nothing." Farrel had regained his old self.

"Shut up, fool!" yelled his friend. "Those women are gonna kill us! Don't you understand? I'm going out there."

The sound of furniture breaking reached them as a scuffle ensued inside the house. It continued for several minutes, and finally one of Farrel's friends stepped out, waving a handkerchief. His arm was bleeding heavily. Paisley didn't recognize him.

"Don't shoot! I'll tell what I know."

Paisley approached him with gun in hand. "Speak."

"Farrel came to us this afternoon and said he'd taken his son."

"We know that much. Tell me something new, or we'll unleash more arrows."

Sweat popped out on the man's forehead. "Please, you gotta give me a minute. Farrel said he'd left the boy on his property. He didn't say where. So help me God this is the truth."

A dark figure stood in the shadowed door. "What he says is true. If we had an inkling about where, we'd tell you. The kid is somewhere on Mahone land."

"That's a big area, and it's dark. Whereabouts?"

"If Farrel were conscious, we'd bring him out and force him to tell you, but he's unable to talk."

For a long moment, Paisley took his measure and felt both men were telling the truth. "If we don't find the boy, we're coming back, and next time there will be no mercy."

"Understood," said the man in the door. "Search around Farrel's property."

Paisley wanted to tell the friend Farrel didn't own any property, but she was in too big a hurry. Satisfied to have a direction at last, she turned and hurried back to the group of women.

Hilda's face was white with fear. She grabbed Paisley's hand. "What did he say?"

"Tye is somewhere on Mahone property. Farrel didn't tell them the exact location."

"Oh God, we've got to find him." Hilda hurried to her horse.

They climbed onto their horses and galloped back to the Mahone place. When they arrived, they split up, yelling Tye's name.

Paisley grabbed a rock and broke the padlock to the root cellar. "Tye! Are you here, honey? Tye!"

There was still no answering voice. He could be hurt. She needed a light. Running to the house, she grabbed a kerosene lamp and lit it. But the light revealed an empty root cellar.

Where could he be? Where would Farrel have hidden him? God help them.

An hour passed, and they'd looked everywhere they could think of, both inside and outside the house. Weary and heartsick, Paisley was standing with her eyes closed, trying to pick up some sense of where Farrel could've put his sweet son. A wafting breeze fluttered her hair and brushed against her cheek. Soft butterfly wings touching her eyelids.

A rider came from the eastern direction, the horse snuffling softly.

"Paisley." The voice was Crockett's.

Her eyes flew open as he slid from the saddle and scooped her into his arms. She tilted her face for his kiss and clung to him with all her strength as tears ran down her cheeks.

Was this something her exhausted mind had conjured up? He felt as solid as flesh and bone.

She melted into his strong arms and welcomed his touch along her spine. A little of the ice vanished.

When he broke the kiss, she glanced up. "I need you. God, how I need you. Farrel somehow got all the men off the ranch. But how did you get back so fast?"

"I hitched a ride in a Model T Ford. They're not as bad as I thought. Essie told me you and the other women rode out and to start looking for you here. Have you found your nephew?"

"We've looked everywhere with no luck. Farrel would tell us nothing, but his friend said Farrel left the boy somewhere on Mahone land. That's all we know." She gripped his vest. "If we don't find him, he'll die." A sob rose. "Maybe he already did. Farrel might've k-k...killed him."

"Hold on to faith." He stroked her cheek with a finger. "You can't give up."

"We don't know where else to search."

"How about his dog Lucky? Have you seen him?"

"No."

"They're probably together. How about holes? You said Joe and Farrel dug a lot of holes."

Hope sprang from her heart. "That might be it. I never thought to look there." She pulled his face down for a kiss, then hollered to the other women. "Bring lights and come with us!"

Her hand in Crockett's, she led them to the ground littered with holes. Everyone began yelling Tye's name, then they grew quiet, listening.

"Mama?" His voice was weak.

Hilda rushed to the nearest hole and hollered down. But that wasn't the one. Gradually, they narrowed things down to the hole with the wooden platform over it. Crockett yanked the boards off and threw them to the side.

"Help!" Tye yelled. "I'm scared."

"It's Mama." Hilda knelt over the hole. "Hold on. We're coming. Are you hurt?"

"Just my arm. I'm hungry."

Deep in the hole, Lucky barked, and the sound brought a smile to Paisley's lips. A weight had lifted from her shoulders. She leaned over to holler. "We're hurrying, sweet boy!"

"We need a rope." Crockett glanced at the women's faces. "I left in a hurry and didn't grab one."

"I have one." Elena Rose ran back to her horse.

While they waited, Crockett laid on his belly and held a light over the side of the foot-and-a-half diameter cavity in the earth. "Tye, we're getting a rope, but you're going to have to put the loop around you. The hole isn't large enough for any of us. Do you think you can do this?"

"I'm scared."

"I know." Crockett rose and motioned to Hilda. "Talk to him and keep him calm."

She nodded, and Paisley squeezed her hand, then Hilda laid on her stomach and began to talk about fun memories. Each time he started to cry, she'd get his mind on something else. Paisley watched with new admiration. So near to breaking herself, Hilda put on a brave front and kept talking.

Elena Rose returned with the rope, and Crockett fashioned a loop that would hopefully be easy for Tye to figure out.

When he was ready, he traded places with Hilda, thankful for the light that let him see the boy. "Tye buddy, I'm going to lower this rope, and I want you to put Lucky inside the loop and pull it snug around the dog. We have to bring him up first."

"Okay."

Crockett lowered the rope and waited. "Do you have it yet?"

"Nope. I cain't."

"Yes, you can. Keep working at it."

Lucky yelped.

"Not too tight. Do you have it?"

Paisley crossed her fingers, her nerves near the breaking point.

Miss Lara moved to her side and gave her a hug, and it felt like her mother was there.

Finally, Tye said he was ready, and Crockett brought the dog up. Hannah took it in her arms and went to get some water.

Next it was Tye's turn, and the tension made it hard for Paisley to breathe. She couldn't imagine what Hilda was going through. Paisley went to her side and gave her a hug. It took longer for Tye to get the loop around himself. He kept dropping it, and then couldn't get it to stay under his arms. They seemed to wait for an eternity. Crockett was eyeing each of them to see who could possibly fit down the hole.

At last, Tye managed, and Crockett pulled him slow and steady. After stopping several times to look at the rope, Crockett brought Tye to the surface.

The boy ran into his mama's arms, sobbing.

Paisley threw her arms around Crockett. "You did it! Thank you for saving him."

"There for a moment, I wondered."

"Farrel thought he'd won, but I guess we showed him. With no horses and some badly wounded men, Farrel and his friends should be right where we left them in a burning cabin."

Crockett grinned and draped an arm around her neck. "If he's back, I'm betting Callahan will gather the troops and head out. I'll probably ride along. It will do my heart good to see Farrel arrested and take his rightful place in jail."

She laughed. "He may need some doctoring." She told him about the mass release of arrows and bullets.

"Remind me never to raise your temper. Honestly, I'm very proud of you for making Farrel and his friends nervous. That must've been quite a sight."

Paisley shrugged. "Us women just did what anyone else would've done."

"No, you used the Legend way, and that had to have been mighty spectacular."

"All this talk is wearing me out." The smile on her face stretched wide. "Let's go home and engage in a little hanky-panky."

"An excellent idea, Firefly." He kissed the tip of her nose. "But that'll have to wait until we round up Farrel and friends. I want to see them behind bars."

"Me too."

Just then, something streaked across the sky in a blaze of light. A sign that their world had moved back to center.

Thirty-five

AROUND MIDNIGHT, CROCKETT RODE WITH CALLAHAN, TWO rangers, and his father, who'd returned from Medicine Springs quite furious about being duped. They galloped toward the place where the women had engaged Farrel and the men, leaving them afoot. His thoughts were on finally arresting the scourge of the earth and making him pay for some of his crimes.

A full moon shone brightly, lighting their way down the narrow trail. A gun rode on his hip within easy access. Although the women had taken the men's horses, they still possessed their firearms, and like a group of badgers backed into a corner, they'd likely try to fight their way out.

Moonlight revealed the shack still smoldering in front. Callahan stopped when they entered the clearing. "You're all under arrest. This is Texas Ranger Callahan. Come out with your hands raised."

"We're innocent, Ranger," a man hollered. "We've been shot full with arrows and bullets, and some of us are in no shape to walk."

Crockett and his dad went around to the rear of the sorry-looking structure and readied in case some tried to escape out the back door. They could hear Callahan clearly.

"Lay down your weapons. We're coming in. The first one to shoot is a dead man!" Callahan yelled.

"I hope Farrel tries to come this way," Crockett told his dad grimly.

"Me too, son."

As soon as they heard Callahan enter the front, Crockett and Houston went in the back. To their surprise, no one lifted a weapon.

But when they had everyone rounded up and all the guns con-fiscated, Farrel was nowhere to be seen.

"Where is Mahone?" Callahan asked. "I want the truth."

A man giving his name as Bob Vinson held a bloody arm. "Farrel left two hours ago, saying he wasn't about to hang around and get arrested."

"Where did he go?"

"Who the hell knows," said another holding his bandaged head. "Good riddance."

"Was he injured?" Crockett asked.

"Took a bullet in his shoulder. The man's a lunatic. Eaten up with hate," Bob answered, lying against the next man.

Callahan took the rangers, Crockett, and Houston aside. "We'll need a wagon to transport these men. They're in pretty sorry shape. I'll leave the rangers here to guard them, but the rest of us need to track Mahone down. I think he'll be headed to even things with the Mahone women."

Blood rushed to Crockett's head. He nodded. "That's a pretty good guess, seeing as how they whipped up on him. I left some ranch hands to guard the house, but Farrel has demonstrated how easily he can evade them in the past."

And Paisley and Hilda were probably asleep. God help them, they wouldn't hear him coming.

❧

The dark bedroom seemed airless and stuffy. Paisley rose from the desk in the corner, pushed back the curtains, and raised a window. A welcome, cool breeze brushed her skin. She stood staring out, reflecting on the hectic events of the last ten hours.

Her nerves were still stretched tight. But now her gut was send-ing a warning.

As familiar as she was with Farrel, she knew they wouldn't

be safe until he was locked up like an animal. And he'd fight for a chance to get even with her and Hilda. He had no horse, but when had that stopped him? She held up the pistol in her hand and stared at it. The moonlight turned the blue steel to silver. It was a thing of beauty, yet it held the power to end a life.

If she had to, she'd kill Farrel for the terror he'd inflicted on his four-year-old. Nothing could excuse that.

Casanova ruffled his feathers and moved quietly in his cage. She'd brought the parrot into her room so it wouldn't disturb Tye's sleep. The boy was exhausted from his ordeal and terrified of the dark. Hilda had to sleep with her arms around him to settle him down.

She wondered if Crockett had managed to slip handcuffs on her adopted brother. Although his house was dark, maybe he'd returned and gone straight to bed. Dead tired, every bone in her body ached. She pulled a chair to the window and sat, resting her head on the sill. Maybe she'd close her eyes for a second.

"Reach for the sky, Pilgrim," Casanova squawked. "You're surrounded!"

Paisley jumped to her feet and whirled to find Farrel padding silently toward her. His eyes glittered with pure hatred.

"I've wanted to do this ever since you were born," he snarled. "I had everything until you came. You don't know how many times I tried to kill you over the years but was stopped. There's no one to help you now." He advanced, the moonlight reflecting on the sharp blade of a raised knife.

Fear gripped her. "You wouldn't let me love you. God knows I tried. We all tried. I'm sorry your mother didn't want you. That must be a horrible thing to live with."

"Shut up! She did want me. She did. Caroline stole me from her because she wanted a baby."

"That's not true." He was distorting everything. Somehow, inside his head, he'd changed all the facts. Her heart went out to the poor lost man who'd lived with such torturous thoughts. "Please don't make me do this." Her blood turned to ice as tears ran down her face. "Please, I beg you."

But he kept coming with the knife, seemingly undisturbed by her pleading.

Paisley aimed the gun at his chest. Her hand trembled, but she knew he'd left her no choice, and to hesitate more would mean her death. "I'm sorry, Farrel. Forgive me."

"Go to hell!" he yelled. "You mean nothing to me."

Sobbing, she pulled the trigger. Orange flame and smoke leaped from the barrel. The bullet slammed into his chest, and in an instant, his shirt turned bloodred.

Farrel slumped to the floor, his hand clutching the hem of her dress. "Damn that parrot," he murmured. As death took him, he lost his grip on her.

Paisley stared in horror, her body quivering.

Tye's bloodcurdling screams echoed through the house.

Hilda came running. "What happened?" She froze in the doorway, her attention riveted on the figure on the floor. "Oh God. Is he dead?"

"Pretty sure." Paisley felt for a pulse and found none. "We don't have to fear him anymore."

Tye's screams showed no sign of stopping.

"I have to get back to Tye." Hilda hurried out.

Boots raced up the stairs, and Crockett burst into the room. "I about killed my horse to get here in time." He took the gun from her limp fingers and pulled her against him, his mouth at her temple. "It's all right. Cry if you need to. It's over."

"Is it? Farrel has more lives than a cat."

"He can't come back from this. Let's go to the kitchen, and I'll make you some hot tea to settle your nerves. While you drink that, I'll get someone to move Farrel out of here."

Before she could answer, the front door busted open as though rammed by a shoulder, and Houston took the stairs two at a time. He stopped at the bedroom doorway. "I heard the gunshot. I see I'm a little too late."

Paisley stepped from Crockett's arms. "I need some hot tea. You can join me, gentlemen."

"Too late. Too late," Casanova croaked. "Bad. Bad. Bad."

∽∾

In the two weeks that followed, Crockett didn't see much of Paisley as she worked with Hilda to help Tye recover. The trauma left so many residual effects—bed-wetting, thumb sucking, and fear of the dark. But time spent with Magic, Lucky, and Casanova proved of tremendous benefit. Slowly the boy began to relax and laugh again.

Crockett rode the train to his office in Quanah several times to hear cases and carry on government business. He was gratified that John Barfield looked to be serving prison time for his role in Farrel's elaborate scheme. Yet it would leave John's wife and kids in a bad predicament. Criminals never learned that others would suffer for their misdeeds and that the arm of the law was long. They always got caught.

In Quanah, Crockett tore out the burned timber of his house and hired a construction crew to rebuild it. He didn't know if Paisley would ever want to live here, but if she didn't, he'd sell the darn thing. In any event, it would have to be fixed up.

He'd had to bite his tongue several times when he was with her, wanting to ask her about marrying him. But he'd agreed to give her time, and that's what he'd do.

Some things it was best to go slow on, and this was one.

He knew she loved him, and that was enough for now.

Thirty-six

SEVERAL WEEKS LATER, AROUND MIDNIGHT, AFTER EVERYONE had gone to bed, Paisley and Crockett rode double to Lone Star headquarters. They laid under the huge bronze star stretched between two poles by heavy, iron chains.

Comfortable on a quilt, they gazed up at the stars, discussing the day. When they'd exhausted that subject, Paisley curled on her side and drew circles along the soft flesh of his wrist. "The legend that a person can learn their true worth by sleeping under the star…does that mean this star or a star in the sky?"

A frown wrinkled his brow. "I'm not sure. I always took it to mean this bronze one." He turned to face her. "Why?"

"Just curious. Not sure it would help me any to sleep under it though."

"Why's that, Firefly?"

"Because I think I already know what I need in this lifetime. I know for sure I'm going to marry you. I don't need a crystal ball to tell me."

He traced the shape of her lips with a light fingertip. "Oh, you do, do you?"

"I also know something else." She grinned and nipped at his finger.

"You're just full of knowledge." Desire darkened in his brown eyes. "What else is this something?"

"I know without a doubt that I love you and that my future would be empty without you."

The unspoken promises in Crockett's eyes made her stomach quicken.

"All of this thinking going on inside that pretty head of yours…
What do you propose we do?" His words came low and husky.

"I want to marry you. Today. Tomorrow." A giddy happiness
swept over her. "The next half hour will be fine."

"My goodness, pretty lady." His lips met hers in a heated kiss
filled with firecrackers and brightly colored fountains. He rolled
her onto her back, and she melted into his arms.

The hungry kiss left her breathless and bursting with love. A
certain boldness came over her. She loosened his belt and slipped
her hand inside his trousers.

A growl rumbled in his throat. "That'll get you into trouble."

"I do hope so." She stared into his eyes as her hand curled
around him. "Make love to me under the stars, Crockett. Help me
claim my worth."

His warm breath fluttering little tendrils of hair, he unbuttoned
her dress. "We don't need stars for that. You're worth more than
all the gold in all the world." He moved the soft fabric aside and
kissed her skin. "You are priceless to me."

There under the stars, Paisley vowed to always love this man of
Legend and stay by his side for the rest of her life and the next one.
As she took her pleasure, huge, colorful fireworks burst behind her
eyelids.

✑

Word got around that Stoker had turned over the ranch to his
sons, and oil company men began lining up outside headquarters.
They came wearing high-dollar suits in their fancy vehicles with
rimmed wheels and headlights.

Paisley watched from across the dirt street as each man marched
up the porch steps only to be met at the door by either Houston,
Sam, Luke, or Noah. Sometimes all four. All scowling. All shouting
so loudly she could easily hear them at the doctor's house.

They'd become fierce defenders of Lone Star land, and no one was going to put any oil wells on it anytime soon.

Paisley had also been approached, and her answer was the same. She'd not destroy Mahone land for money. Oil was black and dirty and ugly, and she wasn't having any part of it. Over time, she'd restore the property and make the water drinkable again. It would be Tye's inheritance.

The section that was hers here on the Lone Star would be kept for any children she might have one day—but she'd make a stipulation that they had to get along with their neighbors.

No more feuding and fighting. She'd had enough of that to last a lifetime.

It had almost cost her a future with Crockett. Thank goodness he'd been persistent.

Dr. Thorp hobbled out on a crutch. "I sorta feel sorry for those oil men."

"Why's that?" She took his crutch after he sat and put it aside.

"Those boys are every bit as stubborn and loud as Stoker. Sometimes I have to look over there to see who's talking because they sound so much like their father."

"You'll get no argument from me."

Thorp grabbed a stick and pushed it inside his cast to scratch his leg. "Tell me how much longer until I can get this blooming cast off."

"I swear, you're as bad as a kid." She laughed. "I'll have to check the calendar, but I think you have another week."

He groaned. "Good Lord! I don't think I can bear this."

"You will."

"When is your wedding? This cast is affecting my memory."

"Seven days. We would've had our nuptials immediately, except the preacher in Medicine Springs was called away." Her attention swung to a surrey coming from the section of the ranch where Luke lived. As it drew closer, she caught a driver, Elena's mother,

Josie, and an elegant-looking Elena Rose. The woman waved as they passed on her way to a new life in Dallas. Paisley had wished her well the day before, thanking her again for helping them take care of Farrel and get Tye back.

"Do you want to bet that Houston is going to put a boot to that oil man's backside?" Dr. Thorp asked.

"I hope so. We need some more excitement around here."

Just then, Houston spun the oil man around and booted him down the porch steps at headquarters, sending the man's hat sailing. Houston picked it up and threw it at him. "And don't come back! Ever! We're happy raising cattle."

"Looks like we both won that bet, Doctor." She got to her feet. Her heart skipped a beat as Crockett rode up, handsome in his tight denims and boots. His Stetson rode low, shading his eyes. He pushed it back with a forefinger, and her stomach turned a somersault. "I'll see you tomorrow, Doctor."

Crockett swung from the horse in one fluid motion. She met him halfway down the walk and slipped her hand in his. The hunger in his gaze set her heart fluttering like a million butterfly wings.

"I missed you."

"You just saw me at breakfast." His deep voice sent a ripple of awareness through her.

"I know, but that was ages ago. How about we ride to the bluff to watch the sunset? I think it'll be beautiful."

"I want anything that makes you happy." He put his mouth to her ear. "Especially if that includes getting naked." He pulled her against his side, and deep love, as warm and sweet as hot molasses, settled over her.

This was the man she wanted, the life she'd fought for, the future that offered her every dream.

ᴄᴂ

With no chapel on the ranch, they decorated the schoolroom. A week later, Paisley walked down the aisle wearing the light-green dress she'd bought from Miss Felicity and the crocheted choker adorned with a solitary pink rosette. A woven crown of flowers nestled around her head.

Crockett turned, and her breath caught in her chest. They'd overcome so much to claim this future. Happiness bubbled over, and she almost stumbled. She'd soon be his wife to have and to hold forevermore. They'd have sorrow, but she'd make sure they also had joy.

"You look very handsome in that new suit, Mr. Legend," she whispered, slipping her hand in his.

"I have to say that you look like a beautiful spring princess, Miss Mahone."

Someone coughed. The entire ranch seemed to have turned out and filled the room. Tye had insisted on Casanova coming and clutched the parrot in both hands, having promised to keep the bird quiet.

The preacher from Medicine Springs stepped forward with his Bible. Just then the door opened. A gasp from behind brought Paisley around.

Dallam stood there in the doorway with pride on his face, handsome in his jeans, white shirt, and boots, his sandy hair combed to the side. His friend Shep turned loose of his arm and Dallam took three wobbly steps all by himself.

The onlookers seemed to hold their breath, and Paisley released a soft cry.

Tears sprang into her eyes, blurring her vision. She clapped her hand over her mouth. "When I first saw him, I never thought he'd walk again."

"Just proves the power of the mind when a strong woman with conviction stands by him." Crockett's voice was hoarse with emotion.

Dallam lost his balance and started to fall but was stopped by Shep's steady arm around him. The gathering clapped as the popular young cowboy collapsed into a seat that someone had quickly vacated.

The ceremony went off without a hitch, they said their *I do*'s, and Crockett slipped a silver ring on her finger. As the preacher opened his mouth to bless them, Casanova escaped Tye's grip and flew to the front, landing on the teacher's desk.

"I do. I do," he squawked. "Man overboard! Man the lifeboat."

Crockett grinned. Splaying his hand across Paisley's back, he dipped her. "I've always wanted to say this: Kiss me, baby."

Epilogue

THAT SUMMER STOKER WENT TO BREAKFAST TALKING ABOUT his wife's fluffy biscuits. He rode out to take some flowers to her grave, and a few hours later, his horse came back alone.

Crockett found him sitting under a tree clutching a pocket watch General Sam Houston had given him after the Texas War of Independence. The ranch went into mourning, and they had the largest funeral in North Texas with the governor, politicians, and droves of the poor attending.

Stoker Legend was the Lone Star and everything it stood for. He'd loved Texas, his family, and he'd loved the land. He'd never claimed to be perfect and owned up to his failings with head held high. When things needed rectifying, he never dragged his feet or hemmed and hawed about it. And he'd treated everyone equal.

Crockett missed his larger-than-life grandpa, even as he knew this was the natural progression of life.

Five years after the funeral, late on an August afternoon, everyone gathered at the cemetery for Stoker Legend's birthday. The happy celebration overshadowed the sadness of losing the man who'd left such a huge mark on his family—and Texas.

Crockett juggled his two-year-old daughter, Caroline, while Paisley cradled their newborn. Joshua was the newest Legend and showed promise as a horseman. Funny how he could be screaming at the top of his lungs and immediately hush when Crockett swung into the saddle with him. The boy loved horses already, which was a good thing, since his father was a cattleman. He'd given up his judgeship and now called the Lone Star home.

Paisley had become a doctor and took Thorp's place when he left. It amazed Crockett how smoothly things slid into place without much planning when they were meant to be.

Caroline patted his clean-shaven face with her chubby hands. "Dada. Love."

He kissed her cheek. "I love you too, sweetheart."

"Down." Caroline pointed to the ground.

"Okay, but don't run off." The minute her feet touched the ground, she squatted to look at a bug. His daughter had gotten an insatiable curiosity from her mother, and he loved that she was always exploring her little world. He glanced away for a moment, and when he swung his attention back, Caroline was putting the bug in her mouth. "No, honey. We don't eat them." He rescued the poor bug and wiped his daughter's hand.

"I'm glad you caught that." Paisley laughed. "Sometimes it takes us both." She inhaled a big breath of air, looking satisfied and happy as she wound her arm through his. "Did I tell you today how much I love you?"

"Yes, and I adore you. This life we're making is everything I always wanted." He slid an arm around her waist, loving the feel of her lush curves. He wouldn't trade his life for any amount of money. This was too valuable.

Houston, Sam, and Luke trotted up and dismounted at the fence, the trio decked out in black Stetsons pulled low on their foreheads, certainly looking the part of cattlemen. They joined their wives—Lara, Sierra, and Josie—who'd arrived in a surrey.

Shortly after laying his father to rest, Sam had retired as sheriff of Lost Point and moved to the ranch with Sierra, reinforcing the strength of the brothers. People near and far said they were a force to reckon with, and Crockett agreed. While the brothers moved ahead with the times, they kept a lot of the old ways that had made the ranch such a success.

Noah had married Violet Colby and moved to Hope's Crossing,

where he started a ranch outside of town. Under Stoker's tutelage, Noah had learned the secrets of land management and was on his way to making a good living.

Hilda Mahone had married a hardworking cowboy on the Lone Star who treated her like a priceless treasure, and they'd given Tye a little sister.

Crockett's sister Hannah had won an Olympic gold medal the previous year in Stockholm, Sweden, with Mister Pete. To everyone's amazement and delight, Dallam had accompanied her. The young couple arrived with Hannah sporting a pretty engagement ring and a wide smile to match. The pair swung from their saddles and strode toward Crockett and Paisley. Dallam kissed Paisley's cheek.

"How are things going, sis?" Crockett asked.

Hannah looked up into Dallam's eyes. "Going fine. We're moving our wedding up to the end of the month. We're tired of waiting."

"I can understand that. When you know you're in love, why waste time?"

"Exactly," Dallam answered with a grin. "I've lost too much already."

"I'm happy to see you doing so well, Dallam," Paisley said. "You sure have mighty strong determination."

"Nope. My recovery has to do with you believing in me," he answered. "You made me believe in the impossible. I just wanted to make you proud."

Paisley laughed. "You certainly did that. I've never felt so rewarded."

A wagon pulled to a stop, and a small crew of men unloaded a tall crate and hauled it inside the cemetery. Houston directed them to Stoker's grave, where the three sons and their wives removed the wooden frame.

Everyone gathered around, curious to see what it was.

Houston spoke to the gathering. "It's taken a while to finish this, but the timing worked out well for Pa's birthday. Me and my brothers present our father, the man who made us who we are."

Sam and Luke removed the tarp. As the life-size statue of a much younger Stoker came into view, Crockett felt tears well up. The stone hat, the guns, the wide stance, the grit on the face of the famous rancher was an accurate representation of Stoker at his peak. Another likeness even bigger would soon grace the front of headquarters.

"Our pa stood for honesty, integrity, and the meaning of a man's word." Sam nodded to his brothers.

Luke picked it up: "He started this, and we're finishing it."

Houston poured a measure of whiskey into three glasses. Each of them took one and raised the glass high. "To Stoker Legend. May his memory live on forever inside our hearts."

"Amen!" Crockett shouted.

Just then, a 1912 roadster came down the road and pulled in. A black-haired beauty got out wearing an elegant silk dress.

Elena Rose.

Avoiding the stares, she made her way to Crockett. "Am I too late, cousin?"

"Maybe just a tad. Our fathers just unveiled Grandpa's statue. It's nice to see you. You look like a beauty queen. I think marriage agrees with you." She'd fallen in love with a cellist who performed all over the world.

She smiled. "I'm just so happy. Marc hated to miss all this, but he had a prior engagement in Italy. My work kept me in New York, so after days on the train, here I am."

"I'm sure you hated for him to leave without you."

"Yes, but he'll be home in a month, and we'll pack up to move to Paris." Elena's gaze found her father. "The family isn't one bit happy."

"I imagine not." Crockett was surprised Luke hadn't already

shot Marc Baschet. "Nice car. It's a good thing we've made it into the twentieth century, or it wouldn't be allowed on the ranch. I bought my first automobile a year ago and taught Paisley to drive. We love it."

"That one isn't mine. Marc arranged for it to meet me at the train depot in Medicine Springs. An automobile is sure is a lot easier than saddling a horse."

"Yeah, but it's missing the bond that I have with my brown gelding."

Paisley stood next to the statue that glistened in the remaining light. She turned. "Oh my goodness, I'm so happy you made it!" She hurried to them, and Elena gushed over little Joshua.

Crockett took the baby, scanning the gathering, his heart swelling in his chest. He blinked hard.

Family.

They were all pieces of Legend, bound by more than fragile dreams, desires, and trials. It was blood that formed the bone-deep, everlasting bond. Each knew their worth, and that knowledge sprang from a place inside where nothing could touch it.

As darkness descended, thousands of fireflies emerged to blink their tiny, magic lights.

Crockett shifted the baby to the crook of his arm and nudged Paisley. "Are you ready to go home, my beautiful Firefly?" He chuckled.

Her eyes twinkled like stars. "If we can find someone to look after the kids, would you be interested in riding to the swimming hole? It's a warm night."

"Are you kidding? I'll never turn down a chance to get you out of your clothes."

Go back to where the legend began...

to LOVE *a*
TEXAS RANGER

Now available from Sourcebooks Casablanca.

One

Central Texas
Early Spring 1877

Deep in the Texas Hill Country, wind sighing through the draw whispered against his face, sharpening his senses to a fine edge. A warning skittered along his spine before it settled in his chest.

Texas Ranger Sam Legend had learned to listen to his gut. Right now it said the suffocating sense of danger that crowded him had killing in mind. He brought the spyglass up to his eye and focused on the rustlers below. All fifteen had covered their faces, leaving only their eyes showing.

Every crisp sound swept up the steep incline where he crouched in a stand of cedar to the right of an old gnarled oak. He'd hidden his horse a short distance away and prayed the animal stayed put.

"Hurry up with those beeves! We've gotta get the hell out of here. Rangers are so close I can smell 'em!" a rustler yelled.

Where were the other rangers? They hadn't been separated long and should've caught up by now.

Letting the outlaws escape took everything he had. But there were too many for one man, and this bunch was far more ruthless than most.

He peered closer as they tried to drive the bawling cattle up the draw. But the ornery bovines seemed to be smarter. They broke away from the group, scattering this way and that. Sam allowed a grin. These rustlers were definitely no cattlemen.

A lawman learned to adjust quickly. His mind whirled as he

searched for some kind of plan. One shot fired in the air would alert the other rangers to his position if they were near. But would they arrive before the outlaws got to him?

Or…no one would fault Sam for sitting quietly until the lawless group cleared out.

Except Sam. A Legend never ran from a fight. It wasn't in his blood. He would ride straight through hell and come out the other side whenever a situation warranted. As a Texas Ranger, he'd made that ride many times over.

From his hiding place, he could start picking off the rustlers. With luck, Sam might get a handful before they surrounded him. Still, a few beat none. Maybe the rest would bolt. Slowly, he drew his Colt and prepared for the fight.

Though winter had just given way to spring, the hot sun bore down. Sweat trickled into his eyes, making them sting. He wiped away the sweat with an impatient hand.

"Make this count," he whispered. He had only one chance. It was all or nothing.

The first shot ripped into a man's shoulder. As the outlaw screamed, Sam quickly swung to the next target and caught the rider's thigh. A third shot grazed another's head.

Damn! The next man leaned from the saddle just as he'd squeezed the trigger.

Before he could discharge again, cold steel jabbed into his back, and a hand reached for his rifle and Colt. "Turn around real slow, mister."

The order grated along Sam's nerve endings and settled in his clenched stomach. He listened for any sounds to indicate his fellow rangers were nearby. If not, he was dead. He heard nothing except bawling steers and men yelling.

Sam slowly turned his head. Cold, dead eyes glared over the top of the rustler's bandana.

"Well, whaddya know. Got me a bona-fide ranger."

Though Sam couldn't see the outlaw's mouth, the words told him he wore a smile. "I'm not here alone. You won't get away with this."

"I call your bluff. No one's firing at us but you." The gun barrel poked harder into Sam's back. "Down the hill."

Sam could've managed without the shove. The soles of his worn boots provided no traction. Slipping and sliding down the steep embankment, he glanced for anything to suggest help had arrived, but saw nothing.

At the bottom, riders on horseback immediately surrounded him.

"Good job, Smith." The outlaw pushing to the front had to be the ringleader. He was dressed all in black, from his hat to his boots. "Let's teach this Texas Ranger not to mess with us. I've got a special treat in mind. One of you, find his horse and get me a rope. Smith, march him back up the hill. The rest of you drive those damn cattle to the makeshift corral."

The spit dried in Sam's mouth as the man holding him bound his hands and pushed him up the steep incline, back toward the gnarled oak high on the ridge.

Any minute, the rangers would swoop in. Just a matter of time. Sam refused to believe that his life was going to end this way. Somehow, he had to stall until help arrived.

"Smith, do you know the punishment for killing a lawman?" Sam asked.

"Stop talkin' and get movin.'"

"Are you willing to throw your life away for a man who doesn't give two cents about you?"

"You don't know nothin' about nothin', so shut up. One more word, an' I'll shoot you in the damn knee and drag you the rest of the way."

Sam lapsed into silence. He could see Smith had closed his mind against anything he said. If he ran, he'd be lucky to make two strides before hot lead slammed into him. Even if he made it to the cover of a cedar, what then? He had no gun. No horse.

His best chance was to spin around and take Smith's weapon.

But just as he started to make a move, the ringleader rode up beside on his horse and shouted, "Hurry up. Don't have all day."

Sharp disappointment flared, trapping Sam's breath in his chest. His fate lay at the mercy of these outlaws.

Acknowledgments

Deepest thanks to Dr. Keith Souter and his book *The Doctor's Bag: Medicine and Surgery of Yesteryear*. This was so helpful in treating snakebite and spinal injuries. And to former medical professionals Dee Burks and D'Lynn Rawls for letting me pick their brains.

About the Author

Linda Broday resides in the Panhandle of Texas on the Llano Estacado. At a young age, she discovered a love for storytelling, history, and anything pertaining to the Old West. Cowboys fascinate her. There's something about Stetsons, boots, and tall rugged cowboys that gets her fired up! A *New York Times* and *USA Today* bestselling author, Linda has won many awards, including the prestigious National Readers' Choice Award and the Texas Gold Award. Visit her at lindabroday.com.